THE TRIPLE SIX

A Savannah Nights Story

J. R. Froemling

This is a work of fiction.
Names, characters, places, and incidents are used fictitiously.
Any resemblance to actual events, locales, or persons, living or
dead, is entirely coincidental.

To my husband, who pushes me to chase all my dreams.
You are my co-conspirator in all things.
I love you.

CHAPTER ONE
Beaches & Bonfires

"C'mon, Angel, It'll be fun. Yer daddy ain't gonna say shit about it," Jackson winks at Shelley with a devilish grin.

Shelley has belonged to Jackson for as long as she can remember. Her dad doesn't like the boy, but Silus had to admit to himself that Jackson was good at whatever he set his mind to. He protects Shelley from the rest of the gang. The crew has been rumbling about her needing a proper introduction. Jackson doesn't disagree with Shelley's introduction. What separates him from the rest of the pack is he is getting her to play along of her own accord. He knows he needs to woo the girl, make her feel safe, and get her to give herself to him. Jackson believes it's a matter of time before Silus Baxter loses control of the Angels of Wrath. Then he could run this biker gang the right way. The way she fusses with the ringlet of blond hair and chews against her lower lip in worry was enough to make him have to shift himself on the bike seat as he watches her.

"I dunno, Jackson, it seems kinda far. I mean... Hilton Head is an hour away, and if I ain't home in time to open tomorrow, Daddy'll tan my hide," Shelley pouts. The sight of the other girls hopping on the back of bikes, beers in hand, and their rides looking at him for the go ahead makes her step closer. Shelley is sixteen and is two years younger than her sister, Faye. She hates being the little sister tag-a-long. She worries Jackson will see her as a kid and blow her off.

"You leave yer daddy to me, Angel. Now get on the bike," he growls at her.

He is not taking no for an answer. Jackson smirks when she is a good girl and steps up onto the back of his bike. He waits for her to settle down against him and wrap her arms around his waist. Compared to Jackson, Shelley is petite and delicate, like a white lily against a black lake of leather. Her blond ringlets whip behind her and her thighs show from the sun dress tugging and rippling in the wind as they race onto the interstate. He and the five other bikers are all pulling along a sweet little girl for a party in Hilton Head.

The sweet mix of whiskey and cigarettes fills her senses, and Shelley gives a sigh of contentment. She could get used to being Jackson's girl, spending her days clinging to him as they ride all over. Her father will be furious. Faye will take the blame, like she always does. Ever since their mother made her take Shelley everywhere, she never let Shelley get in trouble. Lost in her thoughts, Shelley doesn't register the hour that passed from the parking lot of The Triple Six to Hilton Head. Their bikes roll up to the pier access for the public. Shelley is sure her legs are jelly as Jackson assisted her off the bike. "Don't have too much fun without me," he teases.

"What? You're not coming?" Shelley pouts at him.

"I'll be down there soon, Angel. Got some important business first." His irritation is clear in his voice that she is questioning him. He was pretty clear in telling her to go to the beach with the other girls.

His eyes narrow, and Shelley knows she has done something he doesn't like. To cover her mistake, she steps forward and plants a soft kiss on his lips. Her delicate fingers a stark ivory

2

color to his bronzed cheeks. His brows raise in surprise, but he enjoys this brash development. She tastes like watermelon, and the blush on her cheeks only adds to her beauty. Jackson looks forward and motions her off, his temper abating at her adorable attempt to pacify him.

Once she turns and follows the others, he looks at her figure disappearing down the walk. The bounce of her ponytail as she trots to catch up to the other girls reminds him of how precious she is. The way her sun dress flutters in the breeze taunts him with her sexual innocence and it makes him want to take her away from this life. He could leave the gang behind and claim her as his woman, the two of them happy, traveling the open road alone together.

The rev of the bike next to him, reminds him it was too late for that. They had a date with a rival gang tonight. He pulls his gaze from his angel to his buddies and he nods. They roar off into the city proper. Shelley glances back at the noise but is soon being tugged by Faye to forget about all the boys on bikes.

"C'mon, Bratnik. They'll be around soon, or they won't," Faye shrugs. She learned a long time ago to not wait for the boy not coming to the party. "'Sides. There's a group of pretty hot guys already down on the beach willin' to share their fire with us." She laughs at the eye roll Shelley gives her. Faye is the attention grabber when the group goes out. Shelley smiles at her sister and they walk arm in arm towards the roaring bonfire.

The pretty hot guys are four in total. They introduce themselves as Tommy, Jasper, Beau, and Billy. Shelley looked between them and was pretty sure someone pulled up a Chippendale calendar to create them with magic. They are scruffy, tall, and covered in ripped muscles. Sweet Southern charm oozes from their very beings. The four boys shift with excitement, watching the girls approach their fire. The anxious looks they give each other without saying a word suggests they are having a silent conversation, but the looks vanish as soon as the girls are close enough to see anything. They are replaced with bright smiles.

"I'm Faye. These are my friends," she identifies each of them as she points, "Wanda, Taylor, Candy, Veronica, and," she hesitates, "Shelley. Gotta watch her. She is trouble." She flashes a wicked grin at Shelley, who rolls her eyes. Then Faye is gone from her side to sashay up to the boy who introduced himself as Jasper. Faye and Jasper are a mesh of bodies within a few moments of meeting. The shadows they give off make Shelley think they are fornicating. Each has a beer in hand, and their bodies move to the music being played by Billy on his guitar. Jasper's dusty blond hair is all you can see of his head. Before Shelley voices any protest to Faye's behavior, everyone is getting into the groove. Jasper had to decide if he wanted the ample bosom of Faye or the cherry Chapstick lips of Wanda. There were only four boys and six girls, putting the odds in the boys' favor.

Shelley grabbed a bottle of beer from her sister's stash and plopped down on a log. If Jackson caught her dancing like that with anyone other than him, he would hurt one of these sweet boys. She is smiling and enjoying Billy's sweet singing voice. It seems Jasper and Tommy are all about the anatomy lessons they are being taught by the girls they gyrate between. Beau keeps his behavior closer to a gentleman than Jasper and Tommy, in spite of having two women to himself. His hands only roamed so far as he feels proper. There is something about these boys that makes Shelley curious about them. The way they look between each other, and back at her sister's friends. Shelley tilts her head to the side, resting her eyes on Billy. His cheeks are blushing, from the light buzz the beer is giving him. He is trying to keep a safe distance from the claws of Candy. Shelley could swear she saw him roll his eyes at how Candy was throwing herself at him.

"C'mon, darlin', I need to sit down." His voice is low and rumbles like a well-tuned bike. Shelley could listen to him read the phone book. Candy is not ready to give up the merriment, and releases Billy from her clutches. This leaves Tommy, Jasper, and Beau to enjoy the five older girls. Billy sets the guitar aside and turns on the radio they brought. He sat on the beach next to Shelley on the log. She pops up like a whack-a-mole and squeaks. She giggles at her own nerves and how close Billy is to her.

"You alright, Miss Shelley?" His eyes are piercing and she can feel the flush in her cheeks.

"I… I'm a little cold," she squeaks out. He smiles, looking her over. Her fair hair is wind-blown and loose in her ponytail, framing her heart-shaped face that held the bluest eyes he had ever seen. He allowed himself to trail his gaze down her body, then back up to her eyes and pouting little lips. He bets they taste like fruit. Her sudden movements when he sat close to her tells him there's someone else in the picture. Billy wonders what kind of fool lets a pretty little thing like Shelley out of his sight.

Then she did something he didn't expect. She crawls right into his lap.

He freezes, fearing his touch will be deemed inappropriate. Panic wells inside him at the idea of her possibly mounting him like the motorcycles he heard them ride in on. She must not drink much to be affected the way she is by the beer. He swallows hard and shifts his weight to keep her from feeling his excitement. His arm wraps around her in a gentle embrace. It's a bonfire and they are enjoying the crackling fire nestled together. The boys shot any plans they had about shifting and playing in the ocean as wolves when these human girls arrived. Their scents are everywhere. Arousal is filling the air. Billy smiles as he realizes the little one and Faye are relatives based on the similarities of their scents. Her scent is driving him crazy with lust. She smells of lilies and watermelon. He closes his eyes and smiles when she giggles again, she nestles into his grasp. Who is this girl?

"Where y'all from, Mister Billy?" She teases his formality in calling her Miss Shelley. The chuckle rumbles in his chest as he shifts her on him to keep her on his thigh and away from his raging hard on while letting him relax. He looks down at Shelley and flashes a million-dollar smile.

"Savannah. Well... North of it, really," he replies.

"Me too! Though, I'm not sure how we're gonna get home."

"Oh?" His brow furrows and now he's picturing her in the back of his pickup truck, blond curls sprawled on his old blanket. She giggles again, and she is squirming. He gives a small groan and turns as red as a tomato. Billy shifts her in his lap again to avoid jabbing her in the back with his manhood.

"Yeah, it has been like two hours. I don't think our guys are comin' back. *Important business,*" she mocks Jackson's voice while making air quotes.

"If you were my girl, there wouldn't be any more important business than making you giggle like that." He gives her a sappy smile. His hand is stroking her back in soothing circular motions. His attention focuses on the orgy of bodies moving along with the music on the other side of the bonfire. Tommy is missing, and he sucks in a sharp breath. "Excuse me, Miss Shelley. I gotta go knock some sense into my cousin," he extricates himself from her, but not before taking off his flannel shirt and dropping it around her shoulders.

Shelley pouts at the sudden loss of body heat from Billy departing. She couldn't explain it, but she didn't want him to stop touching her. Guilt fills her that she would even look at anyone other than Jackson, yet he abandoned her. He deserves to feel a little jealous, if he ever finds out. The minutes ticked by and slowly the dancing orgy dies down leaving just Shelley at the bonfire. She curls up in his shirt and watches the dying fire. The longer Billy is gone the more she is convinced he found himself one of the other girls. She struggles to fight off the sleepy pull the beer gave her. Couple that with the crackling fire and Shelley loses the battle, closing her eyes to fall asleep.

CHAPTER TWO
Good Little Soldiers

Jackson rolled his bike into the garage they agreed to meet at and frowns at the lack of Angels present. Their business is brutal tonight. They are supposed to be putting an upstart into his place before he can become more of a problem for the Angels of Wrath. He had been running his mouth about shipments and word got back to the Angels. Jackson knew there was trouble the moment he killed the engine. His eyes settled on the men with him, each looking more somber than the next. He is the leader of this group of young bucks, but they fear Silus Baxter more than him. Their unease irritates Jackson. The boys here tonight are all young men, handsome in their own bad boy sort of way. Jackson is tall and muscular. His sunglasses are popped up on his head, combing back his dark brown hair. The men's boots thud against the concrete as the few men that had come to Hilton Head with him gather around.

"Where's the rest of them?" Jackson growls.

"Kid, you always were too impatient," the smoker's gruff of a voice comes from the shadows as a grizzly bear of a man steps forward. Shelley's father, Silus, the head of the Angels of Wrath, lights his cigar as he steps into view. His curly hair cut short and tight. Tattoos span every inch of his visible skin. Silus leveled his eyes on the kid with a malicious disgust. This boy dares to lay claim on his precious baby, and to strike out against other idiot boys without his permission. The rage he contains is clear in his eyes. He knows his girls are at the beach, after he told Shelley she couldn't go. He knew this whelp of a boy wearing his colors had conned her onto the back of his bike. He would deal with the girls when they get home. For now, he needed to get rid of this pest.

Jackson sizes up Silus. The older man is a legend in the pack. His eyes narrow as he realizes there never was a brawl and his brothers-in-arms had were as screwed as him. Jackson frowns, giving a quick glance from Silus to the others around. It confirms they thought they were getting into a fight tonight. He rests his hand on his pistol. He could feel the hammer of his heart in his chest. For a twenty-two-year-old, he puts on a big front. He has suffered the bullshit of the old guard since he could ride. He has killed for these men. Drank with these men. Now, he believes he is going to die by these men. His jaw clenches and he prepares for one hell of a fight. It stings. He could give Shelley a good life. She is a pretty little thing that could be his biker momma. He wouldn't let another soul hurt her, no matter how big a game he talks. He could not understand why Silus Baxter had it out for him.

Silus erupts into deep laughter. "Fuck, kid," gasping between laughs at Jackson's expense. "You got some balls, I'll give you that." He steps forward with all the confidence of a man with his power and clamps a large hand down on Jackson's shoulder. He looks right into his eyes and snorts at him, puffing out hot air from his cigar.

It gives Jackson the image of an enormous dragon billowing out smoke before it breathes fire. He does not break his gaze, or he would show how scared he is of Silus. He believes he is meeting his death and will face it like a man. The twitch of his jaw gives away the contained rage he wants to rally against the older man. He grows even more agitated as the older man laughs and mocks him. Shelley is his girl. He has loved that girl from the moment she appeared in The Triple Six. He has beat every other damn fool who even came near her. This gang is his. The old man just doesn't know it yet.

"Cool your jets, boy. I ain't killin' ya. Yer dumb ass'll be back to chasin' my girl soon enough. I'm trustin' you with somethin' important." He shoves Jackson toward the cargo carriers for the bikes. There are mechanics working to hook them up to the bikes. "You get these to Mexicali without causing me shit and get back without gettin' caught, then we'll talk 'bout your claim on Shelley." He gives him another rough clamp on his shoulder and a squeeze. He is trying to intimidate the boy.

Jackson's brow furrows at the sight of the cargo pulls. He was sending him clear across the country. It would take months to get the deliveries there and get back. Weapons runs are never safe, and always full of danger, especially crossing the entire country this way. There were easier ways to get these weapons to Mexicali, and Jackson knew it. The old man thinks he's getting rid of him. Jackson is smart enough to keep his mouth shut here, nodding in response. He'll show the old man, and when he gets back, he'll put him into the ground and take what he is owed.

The few hours it took to secure all the bikes, work out the routes, and get ready, causes Jackson to realize he will not get to head back to the beach tonight. That makes his temper even more unbearable. Jackson watches Silus while plotting all the ways he could murder him. Silus's smirking face whenever he catches the boy watching only drives him to plot the older man's death in great detail. Once Silus and his old men left, the young bucks look at each other.

"Just what did you do to piss in his Wheaties?"

"Shut the fuck up, asshole." Jackson cuts him a look that only wins his friends erupting into fits of laughter. He throws a punch at the one who made the comment. "What the fuck? Why didn't you tell me what was going on?"

He rubs his jaw where Jackson's fist had connected, then holds his hands up in surrender. "Didn't know either. Old man has it in for you, and us by association. We thought we were going to rumble with those pussies from the island."

Jackson furrows his brow and thumps his fist on the table as they look at the maps in front of them. He allows his buddies to relax a bit, the four of them plot out their ride. His mind is on that adorable little blond that clings to him like all she needed was him when they ride together. The sweet scent of her perfume haunting him even as faint as it is with all the cigar smoke Silus left behind. He wants nothing more than to get her all alone and make her cheeks blush how they did tonight. He has it bad for her.

"Hello!" The three men snap their fingers in front of his face. "Earth to Jackson."

"Hrmph," he grunts at them, coming back to their conversation.

"We good man?" One of them chimes in. "Don't know about you, but I want to get at least a couple hours of sleep before we hit the road."

He glances at his watch. It was already past two in the morning. He hopes the girls have found a ride home by now. He sighs and rubs his neck. Still irritated, he eyes the other men.

"No. Throw this shit out. We need to plan a different route. I'm pretty sure that fuck has people waitin' for us."

"What? Did you fuck Shelley? Is that why he wants to kill us?"

"Nah, not yet. Sweet little thing is playing hard to get," he boasts. "But she'll come 'round soon enough. Now let's look at the maps again." Jackson lays the maps out a second time, and the boys work with him to plot a course that will take at least two months longer but keeps them off the radar of Silus Baxter's cronies. If that old bastard wanted to play dirty, Jackson will give him dirty.

"Man, I'm wiped. We should sleep. We can leave in the morning."

"If we're wanting to beat the weigh stations, we're going to get the lead out of our asses tonight." His finger flies the universal flag to the other men as they bitch up a storm about not getting rest. "We'll sleep at the state line."

They stroll back to where the bikes have been loaded, and fire them up to take off under cover of darkness. Jackson hated this part, leaving behind his Angel. He would show the old man that he had what it took to earn his keep, and if he thought this brief trip would be all it took to keep him down, then Silus Baxter would learn a hard lesson. Jackson let his anger keep him awake as the row of lights lit the dark highway. The three of them roar towards their destination. He couldn't even send her a message to let her know. It's part of the rules to keep them from being caught. Gun running is dangerous enough that few do it with any success. Most runners end up being gunned down by someone trying to screw the deal over. The men riding with him on this trip are the closest thing to brothers Jackson has, and he would be damned if he let anything happen to them.

CHAPTER THREE
Would You Like Butter With That?

Fall 2003

Shelley's Sophomore year was proving to be no more fun than her previous year. Shelley's anxiety is through the roof now that she has spent a year amongst some of the most awful people she has ever encountered and that includes the bikers passing through The Triple Six. Her friends from middle school had decided she was no longer part of the group. Part of that is who her father is, but most of it was her lack of willingness to participate in activities like skipping school. If her father caught her doing any of those things, the punishment would be brutal. The only reason she had any sanity at school was Faye folding her into her friends circle.

Faye had even encouraged Shelley to try out for the cheerleading squad. The perky little blond fit the bill and made the squad without issue. Shelley often wondered why Faye didn't do cheerleading. She always thought her older sister prettier than her. Faye is tall, curvy, and with beautiful strawberry blond hair. Everyone seems to fawn over her and her friends. Shelley always feels like the kid playing dress up when around them.

Shelley misses Jackson, even if she is mad at him for ditching her in Hilton Head after she told him she was not supposed to go. She had not seen him since the night of the bonfire. She knew he wasn't dead as the rest of the Angels of Wrath would be all a buzz about revenge. Her father shrugged and gave her a non-committal grunt whenever she asked him about the boy.

"You worry too much. Your lover boy will be back soon enough." Faye teases her as they get ready to go out. Jackson had always texted her before when had to do club business. She wonders if he is really off with another woman, and this was his way of dealing with her. She kicks herself for kissing him that night.

This particular Saturday, Faye and she had the night off from The Triple Six. Club business at the bar meant only official Angels of Wrath members are allowed. As the Angels had not introduced the girls to the men, or given them colors, they were not welcome. Shelley knows that their business is something illegal, but she has grown up in this world. Their rebuke of authority is as natural as breathing. She does not question when she and Faye are shielded from it. She was not sure she ever wanted to be in the know, either.

Faye had convinced their mother to let them borrow the car. After an hour of hairspray, make-up, giggling and gossip, Faye, Shelley, and Faye's girlfriends from Hilton Head squished into the sedan. They head to the mall near them that had a movie theater in it. The plan was to walk around the mall, window shop, then to catch a movie. Freaky Friday and Jason vs. Freddy are playing at the two-screen theater. They park close to the theater entrance of the mall and pile out of the car. The girls preen and primp one final time before they begin mall crawling.

Mall crawling is the best thing they could do with the little money they have earned. They wander in and out of stores, socializing with their friends who are working. All of this while getting to look at new and shiny things they might buy in the future. While none of the families in Angels of Wrath were poor, they weren't rich either. Shelley and Faye each had about twenty dollars. This is due to Faye's tips she has split with Shelley. As the little pack walks the mall, they attracted attention. They giggle, wave, and pout cutely to garner free food and drink from more than one boy sheepishly smiling in their direction.

The time for the movie rolls around, and the girls enter the theater lobby that opens to the mall. The smell of movie popcorn always makes Shelley smile. Behind the counter, wearing the polo shirt and navy slacks for a uniform, stood one boy from the bonfire. Tommy is the name on the pin. The other three boys are leaning over the counter, laughing and talking with him. Another man, not much older than them, in a suit too big for his body, counting out money to close out a register for the night. The manager looks up over his glasses at Faye as she approaches.

"Two for Freaky Friday." She then steps aside after getting her tickets. Each girl follows suit, buying a ticket for the comedy as well. She hands Shelley her ticket and raises a brow at the weird look on Shelley's face. Shelley had already noticed the boys and was hoping Faye didn't make a big deal about them being here.

"Hey fellas," Faye's musical voice rings across the way. "Small world," she smirks. The other girls come alongside her and it looks like a standoff in the lobby.

"Why hello ladies," Jasper's sweet Southern drawl fills the area. His voice is deep and while he's only twenty, there is something about him that made everyone take notice. Next to him stood Beau with his sweet face and broad shoulders. They looked like they walked right out of a Chippendale's calendar again, only with clothes on this time. Billy stepped to the side, so he could see who his brothers were now peacocking for. He swears he could see their tails wagging in human form. The sweet scent of the girls filled their nostrils and hormones are rising. Tommy sulks because he is working all night. His cousins get to have all the fun. Billy ignores his cousin's whine as is being held enchanted by Shelley's sweet scent.

"What movie ya seein'?" Faye questions in a smooth tone.

"Jason vs. Freddy," Beau offers.

Shelley knew as soon as it came out of Beau's mouth that Faye was going to see that movie. A side-glance at the manager told Shelley there was no way they were getting into that movie. She bites her lip before she whines. "Faye, I don't wanna see a scary movie." Her cheeks blush as now all of them were watching the sisters. Shelley does not want to admit to these boys she is younger due to moping about why she thinks Jackson has ditched her. She wants them to like her too. She is desperate to be cool.

The other girls are already exchanging their tickets, and Faye gives her sister a small frown. "You don't have to. Go see Freaky Friday. We'll meet up after." Faye shrugs as she moves to trade her ticket in. Shelley droops and looks from her sister to the manager, who looks like he is daring Shelley to change her ticket.

She had not seen Billy staring right at her, as if he couldn't take his eyes off of the sweet angel before him. Her anxiety and fear are driving his instincts to protect her to the brink of uncontrollable. "Here, Miss Faye. I'll trade ya. I'll go see Freaky Friday with Miss Shelley." His smile is dazzling as he steps forward. Billy dwarfs Jasper in size, and his easy-going presence makes it hard to feel his dominance. He's the eldest of this group, at twenty-two, but he lets Jackson strut around like the Alpha wolf. He comes alongside Shelley, reaching out to Faye to trade tickets.

"Perfect!" Faye's voice sings as she falls into step between Jasper and Beau. They are ecstatic to have five girls to the two of them. Tommy groans at his bad luck. Billy laughs and steps up to the concession stand. Faye catches Shelley's gaze and shrugs. There is jealousy and mischief in those eyes, as Shelley is getting to go on a real date. Faye and Shelley do not have permission to date outside of the Angels of Wrath. If their parents found out about these boys, there would be hell to pay. Faye's grin suggests that if Shelley doesn't tell, she won't either.

"You want anything, darlin'?" Tommy's already getting Billy a soda and looks from Billy to Shelley.

"You sure 'bout this? You can go to the scary movie if you want to," Shelley cannot contain her smile that he offered to go with her. He smells of cologne and Zest soap. She knows the scent because it's the same soap her father uses. She is admiring how his body threatens to rip through his shirt, and she looks tiny next to him. In the back of her mind, she knew if Jackson saw them, she would be in trouble. Billy isn't trying anything, but she knows Jackson would still be pissed that Billy is even looking at his girl. She tries to justify it to the imaginary angry Jackson in her head that Billy is just offering to buy her a soda. When he nods, she lights up, "Small popcorn and a Sprite."

Tommy looks at Billy with a quirked brow. Shelley catches the weird way they stare at each other and gets the feeling they are having a whole conversation without saying a word again. Billy's cheeks blush and she swears he let out a low growl before Tommy broke the staring contest and turned to face Shelley.

"You want butter on that?" He moves to get the popcorn with butter when she nods at him. Before she can fish out her money, Billy puts a twenty on the counter and shoves it toward Tommy.

"Miss Shelley, you put that money away. What kind o' man would I be if I let you pay for anything." She blushes and picks up her soda, along with the popcorn, to follow Billy into the theater. Freaky Friday is not attracting a large crowd for the late show and the two of them are two of three people in the theater.

For the entire movie, Billy cannot think about anything other than the pretty girl next to him. He stretches with an awkward glance at Shelley. He finishes the motion with his arm draped along the back of her chair. He didn't want to be too forward. His mother would kill him if he were inappropriate with a young woman. He is the son of the Alpha, which means he has to be on his best behavior at all times. It is something he wished his brothers remembered.

"Shit! she is not wearing any panties." Jasper's surprise and excitement through their mind link makes Billy's lip curl in irritation. He rubs his other hand over his face. He was not leaving this theater to stop them, especially not after Shelley snuggles into him. It allows him to put his massive hand on her shoulder. From that moment on, Billy had no idea what was happening on the screen. He only had eyes for Shelley.

Once the movie ends, they shuffle out to the auditorium. Jason vs. Freddy still had a few minutes to go. He smiles down at Shelley. His fingers brush back a stray lock of blond hair. He could get lost in those eyes, and he didn't even know her last name. He takes a slow breath, to not look creepy taking in her scent, but wanted nothing more than to keep breathing it in. Billy opens his mouth to ask her for her number when the rest of them file out of the theater and interrupt them.

Faye is flushed, and the other girls are giggling as they exit. The girls' scents of arousal fill the area. Billy pulls back from Shelley, giving Jasper and Beau a withering look. The silent conversation is enough to make the young men ease away from the girls and clear their throats. Tommy is nowhere to be seen.

"I assume you girls got a ride home tonight?" Billy asks. He is hoping they do not, but he does not want to sound too eager to spend more time with Shelley.

The gaggle of girls erupt into giggles.

"Oh, sugar, of course we do. C'mon Shelley," Faye strides forward and engulfs Shelley into her little pack again, pulling her away from the pouting Billy. With a graceful look over her shoulder, she coos, "Until next time, fellas." She gives a flirty finger wave, and her friends mimic the motion.

"I think I'm in love," Jasper pants.

"Finger fuckin' a girl in a movie ain't love," Beau snickers.

Both yelp as Billy whacks them upside the head. "You treat

those girls right, or not at all. You know how Momma will feel about you two smellin' like sex." Billy growls even though he is thinking about all the sweet things he would like to do with that little blond. Since the night she plopped herself into his lap, he could not shake all the unseemly thoughts he had of her.

"Right... You tellin' me you didn't get Freaky Friday on that little doll?" Jasper cuts his elder brother a look and takes an easy step away as Billy tries to punch him.

Tommy emerges, now clocked out. "What did I miss?"

"Nothing," all three brothers quip while grinning like fools.

CHAPTER FOUR
Just A Kiss Goodnight

It was the perfect plan. Of course, Faye never screws up when she is sneaking out. Only Jasper had mentioned that Shelley needed to be there. In his and Faye's secret trysts, he couldn't help but laugh at how Billy had been pining for the pretty little blond. Faye asked her to tag along to the midnight release of Underworld. Shelley put her anxiety about scary movies aside at the chance to see Billy again. He accepted her. She spent an entire hour messing with her hair and make-up while Faye leaned in the bathroom door, watching her.

"Girl, you got it bad. Here, let me help." She took the eye-liner from her little sister and turned her to face her.

"Close your eyes." She glides the tiny pencil along the line of Shelley's eyelid with expert precision. There is a quiet moment while Faye focuses on her work. Her tone softens. "You haven't had sex with him, have you?"

"Faye," Shelley huffs and rolls her eyes.

"Hold still," Faye chastises. "I'm serious. He's older, Shelley. And he's a Coeh. If Daddy finds out we've been runnin' with Wolf Pack, he'll flip his shit. And what about Jackson?"

"What about Jackson? He hasn't even bothered to text me.

He's probably with some girl."

Shelley teases her sister back. "And you mean if Daddy finds out you've been sleepin' with Jasper. Ow!" As Faye pulls the eyeliner away and jabs her sister. The two erupt into giggles. Shelley smiles at her big sister. Shelley wants to be everything Faye is, beautiful, adored, and so confident. She is not afraid to tell Daddy no and do whatever she wants.

"Alright! Mamma and Daddy won't be home until at least four. The movie will be out in plenty of time, and we'll be home before they know it." Faye repeats for the hundredth time as she glances at her watch. Shelley furrows her brow again and has not been nervous until now. "We should get going. They'll be waiting."

"Wait, we're not driving?" Shelley has a bad feeling about that. If they were on a time limit, wouldn't it be better to drive themselves?

"Go like this," Fay rubs her lips together as she dabs at the watermelon lip gloss on Shelley's lips. Both of them make funny lip faces at each other before they are giggling again. Shelley chose a sun-dress with pink flowers on it, a pair of boots, and a jean jacket. Her curly blond hair is loose about her shoulders and looks as light as a feather, where Faye has the straighter hair, long and sleek. Faye's clothing is racier as she swiped a dress out of her mother's closet. The girls turn off lights and ease out the front door, locking up. Their excitement keeps the smiles on their faces. They walk down the street where the old pickup is waiting.

As it rumbles to life, Faye hops into the back with Jasper, Tommy, Beau, Veronica, Candy, and Taylor. Wanda and Faye had a falling out over just who Jasper was more interested in. In true girl fashion, Wanda is now persona non grata. Jasper gives Shelley a wink. When she turns, Billy is holding open the door for her.

"Your chariot, Miss Shelley." He flashes his megawatt smile at her. His scent is divine to Shelley, an earthy richness mixed with a hint of aftershave. The boys in the back all give little howls and tease the pair of them. Shelley is thankful her hair will not get all messed up on the way there and ignores the teasing.

Everyone settled in to watch the movie, and it is entertaining enough. The boys snicker and roll their eyes at the way the werewolves act when their attention is even on the screen to judge it. Jasper and Faye haven't come up for air once since they sat down, giving everyone around them quite the show. Beau and Tommy are having far less luck with their girls, though there is giggling and hushing going on. Billy keeps glancing down at Shelley. He had rested his arm around her, then smiled a goofy grin when she snuggled into him. Her slightest touch made him want to howl at the moon. She shared her popcorn with him, and the two of them watched the movie. Unlike his brothers, he didn't need to make out with Shelley to enjoy her company.

"Rein it in, lover boy. Remember who her daddy is." Billy sends over the mind link the boys share.

"Fuck off, man. This girl's hot as hell and I'm gonna have a good time."

"Both of you shut up. You're killing my hard on," Beau chimes in.

"I thought it was just you boys going to the movie," Momma Coeh's voice cuts through their minds. All four boys sit up proper and shift in their seats. Any semblance of smooth gone now that their mother is onto them being on dates. They can't hear her laughter, but she would have words with them when they got home.

Shelley raises a brow up at Billy and he offers a sheepish smile. She blushes and sits up as well, a small pout forming on her face at his sudden stiffness. She steals another side glance when he turns to look at the movie and furrows her brow. She shifts her gaze the other way, to see Faye frowning and sulking in her chair. Whatever just happened was weird, and now the boys are acting different. It is like an unseen force dumped ice water on all of them. She would ask Billy after the movie what that was about. The rest of the movie goes without event. Afterwards, the boys are shaking their heads and chuckling about how terrible the portrayal of werewolves had been.

"You girls wanna get something to eat?" It's Beau that asks. His brothers cut him a look.

Faye and Shelley exchange a look as well. The silent conversation of 'can we get away with it?' on their minds. Shelley shakes her head no. Faye nods. Shelley cuts her a dirty look and points to her wrist, as if to check the time.

"Don't worry, Miss Shelley, we'll get ya home safe," Beau offers with a hopeful look, his arm draped over Veronica.

The entire group is looking at her. If she insists, she is pretty sure Billy will take her and Faye home. But they wouldn't get to hang with boys anymore tonight, and Faye might kill her over it.

"Sure," she mumbles, and cuts Faye a nervous look. She catches Billy's smile and her irritation at her sister pressuring her fades. The group pile into Billy's beat-up pickup and they're off to Waffle House.

An hour later, they are laughing and giggling over sodas, waffles, and mysterious meat that the server called country fried steak.

"Looks more like country fried road kill," Jasper pokes at it in disdain. Throughout the meal, he and Faye were canoodling each other. The others groan and throw sugar packets at them when they get too hot and heavy with each other.

Billy's hand had rested on Shelley's knee and her cheeks remained a rosy color from enjoying the touch. He had said little through the meal, and Shelley couldn't help but keep smiling up at him as they listen to the antics of the others. She had long forgotten about the question of the boys' odd behavior earlier tonight.

He could get lost in those eyes. Then he hears Tommy

speaking. "Yeah. It's a gigantic party. Your girls will love it. November eighth. Party starts at four. Don't be late. It's out on our family's land. Pretty casual affair." He is grinning from ear to ear. Jasper, Billy, and Beau all have stopped talking and stiffened again.

"What the fuck, man. They're not wolves," Jasper growls in the link they shared.

"So, humans get rutted too," he flashes a toothy grin back at Jasper.

"I don't know, man. Momma ain't gonna let these girls partake. They could get hurt," Beau whines. It's his first Rutting, and he doesn't want to get in trouble.

"Well, too late now. I already invited them," Tommy shrugs.

Faye, Veronica, Taylor, and Candy all nod eagerly.

"We'll be there! Just give me the address," Faye chimes in. Shelley said nothing, as she saw the looks on their faces. Tommy was out of line inviting them. The way they all stiffened up and stopped talking made Shelley wonder if there was something they weren't telling them. All the boys have resumed their uncomfortable posture, and the mood has grown heavy. Shelley wants to know more about what is going on between them, but then she notices the time on the wall clock and she is more concerned with being caught.

"Faye, we should get home." Shelley hates being the responsible one. If they get caught, she is not sure what her father will do. Billy snatches up the ticket and goes to pay as the rest file out. It's three in the morning when they pull up to the corner at the end of the street where Faye and Shelley live. "I had a great time tonight," Shelley murmurs to Billy.

"Me too, Miss Shelley. I'd love to take you to another movie sometime." He didn't know why he felt so nervous, but he could feel his heart pounding in his chest as he put the truck into park. He's out of the truck and around to her side before she can open the door. It makes her giggle as he helps her out of the pickup.

She gets a mischievous look on her face and motions him closer, like she wants to tell him a secret.

When he leans down close enough, she darts forward and steals a chaste kiss. It is awkward and rough as her sweet watermelon flavored lips press against his. He lets out a low, happy growl and is reaching to pull her in close when Faye tugs Shelley away. He leans against the truck, watching the two girls trot into the darkness back to their house. He sighs and has a goofy grin on his face again. He felt the sparks. He was right, she is his mate.

The whooping howls of the Coeh boys fill the night air as they drive away.

CHAPTER FIVE
The Devil's Ball

It's four in the afternoon on Halloween. Faye had gotten hers and Shelley's costumes. She thought it hilarious that she wore the angel costume and Shelley the devil. Faye is pushing the envelope. She went out of her way and found platform heels that were sparkling, red for Shelley and white for herself. Faye's 'dress' is a sweet baby-doll number with just enough material to be decent in public. Shelley's is a sparkling red romper with shorts that just cover her ass cheeks, hugging right up her tiny waist and ample breasts.

"I dunno, Faye. This is showing a lot o' skin. Daddy's not gonna like it."

"Pssht. You leave Daddy to me. You look hot." She is radiating mischief as she helps her sister into the outfit. Faye follows this up by unzipping the romper enough to show the black lace push-up bra she forced Shelley into earlier. "Just a little cherry red on the lips," she holds Shelley's chin and draws the red lipstick along her lips, "and your horns." Faye hands Shelley the headband with tiny red horns popping up.

Shelley nestles it into her fluffy blond hair and looks in the mirror. She didn't look sixteen in this outfit, and for the first time next to Faye she thought she looked hot.

"Now! For your slippers, Cinderella," Faye giggles again. She already had her heels on, making her six feet tall.

Shelley gives her sister a dubious look. "How am I supposed to wait tables in these?" She slips her feet into them, wobbling like an inflatable banner in a car lot. "These are really high, Faye."

"Don't worry! You'll get the hang of it. You walk like this," and Faye struts around the room. Shelley tries to mimic her sister as she follows her around the room. They go back and forth for several minutes before they plop down on the bed in a fit of laughter.

"You girls ready," Silus bellows up the stairs.

"Silus Baxter, what in the hell are you wearing?" The girls giggle as their mother shouts at their father downstairs.

"What?! It's a costume!" He sounds incredulous but is giving her a grin. The tall man with a square jaw and tight curly hair he keeps cut short turns slowly to show off his costume.

"Puttin' on your damn colors and lettin' a gun hang from your chest ain't a costume! You promised you'd wear the one I got you!" She is pouting as the Batman costume is nowhere in sight. The older woman is dressed in a skin-tight black leather cat suit with kitty ears tucked in her long straight hair, she had painted on a mask around her eyes to finish the Catwoman look.

"Easy, pussy cat. I'm dressed as Johner, from Aliens." He flashes a devilish grin at her. Then he rolls his eyes and throws his hands up in the air in frustration when she turns and huffs out the door to the car.

"Girls!" He barks it up the stairs. They were already on a short leash for sneaking out. Which is why they are working tonight, and not getting to enjoy the party. He is pretty sure there were boys involved. Neither girl would turn on the other, so he left it at grounding them and punishing them for tonight.

The Devil's Ball is an annual charity event for the Savannah Historical Society held at The Triple Six. Silus welcomes all bikers and a select few outside of the biker circle. It's invitation only, but it's a hell of a party. Silus has busted out the smoker. Twinkle lights dot the night sky as they hang from poles. A stage was erected for the local band. Food, booze, and bikers will fill the parking lot, and bar, well into the night. It is a night of merriment and for a good cause.

Faye comes down the stairs first. Her delicate wings bouncing as she struts right by her father. His eyes narrow as he inspects her. The girl is asking for trouble. He rubs his hand over his face and shakes his head. She is eighteen, and old enough to dress like a whore if she wants. He doesn't approve, but anyone who is there tonight knows better than to hurt her.

His gaze turns to the stairs again, watching as his darling baby girl steps down the stairs, her delicate creamy legs held taught by the heels. Step by step, he can feel his blood boiling with rage as she reaches the bottom step. Her breasts are falling out of that outfit. His jaw twitches and he inhales, then exhales. He has half a mind to beat the fool out of Faye right here. He knows damn well his little Angel would never dress like this on her own.

"Get your fucking ass upstairs right now and put some clothes on," he snarls at Shelley.

"Daddy, it's my costume," she chews against her lower lip in fear.

He looks furious.

"Daddy, she looks great! All the boys'll be fawnin' over--"

The back of his hand connects with Faye's face, making her yelp and hold her hand to her face. The crack echoes in the otherwise silent room. He turns his attention back to Shelley.

"Do not make me tell you again. You have five minutes."

"C'mon," Faye mutters, as she takes Shelley, who is now trembling in fear, back up the stairs. "Here. You can borrow this," she says as she pulls out a tiny black wad from her dresser. It takes a couple of minutes to untangle the fishnet body suit and slide it on Shelley. "Perfect!" Faye squeals. She smooths it out in the back, then Shelley slips the red romper back on. She brings regular clothes and shoes, just in case it didn't satisfy their father's view of how Shelley should be dressed.

A few minutes later, the girls are back downstairs. Silus left while they were changing. Their mother is waiting for them in the car.

"Has your daddy seen that outfit?" Paula's voice holds a worried tone as she asks the girls about Shelley's costume. She knows the answer. It was a warning to the girls to not disobey their father without actually telling them to behave. They're teenage girls and no girl wants to look 'cute' on Halloween. They want to look sexy.

"Yes, ma'am," Faye says. Shelley says nothing and keeps her gaze averted. Faye's cheek is sporting a red hand print still. It would leave a bruise. The level of guilt Shelley feels is pretty high that her sister got hurt again because of her. The three women head to the Triple Six.

*****

Susie Coeh is putting on the last touches of her make-up. David and she are a flapper and gangster. The only time she gets him in a suit is a wedding, a funeral, or when he's pretending to be Al Capone. They are taking the Suburban tonight so they could all have a good time and not worry about getting home. The last she heard, the boys were planning on dressing up as some horror movie character in coveralls and a mask, but they were not asking for her help with costumes much these days. It makes her miss when they were little. Susie steps onto the porch to be greeted by a soldier, construction worker, biker, and cowboy. All of them are howling in laughter as they belt out YMCA off key. Sometimes she thinks these boys are too clever for their own good, but it makes her smile to see how happy her boys are. The youngest, Caleb, is wearing his street clothes.

"What are you goin' as?" Susie asks.

"A werewolf," he mutters. His petulant response makes the other boys laugh harder.

"Boy, you know you're gonna need to shred up that jacket, get some chompers, and put on the fluffy ears to make that work, right?" David gives Susie a bemused look.

"Fine. A serial killer then," he growls in irritation.

"What's got you in such a mood, baby?" She comes over and fusses over him.

"Oh, don't mind him, Momma Coeh. The girl he was sweet on told him she had a boyfriend already." Tommy offers through chortles.

"I see. Well, sugar, all the more reason to go have a good time. Find yourself a nice girl and forget all about the one that doesn't deserve you." She softens as she pulls Caleb into a big hug. She doesn't make him change and they all pile into the Suburban, the four boys still singing YMCA.

They are excited about going to this event, as they know at least Shelley and Faye will be there. The night fate brought the girls to the bonfire has led the boys to spending far too much time in Savannah with them. These boys enjoy being relatives of the Alpha, as it had its perks. They getting to go to The Devil's Ball because of that association is just one of the more fun ones.

By the time the Suburban rolls up, the band's already playing. Silus is holding court at the smoker. There are people dancing and drinking. There are costumes of all status on display. The old grizzly bikers are flying their colors, with a few wearing some sort of costume to appease their women. It is a stark reminder that this isn't some hippy joint. Susie cannot help but laugh as the four boys leap from the car and start looking around as if they were hunting prey. It reminds her of watching them when they shifted for the first time. She thumps against her husband's shoulder and motions to them. They try to act casual, but they are looking for very specific people.

It doesn't take long for the boys to track their prey. Drinks in hand, they ease into the bar proper. The pool tables were occupied with Angels of Wrath members hustling each other for money. The barstools are full of old men not wanting to stand around out in the Georgia night. A middle-aged woman that looks damn fine in the cat suit is behind the bar. There are bikers everywhere and the jukebox is thumping out some old twangy tune they like. The four boys stand in the walkway, surveying the room. Their eyes look from place to place and they use their other senses to find what they are looking for. Faye's musical laugh is the first thing they hear related the girls. She is on the other side of the room, setting down food and drinks for the men at the table. One man plays with the hem of her 'costume' while his grin turns lecherous. Jasper's growl is enough for Tommy and Billy to look at each other and go on high alert.

"Easy, brother. She is working, and this is their bar." Billy's voice was low and full of command, but he can sympathize. Any young wolf would lose his cool watching another man touch what he believed to belong to him. "Look, a table has opened up." They settle into the chairs around the table.

"Hey fellas! I'll tell your waitress you're waiting," Faye smirks as she struts up alongside the boys. She is full of energy even with being run all over the place.

Billy furrows his brow at Jasper, who is staring at Faye. A mix of fury, anxiety, and irritation radiates off Jasper like too much perfume on a cheap hooker. He is wearing the pristine soldier's uniform, which serves to make him appear more menacing. Faye didn't stick around as she is being hailed by her tables and this is Shelley's section.

Jasper's eyes never leave Faye as she quickly melts into the crowded room with her little angel wings bobbing behind her. Jasper was here to see her and was hoping to sneak off to relieve her of her costume. She barely gave him the time of day.

Billy's trying to remain optimistic about it, but he can tell something Jasper just saw has his brother on edge. This was causing the rest of them to remain on edge.

"Dude, chill the fuck out. If we start shit tonight, Momma'll kill us. Remember what she said about the guys from up North?" Beau's voice is one breath short of a whine as he tries to calm his older brother down.

"Yeah man. You're killin' the vibe. I mean, if all the waitresses here are hot as Faye, Smurfs will have nothing on my balls. Look at the hot MILF behind the bar. Shit. The Angels of Wrath have all the hot chicks." Tommy's chuckling.

"Jasper, she is worried her momma'll see you guys. Didn't you see her point at the bartender?" Billy motions to Faye, who is emphatically motioning to the bartender with a worried look now that she has emerged from the crowd. Billy breathes out to push his calming aura out to his brother. He clamps a massive hand onto his brother's shoulder. "Easy, man. She is just a girl. You'll live."

"Easy for you to say. That cute little blond only has eyes for you and you haven't even gotten to taste her yet." Jasper grumbles and turns to face his brothers. He didn't want to admit he felt the mate bond with Faye. His mother has already made it clear she does not approve of them sniffing around human girls.

"Hey guys!" Shelley's voice chirps over the noise in the room. All four heads snap up to take in the tiny devil that appeared next to Tommy. She stands there in her platform heels with her hip cocked, is the cutest devil Billy has ever seen. All four have their mouths open and Billy shifts in his seat as his pants get too tight. He cannot take his eyes off of her. The rumbling sound of enjoyment emits from him and her cheeks flush as red as her romper. He is sure his heart is going to beat right out of his massive chest.

Shelley gives Billy a once over look. Billy looks like a weight-lifter pretending to be a construction worker. Broad and muscled shoulders narrowing down to a trim and fit waist give way to his muscular legs and arms. His easy-going temperament and gentle smile makes his stunned face even more adorable to her.

He cannot look away from Shelley. His eyes settle on her chest the possessive wolf nature creeps in. He wants to murder every man in here, including his brothers, for looking at her. His cheeks redden, and he averts his gaze down to the beer in his hand. His mind clouds with the things he wants to do to her. He knows looking at Shelley like that much longer will only get him in trouble.

The low whistle from Tommy followed with, "Hot damn, Shelley-belle. You dress like that all the time and I'm gonna have to find me a hand-basket to ride straight to hell." His comments win him a steel-toed boot to the shin and a rather threatening growl from Billy. He grunts and shifts his shins out of kicking range with a shit-eating grin.

Shelley's blushing bright red and tries to ignore Tommy's compliment. She isn't long at the table as she takes their order and hurries off.

Billy stares at her, suddenly knowing exactly how Jasper feels. Lucky for them, the pool table opens up.

"C'mon. Let's blow off some steam," Tommy chuckles. Tommy is easy-going, like Billy, even if he is also a shit-starter. He has looked up to Billy his whole life They've been best buds since they were little, even if he is four years Billy's junior. He doesn't get all the freedoms the other Coeh boys do as he is just their cousin, but he basks in their glory. He'd be out of high school soon enough so he could fly colors and officially work for the pack. Tommy puts the bill down on the pool table. They commandeer it for the foreseeable future. A few Angels grumble at them, but otherwise let it go. Tonight is for charity, and if Silus catches wind of them starting trouble, he'll have their hides, even if these boys are Wolf Pack.

A few minutes later, Shelley delivers the wings and nachos with beers. No one is asking for ID tonight, and God help the man who tries to bust The Triple Six. She brushes her fingers along Billy's arm as she passes. It's a sweet motion to say she is happy he is here. It puts a cheesy smile right back on Billy's face as he watches Tommy lean down to take the first shot.

Jasper can hear Faye's musical laugh again. He grips the pool cue harder and looks in the direction he can hear it coming from. Near the dart boards, she is laughing and flirting with a man easily twice her age. His grimy paw of a hand comes down and cups along her thigh. Jasper lets out a full growl, his lip snarling. Jasper snatches up his beer and takes a large swig of it.

Beau and Billy exchange a glance and both shift their weight to block his path.

"Oh, Max," she sounds flustered. "Daddy catches you touchin' me like that and you're gonna beg for an angel."

"Well, darlin'. Best iffn ya don't be tellin' him. Why don't you come sit on ol' Max's lap for a spell?" His hand rubs firmer against her thigh.

Faye's used to the attention. She has grown up in this bar and the men know she is old enough to play. They've been talking about 'introducing' her to the club for at least a year now. Silus has been dragging his feet on the matter. This girl should belong to the club, in their opinions, along with her sister. Max's hand is firm on her thigh as he eases it toward her waist, and it's creeping her out. She will be in big trouble if she is caught goofing off. She has felt her father's wrath once tonight and is not going to do anything to attract it a second time.

"Max, stop it," her voice loses all mischief and mirth.

It was all Jasper needed to act. He flies around the pool table and away from his brothers faster than a lightning strike. "You heard her, dick weed, now get your hands off the lady." Jasper puffs up to his full height, his fists open and close with the anticipation of a fight. His eyes held a malicious glint and his lip curls again.

Beau moves to step in, but Billy held his hand up to stop him.

With a few easy steps, he is between Jasper and Max. He put his back to Max so he could focus on keeping Jasper out of trouble. He could see Jasper's pupils have gone pitch black. Jasper is struggling to keep himself from shifting in front of all these bikers.

"Don't do it. Not here." Billy's voice is low and calm, but he means for his younger brother to listen to him. The authority behind his voice is enough for Jasper to focus and stop himself from shifting.

Max shoots up off the barstool and pulls Faye against him, grinding against her to egg on Jasper. He follows it by shoving her to his buddy to get in Jasper's face. "Just what are you gonna do about it, boy? Girl belongs to the Angels. We don't need no inbred hick Coehs stinkin' up the joint. So why don't you run back to your momma's tit?" There are several chuckles as a few other Angels stand up to back Max up. This brings Tommy and Beau to stand alongside Jasper and Billy. Billy sighs and turns to stand next to Jasper to face the drunk Angels itching for a fight. All four boys puff up just as much as Max and his buddies. Billy is hoping their intimidating nature is enough to make the Angels take pause.

"Let it go, man. Let it go. He's trying to get a rise out of you."

"That's right. Listen to that pussy. You fuckin' Coehs are the shit stains of this Earth." Max feels like the king shit when suddenly there's a fluff of blond hair with little red devil horns between him and Jasper. Shelley comes up to their shoulders in her heels, but she means to get their attention.

Her hands are on her hips, and her eyes blaze with anger. "Max, you damn well know there's no fightin' in the bar tonight. Take your shit outside before I get Da-,"

The back of Max's hand smacks Shelley's cheek loud enough the slap sound can be heard over the noise. The momentum is hard enough it sends Shelley to the floor with a crying yelp.

CHAPTER SIX
Dance With The Beast

Shelley hit the floor and brought her hand to her cheek. It throbs with pain. She is surprised that Max would strike her. She doesn't dare to move, for fear he might strike her again. She learned at a young age when someone is raging at you to make yourself as small as possible and do not move. Tears are in her eyes and she is pretty sure her mother is going to come out from behind the bar with the shotgun. She had sent Shelley over here. Faye stares in disbelief as she is held by one of the other Angels. Everyone loves Shelley and while Faye is used to getting knocked around by their father for her antics, she had never witnessed someone intentionally hurting her kid sister.

Jasper's eyes widen. He and Max were puffing up. He was planning on beating the shit out of the man for touching Faye and looking like a big damn hero to her. He never, in a million years, thought he would witness someone abuse a girl how Max just did. The snarl that comes from him makes a few bikers give him and Max a wide berth. He no longer had to fight against Billy holding him back. Instead, he felt Beau next to him snarling, and Tommy had moved with lightning speed to stand over Shelley. He puts himself between her and Max in case he tried to attack her again. Max had insulted their family twice and abused a woman. They didn't care how much trouble they were going to get into, this could not go unanswered, even though the girls are not part of the Wolf Pack. Women are to be cherished and adored. These bikers needed to be taught that lesson.

Billy didn't say a word. His hand wrapped around Max's throat with ease, lifting the large man right up off the ground. Billy's eyes had shifted to an inky black with no pupils at all and with an easy step, he moved from the group of men. His other hand caught the man right at his balls, lifting Max above his head. Before anyone could stop him, Billy is hurling Max through the blacked-out window at the front of the bar. The shatter of glass tinkles as Max lands with a grunt in the gravel. Billy's massive form stalks through the opening without even breaking a sweat. He drops his construction worker's helmet, vest, and tool belt on the ground. His breathing is erratic and his hands are curling into fists the closer he gets to Max. There was no stopping this freight train on a collision course with the biker on the ground.

Jasper and Beau mimic his behavior, coming behind him to protect their brother.

This alerts Caleb, who had been sulking outside. He looks on in shock as he sees Billy plant his steel-toed boot right into another man's chest while the man was trying to get up. The other party goers have not noticed the commotion yet. It is a group of rough and tumble bikers. If there isn't at least one fight, it's not a party. The problem is who is fighting, and Caleb knows if Momma sees this, all of them are in trouble. What the hell did that guy do to piss Billy off? He opts for the safer route and follows his mother's scent, hoping to find her, or his father, before Billy does something he regrets.

Tommy shakes his head as the crowd moves outside, knowing his place is to keep the girls safe should any of this blow back on them. He eases Shelley up and guides her, along with Faye, to the bar. This also traps their mother behind the bar. He saw that shotgun coming out from underneath it. He wasn't about to get one of his cousins shot, or worse.

"Here now," snatching up a clean hand towel and filling it with ice. "Keep that on your cheek." He then turns to look at Faye, his eyes narrowing in on her face. "Who did that?" His voice is darker and full of menace. He realizes now that Jasper must have seen her face earlier, and that is what set him on edge. Tommy can tell the girls are just human but Billy and Jasper are acting a fool about them. He hopes it will be out of their systems after The Rutting, but for now Shelley and Faye are under the Coeh boys' protection.

"Don't worry about it, Tommy. It's nothing," Faye mutters. This was not how she wanted to spend Halloween. She sure as hell doesn't want Jasper to go after her dad.

"Get the fuck out of my way," their mother yells at him, distracting him from understanding who hurt Faye.

"I can't do that, ma'am. I think your girls need you more than those old bikers do," he motions to Shelley and Faye.

Faye is hugging Shelley to her. All they needed now was for Daddy to come barreling in and beat the fool out of them for causing trouble.

She pumps the shotgun and Tommy frowns, holding his hands up to show he is not armed. "I let you go out there like that and it might be one of mine that gets hurt."

Outside, Billy grabs Max by the collar and brings his massive fist down to his face. He only lets go enough to let Max hit the ground from the force of it. It is not a fair fight at all. He is one breath away from shifting into his wolf form in front of all the party goers. His arm rears up, and he slams his fist into Max again. Then again. Blood splatters on the ground and Max grunts in pain at the crunch of a broken nose, then jaw. The Angels nearest them aren't about to let this stand.

Tommy hisses, "Shit," from his position at the bar. As men

jump into the fray and try to pull Billy off of their fallen brother, Jasper and Beau jump them, causing chaos. Tommy looks back at the girls and their mother, making sure all three are alright. It's too late now for Mrs. Baxter to shoot any of them without hitting Angels too. He is through the window and in the fight like a good soldier. All four Coeh boys are now brawling with Angels.

The party goers have stopped in their revelry, circling to watch this one-sided fight between Billy and Max. It's the four Coeh boys versus the Angels. It is punching, growling, kicking, and snarling, all wrapped up with blood and grime from the gravel. Susie, Caleb, and David come barreling up at the same time as Silus and his second in command come into view. Alongside Silus is a petite woman, with dark skin and golden eyes. Her fangs are showing, and her brows raised in bemused surprise. While most people believe it is a costume, Susie knows the woman is likely the most vicious monster in attendance tonight. Mehzebeen is her name, and she is head of the Savannah Historical Society. Her seeing Billy act makes Susie nervous she will lose her chance to become Alpha of the Appalachian Pack.

With a sigh, Susie watches her son, connecting with him via his mind to find the truth of why he would attack a man. Both of her brows raise at the emotions of rage and protectiveness, but no coherent words come from him. The boys are young and prone to brawling. It's what prideful boys do, but Billy was going to kill that man. He is the beloved of the sons because he generally keeps a cool head. For Billy to lose his temper meant something drastic happened and she would put money it is regarding a girl.

"Enough," her voice roars over the crowd. She is the president of the Wolf Pack biker gang as well as Alpha of the Coeh pack. She stands over six feet in height, with long dark auburn hair, and she is not a woman who likes to repeat herself. Momma Coeh as she is called by most was the first woman to become Alpha in the United States. The Coeh Pack is in the southeast.

Her direct family lives out in the national forest, just north of Savannah. A few weeks ago, Mehzebeen and several wolf elders approached her about stepping in to fill the role of Alpha for the Appalachian Pack. The Appalachian Pack covers the entire country east of the Mississippi river and holds a seat at the infamous Tribunal. Peace has reigned since the Civil War, where Sherman and the underworld leaders signed The Accord, a pact to help the underworld protect humanity. Those men are also watching tonight as Momma Coeh tries not to fume at her children brawling like pups in public. It is critical for her to become the Alpha and preserve The Accord.

Billy's hand, covered in blood spatter from Max, halts mid punch. His breathing is hard and there is sweat on his brow from the effort to not murder him. While no one else knows, Billy felt it when Shelley kissed him. She is his mate. The only thing stopping him from murdering Max is that his mother is the Alpha and going against her word could be a death sentence. His fury abates, and he throws Max to the ground, spitting at him. Jasper, Beau, and Tommy do the same with the men they were engaged with. All four of them are now bloody and scraped from the brawl. They stand still in defensive poses, watching the Angels of Wrath members struggling to get up after the ass whooping the Coeh boys handed them.

CHAPTER SEVEN
Time To Come To Jesus

Silus Baxter stood with his arms crossed, watching as the Coeh woman wrangled her mutts. His eyes narrowed, and he has made no sign of opposition to the woman's command.

His second is chuckling next to him. "I'll put fifty on your girls are at the root o' this."

Silus glances sideways at him then snorts in irritation. He was still fuming about the costume Faye tried to dress Shelley in. He tears his eyes away from the boys huffing and puffing at each other and looks into the bar. His wife is at the bar and he can't see the girls. As the party goers are no longer entertained by the brawl, they head back to the twinkle lights and live band. The music kicks back up. It was as if the Coeh boys hadn't just pounded the piss out of several grown bikers. A few minutes later, he nods to his second, and he wanders back off to the party as well. Silus draws in a deep breath and comes forward. "Sit down, all of you." His tone is bordering on a snarl in spite of him being only a human.

Momma Coeh comes and stands where Silus' second in command had just been, giving Mehzebeen an eye roll that suggests the two of them have had multiple conversations about

Silus Baxter and his Angels of Wrath.

"Which one of you Coeh boys broke my window?" Silus didn't ask who started the fight. He also didn't ask what the fight was about. He didn't care. What he cared about was how much that custom window was going to cost him to replace and how many nights it would affect his business. He could not conduct full club business while it is open. Faye and Shelley comes out with the first aid kits. Faye took Max, who was at the end of the line. Shelley walked to Billy on the other end when her father cleared his throat and leveled his gaze at her.

"Them boys can take care of themselves." It was the only warning he was going to give her to not embarrass him in front of the other bikers. He was also protecting her. His boys would not stand for his own damn daughter choosing Wolf Pack over Angels. From the look of her cheek, he was going to have to give someone a beating. For tonight, he needed to be in control of the situation.

Shelley frowns and bites her lip. She was no longer in her devil costume. Her new outfit is a pair of jeans and pink T-shirt that has the bright letters of 'Daddy's Girl' across her chest. She hesitated in front of Billy for a few seconds before she moves to one of the Angels. It wins a quartet of huffs and growls from the Coeh boys. Billy's eyes are on Shelley as she touches the other man, dabbing alcohol swabs along his temple and offering a clean dish towel for his nose. If that man touches her, he will rip his arms out of his sockets. Jasper was doing something similar for Faye.

Susie saw the look on Billy's face and frowns. She follows his gaze to Shelley, then to Silus. It would be the worst possible thing if the two of them were together. Did Billy know Shelley was only sixteen? She crosses her arms and gives a sharp whistle. It is enough to bring the boys' attention back to her.

"What makes you think my boys did it, Silus? It's your man that flew through it." Tommy and Beau snicker. Billy is still staring at Shelley. His hands opening and closing in fists, as he can smell Shelley's fear. It spiked after her father demanded she ignore his brothers and him. Being afraid of her father on that level isn't right for a father and daughter. Another glance at the men Shelley is attending to rewards him their lecherous grins while the two girls tend to them. It makes him want to pummel them all the more.

"Daddy," Faye's voice is urgent as Max's eyes roll to the back of his head. The wail of a siren in the distance as an ambulance approaches causes all the brawlers tense and sit up straighter. Silus comes over and helps Faye with Max until the paramedics arrive. Susie comes to her boys, resting a hand on Billy's shoulder. His muscles are rippling with agitation and his mother's soothing touch helps him keep the desire to shift at bay. Shelley is safe and had moved on from the assholes. Her cheek is red and angry looking and it breaks his heart he cannot comfort her. He never wants to see her hurt. A low whine escapes him, prompting his mother to squeeze his shoulder firmer.

"Silus, we'll come 'round and fix it in the morning. I think it's time for us to head on out, anyway." She jerks her head toward the suburban their father had already gone to get. All the boys and she pile into the vehicle. They pull out before the ambulance gets there. It's at least ten minutes before she says another word to any of them. "Billy, I am disappointed in you. I asked you boys to be on your best behavior tonight. Not only did you not do that, you have given them one more reason to treat us like animals. Was this about those girls from the movies?" She turns in her seat and looks at her son.

Billy's jaw clenches. "That man struck her, Mamma. Men don't do that." His voice is low when he responds. He is struggling to contain his emotions. He knows he did the right thing, and he would do it again.

Jasper is not having it. "Those fuckers put their hands on Faye!

Then they hit Shelley! She wasn't doin' shit. Just tryin' to get us all to stop fightin' in the bar. That asshole hit her *after* he groped my woman."

Jasper's retort is enough that Susie cuts David a look. He sighs and pulls the Suburban over. He puts it into park and puts on the flashers. "Everyone out," she barks at them.

As soon as the boys were standing outside of the vehicle, she was on them like they were rabbits. "Are you going to stand here and fucking tell me this entire fight was over some other man touching two strippers in training? Jasper Dean Coeh, have you been fucking that girl?" Her voice booms through the area as her Alpha dominance rears its ugly head.

All four sons and nephew shy from her. Their father would not intervene. He is a human, and right now she is being Alpha, not mom. David knew these boys had been heading into Savannah every weekend since August. He figured they were chasing girls, but he hadn't thought they were chasing the Baxter girls. Jasper realizes he fucked up yelling at his mother. If he were in wolf form, he would tuck his tail between his legs.

"I love her, Momma," Billy's voice roars through the night air with as much dominance as his mother's.

She moves to right in front of him, pulling him down to her eye-level by his ear. "You don't know what love is, boy. Those girls are human trash and if I catch you near 'em again, I'll make you wish you had never been born." She gives him a jerk, and he hisses in pain. "That goes for all of you. You want to play Romeo and Juliet? Fine. The next one of you I hear about socializin' with the Baxter girls will find out that I'm the mother-fucking Tybalt of this story and I will treat you lot like the Montagues. Is that understood?"

David frowns at Susie. His eyes fall on Billy, who is huffing and his jaw is twitching like he is being electrocuted. He had not hesitated when he professed his love for the girl. That told David all he needed to know and he would talk to Susie for him. Right now, she needed to put down the law. Another roaring growl of pain and sorrow fills Billy as he turns and shifts to run. His form transitions into a massive and beautiful beast with shiny copper fur. He grows to at least seven feet tall and his shoulders are the width of two men. His dark wavy hair and trimmed beard give way to copper fur, claws, and fangs. As he raged into the woods, he was every bit the image of a traditional werewolf. He disappeared into the tree line before any of the rest could comprehend his reaction.

Tommy frowns and looks at the rest of them. "I'll follow him and make sure he gets home." He hesitates only long enough to get approval from Momma Coeh, then he is running and transitioning into his lanky, black werewolf form.

Jasper, Beau, and Caleb file back into the truck in silence, soon followed by their parents. The rest of the car ride is quiet. Not even music on the radio.

"You saw what I saw, Susie," David links her while he keeps his eyes on the road. *"If Jasper was telling the truth, the boys were doing the right thing."*

"Don't." Susie's voice is curt in his head. *"No son of mine is going to get himself tied down to a trailer trash whore of a biker gang. He deserves a nice girl from the pack."*

"Careful there, Susie Q. If I remember correctly, there was this cute little Coeh girl who got herself knocked up by some no-good thug that'd never amount to nothin'," David chastises.

This gets him a dirty look, and he gives her a shit-eating grin. David glances in the rear-view mirror to gauge Jasper's response to the entire situation. He looks irritated and sulking, but he has always been better at hiding his emotions than the rest. He will bury it inside until he blows up like a powder keg. Billy had looked devastated, like his mother had kicked him right in the teeth. It was only eight days until The Rutting. The boys will get it out of their systems and everything will be alright. Those girls will be a distant memory.

CHAPTER EIGHT
Daddy's Little Angel

Billy's pickup truck rolled into the parking lot at eight in the morning. Out front stood Shelley, sweeping the concrete patio. For the first time in his life, Billy contemplated a life without the pack. His mother's command sent a pain right into his chest as he watched the cute little blond doing her work. He leans forward and rests his chin on his hands as they grip the steering wheel. He had spent most of the night running and hunting to ease his broken heart and failing. How could his mother deny him his mate? It wasn't fair, and he was beginning to think defying his mother was better than following her pack rules. He kills the engine and eases out of the truck.

"Mornin', Billy," Shelley calls as she waves at him. Her smile is gentle and everything in Billy screamed to just go wrap her up into his arms.

"Mornin', Miss Shelley," he drawls.

"Shelley, go help your sister in the kitchen," Silus appears in the door, holding it open. Shelley frowns, and scurries by her father to disappear into the bar. Silus remains, letting the door close behind him. Leaning back against it, he crosses his arms to watch the Coeh boy fix the window.

Billy turns and ignores him for the moment. He pulls his tools off the truck and settles them next to the window opening. Then he brings over the sawhorses and large piece of plywood to make a workbench. The last thing he pulls from his truck is a slab sized piece of bulletproof glass. Instead of buying a replacement window that's likely just as flimsy as the one he put Max through, he talked with his father about upgrading it to a more wolf-proof model.

"Mornin', Mr. Baxter," Billy finally says when he acknowledges Silus still standing there.

Silus grunts a response as he watches the younger man. After the party ended, he spoke with his wife about what happened in the bar. She wasn't completely sure, but the short of it was she had sent Shelley to break up the fight between Max and one of the Coeh boys when Max hit her. Then Billy lost his shit and threw the man out of the window. Silus continues watching this beast of a man get his workstation setup. He wanted to ask if he had touched his baby girl. He might murder him if he has, and it would just rekindle the feud between the Wolf Pack and Angels of Wrath. When Susie Coeh took over the pack from her father, she and Silus buried the hatchet. Now her boys are bringing trouble to his doorstep and his men are demanding blood. Silus is feeling his age today. Last night proved to him that time was running out on what to do with his girls.

The popular consensus is to have them become property of the club. He knew what that meant for them. No man wants his little girl to be treated poorly, even if Faye makes him want to strangle her. He also knew that keeping them 'protected' would cause dissent among the ranks. There's a difference between property and wife. The idea of his daughters being used and passed around like they meant nothing made his blood boil. It's why he sent that punk, Jackson, packing. He did not believe for one second that asshole would cherish Shelley the way she deserves, and if he can only save one, she is the one he is saving. If everything goes according to plan, his trek to Mexicali will be his last. Silus Baxter is not a man to trifle with.

Billy could feel the man's eyes on him. He whistles while he works to show Silus is not bothering him. The gloves he pulls on fit snugly, and he moves to the bucket and tools by the window. Billy then gets to work chiseling out the broken glass and cracked wood of the frame with expert precision. He is glad he brought extra materials. It looks like the frame is shot. He pays Silus no mind at all. The work isn't hard, and when it's done, it will be done right. Billy prides himself in always being good at what he does.

Faye and Shelley emerge from the kitchen, each carrying containers of food to be chopped for the cook. They settle on barstools at the bar. Faye can see Billy while Shelley's back is to him. A gentle smile forms on Faye's face. "What are you plannin' on wearing on Saturday?"

"Faye, you know what Daddy said."

"It's a party. You're supposed to dress for fun. Besides, Momma and Daddy will be at the rally in Jackson. What they don't know won't hurt 'em." Faye flashes a grin to her little sister, then winces as her cheek still hurts.

Shelley shifts in her seat and turns her focus on the onions they are supposed to be chopping. Her father spent the better part of last night barking about how those no good Wolf Pack boys would abandon them at the first chance. That they were Angels and should start acting like it. "Faye, maybe we shouldn't. Daddy was pretty angry. What if he has someone watchin' the house? Do the boys even still want us to go?"

Faye steals a glance at Billy, who is working at the window. She is pretty sure she sees him freeze for a second. She shrugs. "Listen, Shelley. At some point, Daddy's not gonna be the boss of everything. And... Well, after graduation Jasper and I are--," she stops. Faye catches herself before she tells her sister she is leaving. There is a guilty look on Faye's face as she turns her gaze back to Shelley.

Shelley's head whips up from her task to examine her sister. Both of her brows raising high as she pieces together the rest of the sentence. In six months, Faye would be gone, and she would be left alone with her parents. Swallowing hard, Shelley sets down the cutting knife. "Faye," she didn't know what to say. She wants to shout and scream at her sister to not leave her here, to stay here and it will all be alright. The look on Faye's face made Shelley hold her tongue. Fear wells in the pit of Shelley's stomach for her sister. *Where would she go? Did Jasper want to take care of her? What did that mean for her own wellbeing?* All of these questions swirl in her mind.

"Shelley. Stop worrying so much. Besides, Tommy invited us and I ain't heard otherwise. The girls and I are going. If you don't want to, you can stay home by yourself. But I wanna go have some fun." Faye laughs it off in her musical way and nudges her serious little sister. "Now. Back to the task at hand. We should get you a new dress. After we're done here, let's go shopping. I'll call the girls." Faye pulls out her little Nokia flip phone. The girls got them a few months ago when some bikers from another gang were sniffing around houses of the officers of the club.

Billy's brow is furrowing at the window. He had heard the entire conversation. He should tell the girls they are no longer invited to the party, but there is a tiny part of him longing for Shelley to be there. Just the idea of her being his mate made his heart skip a beat. His eyes linger and he had not even realized he had paused in his work to watch them. Faye's revelation about Jasper made him grimace. Jasper had no intention of running off with that girl, as far as Billy could tell. The conversation when he got home made him believe Jasper was just having a good time with the girl. That he thought she was pretty, and she is a good lay for sure, but he's not ready to commit. He intends to enjoy whatever woman finds him during The Rutting. After hearing Faye, he wonders if his brother was lying to him. He doesn't want to believe Jasper would be so cruel to someone.

Silus clears his throat, and it snaps Billy's attention back to the task at hand. Silus narrows his eyes and pushes off the door. "Son, I'm telling you right now. You and your kin need to stay away from my girls. If I have to tell any of you again, I'm gonna shoot first and ask questions later. You understand me?" Silus stood a few inches from Billy. The older man clocks in at six foot two. Billy, who is on his knee while working on the bottom part of the window frame, stands. He comes to six foot six inches and turns to focus right on Silus. The way his jaw clenches, and how his chest rises and falls as he debates beating this man with his own arm, is enough that Silus takes pause in invading his space any further. This man hurt his own daughter, and Shelley's fear of her father is palpable. Billy wants to show him what happens to assholes that abuse their children. The two men stare at each other for what feels like an eternity to Billy.

"Yes, sir," he rumbles low. Then, turning to the work at hand, he tries to tune them all out. This is torture to him. Billy promises himself that he would marry that girl. He loves her. No one was going to tell him otherwise. He's a good man, with a steady paycheck. He would cherish her for the rest of their lives. Why wasn't he good enough?

"Girls, finish up what you're doing and get out of here," Silus barks at them as he walks back into the bar.

CHAPTER NINE

Uninvited

The week from The Devil's Ball to the party Tommy had invited them to was torture. Shelley tried to throw herself into her schoolwork, while Faye tried to keep well out of sight of their father. Their plan had worked, as not one incident happened from Halloween to the following Saturday. Instead of leaving them alone, Silus agreed to let the girls stay the weekend with Taylor. He left the arrangements to his wife. Faye and Shelley watched their parents wheel off into the morning sun before school on that Friday. The girls gathered all their things for the weekend as soon as school was out and headed to Taylor's house. Faye had the sedan, so they would have their own transportation to the party. Tommy had informed Faye on the 'dress code' and location. It was all set. Taylor's parents figured the girls were going to the mall and a late movie, as they do every weekend.

Saturday afternoon Wanda, Taylor, Candy, Veronica, Faye, and Shelley are setup at various vanities and mirrors, curling hair, putting on make-up, and having a great time. There is laughing, teasing, and the entire room is bubbling with excitement. This party was going to be pretty big, according to Tommy. The entire Coeh family and a few friends were going to be there. He told them they didn't need to bring anything and to wear comfortable clothes as it's out in the woods. This meant campfire and cookout, in the girl's minds.

"Alright, girls. Time to go. Don't wanna be late," Faye says as she turns off the alarm on her phone.

The six of them pile into the sedan in a hurry, all scrunched together.

Shelley had to admit she couldn't wait to see Billy. She hadn't seen, or heard from him, since he came by the bar to fix the window. It's been three months since Jackson left town. He hadn't even bothered to call her once. All the time she had spent with Billy and his brothers made her feel safe and adored. Billy was the polar opposite of Jackson, sweet, funny, and tender with her. He didn't get angry when she asked a lot of questions, and he always told her she looked so pretty. She is lost in her thoughts as she is squished against the passenger window in the back with Wanda, Candy, and Veronica. Taylor and Faye are comfortable in the front seat. It took an hour to get to the gravel road with the little wolf sign. Once the girls turned off onto the gravel road, it took a good fifteen minutes to find the location. There were bikes, trucks, and cars parked in a field, at least fifty of them. Shelley couldn't believe how many people were here.

They pile out of the car and give each other a last pat down. Shelley can see the anticipation in Faye's eyes. She likes Jasper more than a fling. Faye smooths her skirt, gives Shelley a wink, then the group was heading to the party itself. Beau spotted them first and nudges Jasper who was hanging on a cute little girl with freckles and red hair. Beau had been flirting with a brown-haired girl that never stopped talking and is so perky he can't stand it. She makes his heart race and is a looker to boot. Tommy and Billy were off at the edge of the fray, having heated words. Tommy is still trying to talk him out of taking the mushroom to prevent him from rutting tonight.

Shelley spotted them first. She frowns as she watches the two men have a hushed argument when Tommy throws his hands in the air and shakes his head at Billy storming off. Shelley glances back at her sister and her friends. They were clustered together still, heading toward the drinks. Shelley hesitates, then follows them. A few minutes later she had two red Solo cups in her hand filled with beer from the keg. She slips away from the group unnoticed and starts the same direction Billy had stormed off in. Finding the trail with little effort, she made her way along it with a cup in each hand.

Faye and the girls had caught up with Tommy, who was nervous.

"Eh, I didn't think you girls would come after what happened last week," he rubs the back of his neck. Tommy was not taking part tonight. He still didn't want any of the women in the pack to see him with these girls. He wouldn't need a mushroom to remain celibate if they did. Jasper had draped his arm around his cute little redhead and disappeared further into the party. Beau follows suit with his girl. They weren't about to do anything today to incur Momma Coeh's wrath. The girls are giggling and admiring the surrounding men. All the men here are in varying states of dress, most in just pants. There are very few women around. Then, as if Momma Coeh materialized out of thin air, she is standing behind Tommy.

"Tommy, you need to get back to your family." He leaves without question and Momma Coeh crosses her arms. "You girls need to go home. You're not welcome here."

"We were invited," Faye snaps back, irritated at this woman trying to ruin their night. The other girls hesitate and look from Faye to the woman who is blocking their path. "I'm not leaving unless Jasper says he doesn't want me here."

Momma Coeh gets a malicious glint in her eyes and she shrugs.

"Jasper, you and Beau should bring your dates down to meet the girls here to see you," Susie links to them.

Jasper and Beau frown at each other. *"Momma don't do that. I'll come tell her to leave."*

Jasper kisses the redhead on the forehead then he trots back to the parking area. He comes alongside his mother, and a small frown forms. "Faye, you shouldn't be here. I know for a fact your Daddy said to stay away. He told Billy he'd shoot us if we came around you."

Momma Coeh raises her brow. She could not understand the sudden burst of jealous and hurt energy emitting from Faye Baxter. She cocks her head to the side, to see how this goes.

Faye is shaking with rage. Jasper hadn't bothered to check himself and the smeared lipstick on his lip was enough to tell her what he had been doing before he walked up. Faye, who never seems to be rattled, is now looking at him with a quivering lip. "I... I... I hate you, Jasper Coeh! I hope your dick shrivels up and falls off!" She slaps him clean across the cheek. "You told me you loved me! Gonna take me away from all this! See the world! That I wouldn't have to be scared anymore!" The tears flow even faster now as her friends circle around and comfort her. The death stares from the other girls as they walk away with Faye. Jasper made no move to follow them.

"C'mon. He's not worth it, honey. It'll be alright," Taylor soothes. Faye is outright sobbing as they get in the car, Taylor driving. None of them think to look for Shelley due to how distraught Faye is.

Momma Coeh stands there watching the car leave to make sure it's not all for show. *"Make sure the car leaving does not stop until it's back in Georgia."* She links to the patrols working for the pack tonight.

Jasper watches Faye fall apart. Guilt fills him and he wipes the lipstick stain from his mouth. He had done it on purpose, but it still made him feel like a complete asshole, like he had shattered her entire world. The look on his mother's face didn't make him feel any better.

"You did the right thing, Jasper. Get on back to your girl before someone else claims her." She ruffles his hair. She could feel the pain from him. She was more worried about Billy. She couldn't feel him right now and hadn't been able to for most of the week. He has been keeping to himself. David had talked with the boy, but the only information he would give her is that Billy is still professing his love for the younger Baxter girl. Susie had all but demanded he take part tonight. She knows if he just finds the right wolf, he'll get a pup and this Baxter girl business will be behind them. She tries again to link with Billy and only finds silence in response.

Then the four o'clock horn blares. The entire party shifts from down home cookout to music and dancing. Clothes are coming off and women are sauntering out from the various tents, wearing little to nothing at all. Some of the older wolves choose to walk bare. The Rutting is the annual mating ceremony held the first full moon after Halloween. It's where potential mates are found. A conception from a Rutting means the pair would be mates. Among the wolves, there is no shame in pairing with multiple partners. There are a few who have human mates, and those couples tend to stick together, because of the fragility of the human partner.

Momma Coeh has to smirk at the zealous young wolf approaching David. Both of his brows raise in surprise and he looks to Susie. She nods. She had taken the mushroom this Rutting. Worried about the Appalachian representatives being present, she preferred being available to extinguish fires, fires like the Baxter girl and her little gaggle of friends. At least they hadn't brought the younger one. David sets down his bottle of beer and allows himself to be led away by the young woman. Susie had to laugh at the smirk on his face. He didn't look back to see the faint hint of jealousy and sadness in her eyes.

On the other side of the party, Shelley had been walking for a good five minutes when she saw him sitting in the clearing by himself. His hands on his knees as he plucks at some blade of grass in his hand. She sips her drink in silence, glancing around to see if any of the others are following, or are nearby. There are voices in the distance, but they weren't coming closer. Shelley swallows any fear she might have had about being alone in the woods with him and comes out of her hiding place.

He had picked up her scent before she spoke. He thought he was imagining it. His head whips up when he hears her voice.

"Hey darlin'," her sweet voice carries across the clearing to him. "I have a present for ya," as she hands him the drink and sits down next him.

CHAPTER TEN
The Rutting

The surprise on Billy's face as he takes the cup of beer is enough to make Shelley giggle. Then his megawatt smile appears, and he scoots closer to her. The horn blares in the distance and he looks off in that direction. "I didn't think you were gonna be here. Not after how your daddy was actin'." His massive hand comes to rest on her hip, holding her close. He takes in her scent, sweet and delicious. He can feel his pants tighten at just the thought of getting to rut with her. He cannot bring himself to look away from her. She is divine to him. The way her blond hair flutters at the slightest breeze, her pert little nose and sweet, full lips, her creamy white skin without so much as a blemish on it all makes him want to lick her from head to toe. He could spend a lifetime getting lost in her eyes. He had a few hours before sunset. They could canoodle awhile and he would send her home. She is too delicate and precious to have this be their first time.

His instincts are screaming opposition to this thinking. He battles with himself to maintain control of his hormones and keep from ripping her pretty little dress right from her body. Her giggle pulls him from his silent war.

"Earth to Billy," as she is waving her hand in front of his face.

"Be my girl," he blurts out, then leans down to pull her into a heated kiss. His mouth crushing against hers followed by his tongue darting against her watermelon flavored lips to get her to part for him. Her soft moan as she leans into him, bringing up her arms to wrap them around his neck encourages him to pull her into his lap. Their red Solo cups forgotten and spilled over on the ground next to them. He groans in mild agony as she settles into his lap, straddling him like she would a bike. His hands slide up along her thighs, easing the hem of her dress higher.

"I love you, Shelley," he peppers kisses along her jaw. "I need you," he is panting.

Shelley's skin flushes pink and she mirrors him. Her heart rate increases and her body tingles with excitement. Billy had never been so forward with her before. They had shared a few sweet embraces, but nothing like this. When his fingers brush along the cotton fabric of her panties, she lets out a squeal of surprise. Fear mixes with anticipation. Fear that she wouldn't know what to do, and he wouldn't like her after. Faye had told her to be careful who she gives it to, because she didn't want to be known as a slut.

It makes Billy freeze, tearing his lips away from her tantalizing skin. His eyes are dark and his gaze full of desire for his tiny goddess.

"If you'll have me that is, Angel."

He held his breath. She looks like a scared rabbit. He tries to keep his expression easy for her, but her rejection would devastate him and he fears that more than anything. She has to know the way she torments him. His entire body twitches with anticipation. He hopes she can feel the electricity between them. Her cheeks turn a dark shade of red and for once he wishes any of his supernatural abilities allowed him to read her thoughts without her being a part of the pack.

"Shelley," he coaxes, his shoulders drooping as he eases her off his lap.

"No," she says in an urgent tone, tightening her legs on his hips. He jerks and freezes again. Swallowing hard, she leans in and gives him a tender kiss. "I... I...," she debates telling him she is not eighteen, like Faye made it out to be, and that this would be her first time. The way he looks at her makes her feel guilty for not telling him the truth before. But she didn't want him to treat her like some kid. She wants him as well. "I. mean," she realizes he has asked her multiple things, and she is not being very helpful, "no, don't stop." She leans in and kisses him, eager in her response. Her lips then murmur against his. "I'm just scared I won't know what to do. It's... It's my first time."

Billy's heart explodes with joy and his husky laugh against her skin as he kisses down her neck makes her blush again. "Awe, Miss Shelley, don't you worry about that. I'm sure you'll get the hang of it." His fingers resume exploring her body. His thumb presses against the cotton material again, rubbing in circles until she is squirming on him. His lips part, watching her. They had little time, and he does not want her first time to be with the beast. It will destroy her. "You sure you want this?"

"Mhm hmm," she is biting her lower lip and her eyes are closed. Her hips had followed his hand, making her rock on his already painfully hard manhood. When she opens her eyes and gazes at him, he melts. "I love you too, Billy Coeh."

The next moments are torture to him. He stops teasing her clit just long enough to help her out of the dress. It's then Shelley realizes he's not in a shirt. His muscular, tattooed body had been exposed all this time. They find each other again in frantic and wanton kisses as they tear off the remains of their clothes. All the garments tossed aside and are forgotten as Billy lays her back on the grass and was taking great care to be gentle and sweet. He puts his weight on his elbows, propping himself above her to admire the way her hair fans out on the ground and how much like a goddess she looks.

He could only assume that his mother relented and had told Shelley everything. Otherwise, why would she be here? He lowers his weight down on Shelley, leaning down and kissing away her hands from her covered breasts. His calloused hands coming up and roughly caressing against them, drawing her nipples into tiny perfect little pebbles to be devoured by his lips. Her squeals and squirms underneath him causes his massive cock to twitch in anticipation. His hand easing down and around to pull her bottom off the ground and force her legs to open more. With a skilled shift, he brings the tip to her body, watching her every expression. The scent of fear and excitement makes it difficult for him to keep from mounting her like the beast he is. With a steady push forward and hand holding her in place, he feels the wet and warmth of her. Inch by inch he presses in, savoring the throbbing sensation that's engulfing his shaft. He cannot help but grin as she arches to accommodate him. Her lip was caught between her teeth and her eyes are closed.

The way the sun plays off her skin as it sheathes itself on the horizon is an image he will never forget. This is what he dreamed of his whole life. Sure, he had rutted with a few other women in the pack, but they never looked like this. They never made him feel like this. Her whimpers are driving him mad. His hands tighten on her ass and he rocks in her.

"Breathe, Angel, breathe," he coaxes her as his lips devour hers again. Then he is burying his face against the crook of her neck. Her knees had come up and it let him press in as she opens more for him. A heavy growl of pleasure erupts from deep within. She is so wet and tight around him. He could stay like this forever, in her arms. Her soft lips kissing against his skin and the way she bites against his shoulder as he feels her body shuddering against him, tells him he did his job right in pleasuring her. She can't see it, but his goofy grin is plastered all over his face as their sweaty bodies continue moving in this tender battle.

Shelley doesn't know what to think. It feels so good and hurts at the same time. He's too big, and she wants more. Her body is on fire everywhere he touches her and the way he is grabbing onto her ass makes Shelley think he believes he will lose her. All she can smell is the rustic, earthy smell of his aftershave, mixed with sweat. He covers her and any shyness she had at being naked in the woods is gone under his guiding touch. There is a hint of jealousy there, realizing he knows exactly what to do. She bites against his shoulder to remind him of that. Then her body tensed and all the muscles contract and feel like she is about to be squished into a massive ball of tension. Her moans grow louder and she digs her nails into his shoulder, clinging to him for dear life. His hips pump faster, and it hurts. Now she knows what Faye meant by a good hurt. "Billy," she cries out his name, then she explodes around him, shuddering as the intense, uncontrollable sensations roll over her body.

"Shelley," he moans against her lips. The pulsing of his cock as he unloads his seed into her makes her gasp and the two of them lie still in the slow burn down of their lovemaking.

Billy realizes then it's almost dark. The moon was peeking out from behind a cloud. "Shit," he whispers, pulling out of Shelley abruptly.

"What? Did I do something wrong? You didn't like it, did you?" Shelley's fear is rising and the anxiety of being inexperienced is getting the better of her. Especially when Billy is pulling back further, not answering her. He has turned his back to her. Tears form in her eyes and she brings her hand up to her mouth, her other cover her breasts. She had thought it wonderful, but apparently, he hadn't. Shelley makes a strangled sound as she tries to push herself up and find her dress, now believing he lied to her just to get in her pants. She needed to get out of here, and fast.

Billy lets out a growl and a whine at the same time. "Shelley," his voice is raspier and graveled. It's enough to make her snap her gaze back at him. Her eyes go wide in horror. Billy wasn't Billy anymore. He was changing right before her eyes. His muscles rippled and shifted. Hair came out of every place she could imagine. His snout elongated and his hands transformed into massive hands with claws. She screams a blood-curdling scream as the beast being silhouetted by the moonlight turns to face her.

The delicious scent of fear filled his nostrils. Mixed with the faint scent of blood. He turned to look at the girl on the ground. His scent is all over her, which just turns him on more. He is cognitive of who she is and what they had just done. He had little time to calm her down before the jealous Moon Goddess thrust her desire to procreate on him and he would take Shelley regardless of her desire. Her fear is intoxicating. He takes one predatory step toward her, then another. He couldn't speak to her, not in this form. His dark eyes lock onto her pretty blue eyes and he tries to silently convey it's still him. His hands out to his sides and his breathing labored as he struggles with his instincts to mate. It doesn't help that he is well over seven feet tall at this moment. Covered in copper fur with his mouth open in a pant, and his manhood menacing in its erection, he looks absolutely terrifying.

Shelley is shaking, and she is paralyzed by the fear of seeing the monster before her. Was she hallucinating? Had there been something in that beer? Her clothes are scattered away from her and she pulls herself backwards away from the beast at it approaches her. She swallows hard and rolls herself over to push off and run. She could make it, she believes. Someone would save her. She didn't care about her clothes any longer. She only cared about not wanting to die in this clearing with this beast that appeared out of nowhere.

"Help me," she screams into the night air. Before she could get off the ground, she felt his weight on her and the feral growl in her ear. His hot breath against her skin. "No. Please... No," her tears won't stop flowing and she is struggling under the beast, expecting it to rip her neck out. Another low growl emits next to her. It was different. The tone wasn't that of a monster. A low whine followed it. Before she can scream again, she is being flipped onto her back in an animalistic manner.

She bucks and squirms underneath him. Her tiny fists pounding into his furred chest and he let her. Her soft thighs keep brushing against his aching cock and it's taking every ounce of Billy's strength to keep from just mounting her. If she runs, he'll kill her. She is emitting the prey pheromone so hard that in his state he would see her as that and devour her. This is why humans that aren't a part of this world shouldn't be invited to The Rutting. He realizes now his mother never sent her and she didn't know what she was agreeing to by being in this clearing with him. It breaks his heart to see her looking up at him like this. Couldn't she see it's him? All he wants to do is love her and hold her close. That he would never hurt her on purpose. He emits another growl, looking down at her as his clawed hands catch hers and pull them above her head. In all her bucking and squirming, he had ended up between her legs, and now she was open to him. Holding both her wrists above her head, he stares down at her.

Shelley could not believe what she was seeing, fear, anguish, lust, in the creature's eyes. He had every opportunity to rip her to shreds, and yet he was letting her fight him. Almost like he would rather she beat him with her fists than let her run. Then his hands catch hers and she writhes underneath him, trying to free herself at all. It failed miserably, and she is now at his mercy. She can't catch her breath. She can't move. Shelley can only feel his hard cock twitching against her thigh as he pants above her. His eyes focused on hers. The air had changed. She sucks in several breaths, trying to push her fear down and get out of the situation alive. Then she realized her heart is racing, her skin is hot, and she is throbbing. She tells herself it was the lovemaking she and Billy just had. But the truth was her head is getting muddied with visions of this beast consummating with her. His low whine forces her eyes to flutter open again and his massive head leans down, nuzzling against her neck.

Shelley could not believe what she did next. Something told her that this beast wasn't going to hurt her, that he was trying to protect her. "Y… Y… You aren't gonna hurt me, are ya?" She tries to extract one of her hands and Billy allows her. He holds as still as a statue as her delicate fingers come up, at first to his nose, palm down. He lets out a laugh as she treats him like a dog. When he doesn't bite her, she then moves up along his face to his ears. Her soft fingers brush along them and his entire body shudders. He leans down closer to her then and licks against her skin. Her fingers sprawl into his fur. "It's so soft," she murmurs.

All he can hear is her heartbeat. It's fast and light. His rumbling growl was the same as he gave in human form when she would do something he loved. His clawed hands let her hands go only to slide down her creamy white skin. Her fear is still palpable, but he is aware the pheromones he is putting off are dominating her. When he reaches her supple bottom, his claws dig in, drawing a gasping noise from her. He tilted his body up, looking down at her again. Her eyes are wide and her hands are now on his chest.

"Billy?" Her voice is like music to his ears, even in the whisper of her realization. A single nod is all he gives to her as he lifts her bottom again, forcing her legs wider apart. He wouldn't take her if she stopped him now. He would run off. Billy swears he could control himself enough to. The terrifying thought she would reject him made him hold tighter to her hips. He needed Shelley like a man needs oxygen to breathe.

Then he felt it, her tiny hand on his cock. He whines. He felt her fingers curl around the engorged beast, exploring, and guiding. God, she was guiding his cock to her open body.

"Billy," she murmurs again, more in a demand.

As soon as the tip touched against her wetness, he wanted to thrust. It's agonizing and slow for him to press in with this slow pace. His claws digging into her flesh more. She whimpers and brings her hands up around his neck, which lifted her off the ground and into his lap. That was it. He was undone. She accepted him and it's the last thing he remembers, her face burying against his chest as he thrusts his massive cock into her. His arms coming around her and holding her there as he bucks up. Her muffled screams and cries only driving him further. She is his, only his, and belongs to him. She is made for him. Billy would spend the rest of her life making her the happiest person alive. He bucks harder and harder until he feels his seed erupting into her like a volcano again.

Shelley felt pain and desire. He was tearing her in half and she realizes now she is going to be fucked to death by Billy Coeh, who is a werewolf, like that movie they all went to. She tries to slow him, to pace him, but there was no communication with the beast. He thrust and thrust into her, forcing her to take all of him. Her body and her mind were not of the same opinion. She felt that swelling pressure building again. The more he thrust the more she wanted him to. At some point, fear left her body, and she wanted him to take it all from her. To fill her again and again. She wants his hands all over her. Then shame fills her as she loves the feeling of his fur against her skin and his hot breath as he growls. She buries her face against his chest in shame as her orgasm explodes and washes over her body in tingling fiery waves. She wanted nothing more than to feel this with him forever.

Pausing only a moment to pant against each other, there are no other sounds in the clearing. Their climaxes were intense and burning. Billy eases from her, peppering her sweaty, flushed skin with soft licks. He is being very careful to not bite her, graze her, or otherwise break her skin with his teeth. He didn't want to turn her into a werewolf. She is perfect the way she is. He wasn't about to take that away from her, not unless she asked him to. But Billy wasn't done with her. His muscular hands take hold of her and he flips her around, which elicits a yelping gasp as he makes no hesitation this time and thrusts into her from behind.

She lets out a strangled cry, her body burning and throbbing from the aggressive coupling.

Billy wasn't holding back any longer, and he continues to thrust as hard as he could into her. Her hands had to plant on the ground to catch herself from being pushed face first into it. His clawed hands come around her body as he hunches over her, groping and squeezing against her breasts.

Billy and Shelley made love until well into dawn. Her body exhausted she passed out against him. He shifted back into his human form and kissed her lips before sliding onto the ground next to her, pulling her close.

"I love you," he murmurs as he succumbs to sleep.

CHAPTER ELEVEN
Your Secret Is Safe With Me

Tommy is standing down wind, at the edge of the clearing, his expression is grim. He watched his cousin mount Shelley over and over. The poor girl is covered in bruises and scratches. Her hair is a tangled mess of grass and mud. He is being very careful to keep Billy from picking up his scent. In this state, Billy would attack him to protect what is his. Not being able to shift made it even more dangerous and is why anyone on patrol has a cattle prod in hand. It would force their shifted brothers and sisters to think about the attack.

"Everything alright over there, Tommy?" Susie's voice fills Tommy's mind.

"Yes ma'am. Just a bit of role play." Tommy lied to Momma Coeh. There would be serious hell to pay if she finds the Baxter girl in this clearing with Billy. She might even throw him out of the pack and kill the girl. Billy would go berserk and it would be all out war. Tommy frowns again as he tries to play out any scenario where Billy waking up next to Shelley would a good one. So, he stands and watches Romeo and Juliet have their moment. He had to admit that it felt like he was invading Billy's private world. He wanted to make sure Billy was sated and

unconscious before he moved. It wasn't until the wee hours of dawn when Billy succumbed to slumber.

Billy's body relaxed, and he settled next to Shelley, shifting back into his human form. He rolled onto his side and pulled her close. This makes Tommy grimace again, as it would make things trickier to get her away unnoticed. He steps forward, circling around to Billy's side. He nudges his bare foot with his boot. "Hey," he whispers. No response. Not at all. Billy's heavy breathing and light snore made Tommy chuckle. He had never seen such a content man before. Tommy gathers up any traces of her clothing and comes back to the lovebirds. They had not even moved from the spot where they passed out. He holds his breath as he extracts the girl from Billy's arms, watching the man's face the entire time.

Moments later, Tommy is walking out of the clearing, carrying the sleeping Shelley. He is careful not to head back up the main path, instead he cuts across the forest to where his truck is parked. He settles her in the passenger seat, pulling a blanket from the back to cover her. He tosses the cattle prod into the bed of the truck and hops into the driver's seat. He didn't know where to take her. He could take her home and just deposit her in the bed, letting her think it was all some weird dream. She looks pretty roughed up, so maybe take her to a hospital. He can hear her heartbeat, and her steady breathing. She wasn't in any real danger. The scent of sex and arousal fills his truck cabin, making it hard for him to concentrate. He could call Faye and tell her to come get her. After the shit Jasper did, he was pretty sure that's a bad idea.

"Fuck," he growls as he slams his hand on the steering wheel. How could he have been so stupid as to invite these girls? He knew better. Another glance at her sleeping form and he feels guilty all over again. Rubbing his hand over his face, he knows nothing will come of it. Billy got her out of his system. She'll go back to the biker life. Billy will take over the pack. Everything will be okay. He thought about taking her to the bar and saying he found her like that. Silus Baxter would shoot first and ask questions later. So that ruled that out because he wasn't planning on dying today. He pulls over just before crossing back into Georgia. He needed to think this through further. One thing is for sure, he needs to convince Shelley to stay the fuck away from Billy. As if the Moon Goddess heard him, Shelley groans awake. He gets silent, turning to face her.

Shelley can feel pain everywhere. She is sticky, dirty, and it feels like she has been in a fight. "Billy," she whimpers. Then her eyes settle on Tommy. She is not in the clearing anymore, but she is still naked. Fear wells up again, and she sits up more.

"Easy, Shelley, easy," Tommy's voice is soothing and gentle.

"Where's Billy? Wh… Why am I in your truck, Tommy? Oh God! Last night." Her eyes are frantic and dart from one thing to the next. She winces as she sits up.

"Shh, relax. I'm taking you home unless you think you need medical attention. Why didn't you leave with your sister?"

"Oh God! Faye. She… She… was going to see Jasper. Is he one, too?" Shelley meets Tommy's gaze and there is a dark look in his eyes.

A small growl emits from his lips.

"T… T… Tommy." She gulps. "I am right, aren't I? Billy's a werewolf… right?"

He flinches when she says it out loud.

It was enough for her to know she didn't hallucinate it. "We… We have to go back for Faye."

He felt a pang of guilt at her bravery. The idea she thought they were monsters and she could save her sister made him like her more.

She pulls the blanket closer to her then and lets out a whimper. "You're one too, aren't you? All of you. P… Please don't eat me."

Its then Tommy laughs out loud. He didn't mean to make fun

of Shelley, but the idea of consuming her like a snack made him laugh hard enough tears came to his eyes and the tension he was feeling seconds ago ebbs. "Nah, darlin'. If I were to get my mouth anywhere near ya, Billy would have my hide as a carpet. One he would prolly piss on every day, too." It made her giggle, and that's a good sign. She is not too traumatized in his mind if she is laughing. His laughter fades, and he turns to look away from her. "Put your clothes on, girl. Then we'll talk."

"Okay, I'm dressed," Shelley taps his shoulder a few seconds later. Her mind is full of fear and curiosity. The most pressing is why she is in this truck with Tommy, and not with Billy.

He frowns, watching her. "Miss Shelley. You can't tell a soul what you saw out here tonight."

"I understand," she nods.

"No. I'm serious. Not a soul. Not Faye. Not your mamma, or Daddy. Especially not your daddy. Shelley, there are rules about it. If anyone from the pack finds out you know, they'll kill you." Tommy didn't explain why. He figured scaring the girl off would be the best thing. She would destroy Billy's life and it's Tommy's job to look out for Billy. Which made the next thing he had to say to her the hardest thing he would ever do. "You also gotta stay away from Billy. If his mate finds out, she'll come after you."

"Mate?" Shelley's heart hammers in her chest. That sounds an awful lot like he has a girlfriend, or Wife. Shame fills her cheeks and tears well in her eyes. "What the fuck do you mean, Mate? He asked me to be his girl. He said he loved me."

Tommy runs his hands through his hair and growls. Of course, that idiot told her those things. "Look, Shelley. The full moon, particularly this one, makes us do stupid shit. Like fuck people we aren't supposed to. Humans and wolves don't mix well. More often than not they just end up killing the human. Billy doesn't want that for you. He told me to take you home and make sure you are safe. His mate is a powerful wolf, like Momma Coeh. If you keep comin' around you're gonna get him, or yourself, killed."

Shelley's face crumbles then, and Tommy feels like a complete prick. This sweet little girl didn't deserve this. Billy should be allowed to have her in his mind but Momma Coeh had made it very clear her opinion on the Baxter girls. Tears are clinging to her lashes and she shifts in the seat to look out the window and not face him. Silence fills the truck cabin again and Tommy bites against his lip, watching her. "You weren't supposed to be in that clearin'. It's best you just forget what happened last night and move on."

"Okay," she sounds so broken to him. "What about my sister?"

"We kicked 'em out before everything started. We didn't know you were with 'em."

"Oh," she is giving him a one-word answer, and it's making his guilt feel even stronger. Billy's going to beat his ass. He puts the truck in gear again and they get back on the road. He is pulling into her driveway thirty minutes later.

"Don't forget, Miss Shelley. Not a word to anyone." He didn't know what else to say.

"Don't worry, Tommy. Your secret's safe with me." Her voice held that wavering sound of someone about to burst out loud sobbing. He could see he crushed her by the way she limps to the door from the brutal sex she had, how her shoulders hang, and the way she keeps rubbing her eyes to push away the tears. It is taking all of Tommy's willpower to keep from telling her the truth. He had to put pack before this girl. He waits until she closes the front door behind her before he pulls away.

CHAPTER TWELVE
Hell Hath No Fury

When Faye and her friends got around to realizing Shelley wasn't with them, she called Shelley. Shelley could only sob and blubber on the phone, barely getting out that she is at home. Faye rushed home and found her sister balled up in a towel, fresh out of the shower, her face red and puffy from crying. She frowns and bites her lip as she sees the scratches and faint bruises forming on Shelley's ivory skin.

"Oh, Bratnik," she whimpers. "Who hurt you?"

Shelley just shook her head no and balled up more, hugging onto her pillow so tight.

"Shelley," Faye's voice is full of concern and her boy woes forgotten. Rage fills Faye as she thinks the Coeh boys have done something awful to her sister. If that's the case, she would shoot Billy's balls off herself. "Shelley, you're scaring me. Tell me what happened?" She eases onto the bed and pulls her sister into her arms.

"He… He… has a girlfriend!" Shelley moans into the next fit of crying. Faye's brows furrow. Billy Coeh was the least deceitful person she had ever met. Hell, the man wouldn't even buy liquor for the rest of them. "Told me he wanted me to be his girl.

That he loved me."

"Billy said he had a girlfriend? After he said he loved you?" Faye eases Shelley back to look at her with a stern look, demanding Shelley to think about what she just said, and to confirm it.

"He told Tommy to take me home after... He... We," Shelley's cheeks turn bright red and she sobs into her pillow all over again.

"Shelley," Faye gets a firmer tone, as she is believing Billy may not be the upstanding gentleman he portrays in public. "Tell me what happened right now."

"I... I found him in that clearing. And it was so wonderful. The way he kissed me. How sweet he was. And gentle. It didn't hurt much, just like you said." Shelley is hiccupping and appearing to calm down. She looks distraught as she regales her sister with her first sexual escapade. "But then... Then he changed.. And... It was rougher." Shelley bites against her lip as she remembers Tommy's haunting warning about being killed if she told anyone what she saw last night. Fear is all over Shelley's face and Faye's eyes narrow.

"Go on," Faye encourages.

"Then... I woke up in Tommy's truck. And... He told me everything. Oh Faye, I'm such an idiot. He has a girlfriend. Tommy told me she would kill me if she found out about us." Shelley collapses into Faye's arms, mewling and crying all over again. "I love him, Faye. God help me, I love him. It's killing me to know he doesn't really like me. Am I really that stupid? What's wrong with me that he wouldn't pick me? Is she prettier? Is it because I'm just a kid? Is it because of Daddy?"

Faye lets out a slow breath and pats her sister's back while Shelley word vomits against her. She has a pretty good idea that Billy Coeh doesn't have a girlfriend or told Tommy to do shit about Shelley. What she couldn't piece together was why Tommy would do such a thing. She bets it has something to do with that bitch that chased them off at the party. "You stay here and rest," she soothes Shelley. Then she eases up from the bed and pulls out her phone. She is going straight to the source. Leaving Shelley to sob and cry in the background, she dials Billy.

"Hey Faye, what's up?" Billy's easy going voice comes over the speaker. He sounds pleased as punch to hear from Faye.

"I hope you're fucking happy with yourself, you pig," Faye's voice cuts through his phone. Everyone within fifteen feet of Billy heard what Faye just said.

"What?" Billy's voice sounds stunned. Sitting up more, he sets his beer down. "What's the matter, Faye? Is it Shelley? She alright?"

"Oh, don't you fucking play dumb with me, asshole. What did you do? Lure her in, have a good time, then let your brothers fuck her?" Faye feels so smug with her tear down of Billy and his brothers.

Shelley is coming out of the bed, yelling at her that it wasn't like that and to give her the phone. Faye holds her sister at bay.

"Wait. What are you talking about? Nothing like that happened. What's going on?" Billy is frantic and confused by what Faye is spewing at him.

"Right. You fucking prick. Why don't you take that sweet boy bullshit to your other girlfriend?" Faye retorts.

"What other girlfriend?" Billy roars in confusion. Tommy starts to slink away, his beer half drunk and forgotten.

"You weren't even man enough to tell her yourself. You had to have your bitch, Tommy, do it." Faye jabs in like a boxer taking Billy to the mat.

"What does Tommy have to do with anything?" Billy's voice sounds desperate and just short of a whine. Why would Faye treat him like this? What happened when Shelley woke up this morning?

"Fuck you and all your fucking brothers, Billy Coeh. Stay the fuck away from us. You come near us and I'll tell my old man what you did!" With that, Faye hangs up on Billy.

Billy stares at the phone for a good thirty seconds in confusion. His mind plays back the entire conversation. Then it dawns on him. Tommy has done something incredibly stupid. His gaze snaps up and his eyes go black with rage.

"What the fuck did *you* do?" In a few easy strides, Billy has Tommy by the front of his shirt.

"Well, shit. Now it's a party," says David from the grill. Susie hasn't said a word. She is watching as this soap opera scene plays out before her. She knew those Baxter girls were trouble.

"What the fuck did I do? What the fuck did *you* do?" Tommy gives him a shove.

"No. Don't you play with that stupid bullshit, Tommy." Billy's entire presence changes and fills the area as his alpha dominance bears down upon Tommy. "What happened?"

"I saved you from yourself, you idiot," Tommy snaps back.

"You're supposed to be *my* beta, man. What did you do to her?" Billy's voice sounds hurt and anguished as he thinks Tommy has betrayed him.

"I did exactly what I was supposed to do as *your* beta, you idiot. That girl was trouble, and I saved your ass. You were just thinkin' with your dick and put the entire pack in danger." Tommy snarls back as the pair part and they are shifting. "So, you know what? You want to fucking punch me, punch me. We both know I'm in the right here."

Billy is quivering with rage. He wants to pummel that smug ass look off Tommy's face. The clearing has grown quiet, and Momma Coeh hasn't made one move to intervene. Taking several deep breaths, Billy shakes his head and turns his back on Tommy, walking away. As much as he would like to beat down Tommy for what he did, he couldn't. It rips him apart inside to think that sweet little girl would ever believe he would cheat on her. He continues stalking away.

Tommy is fuming, but then he droops. He turns to follow Billy and apologize.

"Sit your ass down, Tommy." Momma Coeh says it in a quiet tone but means to be obeyed.

Tommy picks up his beer again and frowns, not in the mood to drink it anymore.

Susie and David exchange looks and sigh at each other. She has pieced together that Billy took part in The Rutting, but not with any wolf. It was with that Baxter girl, and she was furious with Tommy all over again for bringing those girls here. While Susie agrees with his reasoning, she does not approve his method. They could have worked out a better solution. Now two of her sons are furious over the loss of a Baxter girl. She could feel Jasper's guilt and sadness at what he did to Faye. David clears his throat, and he's giving her a pointed look, like she needs to fix this. "She is sixteen fucking years old, David," Susie growls out loud.

David lets out a heavy sigh and continues the conversation in her mind. *"You say that like it's the be all and end all. In two years, she'll be eighteen. Will it have matter?"*

"It fucking matters to Silus Baxter. You want to tell him two of our boys have been fucking his precious girls? Or the rest of those backwards hick bikers he calls a gang? Do you remember the last time the Angels of Wrath got shitty with us?" Susie roars back into his mind.

"So, what you're saying is you'd rather break your sons' hearts than go to war for them? We both know you could have worked something out with Silus. Fuck, he was already talkin' about Faye's introduction and how shitty it was she hadn't found someone she liked. I seem to remember, once upon a time, you bending pack rules for a different Angel." David crosses his arms.

Susie's eyes narrow at him without a single word in response.

"Tell me I'm wrong." He gets a grin on his face and points his tongs at her from the grill.

The low growl from Susie was enough to make him shrug in response, turning back to the chicken breasts.

"Remember, Susie. You bore those pups. You can't be pissed when you realize you ain't the only stubborn one in this bunch." David's voice is full of irritation and disappointment as he chastises her out loud.

CHAPTER THIRTEEN
The Boys Are Back In Town

The bike rally in Jackson was a week long. All the prominent Angels went to the event. The bar has been left to a young buck Silus hired a month ago. Faye comes each night to help him out and make sure the bikers who pass through stay in line. Shelley wasn't leaving their bedroom other than to bathe, eat, or interact with Faye when forced to. She had not been in school for two days when Faye finally kicked her out of bed and made her go to school. The last thing either of them needed was the school to call their parents and turn their father's wrath on them again.

The following Saturday, both girls are flitting back and forth with the influx of bikers passing through. The Triple Six is a known stopping point coming up from Florida.

Faye is laughing and flirting as she serves the drinks and takes the food orders.

Shelley, on the other hand, can barely find a smile, but is making sure everyone has everything they ordered. Her heart is heavy. She feels used and empty, like the garbage she keeps having to take out. Billy broke her in just about every way possible. She knew Jackson didn't love her either and just wanted a trophy on his arm. Billy made her feel pretty. He made her feel special. He made her feel safe. Then he threw her aside when she gave him her innocence. Tears well in her eyes again as she sets down the finger food the guys ordered. The bar was too busy to mope, and Shelley knew that. She just keeps pushing through. When her break comes around, she bolts outside and props herself against the wall. She is convinced her heart will never heal, and she is going to die from it.

She closes her eyes. Then an all too familiar sound fills the air. The deep rumble of an old Harley well-loved coming down the highway. Taking slow breaths, she wipes her cheeks and looks to the night sky, praying that this nightmare would end and Billy would come tell her it was all a lie. That there was no 'mate' as Tommy put it and wrap her up in his arms to profess his love for her. Then her senses are filled with the powerful scent of leather and aftershave.

His hand cups her cheek, and he growls in her ear, "Miss me, Angel?" Jackson presses his form into the sweet little thing he has dreamed of every night since he left her on that beach. She smells like berries and beer. The only thing wrong with this picture of heaven before him is the puffiness from crying. "Shh, it's alright. I'm back, baby. And I'm not leavin' anytime soon."

Shelley's brow furrows and her eyes snap down to meet the piercing gaze of Jackson Pruitt. It is cruel that she prays for one man and gets another. She draws in a jagged breath. Then she is angry, so angry she can feel it bubbling up from deep within. First the guy she has mooned over since she cared about boys just up and abandons her, no goodbye, no I love yous, no texts, no nothing. When she allows herself to fall for another guy, he tears her to pieces, ruining her. Only to have the first guy come back and act like nothing has happened. Shelley's shaking with rage.

Jackson takes an easy step back in surprise. He is confused by how she is reacting to him. The last time he saw her she was pouting for his attention. Then her tiny hand darts up so fast he barely registers what is about to happen as she slaps him hard enough he feels it.

"No!" She shouts at him. "No! I didn't fucking miss you! You didn't even fucking call. Not once! Nothing! Just left! And now you're back like nothing happened! Like I didn't move on. Like you just went around the block. Fuck you, Jackson!"

Jackson's eyes narrow as she shrieks at him like a banshee and throws a bunch of bullshit in his face. He has half a mind to back hand her and put her in her place. He knows once he goes there, he can't take it back. "What the fuck are you talkin' about? I swear I make one run and you are all of a sudden tits over ass about me abandoning you. What's gotten into you?" He takes hold of her then, forcing her to face him directly and preventing her from further slapping him.

"Right. One run. You just went for a fucking joyride and I'm supposed to sit around and wait for you?"

"Who the hell has been filling your head with that kind of bullshit? Because they are a dirty liar." He growls. She was acting her age, and it irritates him. "You know damn well I pick up the runs when told."

"Right. What happened to 'showing those boys whose boss'," she mocks him, "bullshit you gave me that night? And now you're callin' my daddy a liar?"

He didn't understand what was going on other than Silus Baxter sent him on that run, expecting him never to come back. Yet here he was ready to claim what was owed to him, Shelley. Only, she is acting like he was off fucking some whore in a motel for the past few months.

"It was your damn daddy who sent me on the run in the first place. So yeah," he growls, "I am gonna call his snake ass a liar."

Shelley throws her hands up in the air, forcing his hands off her shoulders. "Just leave me alone, Jackson. I'm not some dumb kid you can just keep stringin' along," she mewls like the teenager she is. She turns and ducks back into the kitchen door of the bar. Jackson starts to follow her in when a large, heavy hand rests on his shoulder.

"Son, you and I need to have a talk," Silus Baxter's eyes blaze with anger as he stares at this punk kid. He doesn't know what all that was about, but he has never seen Shelley act that way. If Jackson has put his hands on her, he'll kill him right here. He had rolled up during their tryst.

Jackson throws his fist into the wall and turns to follow the massive form of Silus Baxter. They are heading to Silus's office, the big smoker out behind the bar.

"Boy. You're like one o' them damn Yankee cockroaches, you know that?" Silus judges him. This kid has been trying to steal this club from the moment he got his colors. "But I will have to say, I am impressed you made it back with the haul you did. Good to know you can at least do one thing right." His arms cross as he watches the still fuming boy in front of him. The kid wasn't even listening. He just keeps glaring at the bar where Shelley had disappeared. Silus snaps his fingers hard in front of Jackson's face. "You're gonna wanna pay attention to this, you little shit. You wanna try your hand for Shelley? You survive this run, and we'll talk. I'll get you squared up and out by the end of the month. Don't make me regret this."

Jackson's head snaps back to look at Silus and he's breathing hard. He wants to tear him to pieces right now. There's nothing out here to stop him. He could kill him and take the club. But he knows what will happen if he doesn't have more support. He lost two of his friends on this last run, and that's enough to stay Jackson's hand. He growls in frustration.

"Fine," he growls and turns to go into the bar.

Silus let him go, shaking his head. "That boy's dick is thinking for him and it's going to get him killed," he mutters to himself. While that boy is an idiot with the girls, his tenacity is a skill to be used. Silus'll be damned to throw away a good pawn for nothin'. He lingers outside and enjoys the last of his cigar before sauntering into the bar.

Jackson thumps down at a table. His blood is boiling at Silus fucking with him like this. He's entitled to everything in this club. That old fuck hasn't done shit for the Angels in years. Then there she was, coming to his table with the bottle of beer. As soon as she sets it down on the table, his hand whips out, grabbing her by the wrist and pulling her right into his lap. Once upon a time she would giggle and curl into him with a shy smile. Tonight, she yelps and struggles.

"No, Jackson," she whines. "I'm working."

"Not anymore," he growls back. "You're gonna sit here, calm the fuck down, and let me enjoy your pretty ass for a few minutes."

"Jackson," her cheeks flush and she squirms. "Daddy's gonna see."

"Well, let him. We just had a little chat out in his office, and here I am." He gives her a smirk.

"What does that mean?" She looks confused and scared.

"It means you just sit there and look pretty. Everything's gonna be alright." His grip firms around her waist as Faye stares daggers at him from across the bar. He lifts his beer with his other hand to her and winks before he downs the amber liquid.

CHAPTER FOURTEEN

Claiming What Is Mine

Faye comes out the door, heading towards the parking lot of their high school, when she sees Jackson sitting on his bike. She comes to a stop and crosses her arms, narrowing her eyes at him.

He doesn't say a word. In his opinion whatever she had to say she could keep it to herself. He gives his head a jerk, motioning for her to get out of here as he resumes watching the door for Shelley.

Faye huffs in response, but she heads to the car just as he demanded. There is something scary about Jackson Pruitt and for all of Faye's bravado she knew better than to poke that bear. Her father had not stopped him in his pursuit of Shelley, which tells Faye Silus approves, even if he doesn't.

Glancing at his watch again, Jackson tries to will Shelley to come out faster. Then he smiles when he sees his angel appear.

Shelley sighs when she sees Jackson propped on his motorcycle waiting for her. All her friends are a giggling mess at just how hot he is, with those telltale shades and leather jacket, telling everyone he's an Angel of Wrath member. He is handsome and if she were not still angry with him, might find him stalking her kind of endearing.

"I'll call you guys later," she grumbles as she trudges toward him. She could see the sedan was gone, which means he chased Faye off again. She contemplates running to catch the bus home but knows she would miss it. Which means she is forced to ask Jackson for a ride home. He has done this every school day since he came back. Jackson picks her up straight from school and keeps her out until curfew. He keeps pressing her father's rules as far as she will let him. It has irritated her more than anything. She just wanted to curl up and die without Billy. All she could think about was Billy Coeh and how much she wanted to run away and be with him. He didn't force her to sit in his lap. He didn't paw his hands over her when she told him to stop. He didn't threaten to tell her father, who has appeared to approve of Jackson's behavior, when she acts out. Shelley hugs her bag tighter to her and wishes Billy would roll up in his pickup truck and save her.

Jackson's smile turns into a grimace as she doesn't look as happy to see him. He wants to murder that snake, Silus, even more now. She'd be all over him if it weren't for her father. He has been trying every damn day just to get her to smile at him again. His patience is wearing thin and time was running out to woo her before he has to leave. "C'mon Angel, let's get some food before the show."

"Jackson," she whines. "I got a ton of homework and it's a school night." It's a week before Thanksgiving, and while she didn't have that much homework, she still uses it as an excuse.

"And? You gotta eat, don't ya?" He grumbles back at her.

"What about my curfew," she tries another route.

He snorts, "He knows who you're with. Now get on the bike." His bark is enough to make her flinch and do as he asks after she settles her bag on her back.

Jackson is frowning as they drive off. She doesn't hold him like she used to with her arms wrapped tight around his waist. He misses that, and he misses her. He wouldn't tell her it crushes him that she doesn't want him anymore. He believes she will come back around. He just needed to make her fall in love with him again. They eat at the food court of the mall. He can't help but chuckle at all the middle-class people giving him a wide berth. They are worried that something bad is happening to his sweet little Shelley. He can see it in their eyes. Soon after they are heading into the movie theater.

She hopes he is taking her to see Love Actually. When he motions for her to get in line for concessions, she can hear him buying two tickets to Master and Commander, the Russell Crowe flick. "Yay," she mutters to herself and turns to see the guy at the register for her concession line is none other than Tommy Fucking Coeh. "Of course," she hrmphs and moves into the other line, even if it is longer.

Jackson comes walking up and puts his arm around her shoulder, kissing her temple. "Hey, why don't we jump over here, it's shorter?" He is innocent in his question, and for all his warts Jackson is trying. He can't understand why she can't just let it go and get back on board with the plan.

"Thanks, this line has better popcorn," Shelley snarks as she stares daggers at Tommy.

"Okay," Jackson says in the slow drawn-out fashion to not set the crazy girl off further. He can see they are taking popcorn from the same popper. He does what every man does when he wants to get laid, he lets the girl be right. With snacks in tow, he guides them into the last row of the theater. The movie starts, and he's excited. She smells sweet next to him. He takes the popcorn she is hugging like a life preserver and sets it aside while he drapes his other arm over her shoulder. A few minutes later he leans down and nuzzles against her neck, kissing just below her ear. He can't see it, but he's making Shelley's skin crawl.

She tries to squirm away from his affection, and she shakes her head no at him. "Jackson," she hisses in warning. "I'm trying to watch the movie."

He draws a sharp breath in and he clamps his hand on the back of her neck, pulling her close. His lips brushing against her ear. "You're gonna stop actin' like that fucking tease of a sister of yours and pay attention to me. You belong to me, Shelley Baxter."

Fear wells inside of her. She belongs to him? She tenses up and begins to tremble. Jackson means to do anything but watch the movie and she is not sure she could fight him off. Her whimpers and pushing against him is doing nothing to deter him.

His lips trail along her neck again as he holds her in place. "You taste so good," he whispers. His lips find hers and crushes hers as he forces himself into a kiss.

Tommy normally hates doing theater checks. He just wants to chill behind the concession stand, flirt with pretty girls, and get free movies. Tonight though, he is looking forward to being diligent in his duties. The moment he saw the two of them walk in, he watched Shelley like a hawk. It didn't take an expert to see she didn't want to be there. His brow furrowed even more when he watched the man kiss her temple and pull her close, like he owns her. He is flying Angels colors. If Tommy weren't working, he would pick a fight with that asshole. Now he had a choice, he could leave them alone and forget about Shelley Baxter, or he could try to make amends.

He had been trying for the past few weeks to repair the damage with his best friend and cousin. His mother had pulled him aside to tell him to put his balls back on and fix it. She told him that the Alpha has no right to deny Billy his mate, and all he was doing was hurting his own blood. So how does Tommy decide to try and fix it? He does a theater check. He didn't need the light to see the pair as his heightened abilities allow him to see perfectly in the dimly lit theater. He still flashes that light of shame on Jackson and Shelley.

Shelley blinks and squints at the sudden light, and Jackson

pulls away like he was burned, both of them sitting forward. Tommy smirks and moves on to the door, opening it like he left. He leans against the back wall and repeats this process every ten minutes for the rest of the movie. He gives that asshole just enough time to start making out with her again before he makes the next round of checks. If Shelley had seemed into it, he would have left them alone. Then broke Billy's heart to tell him the truth about her. He could hear her protests and smell the fear on her, so he does what he can to keep that guy at bay. He'll deal with him after work.

Jackson is furious. Why does some prick have to kill his chance to get laid with his girl? It's like he knows when Shelley's starting to get into it and flashes that light to cock block him. If he weren't with Shelley, he would beat that boy's ass. When the lights come up, he abandons the forgotten popcorn and jerks Shelley out of the chair. They come storming out of the theater.

"Jackson, stop. You're hurting my arm," she whines. Tommy steps into the path and causes Jackson to plow into him.

"Everything alright, miss?" His sweet Southern drawl amplified as he stares her down.

"Fuck you," tears well in her eyes as she jerks free of Jackson and runs off towards the exit of the mall.

Jackson gives Tommy a hard shove, surprising Jackson that it does not move the boy from his position. "Watch where the fuck you're goin', asshole." He storms off after Shelley. He doesn't know Tommy snapped a picture of him manhandling Shelley.

Tommy sends the picture to Billy with a smug look on his face. Whoever that guy is he is about to get a lesson in manners from the Wolf Pack. Tommy's phone chirps with a reply.

Tomorrow we ride

Shelley is beside herself and is livid by the time she reaches Jackson's bike. She had already climbed on and was sitting there with her arms crossed by the time Jackson comes stalking out of the mall.

Jackson takes a few slow breaths to keep from slapping that bitchy attitude right out of her and climbs onto the bike. The ride back to her home is full of tension and silence. He kills the bike when they pull into the driveway and she hops off it like someone lit a fire under her.

"Hey. Don't I at least get a fuckin' goodbye kiss?"

She whirls on him, "Why the fuck would I give you a kiss after what you just pulled, Jackson?"

"I don't know. Fuck, Shelley. 'Cause I'm leaving tomorrow?" He growls it back at her, but his tone reveals that desperate whine of a man who doesn't understand why his girl is being so awful to him.

"Oh, so now you're all about telling me you're leaving? Great! Go! Maybe you should just... Not come back!" she is crying and her voice raises to the dangerous octave a woman gets when a man crosses the line with them.

Jackson is up off the bike, the bear inside awake now, and stalks toward Shelley as she backs away, fearful, until he has her pinned against the garage. He leans down and crushes her mouth again with his kiss, his hands coming around her and pulling her against him, in what he believes is a romantic gesture. He keeps kissing her, even when she pounds her fists against him and cries out against the kiss. His eyes close and his hands roam over her and savors every bit of his angel. He knows she will melt to him and remember how much she wants him if he just keeps kissing her.

He is panting, and she is whimpering, when he finally releases her lips, which are puffy and swollen from the abusive claiming. "You're my angel, Shelley. Yer daddy already agreed. I'd prefer you want to be my girl, but I'll take what's mine if it's not given freely when I get back." Before she can reply, he pushes away from her and gets back on his bike.

Shelley is so stunned she does not react to his ultimatum. She watches him drive away before she turns to run into the house.

Her father was standing in the dark on the front porch, his arms crossed. She pauses to look at her father when she sees him. She is hoping everything Jackson just said was a lie. He was supposed to protect her and right now she feels like Jackson is getting out of control. Her eyes widen in horror when the only response is her father opening their front door for her to go inside.

CHAPTER FIFTEEN
Tonight We Ride

Billy couldn't stop thinking about the lesson he intended to teach that boy Tommy saw with his Shelley. Tommy filled him in on what he saw and heard when he got home last night. With each pop of the nail gun, cut of the wood, or bang of the hammer he could feel his temper welling inside. The moment he saw that picture, it was all he could do to keep from shifting and running after her last night. It didn't matter what his mother had said, he wasn't going to let anything bad happen to her. He loves her. He would teach that punk a lesson and warn him about what happens to men who put their hands on women.

At three o'clock, his father took the hammer from him. "Go on, get out of here. Your mind ain't in it, and you've ruined this drywall."

"Thanks, pop." Billy sighs and looks at the dent he caused.

Thirty minutes later he's rolling up to the Coeh house. Two honks of the horn, and out of the house come Jasper, Beauregard, and Tommy. He was still pissed at Tommy for what he did to Shelley, but he couldn't stay mad at the man forever. And Goddess help him, Tommy was trying to make it right. Billy had already forgiven the man. He just needed time to get over his broken heart. Only, the longer he stays away from Shelley, the worse his temper is getting. Tommy had been following him around like a lost puppy and Billy could see the silent treatment was taking its toll on his cousin. When Tommy sent that picture, it was enough that Billy had to repair his bedroom wall before he went into work this morning. Billy peels out of the driveway like a bat out of hell once his brothers are secure in the bed.

Mamma Coeh watches the truck haul ass down the gravel drive. She knows they are about to go start trouble down at that bar and she considers calling them back as Alpha. Whatever had Billy in a fit of rage probably deserved whatever they were going to dish out. Plus, if Silus couldn't handle four angry boys, he didn't deserve to be head of the Angels.

Shelley had told Faye what happened the night before, and Faye was furious. She has been picking at her father since they got to the bar after school. Shelley had to tell Faye to knock it off before she got in trouble. Then, it seemed as if every Angel this side of the Mississippi was in the bar tonight. There isn't an empty seat in the house. Jackson had told Shelley he was leaving today, but he must have ridden out while she was in school. Because he was not here much to her relief. The idea of him holding her hostage in his lap all night while her father watched made her sick to her stomach again. She already didn't feel good. The men in the bar tonight, are ignoring her for the most part. They keep their hands to themselves and thank her for bringing their orders. None of them are treating her how Jackson had been.

It's just before sundown when that rumbling old pickup truck crunches onto the gravel and the headlights flicker over the massive window. Faye's brows raise and she leaves her tray on the bar top.

"I'll be back."

The last thing she wanted was one of those Coeh assholes coming in and making matters worse for her sister. If it's Billy

Coeh, she has half a mind to knee him right in the balls. She steps outside with all the authority an eighteen-year-old girl can muster and crosses her arms. "Just what the fuck do you think you're doing here?"

"What? A man can't buy a drink after work?" Billy flashes his megawatt smile.

"Not if he stinks like a Coeh," she doesn't move from in front of the door.

Billy's eyes narrow at the girl, "Faye, we're lookin' for a man named Jackson. Know where he be?"

Faye's surprised expression says she knows the man. She narrows her eyes back at Billy, ignoring Jasper entirely, who is standing right next to him. He looks every bit as pissed as Billy does. "What's it to you, where he's at?"

"Got words for him," his tone shifts to a menacing promise.

"What? Didn't want to send your little bitch," cutting Tommy a dark look, "to do your dirty work today?"

"Is he here, or not, Faye?" Billy growls in frustration.

"If I say no, you gonna get the hell off my property?"

"Depends on how you say no," as he steps forward, towering over her. She lifts her chin in defiance.

Jasper can't help but grin at the little daredevil. It's one of the many things he loves about her. She is fearless and brutal.

"I ain't sayin' shit until you tell me why you hurt my sister," She shifts her stance, anxious he might just toss her aside and go into the bar anyway.

Billy sighs, "That," cocking his head towards Tommy, "Was all *that* idiot."

"And yet, you didn't call her to correct it. Hope that bitch you're fucking is worth it. Now get the fuck out of here." Faye turns to go back inside.

"Just tell me he'll treat her right," Billy sounds desperate. It makes Faye take pause, looking back over her shoulder at him.

Their eyes meet and she can see the anxiety in his expression and the way his muscles twitch as he stares at her. She turns back around to look at Billy. He looks distraught, and she sighs, looking over his shoulder at the three other men pacing behind with violent energy. She swears if they were cats their tails would be fluffed out and whipping hard enough to create a breeze. "Come to the office," she mutters and turns, walking around the building to wait for him at the smoker.

Billy follows and leans against the smoker, crossing his arms. He would hear her out before he did anything.

"No. He won't treat her right. Not at all. He was all over her last night. He's one of those fucking bikers and he thinks he owns her. And thanks to you, she ain't got no one to protect her from him." Faye jabs Billy in the chest to drive home that this is his fault.

"So," he looks at her with a pointed look, "back to the original question. He here?"

Faye frowns and shakes her head no. "He rode out of town on club business. I heard Daddy talkin' about him. He's gonna be gone for at least three months."

"Hmm," Billy grunts. "How's she doin'?"

Faye softens. "Terrible. I hear her crying after she thinks I went to sleep. I don't think I've seen her smile in at least a week. She just... mopes."

Billy looks crushed and lets out another sigh. "I fucked everything up, didn't I?"

Faye is surprised by the pain in Billy's tone. "You better get out of here before Daddy sees you. He's still pretty pissed about Halloween."

"Yeah, I guess we will," Billy turns and trudges back to the truck. "C'mon boys. Let's head home. No huntin' here tonight."

"Where's Faye," Jasper grumbles when she doesn't come back around the corner. Billy shrugs in response and gets into the truck. Jasper waits, hoping she'll come back around the corner.

Beau puts his hand on his shoulder. "C'mon man. Pop's got some o' that shine you like made up."

When Tommy gets into the pickup, Billy's fist connects with his jaw, causing his head to bang against the window. His jaw cracks from the power behind it. "I deserved that."

Faye watches from the shadow of the corner of the building, not watching Billy. Instead, she is trying to figure out what is going through Jasper's mind. She noticed how he paced like a toddler getting ready to throw a temper tantrum. What the fuck did he care about her? He made it clear she was just a good time at that party. She shakes her head, trying to forget all about Jasper Coeh and heads back into the bar through the kitchen door.

Silus catches her forearm as she passes by his office. "What was all that about?"

"Nothing," she jerks her arm free to head back to work. "Just a bunch o' Coeh boys tryin' to see whose dick's bigger."

Silus raises a brow at her choice of words. She didn't smell like sex and she seemed irritated more than anything.

"Mine was the biggest," she quips before turning her back to him and strutting out into the bar.

"That's my girl," Silus chuckles.

CHAPTER SIXTEEN

Truth & Consequences

December 14, 2003

Shelley stands in the bathroom she and Faye share, unable to move from the spot. She stares at the little white stick lying flat on the counter. The positive symbol had appeared a few minutes ago. It was the third test she had taken in as many days. Fear paralyzes Shelley. The only person she has ever had sex with was Billy Coeh. If her father found out what Billy did to her, he would sick all the Angels on him. Jackson had all but threatened to drag her by her hair into a relationship with him as well. She still has two years of high school to finish. Fear is making Shelley hug herself and trembles as she tries to will the little stick to change its mind. Shelley had thought it was just the flu, or something from school. She was so tired all the time, and everything was tender. Then she missed her period. How could this be happening to her?

"Bratnik," Faye's voice is muffled behind the door. "You've been in there an awfully long time. Everything alright?" Faye figures it is just another episode of Shelley's broken teenage heart. After seeing Billy a week ago, she was pretty sure the two of them should get back together. She was worried that if

Shelley knew and tried to get back with Billy, and their father found out. He might do something drastic such as introducing her to the club early. Shelley wraps the pregnancy test in toilet paper with haste and throws it in the trash. Turning on the water and washing her hands, she says nothing at first. She looks in the mirror, and the dark circles under eyes are prevalent. Her cheeks are puffy and red from crying. Shelley splashes some of the water on her face, then buries her face in the towel. "Shelley," Faye's voice sounds more urgent. "You're scaring me. Open the door." Shelley pulls the door open, harder than she means to, and comes face to face with her sister.

Faye looks her over. Red and puffy cheeks, dark circles, hiccupping breaths, all things that are manageable but she can tell there is something wrong with her sister, and for whatever reason Shelley's not confiding in her. "You know I'm here for you, right?" Faye offers.

"I... Oh Faye... I... I don't know what to do. It's awful. God, I need to get out of here before Daddy finds out." Shelley is making no sense and Faye shifts her weight, trapping her sister in the bathroom. Shelley tries to dart by again and Faye gives her a stern push back into the bathroom, closing the door behind her.

Faye looks her sister over again with a more critical eye. Without question, she pops open the lid of the trash can and gives it a light kick, jostling it enough the little stick reveals itself. Faye's eyes widen to the size of saucers, then she looks back at her little sister who is crying again.

"Oh God, I didn't think about that. He takes out the trash. Faye. He's going to kill me. What do I do? This can't be happening."

Faye steps up to her sister and just pulls her in tight against her, wrapping her arms around her. "Hey, hey. Calm down. It's alright. Shh," their father is downstairs watching football, and if he hears a commotion between the two of them, he will come up here and discover Shelley's secret. Faye rubs her hand in soothing circles along Shelley's back as she sobs against her. Her mind is ticking a mile a minute. She would have to tell at least their mother, to explain why they were going to skip school. Her mind begins to tick through all the hurdles of keeping this a secret. Would a clinic even let her get an abortion without her parent? She doubts it, even though she is old enough to give consent in Georgia. "Listen, go to our room. I'm gonna get Momma. She'll know what to do."

Shelley hesitates, but then nods and they part.

Faye comes downstairs. "Hey momma, you got a minute?" Faye lingers at the bottom of the stairs, looking into their living room.

"Can it wait? I'm watchin' the game with yer daddy," Paula doesn't look up from the magazine she is reading next to Silus. She was no more watching that game than Silus was interested in that magazine.

Faye frowns. She doesn't want to rock the boat too hard, but she wants her mother's attention right now. "I think Shelley's getting worse. I'm not sure what to do. Can you come check on her?" Faye makes herself sound younger and worried on purpose, not that it's a hard stretch right now. She wanted her mother to help them and if she has to put on a waterworks show, she was going to do it.

With a grunt Silus indicates he is irritated that Paula and Faye are disrupting football time.

"Fine," she huffs and thumps the magazine down on the table. Paula gets up from the couch and follows Faye back upstairs. The two women enter the girls' bedroom and Shelley is curled against her pillow. Paula comes and sits on the edge of the bed, while Faye closes the door, leaning against it as if she could keep it closed should her father decide to join them. "What's the matter, Shelley?"

Shelley flings herself into her mother and sobs against her.

"Momma. I'm so scared. I don't know what to do. Daddy's gonna kill him. And and... then what'll happen to the baby? What if I can't do it? What if Daddy kicks me out? Where will I go? Oh Momma." Paula blinks and tries to process the rapid fire confession from Shelley. When it doesn't click what Shelley is talking about, she looks at Faye with a furrowed brow.

"She's pregnant," Faye whispers.

"Oh honey," she sounds sympathetic, but she is furious. Now that Pruitt kid has even more claim to her. She couldn't have that little prick ruling the roost. No. "Don't you worry none. I'll make you an appointment. You'll be right as rain before Christmas." She eases her daughter back and brushes her damp hair from her face. She kisses Shelley's forehead, following it by wiping her tears away. "It'll be alright. I'll call the doctor in the morning." With jagged breaths, Shelley nods. Her mom seemed so sure about all this. Faye was right, she did know what to do. With that, their mother leaves the room. Paula decides to not Silus about this. She is pretty sure he'll lose his temper and hurt the girl.

When she comes back down and settles back into her magazine, he raises a brow at Paula. "She alright?" His voice holds that fatherly concern for his baby girl. For all his faults, he does love his daughter.

"I'm gonna call the doctor in the morning. She is running a temp and has the shakes. It's probably just the flu. Better safe than sorry," she lies smoothly.

The next afternoon, Faye, armed with Paula's identification, and Shelley are pulling into a clinic. There are two furious people who claim they are doing the Lord's work by protesting abortions in front of the clinic door. Faye parks the car and the two girls watch them stalk and harass the poor young women coming and going from the clinic. Shelley curls her hands around her stomach on instinct. She shouldn't be here without telling Billy. It's his baby too. Would he take care of her? She hoped he would appear out of nowhere to stop her and save her from this fear. Shelley bites against her lower lip and shakes her head no to chase off the fantasy.

Everything in her being tells her this is wrong. That nagging sense of she can't go through with this, and abortion is not birth control. That she shouldn't just throw away this baby because she was dumb. Maybe it was the protesters, or the lack of sleep, but Shelley was starting to chicken out.

Faye has been quiet. She cannot understand what Shelley is going through. She has been so careful to not get saddled down by anyone in Savannah. Five more minutes pass in silence as they watch the two belligerent people march about. They had not spotted the girls in the car yet and Shelley didn't think she could handle facing them. "Let's get out of here," Shelley sighs.

"You sure about this? What about Daddy?" Faye is looking at her little sister with genuine concern. "You really want to have Jackson's baby?" Faye knew Shelley and Billy had sex. She assumed Jackson forced himself on her and that he was the culprit. Faye was confident Billy was far more responsible than that when it came to sex.

Shelley gives a bitter laugh. "Fuck no," she replies. "This baby is Billy Coeh's."

The sound that Faye makes causes Shelley to jump, it was like someone had hit her. "What?" She hisses it. "Oh Shelley, you can't keep that baby. Daddy won't just kill him. He'll kill you too." Faye cries with this new information. This was the worst-case scenario for her sister.

"Then we just don't tell him," Shelley doesn't sound very confident. "We don't tell anyone until after Christmas. Then I'll tell Billy. And if he is still with that other girl, well, then we'll come back."

Faye, without another word, starts the car and leaves the clinic. The overwhelming guilt at not telling her the truth she learned last week about Billy eats her up inside. She is definitely not telling Shelley now about Billy. After hearing Shelley today, she knows she would just run right back to him and their father's wrath would be unstoppable.

CHAPTER SEVENTEEN
Holly Jolly Christmas

Christmas Eve 2003

The Baxter house is at the end of a cul-de-sac and is two stories with nothing in particular to identify it. It's an older neighborhood in Savannah, and one of the few still without an HOA. The lights had been hung around the porch by Silus, while the girls had decorated the tree in the front yard. The big picture window in the living room sports a well decorated Christmas tree. Presents sprinkled underneath for each person. The Baxters aren't poor, by any means, but they aren't rich either. Paula, Faye, and Shelley have been cooking all morning while Silus has been enjoying relaxing in the living room. They are having an early dinner, so Paula and Silus can have The Triple Six's Christmas bash. It's a time for the Angels to celebrate without kids, or other clubs.

Shelley brings her forearm up to her mouth and nose for the umpteenth time this morning. There is something about eggs that is making her want to puke. Faye and she exchange a look while Paula's back is to them. Shelley has resumed working when Paula turns to face them, trying not to breathe. Shelley, from the time she could hold the piping bag, has always finished the deviled eggs for Christmas. They are her favorite, but today these tiny devils are making her life hell.

The kitchen is quiet other than the sweet sounds of Christmas music pumping from the CD player in the corner. Faye's busy rolling out the dough for rolls as she watches her sister struggle through the eggs. If they switched tasks, it would alert their mother to something amiss, so both girls suffer in silence.

Paula's curvy figure is bopping around the kitchen like she is Martha Stewart. She checks the ham, dribbling the glaze on it. She stirs up the concoction for green bean casserole, and she keeps sampling the rum balls they made last night. "Alright girls, you got this?" Paula turns to face them.

"Yes, ma'am," the girls say in unison. Paula removes her apron and heads out of the kitchen with a fresh glass of sweet tea. She snuggles down on the couch next to Silus, content to get off her feet.

Faye watches from the kitchen entry before she comes and relieves Shelley. "You finish the rolls," she whispers.

Grateful, Shelley moves to the dough, flattening it out and cutting it with a cookie cutter to put onto a baking sheet.

An hour later, all four of them are settling down at the table. Paula and Silus are at the ends, while the girls on opposite sides. They pass all the dishes around the table and wait to eat until everyone has food. Shelley stares down at her food. None of it smells good, and she wants to just go back upstairs to take a nap. She pushes it around her plate with her fork, frowning.

Silus, knowing the deviled eggs are Shelley's favorite, takes the plate that Faye had placed on her side of the table, and offers it to Shelley.

Shelley, not wanting to raise suspicion, takes two off the offered platter. "Thanks, Daddy." She watches the little devils for a few moments trying to will herself to eat one. The scent alone is making her queasy. Swallowing hard, she scoops one into her hand and brings it to her mouth.

Faye's head shakes no as she watches in horror as her sister tempt fate.

As soon as the delicate, fluffy egg goodness touches the roof of her mouth, Shelley regrets her decision to make the effort. She begins to gag and covers her mouth, excusing herself as she rushes to the little half bath tucked under the stairs.

Silus raises a brow as he hears Shelley retching. "I didn't think they were that bad. You didn't change the recipe did ya?" He takes a careful sniff of one before popping it into his own mouth.

Paula furrows her brow, looking at the bathroom door. Her gaze shifts from the door to pierce into Faye.

Faye is fastidious in ignoring her mother by stuffing her face as fast as she can.

"You got a hot date?" Silus asks Faye.

"No Sir. Just so good I can't wait." Faye gives him a cheesy grin as they hear the toilet flush in the background.

A moment later Shelley, red faced from vomiting, returns to the table. She resumes pushing her food around on the plate when she eases back into her seat.

"Everything alright, baby girl?" Silus asks with genuine concern.

"Yeah, Daddy. Still feeling a little ooky," Shelley mumbles.

"You seemed right as rain yesterday," he counters. He reaches over and puts the back of his hand on her forehead. "Don't feel like you're runnin' a temp. Eat something. It'll make you feel better."

Faye is as still as a deer in headlights when Silus reaches over to touch Shelley and question her about her health.

Paula, who was still mulling over what's happening gets a dawning look on her face. She looks from Faye to Shelley and back. She narrows her eyes, sets her fork down, and places her napkin on the table. Then easing up she comes over to Shelley and takes her by the elbow. "With me, now," she barks at Shelley. She does not let Shelley reply as she drags her into the kitchen.

This leaves Faye and Silus at the table. Faye's eyes are locked on the kitchen entry, and she is mid-forkful. Fear for her younger sister is plain as day on her face. Before either of them can speak, Paula's voice raises in a dangerous octave in the kitchen, "... took care of it. That's the reason I made the fucking appointment, Shelley!"

They cannot hear Shelley's response. A moment later, she is dragging Shelley back into the dining room. Shelley's standing there, hiccupping to breathe and her cheeks are stained with tears.

Paula shakes her. "Tell him," she hisses at her. "Tell your father what you did." Silus sets down his fork. He didn't realize he was getting a Christmas pageant with dinner. He leans back in his chair and crosses his arms to see what happens next.

"Please, Momma, please," Shelley begs her mother to not make her do this.

"Shelley Joanne," Silus's voice is low and commanding, which causes Shelley to turn and face him.

She cries harder.

He could not understand her blubbering, but his patience for this drama was low.

"Daddy.. Please.. It was an accident. I didn't mean to. I just couldn't kill it. I couldn't. I went there. Faye took me. There were these women. All I could think about was his daddy and how heartbroken he'd be. I promise I won't be any trouble with it. I'll take care of it. Go to school. Everything!" Shelley's voice is at a hysterical level as she pleads with her father.

Silus's eyes darken with rage as he comes to understand his precious baby girl is pregnant. When he shoots up out of his chair Faye jumps, Paula steps back, and Shelley flinches.

"I'm going to fucking kill that cockroach." He yanks his cell phone out of his pocket and starts dialing.

Shelley runs to him, clinging on. "No, Daddy, please. You can't hurt him. I love Billy."

The room goes deadly silent. The tick of the clock in the living room echoes for everyone to hear as heartbeats stretch on for what feels like an eternity. The first sound to shatter the silence is the little Nokia brick smashing against the wall where Silus threw it.

He turns his wrath onto Shelley. "Billy? Billy who?" His voice drops lower and lower, with the promise of death breathed out.

This causes Shelley to step back. "B... Bi... Billy C... Coeh," her voice is timid and dripping with fear.

The weight of Silus's rage fills the room. Shelley swears he has grown in size right before her eyes.

Faye and Paula stand stock still and silent, watching in fear for Shelley. Neither could get to her before Silus could if he attacks.

Shelley's hyperventilating in front of her father as he puffs in anger.

He raises his hand, as if it is taking all his effort to move at all, and points at the door. "Get. Out."

Shelley, in utter shock and confusion whimpers, "Daddy?" The next thing Shelley sees is the gates of hell open in her father's eyes.

Before she can react, his hand whips out and laces into her hair with his massive fingers palming her skull. He drags her to the front door, ripping it open and tossing her out like a stray cat.

Shelley cannot keep her balance and ends up skidding across the porch into the railing. She lies there on the ground as the tears come again, blinding her.

Silus returns to his seat at the dinner table and resumes eating, as if he had not just thrown out his youngest child.

Faye and Paula look at each other and follow suit in silence. Both are fearful that one wrong move will turn his wrath on them.

It's agony for Faye, the thirty minutes it takes to finish eating. She stares daggers at her dinner plate. How could he treat

Shelley like that? How could he sit there and eat like nothing happened? She doesn't look at him, or her mother, for the rest of the meal.

Paula is also staring at her plate and not wanting to attract unwanted attention from Silus. The sound of the forks scraping against the porcelain is jarring.

When Silus finishes, he gets up, leaving his plate there, and gets his colors. "We're going to the Christmas Party." He stalks toward the garage, Paula following behind him in a defeated and meek manner, leaving Faye to clean up by herself.

CHAPTER EIGHTEEN

Sweet Sorrows

Faye watches out of the window as her parents drive away. They turned the corner at the end of the cul-du-sac, and she yanks the front door open. She is going to look for Shelley, figuring she had run to a friend's house and gasps when she sees her sister still lying on the front porch, unmoving. Had their father hurt her? "Shelley," she whimpers and kneels down with her.

Shelley flinches at first, still afraid to move, broken that her father would look at her like that. She had nothing and nowhere to go. In fact, she was still barefoot, and wearing sweat pants with a T-shirt. She is shivering even though it is sixty degrees outside. The shock of losing everything has put her in this near catatonic state.

"Come on, we have to hurry." Faye forces Shelley up and brings her back inside. She pats over her sister and checks her for any injuries she might not have seen on the porch. Faye then pulls her kid sister into a tight hug. "Don't worry, Bratnik. I got you," she cries against her.

Still in shock, Shelley wraps an arm around her sister's waist and sobs again. The girls stand there crying in each other's arms for only a few minutes before Faye breaks the embrace and takes Shelley's hand. They go upstairs and Shelley gets dressed at Faye's prompting.

Faye goes into her parents' room and gets the big rolling suitcase her mother bought for their trip to Key West a few years back. She plops it onto Shelley's bed, followed by a duffel bag with Shelley's name in glitter on it. Shelley had gone into the bathroom, and Faye could hear her vomiting again. Faye frowns as she pulls open the top dresser drawer for Shelley. She empties the entire dresser into the suitcase without a word. Faye then tears open their small closet, grabbing an armload of little sundresses on hangers and stuffs them into the suitcase. By the time Shelley has come back into the room, Faye has packed all of Shelley's clothing, shoes, and was pulling some of Shelley's favorite knick knacks into a third bag.

"Faye?" Shelley's voice cracks as she watches her sister moving around faster than a Tasmanian devil.

"Go pack your bathroom stuff. Take whatever you want. Even if it's Momma's, or Daddy's, we're not coming back." Faye doesn't look at her little sister. She had sat in that dining room watching that monster enjoy his glazed ham like a fucking king of the mountain. She isn't sticking around to take his bullshit anymore. Sure, it's one thing when she was protecting Shelley, but he threw her out like trash and then finished his fucking figgy pudding. If Faye had been braver, she would have gone and gotten his gun to shoot him. Shelley never hurt anyone, and for him to put his hands on her, Faye wasn't having any of it.

"Fuck them both," she mutters out loud, as if she had just been saying all this to Shelley.

Shelley remains silent, watching her sister move at this frantic pace. She feels guilty for causing all this and ruining Christmas. She hiccups again, trying to hold back her tears, and Faye whirls around.

"Oh, Shelley, no. Not you. Oh, man. I'm sorry. Look. We don't have time for this right now. I need you to pack the bathroom stuff, mine too. Then get whatever you want from Momma and Daddy's room. We're leaving as soon as we have everything. They won't be back until way later, so don't panic. I won't let anything bad happen to you." She comes over and hugs her sister again, squeezing her tight.

Shelley realizes what is happening and hates that Faye is leaving too. She nods in understanding, then disappears back into the bathroom.

Faye only hesitates long enough to see she is packing things and turns to under her bed. She pulls up the single duffel bag. She tears through her clothes like a demon possessed, grabbing only the most important things, and the stuff she likes. She had packed three full bags for Shelley, and was starting a fourth, but Faye only needed the one. She tucks the photo box in the bag with care, and stuffs in the remaining clothes. Then she darts out of the room to her parents' room. Faye flings open the door to their walk-in closet. She plops down and begins turning the combination to the safe.

Paula had written it in her little address book in case she forgot, and Faye's now staring at just what she needed. There are four bundles of cash totaling ten thousand dollars and a nine millimeter pistol with angel wings etched in the grip. She tucks it into the back of her pants and grabs the box of bullets next to it. Faye then snatches an old purse off her mother's shelf and stuffs the cash along with the bullets into it. Then she turns to her parents' dresser. She snatches up any jewelry she wants and brings all her treasure back with her, dumping it on her bed. Shelley has set Faye's bathroom bag in her duffel bag and placed hers in her own.

"You want any of this?" Faye motions to the jewelry.

"Faye, that's stealing. You know that's Momma's stuff,"

"FUCK MOMMA!" Faye roars at her sister. "Don't you get it, Shelley? They sat there and fucking ate dinner like nothing had happened. Like you hadn't been begging for their help! He fucking sat there and enjoyed Christmas fucking dinner while you laid on that porch suffering. So fuck them! I'm taking what I want, and they can fucking rot in Hell for all I care." Faye is breathing hard and kicks her nightstand over in frustration. It makes Shelley jump. "We're never coming back, don't you get that? If you want any memories, you had better get them now. 'Cause if Daddy sees you again he'll likely kill you."

Shelley hugs herself and watches her sister meltdown in front of her. Faye is losing all sense of composure, and Shelley doesn't know what to do to stop her. She had spent her whole life hiding from raging people, just like Faye had taught her. Memories of hiding under the bed while their father took a belt to her sister flash in her mind. She also remembers how he backhanded Faye not more than a few weeks ago. Shelley's shaking again and nods. She comes over and takes a few pieces of her mother's jewelry. She stuffs them into her pocket.

Faye frowns, trying to rein in her temper, but only finds she is full of rage with no outlet. She finishes stuffing a few last-minute things into her bag and slings it over her shoulder. She helps Shelley with the four bags as they head downstairs.

Christmas dinner remains where everyone left it. She hadn't even bothered to put away the leftovers. Shelley watches in fascination as Faye tears through the pile of presents under their Christmas tree, snatching up all the ones labeled for each of them and stuffs them into Shelley's arms. "Go put all this in the car."

Shelley nods and turns, walking through the kitchen and into the garage where the old sedan is. She gets the packages into the back seat. Then she comes back for the bags when she hears shattering glass. "Faye!" She comes running to see what happened and stops dead. Faye's standing in the living room, breathing hard. Silus's bowling ball is nestled in the TV, having shattered the screen. "Oh, Faye. What have you done? He's going to kill you!"

"Fuck him. He has to find me first. Come on." Faye grabs the bags at the bottom of the stairs and brushes by Shelley to load them into the car.

Shelley is dumbfounded, staring at the destruction and chaos created by Faye's outburst. Her father is going to think she did it. There will be no forgiveness now. He won't believe her. She cries harder, realizing there was no coming back after this.

"Hey, it'll be alright, come on. We need to go." Faye touches her shoulder and Shelley droops, stepping around Faye to go get in the car. Faye looks around and snatches a piece of paper out of Shelley's backpack.

I hope you're happy with yourself you fucking monsters. You won't ever hurt us again. - Faye

She leaves both their phones on the table at Silus's seat with the note tucked under them. She doesn't even bother to lock up. Faye grabs Shelley's backpack on her way back to the car. She slams the door closed as she plops into the driver's seat, presses the button to open the garage, and backs out. Faye pauses the car to roll down the window and tosses out the little remote for the garage. She rolls the window back up and backs out the rest of the way to drive away from the house.

Neither girl has said a word as the sun sets. They cross the state line into South Carolina and Faye keeps stealing side-glances at Shelley to assure herself she is alright. The two-lane highway is dark as it cuts through the national forest. Faye knows exactly where they are going, and what she has to do to make sure Shelley is safe. Then she is disappearing. She will start over somewhere no one knows her, and where the Angels of Wrath can't touch her.

When Faye stops the car again, she has parked in front of a driveway with a wolf howling at the moon hanging from under a mailbox. Faye kills the engine, then she pulls all the presents from the back seat up front. All the rage she had in the house is now being consumed by grief. She believes this will be the last time she will ever see her kid sister. She divides the packages while Shelley looks on.

"We're going to have a good Christmas," Faye whispers out, as if she could just will it by putting it out in the universe. "We're going to open presents, and then you're going to walk up that driveway to your new life. Okay?" She was trying to will a happy Christmas into existence for both of them. "Listen. Billy never had a girlfriend. Tommy was being dumb and was jealous. Billy's been asking about you for weeks. He came by the Six to beat the shit out of Jackson and I'm sorry I didn't tell you." Faye's voice cracks with the tidal wave of emotions as she confesses her secret.

Shelley couldn't believe what she is hearing. Had she been knocked unconscious back on the porch and this was all a dream? Or had she died? Can you die from a broken heart? Fear consumes Shelley. She had just witnessed her sister rage like her father, and they are now sitting in a stolen car in South Carolina. "What do you mean by a lie?" Shelley's voice is fragile and small as hope tries to bloom. She wants to believe Faye, but she doesn't want to get hurt again.

"Exactly that, Bratnik." Faye pulls her into a tight hug. "That asshole, Tommy, made all that shit up cause he's a prick. You kick him in the balls when you see him, okay?"

"Why didn't you tell me?" Shelley breaks free from the hug and looks at her sister with a hurt expression.

"I... I... Oh, Shelley, I'm sorry. I was scared if Daddy found out... I didn't want him to hurt you." Tears stream down Faye's cheeks.

Shelley hugs her sister again and the two girls cry in each other's arms. It takes several minutes before they are able to calm down. It's Faye who breaks apart first this time and she motions to the presents. The two girls open them in silence with slow and careful motions, as if they could make this moment last a lifetime. Each girl got shiny iPods, and new phones.

Faye took the phones. "If you want a phone, get one that he doesn't own. So he can't turn it off or find you." She tossed them into the backseat. They got other trinkets, and clothes as well. Shelley had gotten Faye the charm bracelet she had been eying at the mall, and the two girls hugged tight again. Then they get out of the car. Faye helps her unload her bags, stacking them so Shelley could drag the suitcase with all the other bags on it. Faye helps Shelley slide the backpack onto her shoulders, then closes the trunk without getting her bag out.

"Wait. Aren't you coming with me?" Shelley frowns, realizing Faye's bag is still in the car. Panic starts to fill her. She hadn't registered that Faye was leaving her. She had been so caught up in everything Faye had said.

Faye doesn't want her sister to worry, so she lies. "I'm gonna go ditch the car far enough away so daddy can't find us. I'll be back. Go on up to the house and get settled. It's cold out here." Faye hugs her sister tight enough Shelley is struggling to breathe. Shelley clings to Faye, not wanting to let go. She knows, deep down inside, that Faye is never coming back and just lied to her.

"I love you, Faye," Shelley whimpers against her big sister. She wants to tell her sister to not go, and to stay with her, but she knows that Faye has already decided.

"I love you too, Shelley."

CHAPTER NINETEEN
Matters Of The Heart

The house is large and set a fair way back from the road. Susie's great grandfather built it when he settled in South Carolina. It's seven in the evening and the Coeh family is sitting down to the massive table to eat. It is Susie, David, their seven sons, three wives, eight grandkids, Susie's sister, her husband who is the pack's beta, and their son, Tommy. The tree shoved off into a corner has a mountain of presents that hides the entire bottom half. Susie's great grandfather had always intended this house to be for a large family. As each generation takes over the pack, they inherit the big house. It's not a pack house, but it's the house the Alpha always lives in.

Pack business is done at a neutral place, and always in public. Susie tries very hard to keep the pack and family separate. She has raised seven alpha males, which is no small feat. She leans in the kitchen door, holding the fourth bowl of rolls for dinner and watching them. Beauregard and Tommy are snickering over something Caleb just said. While she can see the resemblance in the two, it's one of the few secrets she will take to the grave. As far as she is concerned, he is her nephew, not her son. Her sister's happiness is more important than laying claim on the boy.

This was going to be their last Christmas with her as the Alpha. She hadn't told the family yet, but she was tapped as one of the three candidates to fight for the Alpha position in the Appalachian Pack. Mehzebeen had informed her of the Tribunal's support for her candidacy that morning. She hadn't even told David yet. She wanted this Christmas to be about family. She watches her sons down the line and sees qualities in each of them for leading this pack. She had hoped to spend some time with them individually and test who was worthy of being Alpha.

After talking with the pack elders, it's clear that only natural born wolves will be accepted as Alpha. This leaves Matthias, Billy, and Caleb. Tommy is natural born, but the pack would revolt if she put that schemer in as Alpha. He's a good kid, but his brain runs away with him. Her gaze settles on Billy. He is sitting off to the side, Jasper next to him on the end of the big bench seat they brought in for all of the extended family in attendance. Both boys are pushing their food around like it's a chore to even be at the table. It draws a small frown from Susie. She knows why they're moping, those fucking Baxter girls. How her boys could be wrapped up with such trash is beyond her. One thing's for sure, Billy's temper has progressively gotten worse since The Rutting.

"Not hungry?" She speaks through the mind link. *"I thought that stuffing was your favorite, Billy."*

Billy responds with a smile as he shovels in a large forkful. She can see his heart isn't in it. Then her gaze settles on Jasper who sulks without looking up. He was angered beyond reason with her for being denied his request to accept Faye as his mate. He is not a child, and he doesn't need her permission, but he loves his mother, and he became a wolf when he turned eighteen. Which means he would follow her rules so long as she was Alpha.

Then their eldest brother, Matthias, throws a roll from the newly placed bowl and pings Billy in the head. "What's the matter, Billy boy? Girl still got your balls in a sling? From what I hear, you got yourself a looker at The Rutting. When are we gonna get a whiff?"

"Matty!" His wife hits him hard in the arm. She had talked with Susie about Billy. She married into this family twelve years ago, and the two of them had grown close. If he knew he was poking the bear, he might not have tried to lighten the mood.

Billy lets out a threatening growl. The entire table stops and turns to look between the brothers. Susie sits down at the head of the table, taking a large swig of her beer. Her eyes level on Billy and she shakes her head no.

This makes Jasper pound his fist on the massive oak table. "What the fuck do you have to be shitty about? At least you got to fuck Shelley. Heaven forbid Billy Coeh doesn't get what he wants. Or any of us get to be with people we love. Only Momma gets that luxury, apparently. Forget that girl and move on already," Jasper snaps at Billy with as much growl in his voice as Billy had in his.

There is no fighting at Momma Coeh's table. Not when they were little, not when they were bigger, and sure as shit, not now. Susie watches as Billy rises and steps out of the bench, taking one of the festive holiday napkins and smacks Jasper in the face with it, letting it fall from his hand as he walks outside.

The gauntlet is thrown.

The table watches with anticipation as Jasper processes what his brother just did. He shoots up off the bench and starts like a freight train for his elder brother. The single low growl from their Alpha causes all the rest of them to grumble and plant their butts back in their seats. She is not providing a dinner show for the whole family tonight. The boys sulk at not being able to see outside.

Jasper leaps from the porch, fist in the air, with every intention of hitting his brother from behind.

Billy's fast and turns in time to catch Jasper in the gut as his younger brother's fist connects with his jaw.

The two men meld into one massive ball of fists, teeth, and shredded clothing as they shift into their werewolf forms. Claws slash at each other. Teeth tear at skin. They both growl and snarl, with the dominant power oozing from them. This aggression has been building for weeks now.

Susie and David exchange a glance and Susie moves to get up from the table. They were silently trying to decide which one of them goes outside to break up the fight.

"No, I got it," David sighs. "Trust me darlin', you ain't got the slightest idea of how to talk to lovesick male pups," as he kisses her on the temple on his way out to settle the fight. David takes a leisurely and strolling pace to the combatants. He pauses to find himself a weapon that will suffice his needs. The last thing he wants is to be ripped to shreds by his own sons in a fit of rage. His calloused work hands curl around the handle of a shovel and he pulls it up like he's the mighty Babe Ruth.

A couple of ringing bongs later, both men are naked on the ground, holding their heads with David standing over them, leaning on the shovel. "Now that I have your attention," he starts. "You two assholes are brothers. Ain't no one else in this world more important, not even your mates. Well, except maybe for the other assholes at the table. You two are pining after them girls. So you have to ask yourself, are you just gonna keep pinin'? Or are you gonna do somethin' about it?" He flashes them that debonair Coeh smile. "Just remember, it's always easier to beg forgiveness than to ask permission. Now get your asses inside, get dressed, and eat your damn dinner. She slaved all day in that kitchen for you ungrateful pups."

"Yes, sir," they reply in unison and watch as their father goes back inside.

Billy starts to head to the front door, when he sees Jasper making a beeline for the barn. He catches up to him, "What are you up to?"

Jasper doesn't say a word as he scrounges up a fresh set of clothes. He then wheels his bike out of the barn.

"You're going after her, aren't ya?"

Jasper still says nothing, continuing to walk his bike down the driveway. He doesn't look back. He didn't just ride off because it would have alerted Momma and she would stop him.

Billy watches in silence. He understands the urge. Everything in his being said to do the same thing. He wants to ride with him and get his Shelley. Jasper has always been the wild one to buck authority. A glance back at the barn and he takes a step towards his bike. Then he stops, frowning. His responsibility to his family is too strong. He can't break his momma's heart. His shoulders droop and he is thankful he was out here alone. He lets out a mournful howl before he forces himself to walk back into the house. Billy avoids most of the family and keeps his hand over his manhood while he trots upstairs to get dressed again, ignoring the squealing giggles of the younger pups in attendance.

Jasper was already on the two-lane highway and had mounted his bike when he saw the headlights in his mirrors. He takes pause and adjusts the mirror, recognizing that old sedan. He watches in the dark to see what is happening. The two girls appear to be exchanging gifts and talking. His brow furrows more when he sees them get out of the car and unload luggage. He tilts his head up as he inhales. They're upwind of him and after a minute he realizes what is going on. Shelley's scent differs from before, and she's terrified. Billy's scent is on her as well.

"*Momma, you have a visitor,*" He links to his mother as he waits on his bike to see what Faye is doing. "*Be nice. I love you.*"

He blocks the link after that. He sits in silence to watch the sedan drive by him and confirms it is Faye. He starts his bike up, without turning on the lights so he can follow in the dark. He didn't need lights to see.

When she pulls off into the abandoned gas station about twenty miles later, he stops far enough back so she won't see him. She takes a long time to get out of the car. He watches her toss the keys into the car, lock it, and close it. Then turning on heel she continues walking on the shoulder of the highway. He gets a wolfish grin and eases back onto the road as he flicks the headlamp on.

Jasper pulls alongside her and leans on his handlebars, "Hey darlin', wanna ride?"

CHAPTER TWENTY
Christmas Miracles

Shelley does not watch Faye drive off. She would run after her if she does. She takes all her bags and begins trudging in the dark up the gravel drive. The massive house lit up in the distance looks warm and inviting. She is still crying, and the walk feels like it takes forever. Her muscles are tired, and she drags the massive suitcase up the steps with all the grace of a turtle on its back. She tries to get herself under control, which results in hiccups and whimpers. No matter how hard she tries, wiping her cheeks does her no good. She forces herself to take slow and deep breaths. Faye had told her she was safe in this place. She had to trust her sister. She does not know whose house this is, or what's going on inside, other than it's full of laughter and squealing. She stops to take stock of everything around her. She didn't want to interrupt their family time. It stays her hand at the door, preventing her from knocking as she realizes she is about to be someone else's burden.

Before she can back out of this idea and flee, the door pulls open. Momma Coeh stands tall and fearsome before Shelley. They lock eyes, and sharp inhale from Susie tells her everything she needs to know on the matter. Any hardness on Billy being with Shelley Baxter melts away as she moves forward and pulls her into a tight hug. "Oh, baby girl," she coos, as a mother should. Shelley breaks down again and clings to Momma Coeh. She smells like whiskey and cookies. "Come on in, sugar. Let's get you some food. Boys, make a place for Miss Shelley." Susie takes the bags from Shelley and hands them off to Caleb, who appeared by her side. "Put 'em in Jasper's room." She keeps her arm around Shelley as she guides her into the dining room. The 'adults' table falls quiet watching the pair walking in. There is a mix of emotions and expressions.

Tommy's eyes widen and he starts to smile, then sees the state Shelley's in and lowers his gaze. Guilt fills him all over again. She looks like hell. The boys, and their wives, slide down the bench, allowing Shelley to sit near David and Susie. Without hesitation, the table resumes their conversations, albeit muted, and they fill a plate as they pass it down to Shelley. Matthias offers the tray of deviled eggs and Shelley covers her face, gagging. She holds her free hand up and shakes her head no.

"Well, she doesn't like deviled eggs, she is out," he flashes a grin and flinches as his wife whacks him again.

"Oh... No. They are my favorite," Shelley mutters from behind her hand. "It's just... they're making me... that is... It's awful," knowing chuckles come from the women at the table.

"It's alright, honey. We all get weird when we're pregnant. This brute is just teasing you," the woman whacks Matthias again.

Caleb picks up the bags and heads upstairs. He still didn't get why she would go into Jasper's room. Doesn't Jasper need this room? Wasn't she Billy's girl? Shouldn't she go into Billy's room? He does not argue with Momma's decision though. He is entering the room about the time Billy is coming back out of his room with great reluctance. He had been moping in solitude when his mother linked him to come back downstairs. He looks defeated. His hulking shoulders droop and his expression is blank. He feels empty inside without her and believes himself a coward for not wanting to stand against his mother's wishes.

That's when he gets the scent. The sweet watermelon mixed with lilies scent of Shelley. It makes his entire body roar to life with longing. He looks back and forth, confused. It's so strong and fresh that he could swear she just walked by his door. He sees a light on in Jasper's room, which makes him raise a brow. His feet are carrying him into the room before he could realize he was bursting through the door. He expects to find her standing there. Only he finds Caleb, picking up the laundry Jasper had left strewn everywhere and putting it in the hamper right by the door. Billy's eyes narrow and he looks from Caleb to the luggage and back.

"What? Momma told me to put her--," Billy didn't wait for him to finish the statement.

Shelley hears is a freight train coming down the stairs at a fast enough pace it's rattling the pictures on the walls. Everyone at the table is bemused by this horrifying sound and Shelley shies in fear.

"Don't worry, girl. It'll be alright," she hears David's sweet drawl over the commotion. Shelley barely swallows the bite of food she put in her mouth when she sees Billy.

His eyes are darting back and forth, searching. He is breathing hard and frantic. She is here. He knows it. He can smell her. With a yelping sound that startles him, he turns just in time to see the tiny blond leap into his arms. His massive arms wrap around her and pull her right to him. Billy buries his face against the crook of her neck and thanks the Goddess Shelley is here and wants him. He can feel her tiny body shaking from crying against him. She clings to him. He is so over the moon that she is here he does not register her whimpering against him. He isn't letting go for dear life.

"Shelley," he huffs out.

"Billy," she whimpers against him.

"Alright, love birds. Sit." Susie cuts across the sappy reunion, but there is a smile on her face. All the women at the table are looking on with a matching sappy smile. Susie sighs and shakes her head as she watches the two of them. She decides, right then and there, that she would go to war for Billy's happiness. Silus will just have to get over it. She imagines Shelley being here means something has gone awry at the Baxter residence. She catches David's smirking face, and she has to laugh. She hates it when that man is right.

Billy carries Shelley back to the table, taking up the seat she had occupied, and forcing his brothers to scoot more because of his size. He keeps her cradled in his lap and rests his hands around her. He doesn't care how foolish he looks, he wasn't ready to stop touching her. He lets her nestle into a comfortable position and resume eating. Her appetite finds its way back to her as Billy's fingers trail patterns along her back to soothe her.

His brothers and wives wrangle their children to their rooms to settle in for the final preparations of Santa coming to visit. This leaves the beta Jacob, Susie, David, Billy, and Shelley at the table.

"Now," Momma Coeh begins. Billy braces for her to tell him he's out of the pack, and they would only get to stay the night. "You're a damn fool, you know that?" She points at her son. "This is a right pickle you put this little girl in. So you're gonna make this right." She turns her attention to Shelley for a moment, then looks at her brother-in-law, who is chuckling. When she faces them again. "You're gonna make sure she gets to and from school every day, as well as the work you do for your daddy. You're gonna marry her," she pauses and narrows her eyes, "*After* she finishes high school. Until then, she'll stay in Jasper's room. As long as this is my house, you two had better not let me catch you fornicatin', that understood Billy James Coeh?"

Billy turns a bright shade of crimson at his mother calling out that he has had sex, in spite of him being an adult. "Well, then we ain't gotta wait long. You graduate in May, right?" He looks radiant with hope and excitement only to be met with his mother's bemused grin.

"About that," Shelley mewls and shifts.

"Oh. You were held back. No worries, one year won't be too terrible," Billy is ever the optimist.

"Uhm, no. Never held back," Shelley sounds even more nervous now. "I... Uh... Well, you remember how Faye said I was eighteen," she bit against her lip in fear that he might throw her out for lying.

Susie can't take it, neither can David. "You idiot. That girl's only sixteen!" The pair of them say it in unison.

"Oh." Billy looks like a kicked puppy as he realizes Shelley had lied about her age. "Well, I guess we're waitin' then."

It's now Shelley's turn to blush, and she clings to him with the need to be in his arms. "I'm sorry. I didn't mean to lie. I just didn't want you to think I was a kid. And well, it never came up again. And Faye said it didn't matter." Her voice is timid and full of anxiety. She is used to people flying off the handle when she does things. The level of fear that radiates from her makes all the wolves in the room tense. It makes Shelley shy, expecting him to hit her, or throw her off his lap.

Billy pulls her in tight and soothes her. "So what if you're sixteen? I'll wait. You're my girl."

CHAPTER TWENTY-ONE
Who's A Good Boy

Christmas starts at sunup. All the small children began at one end of the house, running to the other howling at the top of their lungs that Santa had been there. David's bite in the cookies and half-drunk milk was all it took for the magic to happen. Couple that with parents sneaking in last minute 'Santa Only' presents onto the pile by the tree, it is quite adorable, other than Shelley has barely slept a wink. She is in a strange bed, in a strange house, with the guy she is sweet on with just beyond the door. She has every intention of staying in that room until they were done opening presents, as the memories of what she has lost were too much for her.

"Shelley," Billy's voice calls through the door. "They can't open presents until everyone's downstairs." She can hear the gaggle of small children capering around him.

"Yeah! Hurry, Shelley! We wanna open presents," their whining and pleading is so cute. Billy looks like a giant among them.

Shelley sighs and pulls herself out of the big soft bed. The kids cheer and squeal in delight when she opens the door. Billy's sweet smile fills his face, and he is quite taken at how beautiful she looks disheveled. He pulls her closer, leaning down to kiss her good morning.

It makes Shelley's cheeks flush hot and melt right to him. The tension of the past twenty-four hours starts to wash away in his grasp.

"Mhmm... Keep wakin' me up like that and I'm gonna pretend to sleep all the time."

His chuckle is husky and his cheeks are rosy from the blush her retort brings to them. But he guides her downstairs instead of sneaking back into the room with her. The main room is full of sleepy adults all clutching to cups of coffee while their children run amok looking at all the presents. Billy settles her into a spot on the couch while he goes and gets himself a cup of coffee, bringing her back hot tea with honey in it as well. With an easy motion he has her in his lap again. It makes her giggle and be shy, but no one is paying them much attention. She is content to watch the Coeh family open presents. Billy loves the way her face lights up in surprise at there being presents for her under the tree. She had only been here a total of twelve hours, but the kids aren't lying when they read her name on the tags. There are a dozen presents just for her.

It brings tears to her eyes. Guilt fills Shelley at having such a happy Christmas when her sister is alone out there and her parents will come home to find their house destroyed from Faye's wrath. Try as she might to hide those feelings, she still has to wipe the tears away.

"What is it, Angel?" Billy asks with concern. His massive hand rubs against the small of her back.

She shakes her head and wipes the tears, offering him a big smile.

"You sure?" His dark brown eyes remain focused on her, looking just short of panic at her tidal waves of emotions.

She nestles into his lap more and rests her head against him. "Just touched that you guys thought of me," she murmurs.

"Happy tears."

Billy, Tommy, and Beauregard rushed about, finding any place open late last night, and gathered up what they thought she might like. A few gift cards, some cute silver earrings, some scarves, and a book all made the stack of presents. None of it was overly specific to her, but still gifts they thought she would like.

It took hours for all the presents to be opened, and the living room is flooded with wrapping paper and ribbon. Kids are playing with new shiny toys and empty boxes. Adults are laughing and talking. A large spread of fruits, pancakes, and bacon has been put out for people to graze on.

"Let's go somewhere quieter," Billy murmurs in her ear.

With a nod, she follows him.

They head out the front door and keep walking toward the woods. A trail reveals itself on the other side of the yard, then they are shielded by the trees. He keeps his hand in hers, and Shelley guesses he's afraid if he lets go she will disappear again. When they stop, they are at the edge of a private lake. The cleared area for fishing is nothing more than a patch of grass without trees and a few folding camp chairs left propped against a rotted wood dock post.

"It's beautiful."

Billy takes a seat and pats next to him.

Without hesitation, she settles down with her legs crossed and leans her head against his shoulder. They enjoy the serene sounds of the water lapping against the shore. It reminds her of the night on the beach in Hilton Head. Shelley had thought he brought her here to make-out with the way he murmured it but is glad he isn't forcing himself on her. It leads her to thinking about that night in the meadow, how they had made love. Then her thoughts drift to how he had changed into the beast, and how afraid she has been since. "Can I ask you something?" Shelley disturbs their silent revelry.

"Anything," he rumbles back.

"Will the baby eat his way out?" Shelley has been fretting about this for weeks. She didn't know how to learn about werewolves because Tommy told her they would kill her. Now that she is here, among them, she is going to learn everything so she can be the best werewolf mom there is.

Billy's laughter echoes over the lake. "No, darlin'. That baby's gonna come out just like every other baby in the world. We don't like humans for food. They're gamey." He flashes a grin.

Shelley blushes and swats Billy's arm. "Don't make fun of me. I was scared! And Tommy said y'all would kill me if I talked about it."

"You should punch that idiot the next time you see him. Right in the jaw. We don't kill people. I would be surprised if anyone believed you, and if you were believed, they would hurt you before we would. I will never hurt you, Shelley. You're my mate." Billy gives her a serious look. "I would die to protect you."

Shelley feels the butterflies in her stomach at being called his mate. "Is that like a wife?"

Billy shrugs, "Not exactly. It just means we were made for each other. No other people will ever make us feel the way we do about each other. You'll be my wife too. We'll do it right, and in a church if you want. But I'd love to do it under the stars. Maybe on the beach?" He gives her a wistful look, imagining her in a pretty white dress and barefoot as she comes down the aisle. "You're stuck with me. Angel."

"Promise?"

"Promise." Billy gives her his megawatt smile.

There is another long pause before Shelley asks, "Can I see your... werewolf?"

Billy gets a sheepish smile. He was worried she was terrified of that part of him. It would sting if she didn't accept all of him, but he would keep his wolf at bay around her if that were the case. He gets up and steps a few feet away from her before he kicks off his boots.

She tilts her head watching him until she realizes he's getting naked. "Billy!" She giggles and covers her eyes.

"What? You want me to tear up my clothes? Besides, I see you peeking," he wiggles his ass at her as he continues to strip down. Once his clothes are off, he shifts. It's not painful, like the movies make it out to be, and he has well practiced shifting. Before her now stood the massive beast with claws and a long snout. She comes to her feet and her heart is racing. His coppery fur shimmers in the sunlight, making her think of a fire smoldering. He is casting a shadow over her. She swallows hard and eases forward. His piercing gaze never leaves her and he stands still. His ears are twitching with hesitation, wanting her approval. Another step forward and she was standing right before him. She keeps her eyes up, as his massive manhood is hanging there for all to see. Her cheeks are bright red and she has to keep her face tilted up to not have his manhood right in her face. Her fingers brush against his muscular torso. The fur is soft and feels wonderful under her touch. She explores every inch of him innocently. Fingers trailing over the furred skin followed by her leaning up on her tip toes to nuzzle against his stomach.

He is instantly hard. He can't help it in this form. All the emotions and instincts are primal. His mate is touching him, learning him, and he wants to bury himself deep within her again. His restraint is bringing a low growl from him. Her heart beating a mile a minute isn't helping either. She gives off the prey vibe, and he is having to will himself to remember she is not prey.

"Can you understand me?"

He nods once and leans down and licks against her which chases some of the fear away.

She giggles and squirms.

It makes him whine, and he turns from her.

"No, don't go. It tickles, that's all."

He looks at her over his shoulder with that pointed look to say she knows why he's whining. He points down to his groin.

The giggling fit from Shelley makes it worse. "I'm sorry, but I think Momma Coeh might kill us if I help you with that."

He gives a snort and steps a few feet away again.

"Can... you... change into anything else?"

That makes him stop and look at her again. He hadn't shown his wolf to any girl before. He rolls his shoulders and his body contorts down into the four-legged version of himself. He stands five feet tall on all fours. He's the size of a horse next to Shelley.

"Oh!" She squeals in excitement. She cannot resist running her fingers through his fur as he comes closer. Soon enough the pair are on the ground and he's nestled around her while she pets him. He loves feeling her delicate fingers running through his fur. The tingling sensations all over his body are like nothing he has experienced before. He could stay like this forever. He licks against her cheek and she giggles. It's like little bells chiming in the air.

Billy doesn't know how long they stay there, curled into each other. He had drifted to sleep at some point. The way she pet along his ear had lulled him. He felt her shift and sit up, so he cracks an eye open. She looked like she was lost in thought, the small frown on her face made him curious, but he didn't want to lose the moment, so he pretends to stay asleep.

Shelley looks down at her stomach and rubs against it, even with it still being flat. She whispers, "I'm gonna love you, baby, no matter how you come out. You aren't ever gonna be afraid. I promise." Billy is over the moon to hear her accept their pup no matter how he is. He is also heartbroken to know she has not had the same kind of love from her own parents. He promises himself to never make her feel unloved, or unsafe, ever again.

CHAPTER TWENTY-TWO
Happy Wife Happy Life

Paula and Silus didn't get home until almost four in the morning on Christmas Day. Neither of them enjoyed the party at the bar. Both are drunk enough they should not be driving. As they rolled down the street to their home, Silus knew something was wrong. The garage door is open, the lights are on, and the car is gone. Paula was nestled against his back, using him as a human shield against the cool Georgia night air.

He pulls into the garage and kills the bike. Paula hops off and frowns. "Where's the car?"

"Wait here," Silus mutters. He moves into the kitchen with caution, as the door into the house is open. The first thing he sees is that the kitchen is still a mess. With a few more slow steps, he sees the dining room table. His brows furrow in mild confusion, then his temper builds. He thinks Faye has taken the car to go look for Shelley. He will beat that girl senseless if she tries to bring his slut of a daughter back home.

Then his eyes drift to their living room.

The massive big screen television he had spent a lot of money on was nothing more than a shattered mess, his bowling ball nestled in it. "Faye Noelle," he roars.

Paula had come inside when she heard him call for his daughter. She sees Silus standing between the table and the living room. His back is to her, but she can tell he is murderous. His posture suggests the hulking man will punch the first thing he can, if approached. She looks around the room and sees the phones on the table. With a quiet step closer, never taking her eyes off the hulking man staring at his television, she picks up the note.

"No!" She lets out a strangled yelp and sinks down.

It causes Silus to whirl around and look at his wife. He snatches the note from her hands and leaves her on the floor. Then he's throwing the dining room chair into the wall with rage. He stalks upstairs, finding the girls' room ransacked, and Shelley's dresser left open and empty. He continues into his and Paula's room to see the closet door open, followed by the safe open.

"Un-fucking-believable," he snarls. He walks over to his house phone and calls 911. "Hello, I would like to report a burglary." His voice is eerie and calm, despite the rage bubbling through him. His own daughter had the balls to steal from him. He wasn't letting this go. She wants to play this bullshit game? Fine. He'll let her rot in jail for it.

Fifteen minutes later a police officer is taking their statements.

Silus stands with his arms crossed and a scowl on his face.

Paula is red eyed and sniffling from crying. She refuses to say anything against her girls.

"I gotta tell ya, Mr. Baxter, ain't much we can do here legally speaking. Faye's got a right to be here, and with no proof she took anything, I can't just arrest her. Do you even know where she is?" No one has mentioned Shelley in all of this, and the officer assumes Silus only has one daughter. Silus snorts and takes the card for the police report.

"If she hasn't shown up after forty-eight hours, we will treat it like a missing persons case."

Silus shoves the note Faye left into the officer's face. "What about this shit?"

The officer takes the note and frowns. He looks between Silus and Paula, then back down to the note. The first thing he notices is it talks about more than one person, so the man before him isn't telling him everything. His eyes settle on Paula again, questioning her without saying a word. He has a bad feeling about what has taken place in this house. With a resigned sigh, "Get me a list of their friends and phone numbers. Maybe they're just cooling off there."

This answer satisfies Silus. He lets Paula handle giving the police officer all the details and watches the man as he leaves. The house is quiet as the two of them look at the wake of Faye's wrath. Neither of them think Shelley could do this.

Paula starts to cry again as now both of her girls are gone. "Get the fuck out," she hisses.

"What did you say?" Silus narrows his eyes at Paula. His wife never talks back to him. She knows how it riles him up and causes him to lose his temper with her.

"I said... Get. The fuck. Out!" her voice rises a decibel with each word until she is shrieking at him. "I don't fucking care where you sleep, or who you sleep with. Since you want to be a bad biker motherfucker, then you go let those fuckers put up with your shit. Until my daughters are home and safe, you don't get to have a family! You don't get to have a home. You can go rot in your fucking precious club house. Now get the fuck out!"

"You can't fucking tell me to get out of my own fucking house," he snarls in response. He closes the distance between them and his hand rears up like the sword of Damocles over Paula.

She snatches the carving knife off the table. Her wild slice through the air tears open his exposed arm, forcing him back without hitting her.

"Get. The. Fuck. Out." Her eyes are wild, and she looks

barbaric, brandishing the knife before him.

He knows he could overtake her with ease, but it would result in one of them getting hurt. Their emotions are high and while he wants to murder Paula right now, this is the mother of his children.

"You know what? Fuck you. Fuck the girls. Fuck all this bullshit." He storms by her without another glance and out to his bike.

She stands frozen, brandishing the knife at the empty room until she hears the rumble of the bike as it heads down the street. The knife tumbles from her trembling fingers as she sinks to her knees. She brings her hands up to her face and sobs into them, mourning the loss of her family.

Silus roars across the dark Savannah streets, the pain in his arm only fueling his rage and sobering him. When he pulls into the gravel parking lot of The Triple Six, he can see the boys are still celebrating with no hint of slowing down by the number of bikes lined up in front of the bar. As soon as the door crashes open in his wake, the bar goes silent, other than the jukebox playing some old honky-tonk song. Silus stalks across the room, not saying a word as he goes behind the bar. He pulls down a bottle of vodka and a bottle of tequila. A quick glance at the wound on his arm, and he pops the cork on the vodka to pour over it. He doesn't care that he's dripping blood into the wash sink his arm is over. He sets the vodka down and pops the cork on the Tequila to take a swig. He follows this by pouring another round of vodka over the wound and grunting in pain.

His lieutenant, who is manning the bar at the moment, shakes his head and pulls out the first aid kit. "Sit down, you damn fool. Let me patch that up."

Silus cuts him a murderous look, but then settles on a barstool. The other man comes around and takes a fresh towel to dab at his arm. He takes a few alcohol swabs and makes quick work of cleaning up the bloody wound on Silus's arm. He doesn't stop

Silus from drinking the Tequila. The priority is to patch the man, then get the story from him.

It's several minutes while the lieutenant stitches the wound closed with expert precision. He finishes by wrapping the bandage in gauze. Once free of him, Silus turns and looks the other men and women over. They are still looking on in silence, a mix of fear and anger across their faces.

"I need three of you motherfuckers that think you're worth your shit."

Three men step forward, and he looks them over before taking another swig of his Tequila. "Faye's stolen from us and is on the run. I want her found and brought back alive. What happens on the way home is between you and her."

The lieutenant frowns more. He won't contradict Silus in front of the rest of the gang, but Silus has to know they are going to hurt Faye as they bring her back. Thieves are not tolerated in the Angels of Wrath.

"You got it, boss," the men leave right then.

Silus pushes off the barstool then and stalks off to the actual office in the back of the bar where there's a couch with his name on it. Sometime later his lieutenant comes walking in. By the quiet sounds in the bar, Silus can gather he sent everyone home.

"You wanna talk about how you got that?"

Silus grunts and takes another shot.

"Did Faye give you that?"

Silus shakes his head no.

"Shelley?" His voice sounds surprised even in the question.

"Ain't none of your fuckin' business," Silus finally snarls.

"The fuck it ain't. You come stormin' in bleeding like a stuck hog and sick the Angels on your eldest daughter. What the fuck is going on, Silus? Where's Paula?" His voice now laced with concern that Silus may have hurt Paula.

Silus, in true fashion, throws the bottle at his lieutenant, who swats it away as he's not as drunk as the man before him.

"Fine! Be a sulking pig. But whatever this shit is," he loops his finger around. "Get it under control." He pauses to make sure he has the undivided attention of Silus. "Or you're gonna open the fuckin' door for that little cockroach to take your club from you. That what you want, Baxter?" His lieutenant knew how to poke the bear and Silus roars up off that couch ready to murder the man. The lieutenant shoves him back onto the couch. "Sit down, asshole. You're too damn drunk for a proper fight. Sleep it off. We'll finish this talk in the morning."

CHAPTER TWENTY-THREE
History Lesson

The few days that passed from Christmas allowed Shelley to see just how different the Coeh family lived from the Baxter family. At present, all brothers are in the house along with their families and the chaos it adds to the routine. Matthias, Samuel, and Brandon are leaving in the morning. Susie approved of them running with their younger brothers for patrols. Patrols aren't really anything other than the boys running amok around the forest to make sure there wasn't any trouble. Then they will all convene at a bar and drink a few cold ones. Since The Accord, danger in the pack lands amounted to drunken teenagers at a campsite in the National Forest most of the time. The stampede of men, all seven Coeh boys, as they raced each other out the door, left Shelley in a whirlwind. The wives and other kids were off visiting their various families in the pack, and Susie has business in Savannah proper. Shelley is in the kitchen, rummaging in the pantry. If she is being left to her own devices, she is going to curl up with comfort food and find something to watch on the television.

Susie and David told her this was her home now, and she doesn't have to ask permission to eat the food. Susie also made it clear she would have chores, like the boys, but she was not a servant in this house. That she is Billy's mate, and the only reason they aren't getting married right now is her age.

"What are you lookin' for, darlin'?" David's voice is smooth as it fills the room.

"Mac 'n Cheese and Manwich. I found the pickles already. I was gonna brown up some hamburger meat. Want some?" Shelley is on her tiptoes as she tries to reach the small can of Manwich on the top shelf.

David can't help but smile at the girl. He can see why Billy liked her. She is stunning, even this young. It broke his heart to see her at their door on Christmas. It meant Silus was being his usual pig-headed self. He could only hope Silus didn't bring any trouble here after the girl. While Susie let him blow smoke down at The Six, she would not tolerate that toxic bullshit in her home.

"Hmm. Usually, on patrol night, I rent a few movies, order a pizza, and have a few cold ones. Seein' as you aren't drinkin' beer anytime soon, I think I might pick you up some soda on my way back." David steps into the pantry and retrieves the can for her. "You want to come pick out some movies with me?"

Shelley is holding two boxes of Kraft Macaroni and Cheese and takes the can from David, "Thanks. I think I might put a step stool on the next grocery list." She is a pygmy among these giants. She then realizes what he offered, and nods enthusiastically. "Just let me put these on the counter. How about we forgo pizza and I cook when we get back?"

"Deal," he says with an easy smile. He plucks the Suburban keys off the hook and waits for her to follow. The two of them are browsing movies at the local Blockbuster twenty minutes later. David grabs a few action movies and looks around for the fluffy poof of curly blond hair. He smiles when here she comes with several movies in her arms. As she hands him the DVDS he shuffles through them, "What's all this? Is Horror your thing?" His bushy eyebrow rises in question. She struck him as a romantic comedy type.

"Er... well," she gets shy as he looks from her down to the stack of movies again.

"Bad Moon? Teen Wolf? Silver Bullet? American Werewolf in London? The Howling?" He is grinning as he picks up on the werewolf theme and waits to see why she chose all of these movies.

"Educational purposes," she bites against her lip and David erupts into a deep laugh. Her cheeks flame red and she huffs.

"I'm sorry. Oh, honey. No. These are all garbage. C'mon," he leads her back down the aisle and puts back the movies. He retrieves a few older ones and is still chuckling when they check out.

Once back at the house, he takes a seat while she gets to work on her gourmet cooking. He watches her back while she cooks, sipping his beer. Susie had told him that Jasper had Faye with him, wherever the two of them have run off to. He wants to know what Silus did to make both his girls run. He's been meaning to get Shelley alone and get her to open up about it, but by the state of her emotions, he has given her a few days to adjust.

"Shelley," he starts quietly. "Did Silus hurt you girls?"

Shelley's body tenses, and she bites against her lip. She didn't want to talk about what happened, as if it would summon her father right to the Coeh house. "He kicked me out when he found out it was Billy's baby. I don't know what happened after that. Faye picked me up off the porch and helped me get my stuff. Then she... well... She was angry at daddy. She stole a bunch of money and put a bowling ball in his big TV. Daddy's gonna be so pissed." She has shifted her posture so she could see David and her cooking at the same time.

David knows that posture. This girl is used to watching for danger. It makes him frown more, and his blood boils. This sweet little girl is afraid of someone losing their temper and hurting her. David takes another sip of his beer, reigning in his anger at what has happened to her. The description of Faye's behavior catches him off guard, and he almost spits his mouthful of beer onto the counter. "Yeah. That apple didn't fall far from the tree."

Shelley is putting a far too healthy chunk of butter into the macaroni and cheese and her sweet face draws into a confused look. "I thought you Coehs weren't friendly with my daddy?" She then turns back to her noodles, stirring in the butter.

David chuckles, "My brother always was a hard-headed prick." He is still grinning when Shelley stops dead and turns to face him fully. He waits for the words to sink in. A mix of fear and curiosity crosses her face. "Don't worry none. We're step brothers. My old man married his momma when we were about seven. We weren't too sure about each other at first. One good toad hunt later and we were thick as thieves."

Shelley stirs in the milk and orange powder in, puts the lid on the noodles, and turns the burner to the lowest setting. She then takes the pack of hamburger meat and squishes it out onto the skillet. "So, what happened? He ain't ever mentioned havin' a brother. Let alone it being a Coeh."

"The short answer… Susie." A small frown forms as David thinks about the day Silus and he last saw each other as brothers.

"And the long answer?"

David chuckles again. He could see a youthful version of his stepmother in Shelley. She had been a looker too. "You weren't born yet but were soon comin'. Faye was a cute little bundle of pigtails and fearless. Momma died a year before from a heart attack. Dad died from a broken heart." He grows quiet then, thinking on how to tell her about the history Silus has tried to erase. "Tell you what, you finish that up, and I'll be right back." He leaves his beer on the counter and heads out of the kitchen.

It takes ten minutes to finish browning the meat. She then drains the grease, mixes in the Manwich, finally combining the macaroni and cheese with it. She pulls out the dill pickle chips and sprinkles them on top of the two bowls. She expertly balances his beer, her soda, and the two bowls in her hands as she heads into the living room. She doesn't see David anywhere and crinkles her nose. Shelley deposits his food on the coffee table and takes up residence on one end of the couch. Not waiting for David, she digs into her concoction. It was still too soon for the cravings, she just loved the dish. If they chalked it up to her pregnancy, she wouldn't say otherwise. She keeps glancing to the entrance of the main room, wondering where David had gotten off to.

When David finally appears, he is carrying a pretty hefty box. Draped across the top of the box is an old Angels of Wrath jacket with the Baxter sigil blazing at the shoulder.

"You... Were an Angel?" Shelley nearly chokes on the bite of food in her mouth.

David flashes her a devilish grin. "Oh, darlin'. I was much more than that."

CHAPTER TWENTY-FOUR
Hoist The Colors

David and Shelley eat in silence after he brought down the box and his old Angel jacket. He could see the swirl of questions in her gaze, and the conflict of not wanting to be rude. He lets her stew while they eat. He has to admit the food wasn't half bad, maybe he could talk Susie into trying it in the future.

"Now, where to begin?" he groans as he stretches.

"I haven't seen my brother since our father died." David and Silus never referred to the other as step-brother. While David's father was a son-of-a-bitch, he loved both boys, and took care of them equally.

"Wait, you were at the Halloween bash. Daddy was there too." Shelley's brow draws in confusion at his obvious lie.

David gives a tight smile and nods. "Yes, Silus was there, but that man ain't the brother I lost. That asshole you call Daddy is someone entirely different. Now hush up so I can get through this." He settles back and rubs his hand over his face. Shelley turns and tucks her knees up under her. David thinks she looks so young and he was relieved Susie accepted her. It would have killed him to have to stand against his wife on the matter.

"We were young and dumb, but you couldn't separate us.

Where Silus was the bruiser, I was the brains. Our dad was the head of the Angels and there wasn't no one could talk shit to us without fearing him. He had dumped all his savings into that bar and was using it for the club. Momma didn't like it much, but Pop wanted a place where he and the others could relax and talk business safely." He pauses, taking a sip of his beer. "Then, as if the fates themselves smiled upon me in walks this hot little number. Dark hair, bright eyes, and cocky as hell. She and her old man strolled in like they owned the place, flying the Wolf Pack colors. You should've seen us. We both acted like fools. It was a competition from then on. If he took her to the movies, I took her to the drive-in. He'd pick her up on his bike. I'd let her drive mine. Silus never had a chance. The thing he never learned about Susie is she has to be the boss and that isn't ever going to change."

"But you seem to be in charge just as much as Momma Coeh," Shelley challenges.

David smirks and taps his nose as if she hit it right on the money. "That's cause she lets me," he wriggles his brows. "Needless to say that's how I won."

Shelley's face draws into a pensive frown and David continues on.

"Silus changed after that. He was meaner. Getting into fights and raising all kinds of hell in the club. We still hung out, but Silus didn't want Susie around so it wasn't often. One night, we were shootin' pool at the Six. The cutest little thing had recently joined the club. Don't know where pop found her, but she was there and a few boys thought they would show her what it means to be club property." David gets a dark look on his face at the thought.

"Paula hit the floor, and your daddy took a pool cue to the back of that man's head. The next thing I knew he had claimed her, making her exclusive to him. Pop let him. Don't you let your momma fool you none. She is a crafty little minx. And it was the smartest damn thing she could have done in her situation." David is wagging a finger at Shelley.

"What did she do?" Shelley's leaning forward, thoroughly engaged in the story.

"She asked Susie to help her hook ol' Silus. Susie won't admit this, but I'm pretty damn sure she is the one that told her to poke those holes in that condom." He couldn't help but laugh at the dawning look of her mother having trapped her father into a relationship with a pregnancy. "It was a terrible gamble, and she was damn lucky Pop made Silus do the honorable thing. They got married before your sister was born. But that's beside the point. Everything was fine. We started hanging out again. I hung up my Angel wings and took up the Wolf." He sighs and runs his fingers through his hair.

Shelley tilts her head, watching David. She could see the sadness forming on his face.

"Then momma died," his voice drops. "Little Faye was two. The cutest little button of a thing. It broke Silus, losing his momma. He and Paula got into a fight after her wake and she called me to come get her and Faye. When I got there, she was holding a bag of peas to her face, and Faye was cowering against her. Susie took 'em somewhere. I beat the shit out of my brother, reminding him the entire fucking reason he met Paula was some man thought he could put his hands on her like that. It took all of a week before Silus came crawling to her and she took him back." David softens. "Your daddy loves your momma, no matter how much of an asshole he is. He loves you girls too."

Shelley says nothing, but she doesn't believe that right now. She saw the look in her father's eyes when he threw her out. He hated her. She wonders if David knew that he still hit momma and Faye when he got angry.

"Our dad died a year later of a broken heart. By this time I had been Wolf Pack for a few years. I had even taken Susie's name. We had the boys by then, and she was pregnant with Caleb. Your dad had been given the Angels and was making all the arrangements for the funeral." David pauses and takes the final swig of his beer. He gets up and goes to get himself another one, as well as bringing back Shelley a soda, before he continues. He looks down at the jacket. "Had I known how important it was then, I would have just worn the jacket. But we were both grieving, and I just didn't think about it. We walked into the funeral home and Silus came undone. I had never seen him like that. Paula wouldn't even look at us. He just exploded. And Susie, hot damn, she wasn't having it. It didn't matter that she was pregnant, she got right into his face and he started shoving her. I saw red."

Shelley's eyes widen, and she is hugging a couch pillow. "What happened next? Did Daddy hit her?"

It breaks David's heart to realize that is the first thing Shelley thinks her father would do. "No. He reared back to backhand her, and I put him on the ground before he could follow through. Next thing I knew we were both throwing punches and brawling like drunkards at the Six. Right there in front of my father's corpse. We got surrounded. Angels were everywhere, except Susie. She stood there in her Wolf Pack colors with her arms crossed. She didn't lift a single finger while my brother and I beat the shit out of each other." He grunts and rubs his jaw, as if he could remember how he felt afterwards still. "I was too angry and stubborn to let it go. I didn't just lose my dad, I lost my best friend and brother. Ain't never forgiven the man. Silus beat me to within an inch of my life and Susie was there to pick me up when he finally stopped. Guess I was just like him in a way."

Shelley frowns and shakes her head. "Oh no, Mr. Coeh-."

"David, or Papa Coeh, yer family."

"David," she corrects. "You're nothin' like daddy. Daddy's scary and gets angry at everything. Especially Faye. You... you love all your sons." She looks like she is about to start crying and

David frowns, shifting he offers an open arm for her to snuggle into. He gently pets along her back when she curls to him.

"Honey. We both learned how to raise kids at my daddy's knee. It took Susie setting me straight for me to not raise my boys to be wrong like me. Like I said. She lets me be in charge when it suits her." He remains quiet after that, letting Shelley settle against him. "That, darlin', is some of why yer daddy was so bullheaded about what happened to you. I have to say, of all the boys I thought would get himself into trouble, I didn't think Billy would be it. But you picked the best of 'em. That boy would shoot the moon for ya, if ya asked. It's been killin' him not having you here."

Shelley smiles at the revelation "I didn't mean to trap him," she says quietly.

"Now you listen here, Shelley Baxter. You were too young to be at that party where Billy and you rutted. But I promise ya, that makes Billy the happiest wolf I've ever seen. The ceremony is called The Rutting. It's meant to help young wolves procreate. It makes 'em crazy with lust. Any other full moon they can keep themselves in check. But on that night, somethin' happens to 'em. All the boys wanna do is find the nearest hole to put their dick in and the girls just wanna roll over an' let 'em. You come away pregnant from one of those, it means good fortune and that the jealous bitch that cursed 'em all let you find your soul mate."

CHAPTER TWENTY-FIVE
Stop Looking At Your Watch

Susie walks into the kitchen to see Billy hovering over paperwork with Shelley. Both of them are engrossed in the document as Shelley fills out the answers. "What's all this?" Susie peeks over Shelley's shoulder.

"We're fillin' out the transfer paperwork and change of address so I can switch schools," Shelley gives an enthusiastic reply.

Before either of them realizes what is happening, Susie snatches the paperwork off the table. "That so?" Susie looks between the two of them.

"Yes, ma'am," Billy replies with a smile. "Since Shelley doesn't have a car, and her school won't send a bus out here for her, we thought it would be a good idea."

"You think ol' Silus is going to help Shelley out by filling out any kind of paperwork?" She is looking pointedly at Shelley. "That man would rip this form apart just to spite you and force you to go to the school you're enrolled in, or be a dropout and you know it."

"Then I guess I'm dropping out," Shelley sounds defeated. She had already decided she could get her GED if she had to.

"The hell you are," Susie retorts. "You," pointing at Billy, "You put that baby there, you're gonna take care of its momma. I expect you to get her to school on time every morning before you head into work."

Billy chuckles. While it will be an inconvenience, and Shelley is already groaning at just how early she'll have to get up, Billy doesn't seem put out by this new decree from his mother. Shelley doesn't understand his mother the way he does, and he is mildly excited to get to start his day alone with Shelley. His mother was being both mean and nice at the same time. He gently squeezes Shelley. "We'll make it work," he murmurs to her as he kisses her on the temple.

A few days later, Billy has realized his mistake far too late. He had plotted in his head that if they leave by six thirty, he will get her there on time. He had the perfect morning planned. No one else needed to be up that early, so he made her breakfast. He had heard her alarm at five and heard her snooze it. He just assumed she would get up in a few minutes. At five thirty she had not come down, and he thought she might be in the shower. Then he is casually walking up the stairs, a plate of breakfast for her in his hand, and he knocks on her door. "Angel," he rumbles gently. "It's six. You almost ready?"

"What?!" the sudden panic muffled from the other side of the door causes him to barge into the room. She is sitting in bed with her hair plastered to her face, her eyes blinking in disbelief. "What time did you say?" She looks at her alarm clock and she groans as if someone had kicked her. "Why'd you let me sleep so late? We're never going to get there on time!" She flies out of the bed and is rushing into the bathroom.

Billy watches the blond hurricane brush by him without so much as noticing her breakfast. He would chuckle at the sight, but the level of anger rolling off of Shelley makes him keep his trap shut. He strides over and settles on the edge of the bed, resisting the urge to eat a piece of bacon. He can hear the shower and can still feel the panic washing over her. At six fifteen, the shower had stopped, but he didn't hear much else. At six twenty-five, he gets up, knocking on the door. "We need to get going, Shelley."

She rips the door open and stares daggers at him. Her hair still in a towel, and she is half made-up. "I'm goin' as fast as I can," she snaps, slamming the door in his face.

He can't help it then and he chuckles. She is the cutest thing when she is angry. Which results in her yanking the door back open.

"You think this is funny?! How am I supposed to get ready in thirty minutes? That's not even enough time to take an actual shower. Let alone style my hair and put on make-up! Some of us actually care about how we look!" She slams the door again.

"Would you two be quiet," Caleb groans from the other room.

Billy's not sure if he should laugh or scold her, but he is mildly afraid of the level of anger that has now erupted from his mate. "I can shower in thirty minutes," he mutters to himself as he looks at the plate of cold food in his hand.

Two seconds later the door rips open again, and she snatches the plate. "Thank you." Slamming it again with the heel of her foot.

Billy huffs at the rough treatment, "I'll be in the truck," he grumbles as he stomps downstairs. At six forty-five, he honks the horn in irritation.

She comes running out with a backpack, jacket, pulling her shoes on, and still looking like she is going to murder him. With a grunt, she pops into the seat and buckles up. "Well, what are you waiting for?" She growls at him.

Billy doesn't even look at her, a shit-eating grin on his face, "Yes ma'am, Miss Shelley," as he puts the truck in reverse. When he glances over about twenty minutes later, she is sound asleep against the window. He can't help but chuckle. "Good to know, actually wake her up at five."

"You do that and I might cut off somethin' you like," she

grumbles as she cracks an eye open.

This wins an outright laugh from Billy then. "You're awful sexy when you're angry." The devilish stare she gives him only makes him laugh harder, causing the truck to swerve.

"You're going to kill us if you keep that up, Mister Coeh," Shelley whips back in response, but is blushing and his laughter is infectious. It makes her smile, and she settles back down, falling back asleep.

His sour mood is now dissipated as he makes this long drive into Savannah to take her to school. He lets her sleep the rest of the way. Before they roll into the actual parking lot, he reaches over and gently nudges her. "C'mon baby, we're almost there. Please don't cut anything off," he teases.

"Mhmm," she hums, rubbing the sleep from her eyes gently to not ruin her makeup. She smiles at his hand still on her knee, his thumb playing little circles over the jeans. "Oh Billy, I'm sorry," she finally says.

He pulls into a parking spot and turns to face her, grinning then. "Nah... Don't be sorry. We'll get it right. I promise," he brushes her hair back. He then leans in and kisses her. "Have a good day. I'll be here to pick you up when you get out."

Shelley hops out of the truck reluctantly, then hurries across the parking lot, so she won't be late. She hadn't even realized he sped like death was chasing him to get her there on time. Faye's friends are waiting near the door to the school, "Hot damn, Shelley. Is that Billy Coeh?" Their gaping looks are a mix of shock and awe. "Your daddy's gonna tan your hide, if he found out that boy's bringing you to school. Where's Faye?"

Shelley had put out of her mind that Faye still had a semester to go of school when she left. It was like a kick in the stomach when her friends ask after her. Shelley glances back over her shoulder to see if Billy had left yet. She wanted to run back to his truck and hide facing people at school. He has already pulled out onto the street, slow-rolling to make sure she gets into the building.

"Hey... Earth to Shelley. Where's Faye?"

Shelley looks back at Veronica. Then she looks to the other girls. "She... left," Shelley finally confesses. "It's a long story. I'll tell you at lunch." The gaggle of girls enter the building and hurry off to class.

Billy frowns when he rolls up to the stoplight. Whatever was going on with Shelley, she was suddenly anxious and sad. He guesses it is her friends asking how break was. He wishes he could just barrel in there and wrap her up in his arms all day. The last few weeks have been heaven. He had been trying very hard to wash away any sadness her family had brought her. Now he is sitting here helpless. All this power and strength, and all he could do is hope he is enough comfort for her when she gets out of school. He would pick her up her favorite treat after work today. He contemplates being late to work to go have words with Silus and Paula about Shelley. But he last thing he wanted was to leave his mate high and dry while he rots in a cell for murdering her no-good father. The car behind him honks angrily, pulling Billy from his silent destruction of Silus. He waves a hand apologetically and drives off toward his work site.

CHAPTER TWENTY-SIX
Help Me Help You

Billy and Shelley easily fall into their routine. As the pregnancy progresses, Shelley cares less and less about her appearance and more about sleeping in. Billy still knocks on her door at the appointed time every morning, sweet as can be. Shelley's life at school has become Hell on Earth. Without Faye there, Wanda, Candy, Veronica, and Taylor have stopped talking to Shelley. The few girls she talks with in cheerleading are nice, but, for the most part, Shelley is alone. She looks forward to racing out the school door into Billy's waiting arms every day. She does miss a few days because of appointments. Susie relented and allowed Shelley to see the pack doctor versus a regular doctor. While their offices aren't much different, he is more discerning about his patients. He is also aware of the situation that has led to the girl being here. With a few quick phone calls, he gained Shelley's insurance information from Paula.

It's early in the morning, late in April, about a half hour before Billy and Shelley need to get ready when Billy feels the soul-crushing sadness in his chest. He immediately gets up and treks across the hall to Shelley's room, quietly opening the door to check on her sleeping form. Sure it's creepy, but she looks so beautiful when she sleeps, he can't help himself. Billy doesn't find her sleeping at all. He finds her sitting on the floor, her hair in rollers, and partially in her cheerleading uniform.

"Angel," he murmurs as he comes closer.

"I'm too fat," she hiccups. "It won't zip."

This makes Billy frown. He always thought Shelley was on the skinny side. Their sizes are comical next to each other with such a height difference between them. He thought being pregnant had helped her fill out nicely. "You are definitely not fat," he snorts, and sits on the floor with her. He pulls her into his lap and cradles her.

She immediately curls into him and sniffles. "I am fat. Nothing fits. And I have a game tonight. We're supposed to wear our uniforms and I can't even get mine on," she mewls against him.

Billy knows better than to laugh out loud. He learned that lesson the hard way. His lips curl with a hint of a smile at her woes. "You're pregnant, not fat. You are the most beautiful thing I have ever seen. Even if you were fat, I'd still love you. You were made for me. Now, why don't you get dressed in something comfy, and just ask your coach for a bigger uniform when you get to school?"

The ride to school is quiet and Billy is beside himself with how sad Shelley is. He struggles with handling her tidal wave of emotions and because she is hurting he wants to tear the world apart.

She curls into his lap, wrapping her arms around his neck, when they arrive at the school. He brings his arms around her tiny waist. Both of them can feel the sense of calm that rushes over them. Shelley isn't sure what's going on, but she knows when Billy holds her everything is better. She is afraid to tell him everything, that he'll decide she is too much trouble and throw her out.

Billy doesn't say a word, just keeps holding her. He didn't know how to talk to her, other than to tell her how much he loves her and that from the moment he saw her he knew they were fated to be together. His instincts are to protect her and beat anyone that makes her feel anything other than perfect.

Shelley eases out of his embrace and gets out of the truck. "I'll be here for the game," he offers with a smile. She smiles back at him and trudges into school.

Billy heads out, the heavy emotions of his mate in his chest. He takes a good hour to get to his work site for the day. His father is already working, as are a few other guys from the pack. Billy grabs his tools from the bed of the truck and begins working on the cabinetry he had started the day before. Wolf Pack Construction specializes in custom builds. The level of craftsmanship they provide is unrivaled. Billy has been working under David from the moment he could pick up tools. He didn't join full time until he graduated high school a few years ago. Normally, Billy is chipper and friendly. The man takes everything in stride. The past few weeks have proved otherwise. The determined scowl on his face and the low grumble of irritation when any of them tease him about Shelley had made the group take notice.

"C'mon, man. Are you tellin' me your little mate has you all worked up again?"

Billy shrugs as he keeps working. "I don't know what to do with her. I know she is hurting. I can feel it. She is scared as hell. I think she is really lonely with her sister gone. She has been through a lot of crap the past few months. I've tried everything to cheer her up. It's killing me not knowing how to help her." Billy is honest with the guys. They're ranging in age from him to his father's age.

David chuckles from his workstation and feels for the boy. "Sometimes, you gotta let her work her stuff out. She is a teenager. Her hormones are in overload even before you throw in the pregnancy hormones. That makes everything ten times worse. Just be there for her, son. She'll be alright. Trust me. The more you try to help the worse you're making it. 'Cause right now, it's all your fault. You did this to her, and until she sees that baby in her arms, you are the devil." He gives his son a grin to show him he's half-teasing.

A few of the older ones nod their heads in agreement. The younger ones shake their heads. "Sounds like she is got you pussy whipped there, Billy. She even bothering to take care of your needs?"

Billy leans up from his bench and gives a low growl as he comes to his full height. It makes the others take a step back.

"Settle down," David grumbles. If these boys start duking it out on the work site, they're likely to get themselves exposed. "Get back to work, all of you."

The rest of the day, Billy couldn't shake the feeling that something bad has happened. He gives in to his instincts and tells his father he's cutting out early. The entire drive back to Shelley's high school has him agitated and anxious. On game nights, she wouldn't come out this way. Instead, she would head to the field. He comes up to the fence between the parking lot and the field, leaning over it. The cheerleaders were already out there practicing, but there was no sign of Shelley. He furrows his brow and casually walks back towards the door she normally comes out. He waits against his car, glancing at his watch. The students trickle out with most of them ignoring his presence.

Taylor notices him and she frowns. As the group passes him on the way to Veronica's car, she stops, "she is in the nurse's office. Rumor is she got kicked off the squad, and she is having a meltdown."

"Thank you," Billy responds, and he quickly heads into the school. He had never been inside this school, so it took him several minutes to find the nurse's station. The volume of scents that bombard him at the nurse's station makes him shake his head a little, but Shelley's sweet scent is strong in here. "I'm here to pick up Shelley Baxter," his voice is gentle and concerned.

The nurse looks him over and narrows her eyes. "Are you a parent, or legal guardian? I called two hours ago and left a message to come get her."

"No ma'am. Her parents are out of town and when I didn't hear from Shelley I came to the school looking. I'm Billy, Billy Coeh. Here's my number in case she has an emergency in the future. I'll be sure to have her parents call and update the records to add me." He offers an easy smile. "Here's my ID," he offers as well, hoping to dissuade any thoughts of him being nefarious.

She looks at him with suspicion and has him wait there. He watches her disappear into another room before she comes out with Shelley in tow. The nurse looks between the two of them and Shelley ignores her as she hurries over to Billy, hugging him tight.

He gently rubs the small of her back as he takes his license back from the nurse. Without saying another word, he scoops up Shelley's backpack, and walks out with her. They get into the truck and he pauses before pulling out. He can see she is hurting. "Miss Shelley," he starts, afraid of what she might say when he is done.

"They kicked me off the squad," she interrupts and begins to tear up again. "She was like 'I ain't got no insurance for if you get hurt while pregnant. And I'm not gonna be responsible for that.'" Shelley's voice takes on even more of a drawl than she naturally has as she mocks the coach's voice. "I don't have any friends now that Faye's gone. And really... I just want to not come to school every day and have them all look at me like I'm a slut. Can't we talk to your momma? I'll take all the GED courses, and the test. Either that or I'm sure I could talk my momma into signing all the transfer paperwork. Please Billy. I hate it here."

Billy swallows and exhales the breath he hadn't realized he was holding. All her unhappiness had nothing to do with him. Maybe his dad was right and he should just let it ride. He pulls out of the parking lot and drives through her favorite place,

McDonald's. Instead of taking her home, he drives on and takes them to Hilton Head. It's getting close to sunset. He parks at the public beach where they first met, letting her carry the food and drinks while he gets the blanket. He motions for her to follow him. Billy shakes the blanket out as he settles down and pulls her in between his legs. They eat in silence and when they're done he pulls her close, wrapping his arms around her. The sunset is gorgeous with pinks and oranges across the sky.

"I love you more than life, Shelley." He murmurs against her ear. "I want you to be happy. I can feel everything. When you're happy, sad, scared, angry, and even when you're aroused. It's a perk of being mates. I'm pretty sure you can feel it too, and I think I've been making you more upset." He nuzzles against her and breathes in her sweet scent. "Just tell me how to make you happy and I'll do it."

Every time he says he loves her it makes her heart soar, and her stomach light with butterflies. She has been lucky that Billy's family are good people. She never thought Billy would feel this way about her. Shelley has been conditioned to think she is a burden. She closes her eyes and turns to nestle into him. "I love you too. And you make me happy. Just holding me like this. Don't ever let me go. Promise?"

He chuckles and kisses her temple, "Promise."

CHAPTER TWENTY-SEVEN
Born On The Fourth Of July

June 2004

Shelley finished her sophomore year of high school with little additional fuss. She decides to confront Susie on the matter of changing schools again. She is not going back to that school. It puts too much stress on her, on Billy, and they are going to have a baby by the time she starts her Junior year. She even has all the paperwork filled out and asks Susie to go with her to get her parents to sign it.

Susie balks at it. The last thing she needs is another confrontation between the Angels and Wolves. She tries every counter point she can think of, and she finally resorts to using the Alpha command on Shelley in an effort to make her let it go.

David, Billy, and Susie all look on dumbfounded when Shelley stands her ground, the Alpha command failing.

"No! You do not get to dictate to me because you are the leader of the pack. I am not part of your pack yet. You and yours have been the nicest people I have ever met, but I'm not going back to that school. You can either help me, or you can just watch my taillights as I face my daddy on my own." She lifts her chin in defiance.

"You listen here, missy," Susie stands to her full height. "I am the head of this household. You come in here and eat my food, take up one of my rooms. You run my son ragged with your damn teenage angst. Now you're gonna have the balls to stand there and tell me how it's gonna go?" Susie instantly regrets it as her growl in her tone triggers Shelley.

Shelley falters, her lip quivers, and tears are in her eyes. She teeters back, afraid Susie might strike her. Then she turns and runs, bolting out the front door.

This brings a growl from Billy, who cuts his mother a dirty look, then chases after her.

"What's the harm in letting the girl transfer? From what Billy says, they've alienated her at that school, and kicked her off the cheerleading squad because she is pregnant. Why don't you really want her to transfer? Is it because she is not a wolf?" David crosses his arms as he looks up at his wife.

"Fuck," Susie mutters as the two kids run off. "What? No. I just... It raises a lot of legal questions about why she is going to a private school so far from home. Or why her address has changed. And so on. We both know how vindictive Silus can be. You really think he'll sign the paperwork?"

"We should at least let her try, Susie. That girl's gonna drop out and never go back if we don't do something." David counters patiently.

*****

July 4, 2004

The entire Coeh family is in town to celebrate Independence Day. The field has been cleared and thoroughly watered to keep from catching fire from stray sparks. All the big fireworks have been set in place for the massive show they have planned. Smaller fireworks and sparklers have been set aside for the kids. Shelley's helping put all the food out on the buffet tables. Her belly is so round it's comical watching her try to do anything. She waddles along like a little blond toy. Billy is ever in her line of sight, not quite hovering over her, but close enough he can attend to her every need. When he gets close, his fingers sprawl over her perfectly round belly. They both laugh when the baby kicks his hand in response.

Today she is stopping often and rubbing her belly. She is not due for another few weeks, but she is having awful pains every few hours.

"You alright, Angel?" Billy asks for the tenth time today.

"I'm fine," she gasps as she doubles over.

"Uh huh," Billy replies with a raised brow. "You don't look fine." He deftly takes the deviled eggs from her before she drops them and sets them on the table. He sniffs lightly and when she relaxes, he comes closer, rubbing his hand along her back. "Why don't you go sit down. I'll bring you some sweet tea and make Caleb finish bringing the food out."

"I don't want to be useless," Shelley whines. "Your momma is still mad at me."

"She can be mad," Billy snorts. "Now sit, before I tie you to a chair."

Shelley cuts him the dirtiest of looks but sits down in a lawn chair, rolling her eyes at his megawatt grin. It is a great relief. The pain is getting worse. By the time Billy comes back with the sweet tea, she is whimpering in her seat. "I think I need to pee," she struggles to get back up until Billy easily pulls her to her feet.

That's when it happens.

She lets out a squawk and squeezes Billy's hand so tight he thinks she might actually hurt him. They both look wide-eyed at each other as liquid gushes down her legs.

"Shit," they say in unison. Then she is crying out in pain. Without hesitation, Billy is scooping her up into his arms and running for his truck.

"What's going on?" Susie comes out the front door, having

heard the noises, but hadn't put two and two together yet. Her eyes level on Shelley. "Shit, I'll call Doc."

Billy gets Shelley settled in the passenger seat and buckles her up before speeding around to the driver's side. They're racing to the hospital in the nearest town. It's a whirlwind of doctors and nurses once they get there. Billy could feel the pain from Shelley, and remained as close as they let him, his mere presence soothes her. They get her hooked up and the contraction passes. He remains in the room with her, gently trying to calm her as each contraction passes.

Then it's show time.

The doctor is there, and they are putting Shelley in the stirrups. The whole ordeal only takes about an hour in total. Between Shelley's breathless cries to make it stop, and the grunting pain, Billy is a hot mess. He doesn't even feel his hand anymore where she has squeezed it tight enough to leave bruises. He watches in awe as she works to push the baby out of her body. They had planned for an epidural, but she is too far gone for it to be of any use by the time they got there. So it's natural, and painful. Billy kisses her temple and murmurs encouragement in her ear.

Then he hears the wailing cries of their son. A son! Billy's heart is about to burst at having a boy. He couldn't wait to run the forest with him, or to howl at the moon together.

They wrap the not-so-tiny baby in cloth and hand him to Shelley. She lets him rest against her bare skin. She looks tired, and is covered in sweat from the exertion, but she has a euphoric smile etched on her fatigued face. Tears cling to her lashes as she looks up at Billy. "He's perfect," she murmurs.

Billy swells with pride again and he wants to hold the baby so much but doesn't want to take him from Shelley.

"What's his name, dear?" The nurse is waiting to fill out the information for the baby. "Frances. Frances David Coeh," Shelley murmurs.

Billy grumbles but doesn't argue the point. He'll just call the boy Frank. Then he can barely contain his excitement as Shelley offers the baby up to him and eases back, letting her eyes close. While the nurses and doctor are tending to Shelley, he ducks out into the hall. He can hear his brothers yapping and with a cautious look he sneaks Frances to the waiting area with him. He's then swarmed by his family. All want to get a look at the newest Coeh member. Even Susie can't help but melt at this cute as a button baby. He is definitely going to be a heart breaker.

They all groan and laugh at the name Shelley gave him. David is beaming at her choosing his name.

"Alright, you mutt," the doctor teases Billy. "You put that baby back in the room before I whoop you."

Billy reluctantly takes the baby back to the room and hands him to the nurse.

She chuckles, as she knows how exciting it is to have a new baby. "Don't worry, pup, he'll be back in a few hours to feed. Then we'll get a bed set-up in here for him. Then you can show him off all you want."

Billy nods and takes up residence in the recliner chair that's far too small for him. He doesn't care. He's a father now. He has a beautiful mate, and perfect son. He couldn't ask for anything more in life.

An hour later, Shelley rouses. Billy is reclined in the chair, watching a random cop show. "Hey you," she smiles at Billy.

"Hey there, momma," he smiles back. "Whatchya need?"

"Have my parents come yet?" She asks in such a hopeful way.

"They're not lettin' visitors in yet, and I ain't been out to the lobby in a while. You rest your pretty little head. I'll let you know when they show up." Billy knows her parents hadn't been there. The texts between his mother and him said as much. Billy promises himself he will make it right with her family. He has spent too many nights hearing her cry at the loss of her family to let it go unanswered. If he has to beat the shit out of Silus Baxter to get him to accept his daughter, so be it. For now, though, he is content to lie to her about her parents and enjoy this sweet moment with her and the baby.

CHAPTER TWENTY-EIGHT
Sleep Is Overrated

Billy spent the few weeks Shelley and Frances had to stay in the hospital getting everything ready. He moved all of Shelley's things into his bedroom and made a crib for Frances. Billy wrangled his brothers and father into painting Jasper's room, converting it into a nursery. All of Jasper's things were boxed and moved into the attic. Billy didn't care about Susie's grumbling regarding Shelley's new sleeping arrangements. She understands why he did it. Billy is already married to that girl in his mind. The baby will need its own space. Plus, with a new baby they aren't going to do anything anyway. So she lets it stand. David and she spent an ungodly amount of money on things for the baby. They were going to surprise her with a baby shower after the Fourth, but Frances had other plans.

When Shelley and Billy finally come home, Susie had commandeers the baby, and has been rocking young Frances ever since.

Shelley didn't think about it, as Billy ushers her upstairs to show her the nursery. She wraps him in a big hug and sealed it with a passionate kiss to say thank you. Soon enough they are back in the living room with Susie, David, and Beau. Caleb is on patrol, and the other brothers had already headed back to their homes.

"Now, don't you think for one second you're getting out of taking care of this baby," Susie snaps at them. "I'm not gonna be the one who gets up with him in the middle of the night. Ain't gonna change his diapers. Not going to be the one who feeds him. Nope. You two made this, you take care of it." Susie sounds stern.

David raises a brow at Susie, trying not to laugh. She hasn't put that baby down since he came through the door yet she is sitting there lecturing the two of them about how she was not going to take care of him for them. He watches the way she positively glows looking at her grand-pup. It's not her first one, but it's the first one that's going to live with her. He can feel her longing to have another one. He cut her off at seven. They made seven boys when the two of them were young and broke as hell. Pups are expensive as hell. He is pretty sure these boys eat more than Costco stocks in a week. He is too old to still be making pups, in his mind, even if he feels how she longs for another one. "Why don't you let his momma take him, Susie? He's fussin' for a meal and you ain't got the right stuff." He winks at her.

It's adorable how his big bad Alpha pouts but relinquishes Frances back to Shelley.

"And you," David points to Shelley. "You don't let her bully you. It's *your* baby. She is not the boss of him." He flashes a grin at Shelley as Billy snorts a chuckle, and Susie scoffs in indignation.

In the following days Shelley and Billy learn what it means to be sleep deprived. Frances David had no intentions of sleeping, ever. Every night, he fusses and cries, waking both his parents. Every little sound he makes into the baby monitor pulls Shelley right from the bed. At first, she wanted to do it all herself and not bother Billy. Between the painful feedings, lack of sleep, and Frances only crying louder as she paces the room with him, she is ready to give up and beg for Billy to take him.

Billy, as if he could hear her silent plea, swoops in to save the day. "Come here, Frank," he coos and gently places the tiny infant against his broad chest.

Like magic, Frances stops fussing. Billy gives Shelley a gentle smile as he takes her in. Her hair is a tangled mess. Her eyes have dark circles under them. He's pretty sure she has been in the same pajamas for three days. "Go take a shower, Angel. I got this," he nods toward the bathroom. It's positively adorable to him how she frets and fusses, and even in her disheveled state he thinks she is the most beautiful thing to walk this Earth. He sighs in relief when she does not argue and trudges into the bathroom.

Shelley cranks the shower as hot as it will go. She stands in the steaming bathroom, letting the weary apathy wash down the drain. She is pretty convinced the baby hates her. Inspecting her nipples, they are an angry red color, and chapped. She lathers up and lingers under the hot spray of water to enjoy it. In spite of how tired and scared she is, she can feel giddy joy pulsing through her. She can only guess it's Billy's emotions. Their bond has gotten stronger since the baby was born.

She finally retreats from the shower and comes back to the nursery to find the baby lying on a blanket on the floor and circled around him the massive copper wolf that is Billy.

He lifts his head in response to her entering the room. The infant is sound asleep with a fistful of fur in his clutches. Billy's tail wags and it brings a smile to Shelley's face.

She comes over and curls into Billy, the chill of leaving the shower instantly replaced by his calming inferno. The three of them doze to sleep. Billy and Shelley get about forty minutes of sleep like this when Frances lets out an ear piercing wail from the floor.

******

* * *

Two weeks later, Frances has not slept through the night yet. It is seven in the morning and Billy is pretty sure he laid his head on the pillow at six-thirty. "Fuck," he groans. "That's it. Get dressed. We're not doing this five am shit if we can't sleep." Billy flings himself out of the bed. He is on a mission. If only to get the paperwork signed by the Baxters so Shelley and he don't have to drive into Savannah every day. They won't make it otherwise. He's already exploding at the smallest things and has growled at Shelley twice over nothing. It has made her a nervous mess, which adds to his already frazzled nerves.

Shelley immediately springs from the bed, in spite of everything hurting, and being so tired she is sure she will pass out standing still. Billy's getting frustrated and angry with her. He growled at her the other day for trying to get the sheets from under him. She is on the verge of tears, and Frances is wailing into the baby monitor. "No. I got it. Just go back to sleep. I'm sorry. I'll get him to quiet down." She hurries from the room and into the nursery.

"Hey there my little moon prince," she coos. "Don't worry, momma's here. Even if ya hate me."

She scoops him up and takes him to the rocker, not even caring who sees. She peels her tank top off and tosses it aside. Then she situates him and gasps as his chubby little fists clamp onto her breast and his gums onto her nipple. Shelley hisses in pain and tries to get comfortable. "Frances, ya gotta let us sleep," her voice is soft and sweet to the baby. "Your daddy's gonna throw us out, and we got nowhere else to go. He's so mad at me. I've ruined his life." She can't help but hiccup as her voice cracks from crying. "But he loves you so much. Just be good, so he lets us stay. Please."

Billy freezes, staring at the baby monitor. He feels guilty for eavesdropping on Shelley, and he is pretty sure she has forgotten all about the monitor. It's like she took a silver knife and stabbed him right in the chest. How could she think any of those things of him? He would never throw them out. They're his entire world. He sits on the edge of the bed, listening to her continue on. He can hear every jagged breath as he imagines she is crying. He rubs his hand over his face. He's so tired. Yes, he is frustrated, and angry, but not once has he ever thought about living his life without either of them. She has not ruined his life. It has only gotten better since Santa delivered her to him.

This adds to his resolve about getting those papers signed. He will never let her go live with those monsters again. They have abused Shelley to the point she is too afraid of upsetting anyone. She is running herself to death trying to please everyone. His fists curls in rage just thinking about Silus hurting her. He is lost in his thoughts and hasn't realize he is huffing with anger, or that Shelley had come back and was now looking at him with fear in her eyes.

"Billy?" She whimpers. "I'm sorry. I don't know what to do. He hates me. And I just can't make him stop crying... I know I've ruined your life. Please don't throw me out. Please. I promise I'll do anything. I'll take care of Frances. I'll sleep in there so I can get to him faster." She is covering her face and sobbing.

Without hesitation, Billy moves and pulls her into his arms, holding her tight. He whines in pain and murmurs against her, sounding frantic. "Fuck. Shelley. No. No, Angel. It's not that at all. I'm never gonna let you go." His voice breaks as he cradles her against him. "I'm just tired and grouchy. I can't even begin to imagine how tired you are. I... I was just thinking about getting your paperwork signed, and maybe getting out of the house with Frances for a bit. Let your parents meet their grandson. I'm sorry I ever growled at you. Please don't be afraid of me. I won't ever hurt you. Not ever. You're the love of my life."

******

* * *

The two of them stand on the front porch of the Baxter house with Billy holding the carrier while Shelley rings the doorbell. The door opens to reveal Paula, who is holding a phone in one hand. She blinks in disbelief at the massive Coeh boy standing next to her petite daughter. Billy, before she changes her mind, plays dirty. He brings the carrier up and practically thrusts it into her hands.

"Meet your grandson, Frances David Coeh." He pulls Shelley into the house with the other hand. With a kick of his foot, the door closes behind them and he watches Paula carefully.

She takes the carrier and walks into the living room, her eyes never leaving the small child within. Without paying much attention to the other two people in the room, she scoops the sleeping infant out of his carrier. "Oh, he is precious, Shelley."

Shelley tentatively enters her childhood home and immediately notices the differences. A lot of the things her father loves are gone, replaced with pastel colors and much more feminine decor. The television Faye went bowling with has been replaced. Shelley looks at her mother with hope when she takes a seat next to Paula and Frances.

Billy can feel how much Shelley wants her parents back in her life. It makes him furious they would treat her this way. He stands not far off, his arms crossed as he watches the two women. The roller coaster of emotions he is getting from Shelley is making it hard to focus on his goal of reconciliation. But he does not want this to be about him. He wants Shelley and Paula to reconnect. He wished Silus had been here as well, but beggars cannot be choosers.

"Oh, baby girl, I'm so sorry," Paula pulls her daughter into a one-armed hug, squishing the baby between them. "I've missed you so much. Are they taking care of you? Are you eating enough? Are you going to school? Please tell me you're alright with them Coeh boys." Paula fusses over Shelley and both women are crying in no time. It's then Paula hears the garage door, and she frowns.

Shelley's eyes follow her mother's and panic wells inside of her as she hears the rumble of her father's Harley pull into the garage.

CHAPTER TWENTY-NINE
Bikers & Babies

"Momma," Shelley croaks out. She tries to take Frances back but her mother is already up and moving. Paula is excited to show Silus their grandson and doesn't even think about the fear Silus's presence might cause Shelley. She couldn't see Billy, but the moment Shelley's fear peaks he goes feral. Shelley's movement to follow her mother sets him off further. He moves forward with all the speed and grace of a predator, letting out a low and violent growl. While he was able to keep himself in human form, it was just barely so. He is a step behind Paula.

This causes Paula to stop and turn to see what the commotion is behind her. Something deep in her subconscious picks up that a violent predator is too close for comfort. Her arms tighten around the infant and she shies from Billy, letting out a squawk of fear. Looking up at the massive man that is Shelley's boyfriend all she can see is the murderous gaze he is giving her. Was he this way with Shelley? Her eyes barely leave his to try and look at her daughter who is behind him, blocked by his size alone. Paula could swear he has grown in size since he walked in the door.

About that time the distinct click of a twelve gauge echoes in the room. Silus had been thankful Paula hadn't swept the garage, and he had a weapon to defend her. When she called, she sounded afraid that Billy Coeh was at their door. Even if the two of them had not been talking much since Christmas, he would not let anything happen to her. Silus would like nothing more than to put that boy into the ground. He stole his baby girl from him. He and his family could rot in Hell for all he cares. As he rounds the corner from the kitchen, he sees Paula's back to him and Billy towering over her like he is about to throw her to the ground. He takes aim, his finger is resting on the trigger. He has every intention of murdering this son-of-a-bitch.

"No, Daddy! Please! Please," he can hear Shelley from behind the large man.

Frances, who had been sleeping happily, was now being squeezed and jostled around. He doesn't like it one bit. He lets out a shrieking wail of a noise, which makes the whole room freeze.

Billy's eyes never leave Paula and Frances. He doesn't shift to let Shelley through either, protecting her from her father, who is pointing the shotgun right at them. He knows he can take the shot. It will hurt like hell, but he'll heal fast enough. It won't kill him, but Shelley wouldn't survive a shot gun blast to the chest. His lip curls as Paula turns to face Silus, another growl escaping him.

Silus looks at the infant in Paula's arms, and his eyes narrow. "Who's fucking baby is that?" He hasn't lowered his aim at all. He has to admire the balls on Billy Coeh, as he watches the man stand to his full height and square his shoulders.

"Put the fucking gun down and maybe I'll let you stay long enough to meet your grandson, jackass. Or is the couch at the Six that comfortable?"

Silus gives her a narrowed gaze. In spite of how angry he is, he misses her. He misses his girls. When he draws his gaze from Paula with the infant, he realizes Billy is much closer than he was a few seconds ago. How in the hell did the boy move without him noticing?

This gives Shelley the chance to follow and come from around him. Her instincts are in overdrive to protect Frances, but fear of her father keeps her at bay.

Silus can see how Shelley is reacting to the situation. He lost his temper at Christmas and didn't want to do that here. So he lowers the shotgun and finally sets it on the dining room table.

Billy gently wraps an arm around Shelley as she comes forward. Still protective but trying to diffuse the tense situation. His entire body tenses as Paula moves closer to Silus, gently handing the screaming Frances to him. He watches as the older man takes the boy into his arms, lightly cradling him.

"Hush now. What are you fussin' for?" Silus growls gently down at Frances. He brings his other hand up and lightly brushes against Frances's belly. Within a few seconds, the wailing subsides to little hiccupping breaths. "You got a pacifier?" Silus asks, without looking up.

Shelley's trembling with fear. Her nails dig into Billy's arm with the way she clings to him to prevent rushing her father to take the baby back. "Daddy," her voice barely a whisper. Shelley begs him not to hurt Frances with the tone of her voice. She wasn't really registering what he just asked.

"It'll help soothe him. And my finger ain't clean enough to stick in his mouth," he says.

It's Paula who moves then and retrieves the pacifier from the car seat. She knew the grizzly biker would melt into doting grandfather when he saw the baby.

Silus takes it and immediately Frances sucks on the little plastic nipple, sated for the moment. The little scrunched-up face Frances makes tells Silus the baby knows it's not his momma. "There, there, big fella. She'll feed you soon enough." He moves, as if they hadn't just been in a standoff with a shotgun and finds a comfy place on the couch. His jaw twitches in irritation, and while his demeanor remains calm, the rage monster is just below the surface.

Paula takes up residence next to Silus, and she lightly brushes her fingers over the baby's head. "He's so perfect, Silus. Look at him."

"What's his name?" Silus grunts.

"Frances David," Shelley says. She and Billy had followed Silus into the living room and were now sitting across from him. She is on the edge of her seat, and Billy's entire body language suggests he is ready for a fight at any second.

"What kind of name is that?" Silus chuckles as he looks down at the infant again. "Your momma wants you to get your ass whooped in school."

"Silus," Paula swats him. "I think it's very sweet she named him after your mother."

Silus furrows his brow when he looks back up at Shelley. She looks healthy, and like she is not wanting for anything. And, in spite of his long hatred for Susie Coeh, it would seem Billy Coeh is going to do right by his little girl. "You still in school?" Silus grumbles the question. He shifts and lets the infant rest against his chest, rubbing his back gently.

"Yes, sir," she replies with reluctance. "Might not go back this year." She bites against her lip and her mother sighs, then looks at Silus with an angry expression.

"You're gonna go back to fucking school, Shelley Joanne! What? Those Coehs boys got you locked up in a cellar?" He jabs.

"More like a tower," Billy retorts. "That's the other reason we're here. Shelley needs you to sign the paperwork to allow her to enroll in a private school near our home. The drive to Savannah is too far with the baby and Shelley doesn't wanna go back to that school." Billy fishes out the papers and hands them over to Paula.

Paula frowns, and asks Shelley, "So you're not going to come home? You'd be able to finish at this school then. Don't you think it would be better for you to be with your family? Did something happen at school? Isn't Faye watching out for you?"

Shelley, who is buckling under her parents' questioning, "Well, they're mean to me, Momma. Faye's gone. I ain't got any friends there anymore. My cheerleading outfit didn't fit, so they kicked me off the team. They treat me different since I got pregnant. And I have to get up so early. Frances hates me and won't let me sleep. It's making Billy mad at me. I just wanna go someplace people will like me." Shelley breaks down completely into tears at this point. She completely forgot about the question of her coming home.

"Oh honey," Paula frowns and gives Silus the angry expression again as she gets up and moves to comfort her daughter.

Silus narrows his eyes at Billy. "Is this how you take care of my daughter and grandson?" It doesn't matter that he threw her out to fend for herself. It's tearing him up to see her suffering now.

"She and I have been making do and learning to live together since someone thought it appropriate to throw a teenage girl out of her house with nothing but the clothes on her back on Christmas Day." Billy has not had enough sleep to be diplomatic today. "Which is why we brought the school transfer paperwork. The school's a ten-minute drive from our home, not an hour. Tuck your damn pride and give your daughter something that will actually help her. Coming back here is not an option."

Silus pats the baby, keeping the calm pressure to soothe young Frances. He can tell the baby is partially fussy because of his parents' states. He forgives the boy his shitty attitude, knowing how little sleep new parents get. Silus just can't accept he did anything wrong. "You watch your tone, boy. I have no qualms putting this baby down and whooping your ass for disrespecting me in my home. Now, tell me about this school and why I shouldn't just bring my daughter *home* to take care of her."

"What the hell do you mean, *your home*?" Paula snaps at him from where she is comforting Shelley. "I ain't decided to let you move back in yet. You make nice with your daughter and sign the fucking papers. Then we'll talk about lettin' your no-good ass sleep on this couch, instead of the Six's."

"What?" Shelley asks as she looks to Billy with a surprised expression at what they just learned.

"Oh yeah! That son-of-bitch called the cops on your sister when we got home. And—."

"Woman shut your--" Silus tries to interject.

"Fuck you. Sit there and hold that damn baby, or I'm gonna show you again whose house this is." Paula retorts. "Now. Your daddy has an anger problem. Earned himself a scar, I'm sure," as she cuts Silus a look.

Shelley is dumbfounded when her father doesn't beat her mother and sits there quietly grumbling at the baby.

Billy is looking between the two of them with a grim expression. "You will sign those papers," he demands, his alpha personality coming through now. "If you don't, we'll go to court and let a judge settle this matter. Shelley's home is with me. She and our son are safe and cared for. Her happiness and safety are my concerns now, not yours." Billy is not about to let Shelley be trampled over again. His mate has suffered enough. It is high time someone fought for her and he sure as hell knows how to fight.

CHAPTER THIRTY
Once Upon A Time in El Paso

The sun's high in the sky, and the temperature is sweltering hot.

"Are you fucking kidding me? You only paid a thousand for that truck. Why would you spend a thousand more to fix it?" Faye growls at Jasper.

"'Cause once it's fixed, it'll be good to go," he barks back angrily, as if she should understand this.

"Until the next thing breaks. If we bought a newer truck, we wouldn't have all these problems," she snarks at him.

"You got cash hiding somewhere for that, princess?" He smugly counters.

"Ugh, dog," she grumbles and storms out the door.

"Hey, I resemble that remark," he quips, following her. The mechanics who were pretending to not hear their spat are chuckling at the young couple. Jasper looks left and right for Faye, then rounds the corner to find her pacing behind the building. "Don't walk away from me when I'm talking to you." He growls.

"Or what, Jasper? You gonna cry about it?" Faye mocks him.

He steps forward quicker than she realizes and is shoving her against the wall. "Or I might have to spank you," his growl is low.

"You wouldn't dare," Faye challenges him. Her chest presses against the wall, but she pushes back just enough to feel he's aroused.

"I wouldn't, would I?" his voice purrs against her ear. "Mighty strong words from the girl pinned against the wall," as he kicks her feet apart and holds her against it while he fishes himself out of his pants.

She squirms and struggles but knows where this is going. Something about arguing with him sends them both into a tizzy. Seconds later, she can feel him hiking up her dress and brushing aside her thong. "You aren't getting what you want this time. I'm right." She gasps and squirms more.

He slaps her ass hard, causing her to yelp. His body presses against her to lift her into position. He forces her to be sandwiched between him and the wall. With a hard thrust, he buries himself deep in her. He brings his hand down and grasps her hip as he pumps into her tight little body. There is nothing sweet, or romantic, about how he fucks her in the back alley of the mechanic's shop. Their skin is glistening from the heat. She tries to curl back against him and he roughly takes her hands, slapping them against the wall.

"No. This is your punishment," he nips her ear and groans as his words make her milk his cock harder.

He kept her held like this, driving into her until he feels himself about to explode. He jerks out of her without warning and spins her around. His hands are pushing her down to her knees.

She gives him the dirtiest of looks, but her lust is dominating her anger. She sinks to her knees.

He smirks and laces his fingers in her hair. "No biting," he warns.

Then Faye's sweet lips are around his raging hard cock. She

sucks him in without warning, or gentleness. Her own fingers sliding down to please herself.

"Nuh uh. Punishment," he breathes out. It makes her whine against him. "Fuck Faye, I love making you whine. That's a good girl." He thrusts into her mouth with great gusto.

Faye's an expert with her mouth, and as he fucks her face his eyes flutter closed in enjoyment. She can feel him throbbing as her eyes flutter open again and she looks up to watch his face. The sweet and salty taste of him coupled with her, arouses her all the more. Just before he can erupt, she pulls back suddenly and allows her teeth to graze over his engorged head.

"Fuck," he gasps as his entire body shiver. "I said *no* biting," at which point she sucks in a deep breath before he thrusts himself fully into her mouth and down her throat, burying her nose against his body. Then he's erupting in her mouth, holding her head against him until she swallows it.

Jasper steps back, and he tucks himself into his pants. He is tender as he helps her right her clothes and picks her up from her knees. "You make me so fucking crazy, you know that?" He murmurs against her.

"Ditto," she breathes out. She is still aching and unsatisfied. Jasper using sex as a punishment turns her on as much as it irritates her.

As the two of them stand there, breathing hard and coming down from the euphoric high of fighting and fucking, they don't say a word. While Jasper was demanding, and forceful, he would never hurt Faye. He would give his last breath to protect her. He realized pretty early that she liked it rough. The small smile on her face tells him she has already forgiven him for not letting her orgasm.

"For that, we're taking the bike into town. I'm hungry."

"But I just fed you," He gives a wolfish grin.

"Asshole," She swats him.

He has a goofy grin on his face watching her strut away. He is pretty sure if he were in wolf form he would be panting.

On their way into town, his grin broadens as he feels her shudder against him on the bike. He pulls into a small diner in El Paso proper. They aren't very far from the Mexican border.

She kisses Jasper, then turns to head to the bathroom once inside. She pays little mind to anyone around her as she enters the bathroom. Once in the stall, she quickly pulls her panties down. As she suspected, when she orgasmed, it was more. She had started her period. As she sat there on the toilet, she cried, relieved. It had been more than a month since her last period and the last thing she wanted to be right now was pregnant. She and Jasper have been having so much fun since Christmas, but she knew this couldn't last. They've been fighting more and more. She still has the money she took from her father, but Jasper seems to always have money, and hasn't let her pay for anything. She wads up the bloody panties and wraps them in toilet paper. Thankfully, because of Jasper and she having random public shenanigans, she has kept a spare pair of panties in her purse. Fishing out a tampon, she gets herself cleaned up and freshened. It takes about 10 minutes in all.

Jasper thinks nothing of it. He is grinning about making her have to get cleaned up. His eyes wander over the menu, but all he can think about is having her on all fours, begging him for more. He didn't even see the man sitting at the table near the restroom.

When she comes out of the bathroom, she nearly runs into a guy. "Hey watch where you're--," she looks up to see Jackson Pruitt blocking her path.

"Why hello there, Miss Faye," his voice is smooth. His grin was full of malice. "Awful lot of people been lookin' for ya." His hand is on her forearm and he's pushing her to the exit quickly. "Your daddy's gonna be so happy I found his darlin' daughter."

"What? No. Jackson, let me go," she yelps out and jerks her arm to free herself of him. She hadn't realized he was herding her out the back of the diner, away from where Jasper sits.

Jackson wastes no time in pushing and dragging Faye toward his truck.

Faye isn't having it. She is raising holy hell in the parking lot and even bites Jackson.

"Fucking bitch," he snarls as he backhands her. It sends Faye to the ground. Jackson's hand laces into her hair and pulls her back to her feet. "You got two choices, Faye. You come along quietly and I'll make sure your old man doesn't have any say in what to do with you for being a thief. Or you fight me and I put two bullets in lover-boy's head and make sure Silus knows exactly who you ran off with. It's up to you."

Faye has never been great at doing what she is told. Fear washes over her. She was convinced Jackson would definitely kill Jasper. Had she known what Jasper was, she might have acted out and screamed. She tries to get her head free of his grasp only to whimper more when he jerks her back.

"Hard way it is then," he swiftly punches Faye in the stomach, causing her to double over and turn red as her diaphragm has stopped working.

Tears well in her eyes and she stumbles with Jackson as they approach a big box truck. She tries to catch her breath, while he jerks open the back of the truck. His one hand had let go of her hair and he hoists her up into the truck with them. He tosses her roughly against a crate. She pushes up and tries to make a run for it. His arm darts out and catches her again.

"I'm beginning to think you like being beaten, Faye." He throws her down again and straddles over her now with the twine used to secure items to the sides of the truck. He pins her down, ties her hands behind her back, then her ankles to her hands. He takes his bandana from his jacket and stuffs it into her mouth, taking more twine to wrap around her mouth and keep her gagged.

She cries and struggles. The way he tied her makes the twine tighter, and cuts into her skin.

He hops down out of the truck and gives her a wink. "Now, be a good girl and don't move around too much." He pulls the door closed and locks it in place. Moments later, his truck is rumbling as it pulls out of the diner's parking lot.

Jasper had been ignoring the emotional bond between him and Faye when relief washed over her. He wasn't ready for a baby either. In the future, they would have a ton of pups. For now, they're just going to ride. He was lost in his daydreams of future pups when he felt a mix of pain and fear from Faye, enough to make him growl and come up out of the booth. He stalks towards the women's bathroom but stops when her faint scent heads toward the back of the diner. He couldn't understand why she would go to the back of the diner. But the amount of fear he feels from their bond is enough to make him turn and pursue her scent.

CHAPTER THIRTY-ONE
Don't Leave Me Alone

Jasper speeds down the two-lane highway where he can smell the coffee and cocaine. He no longer could smell Faye's mix of citrusy smells. He bounces between fear and fury about her being taken. He should have been more alert. He didn't protect her and he'll never forgive himself if anything happens to her. As the afternoon passes, his mind drifts to New Orleans and the night he knew Faye was his forever.

The two of them had rolled into New Orleans in time for Mardi Gras. He had only ever heard rumors of New Orleans. The vampire that rules the city is a cruel monster, and to cross Louise Deveroux is a death sentence. So when Faye begged him to go to Mardi Gras, he had agreed but had been keeping his head down. A wolf in vampire territory could find themselves no longer able to howl at the jealous moon. Mardi Gras was everything the two of them hoped. They drank and partied and fucked. He never wanted his life to change if he could spend it with her this way. As a young pup, he had heard a few of the Wolf Pack talk about La Diable Coeur. The rumors were it was a place a young wolf could test his mettle. They weren't leaving without at least looking. He had already decided to fight.

He frowns as she shifts lanes. He remembers her scared face when he was getting ready in the little locker room. How she had quietly begged him not to get in that ring. Jasper had to show her how much he could protect her. He wasn't worried about any vampires in a fight club. He did regret not having anyone to watch her while he fought. He wanted to show her he could provide for her and winning a few rounds here would easily give them a cushion. Faye didn't want to live without him. He couldn't find the words to tell her just how happy that made him when she confessed it to him in the locker room. He kissed her like he was going to die and put his jacket gently on her shoulders. Several hours later, he was back in that locker room bending her over the table in the center of the room, when Louise Deveroux walked in. She interrogated him while he fucked Faye, not even bothered by the show.

As the sun starts to set, he finds a place to pull off and hide the bike. His heart is hammering in his chest. Wherever Faye is, she is terrified and hurting. He is going to murder whoever took her the moment he catches up with them. He knew he wouldn't be able to deal with them on the bike. Not to mention his senses would be amplified tenfold in wolf form. He strips down and neatly folds his clothes. He puts them away in the little bag on the back of his bike. Inside he finds the picture the two of them snapped at the French Quarter during the parade. She had paid a street vendor far too much for the instant photos. It didn't matter now. Those pictures were worth it. He lets out a growl, closing the bag up. Then he turns and starts to run, shifting down into his full wolf. Jasper has always hated the color of his fur. To him he just looked like a mangey mutt. His brother, Matthias, got the sleek, black badass coat. Billy even looks sharp in his copper red. But Jasper? No. He is a dull gray.

The dirt kicks up as he takes off at a dead run. He is moving much faster than a regular wolf, and fast enough to gain ground on the truck he can smell. The closer he gets the angrier he gets.

How dare that asshole touch his woman. He is fantasizing about beating the man to death with his own arms when the scent gets overwhelming. Jasper doesn't have a plan, other than to stop the truck and get Faye back. As the tail lights came into view, he veered his path enough to allow him to turn and start barreling straight for the big box truck. They thought they were so clever, hiding their drugs amongst the coffee beans. Instead, it had been the homing beacon he needed to find her. On this little two-lane highway, there are no lights to alert a driver when an animal is about to cross their path.

The next thing Jasper knows he is flying through the air and shifting up into his werewolf form. The dull gray wolf went from about five feet tall on all fours to over seven feet tall. By the time his muddy gray form completely shifted, he collides with the side of the truck, sending it careening with his momentum and squealing along the pavement. The tires on the other side collapse from the shock. This causes the truck to roll on its side and metal wails like a banshee along the pavement as it comes to a stop. Jasper is sent flying from the truck and rolls along the pavement. Sharp pain sears his body as bones shatter from the impact. He groans, "Fuck. That's gonna hurt in the morning. Note to self, fast trucks hurt." He can feel his bones mending immediately and his muscles twitching in pain as his body repairs itself.

Jackson had been in communication with his buddies back in Savannah the whole time he was on the run. It was against Silus's rules, but Jackson didn't care. He was keeping tabs on Silus, as well as to let them know about this shit run. That fucker had intended to kill him with this run. When he got word about Faye, he could take it or leave it until she walked right by him. Now, he had all the leverage he needed to take over the Angels. He is going to get everything he wanted with bringing Faye back and completing the impossible run. He had just turned the radio on when the next thing he knows, he is hanging from his seatbelt and the truck is on its side.

"Fuck," he grumbles. He gets himself free of the seatbelt, kicks out the windshield, and crawls out of the truck. Whatever hit him had to be massive. Jackson checks the clip in his gun, he scans the road. All he sees in the moonlight is a mass of gray, fur-covered flesh. He rubs his eyes to make sure he sees what he is looking at properly. Jackson doesn't hesitate then. He lifts his pistol and pulls the trigger until it stops going bang. As he stalks towards it to make sure it's dead, he's retrieving the backup clip from his jacket to reload the gun. Jasper gasps and growls in pain as his back is now riddled with bullets.

"At least they're not silver," he mutters. In this form, it's just heavy growling noises. He can hear the clip being put into place and realizes that idiot walked right to him. He lets Jackson kick him to roll him onto his back.

"What the fuck is this shi—," Jackson's eyes widen in horror as he is looking down at what can only be described as a werewolf.

It's about that time Jasper snarls and his elongated claws slash right across Jackson's belly. This is followed by Jasper springing to his feet and tearing part of Jackson's throat out before he tosses the gurgling man aside like a rag-doll. Faye has to be here somewhere, he can smell her. As much as he would like to rip that man to tiny pieces, he has to find her. Panic fills him as he limps to the truck and tears through the metal of the truck like it was tissue paper. He can feel his connection with her fading. His eyes dart back and forth trying to find her. Crates of coffee, hiding the cocaine, shatter against the pavement as he tosses them over his shoulder. He's frantic in digging to find her.

Then he sees her.

The crate had fallen and is crushing her form. All he can see is that pretty little dress he bought her in Memphis. It's one of those cute little floral numbers. The white is stained red with her blood. His mournful howl pierces the night sky as he reaches down, using his claws to free her broken body from the twine.

He scoops her up and cradles her to his chest. That's when he feels her heartbeat, faint, but present. He doesn't hesitate. His jaws close on her shoulder, piercing all the way to the bone.

He doesn't care that he has just broken every rule in existence for the Wolf Pack. He isn't going to live without her. He waits with bated breath, his jaws still clamped into her creamy white skin. Tears clinging to his black eyes and praying to the Moon Goddess that this would be enough to save her.

At first, nothing happens and he whines. It's silent on this dark road, and he is sure his heart is going to stop beating with her.

A faint breeze encircles them. He relaxes his jaw in defeat. His sweet, beautiful mate is dying. All because he was careless and reckless with her safety. He could hear his mother growling at him all those times when he didn't have a care in the world. If only he had taken her words to heart. Keeping Faye held against him, he lightly licks over where he bit and buries his muzzle against the small of her neck. His arms are wrapped tight around her.

It's then he felt her heart beating harder and faster. Hope fills him and he rises to his feet, still cradling her.

"You cannot leave me alone," he begs her in his mind.

She screams. She spasms and writhes in his arms and he took off running with her. He makes a beeline in the bike's direction.

He can feel her body healing itself. Her skin is feverish, and her heart is beating so fast, he is convinced she is going to have a heart attack.

"You are safe. I love you. I know it hurts." He tries to soothe her as he runs with her.

He is nowhere near as fast as in his wolf form but is still moving at a good clip. He is exhausted but digs deep to press on. She hasn't opened her eyes yet. Her body is going through so much right now. He didn't want it to be like this. He had wanted it to be her choice and had hoped she would love the idea of being a wolf as much as he had for the past two years. It's too late now to take it back. Jasper would rather have her alive and furious with him, than to lose her to death.

CHAPTER THIRTY-TWO
Second Chances

A tiny female figure in a blood red biker jacket watches the horror scene before her unfold. She has been stalking this lone werewolf since he waltzed into New Orleans. He had earned enough respect from Louise to be allowed to leave, but she had been tasked with seeing what he was up to. As if that was not impressive enough, he stalks and destroys a box truck. She could not understand why he would do this. Not until she saw him kneeling on the ground, rocking the human girl he had the balls to bring into a Vampire bar. Her heart sang for the young wolf. He seems to really like that girl. She was about to approach and offer to turn the girl when she witnesses, in wide-eyed fascination, him sinking his fangs into her and whines like a puppy begging for attention. She had never seen how a werewolf turns a human into one of them. It is shockingly similar to how vampires turn their victims. Then he was off and running again, and she is left to see what else he abandoned in the road.

Much to her surprise the man is still alive. This assumes one was generous with the definition of alive. His hand had come to his throat, and his eyes are dulling. She can feel his heartbeat slowing. As she stands over him, eyes as crystal clear as the

Caribbean sea, shine with mischief.

"Too bad. You're kind of pretty in that bad boy gone wild sort of way." Both of her brows raise in surprise when he starts to lift the pistol weakly in his other hand, intending to shoot her of all things. "Oh, sugah, you're feisty. I like dat. I'm hopin' you fuck better dan ya fight." With that, she drops to her knees and leans down over him. She bites her lip hard enough to draw blood and kisses him passionately.

He squirms and struggles as he can see the dark spots of unconsciousness taking him. This isn't how he expected to die. His eyes flutter closed and his thoughts drift to Shelley. Her pretty eyes and soft blond hair. The pert nose and sweet full lips. How she looked the first time he saw her, with the sun setting behind her, and giving her an angelic glow. A small part of him is sad he will die without having been with her or known her love. A tear escapes his closed eyes, and he regrets how he left things with her. Then he fades to darkness.

The young woman leans up then, licking her lip to make the bleeding stop. "Don't move," she pats his cheek with a sadistic chuckle. Adelaide eases up off Jackson and heads down the road. There are a few screams faintly heard, then she is back by his side, tilting her head as she watches him. She knows he is not dead, she can feel him. The young girl she has with her standing in her nightgown with fogged over eyes teeters from foot to foot. "C'mon Prince Charming, you need to feed so you don't go bat-shit crazy and murder the whole town."

She giggles when he groans, like a kid asking for permission. Adelaide was sixteen when she was turned. Perpetually left in this blossoming state of innocence, her eyes reveal she has lived just shy of two centuries. She gently pets the little girl as she patiently waits for Jackson to get up off the ground. His neck had healed while she was fetching him food, and his abdomen was almost completely healed. She was right, and he is handsome. "Iffn you don't be gettin' up, you ain't gettin' no coffee from dat truck. And den I'm gonna have ta be eatin' yer dinner." She brushes her fingers along the girl's cheek, who mewls, but does not otherwise move. Tears are streaming down the girl's face, the only sign of her state of mind.

"Who the fuck are you?" Jackson rasps from the ground. He is positive he was dead, and this is Hell. As his eyes open, he looks up at the starry sky. A sudden, crushing need fills him. He swears his heart is beating a mile a minute, and fear is permeating the area. Narrowing his gaze, he realizes it's not his heart, or his fear. He brings a hand up to his neck and his eyes widen in surprise. The smooth skin no longer wet with blood, the faintest hints of the claws that had ripped his throat out remains. As he sits up, he blinks in disbelief. A girl in a red leather jacket and another girl in a nightgown are standing before him.

Adelaide smiles and gently pushes the girl with the nightgown forward.

Jackson doesn't understand what is happening. All he can think about is the pulse he can see in the girl's throat. She smells divine drenched in fear. The crushing need fills him again and his eyes start to redden. He springs to his feet and, before he can fathom what he is doing, he is sinking his fangs into the girl. His arms wrap around her like a needy lover. The girl lets out a shrill scream followed by a moan. As Jackson groans against her throat, he suckles the tender skin. The warm coppery liquid fills his mouth, and he drinks eagerly. His senses are being inundated and causing him to be overwhelmed. All he cares about is making the need stop. The more he drinks, the better he feels.

"Dat's enough," Adelaide coos to him, petting him gently. "You can't be killin' the cattle, as much fun as that would be. I'd be mighty put out iffn hunters gotcha so soon." He ignores her, and she rolls her eyes. They're always greedy when they first turn. She narrows her eyes at him and usurps his will, forcing him to release the girl. Adelaide shoves him away, then licks her thumb and runs it over the puncture wounds. When he tries to get to the girl again, Adelaide throws him into the truck.

"No! Bad!" Scolding him like he is a dog. She leaves the unconscious girl on the ground and stalks toward him. "Look. You went and pissed yerself off a werewolf. You're lucky I was here, or you'd be deader than a doornail, cher. Anything in this truck you be needin'? Best be gettin' it so we can get on outta here."

Jackson is still trying to process what is happening. How did this tiny girl throw him into the truck? It's then his eyes settle on the truck. "What the fuck happened to the truck?" He turns and looks all around. No sign of Faye. "Where is she?" His voice is graveled and hissy sounding as his fangs are extended. He frowns and brings his hand up, surprised to feel his incisors are much longer and sharper than before. He finally levels his gaze on the young woman dressed in the red jacket. The amused look on her face irritates him.

"Oh, sugah. You made dat big bad werewolf howl at the moon. Don't you know no better dan ta fuck with a wolf's mate? She is long gone." Adelaide giggles at Jackson. Still amused that every new vampire reaches up and touches their fangs in surprise.

"What's so fucking funny? Werewolf? That shit ain't real. Now get the fuck out of here, little girl." He turns and starts to work out how he's going to get his bike out of the crate, and any of the product that's salvageable.

It's then Adelaide steps up to him and while she is not tall enough to hold him off his feet by his throat, she is strong enough to take him by the throat and throw him down.

With a grunt, he hits the ground. He tries to come back up and she slams him down again. His eyes widen in a mix of horror and excitement as she bares her fangs at him. There is something about her that made him want to submit to her. Another part of him wants to fight her with all his might.

"I'll show you little girl." She snarls at him, holding him down by his throat as she stares at him. Her eyes are the most brilliant blue he has ever seen.

"What... What the fuck is happening to me?" He feels the need building again and a new-found fear of the girl holding him down. Jackson had prided himself on his fighting skills and yet he's being held down by this little girl. He frowns and tries to relax under her, but his agitation is high. It's freaking him out to hear a heart beating near him. The slow and steady thump banging like a drum in his ears.

"I made ya a fangy, as we like ta call 'em back home. Vampire. You were gonna die, and I thought you looked too pretty to let that happen. Now. Get the fuck up, get whatever shit you want out of the truck, and let's get the fuck outta here. We only got a few hours 'fore sunrise." She jerks him back to his feet by his throat and shoves him toward the truck.

He rubs his throat and grumbles. If he wasn't scared half out of his mind, he might've been turned on by the girl's forcefulness. He turns to the truck. It's a total loss. Crates are scattered all over the place. The coffee and cocaine strewn about the road in mixes of beans and white powder. He makes his way in and finds the crate with his bike. He purses his lips as he rummages until he finds the crowbar. As he picks it up, he swears he can hear her laughing. He pries the crate open and is relieved to find his bike fairly well intact. He is also confused at how easy that was to open.

From outside of the truck, "What's takin' ya so long? You got another one o' dem girls tied up in there to fuck? Jus' what kind o' fuckin' pervert are you? You promise ta tie me up later?"

He laughs at her dirty mouth. "Only girl in here is the one I'd give my life for," as he pushes crates out of the way to make a path.

Adelaide sighs, in spite of not needing to, and steps into the truck. A few seconds later she launches the crates out of the truck, much like Jasper had done a few hours ago. Another glance at her wristwatch and she frowns. As Jackson wheels the bike out, she shakes her head. He is then moving around the truck to retrieve his go-bag from the cab.

Jackson carefully walks the bike away from the truck, following her. Once fully clear of the wreck, he starts up, and waits for her to hop on the back.

She tilts her head with a perplexed look, then shakes it, chuckling. "Your awful pretty, but ain't very bright," she muses as she curls into him on the back of the bike.

He grunts a response as the two of them ride away, leaving the girl he fed from lying in the middle of the chaos.

CHAPTER THIRTY-THREE
Baby Steps

Jackson and Adelaide made their way back to New Orleans the slow way. Adelaide had broken down and confessed to him that they could travel at the speed of their thoughts, and it was silly to still use the motorcycle. He told her to fuck off with that nonsense and that nothing comes between him and his bike. He still didn't fully understand what had happened to him that night. All he knew was that he had this uncontrollable urge to drink blood. He could feel the rage inside of him, like a dark monster shifting about in his skin. He and Adelaide had been fighting. He thought it disgusting to drink blood. Then she started with all the rules. It's more rules than the frigging military.

He rolls his eyes and has had enough when he storms out of the hotel. He has only taken a few steps when he felt the urge and rage rising once more. He didn't know what he was doing until he had the girl in his arms in that dark alley. His fangs greedily sunk into her neck as he sucked her like a juice pouch. She screamed and writhed. All of his anger and regret poured into her. Her screams called to the dark monster inside. The chaos of everything happening around him gives him a thrill. His eyes close. He savors the sweetness of the thick liquid but then the blood no longer tastes good. He pulls back, disgust on his face as he spits out the bitter mouthful. His eyes look down at her and panic fills him.

For a fleeting moment, he thought he was staring down at Shelley's lifeless body. This little girl's blue eyes had gone dull. Her body lies still as he lets her slip from his arms. He scrambles back in fear and disgust. His hand coming over his mouth as he can't think. Adelaide had not made herself known, still in the shadows, watching him struggle with his new life. It wasn't until she was sure he would listen that she steps forward, allowing the shadows to dissipate from her. She pulls him into a gentle hug.

At first, he doesn't respond. He doesn't want this crazy bitch to hug him. He wants to go back to his life in Savannah, to his girl. He wants to take over the Angels of Wrath, and live out his days on the beach, or on the open road.

"You be too young ta be wonderin' off, baby fangy. Ya can't control dat hungry ol' bastard inside ya. It's why we hunt tagethah. So I can help ya pace yerself."

Her tone is gentle and Jackson finds her soothing.

She calms the beast by being close to him. Adelaide rubs his back gently before breaking the embrace. "Go on back to da hotel an' wait for me. Ah'll take ya out right."

"What about her," he voice is raspy with regret.

"You don't worry 'bout her none. I'll take care o' her. Now, go on."

*****

In a tiny motel room, not too far from the body shop where their truck is being fixed, Jasper and Faye are resting. He had brought her back here, bathed her, and burned the dress. She slept off and on for the better part of three days. He was growing worried that he was too late in turning her. That she is going to die a horrible and painful death as her body rejects the poison from his fangs. Every whimper and every whine from her, breaks his heart. He is beside himself watching her suffer this way. Finally, having remembered them talking about mates in school, he strips them both down and crawls into the bed with her. He engulfs her smaller frame by pulling her against his body.

"Come back to me," he murmurs against her ear, kissing just below it. The teachers had talked about certain mates could heal each other just through touch. The comfort of their soul mate overpowering even the worst of wounds. If she isn't better by morning, he will call his mother and confess what he had done. He will get his mother to save Faye, even if it meant he was banished for life.

At some point, he had drifted to sleep. Faye's eyes are open and watching him sleep. Her mind is a holy hot mess. She remembers Jackson tying her up and tossing her in the truck. Then she remembers being crushed under the heavy crates and feeling like she was going to die alone in the dark. Jasper would never know what happened to her. Then there was a monster, a massive gray beast, the thing of nightmares, and it bit her. Everything hurt after that. The beast stole her away from the truck. She swears Jasper had talked to her in her mind. Silently she watches him, taking in the small frown on his face as he is dreaming of something he doesn't like. Her body feels like she is on fire. She hurts and aches but looking down she has no wounds she can see. His skin is warm and delectable against hers. She can't help but smirk at them both being completely naked.

"No, I didn't do anything unseemly. Jesus, Faye. What kind of monster do you think I am?" He growls in a sleepy voice. His pulls her closer and rolls over to pin her underneath him. "But now that you're awake." He smirks. She accommodates him and rolls her hips to meet his. She gives him a small frown due to him plucking out of thin air exactly what she was thinking.

"It's a perk," he leans down and gently kisses her forehead. "Among other things." Another kiss to the tip of her nose.

"Perk? What are you talking about? How did you find me?"

She wriggles and for a moment he's lost in looking down upon her beautiful figure. Her eyes shine bright, and her hair is softly fanned around her like a halo. Her creamy skin was nearly flawless, except for the fading bite mark he left on her. He can't help but be in awe of watching her. He nearly lost her and it all but destroyed him. He would spend the rest of his life making sure she never suffers like that again. As much as he wants to mount her right then and there, he was going to have to explain so much. She hasn't even had her first shift yet. They should probably get that over with sooner rather than later in case it goes wrong. He isn't sure when the next full moon is.

"I'm talking about how I saved your life. And I will always find you. You're my girl, Faye. Ain't nothing on his Earth that'll keep me from you." He kisses her tenderly then and eases off the bed. In spite of the raging hard on, he pulls his boxers and pants on. "Let's get breakfast and I'll explain everything."

*****

The reunion with Silus and Paula had gone well enough. The bridges aren't fully mended. Shelley, after having lived with the Coeh's for these months, doesn't want to go back to that life, ever. She hadn't realized how afraid of everything she was until she was encouraged to grow here. Shelley is leaning against the opening to the Coeh living room, watching Susie with Frances.

Susie is sound asleep in a recliner, tilted all the way back, with the chunky little baby nestled contentedly on her chest. Susie has been over-stepping her bounds with Frances. Twice now she has taken him with her to wherever she is going without telling Shelley or Billy. Shelley was starting to feel like Susie was going to take Frances away from her, but she didn't want to start a fight with Billy about it. It is isolating to know that if things went sideways here, she won't have anyone to help her.

Quietly, she eases forward and scoops up the sleeping infant.

"I don't mind him," Susie murmurs as she stirs.

"I can take care of him," Shelley replies, sounding harsher than she means to.

"I didn't say you couldn't, baby girl. I just said I didn't mind him sleeping on me." Susie's tone took an irritated tone.

"I understood what you meant. Just cause I'm young doesn't mean I'm stupid. He's my son. I don't appreciate you treatin' him like he's yours." She turns to walk out of the room with Frances.

"Don't you walk away from me, missy. You get your ass back here." Susie's up out of the recliner and stalking toward Shelley.

Shelley whirls back around, anger blazing to life on her face. "No. Now you listen to me. He's my son. Mine and Billy's. While I appreciate everything you have done, you don't have the right to do with him as you please. It ain't right for his own momma to not know where he is. Or to be panicked that someone took him. It's bad enough I ain't got anyone but Billy, and even then he bows down to you when you start actin' like the queen bee. I don't know what it is about this wolf stuff that makes him do that, but it's bull puckey! I'm not a dumb kid that can't take care of her own son! If you can't treat me with respect, then I'm takin' my son and we'll find somewhere else to live." Shelley's voice is rising as she rails into Billy's mother. Tears cling to the corners of her eyes and her skin flushes bright red to match her flaring emotions.

As if on cue, Frances starts to wail.

CHAPTER THIRTY-FOUR
Fighting Words

David has heard this storm brewing since the baby came home. He has gently tried to warn Susie that she is not the mother of that baby. She should let Shelley take the lead, but Susie is a strong-willed woman coupled with being the Alpha of a pack. He emerges from his office with caution and comes into the living room where the two women are standing off. Shelley is turned sideways with Frances away from Susie. He would laugh if this weren't a pretty serious situation. Shelley only comes to about Susie's shoulder. The two women couldn't be more different. Susie stands tall and confident, where Shelley has an innate meekness about her. David moves with a cat-like grace to referee and puts his hand on each of them, pushing them apart. "Now, now, girls. Let's talk about this like adults. We're all family here." His tone is soft, but it's reproachful to Susie. The look he gives her tells her she should know better.

"Can't have adult conversations with emotional little girls," Susie spits.

"Or old hormonal bitches," Shelley claps back.

David shouts, "Enough."

Susie's eyes widen. It is very rare David raises his voice. The last time she saw that was at his father's funeral.

Shelley has been trying to get Billy to talk to his mother. She told him how it makes her feel, and how she doesn't enjoy feeling like they are going to take her baby from her. Billy, having not been very versed in dealing with his mother with other women, tried to assure Shelley that wouldn't happen and to accept the help. Shelley has taken this as he is taking Susie's side. Shelley has had enough of this matriarchal nonsense.

"No! It's not fucking enough!" Her voice cuts through the room like a knife. "This is *my* fucking baby. We are his parents. We get to say where he goes and when he goes there. We are the ones who take care of him. You don't get to run off willy-nilly with my child! I don't give two shits if you are the Queen of England, you will ask me for permission to take *my* baby, period."

David's eyebrows raise to his hairline. Very few people have talked to Susie like that and survived. *"Well, she is a fated mate of a potential Alpha."* He links with Susie, hoping a joke will help her see how much this is affecting the girl. It's all he can do to stop from laughing and causing the situation to spiral further into chaos.

Susie lets out a low and menacing growl. No one disrespects her like this. *"Who the fuck does this kid think she is? I'm going to rip her arms off,"* she roars back in his mind. Susie steps forward.

Shelley squares up and lifts her chin defiantly, as if to dare Susie to say something.

David quickly steps between the two, facing Susie, locking eyes with her. The weight of his gaze and the emotional connection between them tells her that he is not okay with her behavior in this situation. Without saying a word, Susie immediately knows that David agrees with Shelley. He is giving Susie the respect of not saying it out loud.

"I can damn well take my grandson anywhere I see fit, young lady. This is *my* house. You came to *me* as a lost little pup. You're not even a fucking adult. We feed you. We make sure you get to school. Just who do think a judge would grant custody to?" Susie snarls.

David takes a deep breath, because that was absolutely the wrong thing to say. What happens next fills David with dread.

"I see," Shelley whispers out.

When he breaks his gaze with Susie, he sees Shelley walking away with Frances, who is still shrieking and crying. He lets out the breath he drew in and looks back at Susie. David pulls out his phone and calls Tommy.

"Yes, sir?" Tommy answers.

"I need you to get over here as quick as you can. Shelley needs a lift." He waits for confirmation from Tommy and hangs up. He then turns his back on Susie and heads to his office.

Susie watches in fury and frustration as her mate turns his back on her. He might as well have punched her in the gut. She can take care of that baby better than that girl. Like it, or not, her grandson is part of this pack and that girl will follow the rules. She crosses her arms and is breathing hard. She is going to hurt someone with how angry and hurt she is. David has always been on her side, in everything. She turns and storms out the door, slamming it behind her. She blocks the link between her and David.

Shelley set Frances down in the crib, letting him scream and cry. His little face as red as a tomato. It's tearing her apart, and she is blinded by the tears filling her eyes, but she was not going to take this anymore. She is terrified and depressed. Her entire life is in shambles, and while she thought this was going to be her happily ever after, she can see it's only that way if she gives up anything she wants. She hurriedly stuffs baby clothes, diapers, and anything else she can fit of his into a diaper bag. She doesn't trust leaving him in the crib, so she scoops him up, and takes him into her and Billy's room. She buckles him into his car seat and finds a pacifier for him. It soothes him until he's left hiccupping and sucking on the pacifier in loud, angry pops.

She pulls out one of the duffel bags she brought with her and quickly stuffs her clothing in it. She is crying harder now and is starting to panic. Shelley has a stash of money. She found it in her backpack, and it made her miss Faye all the more, but that wouldn't be enough. Now she would have to drop out of school and get a job. With a grunt, she slings the bag over her shoulder, scoops up the carrier in one hand, and the diaper bag in the other. She comes out of the bedroom and hurries down the stairs. Shelley assumes they would try to stop her, so she is running for the front door as fast as her feet will carry her. When she gets out the door, she sees Tommy getting out of his truck and stops. The look on her tear-stained face is of distrust and fear.

Tommy's frowning. What the fuck happened while Billy is out on patrol?

"Miss Shelley," he moves forward cautiously. "I was told you needed a ride."

"Mhm hmm," she nods, keeping her mouth closed. He looks down at her and his heart breaks. He can feel the pain radiating from her. Billy is going to be pissed. He loads her and the baby's bags into the truck while she buckles the car seat into the backseat of the cab of his truck.

Tommy gets into the truck with Shelley and takes off. He imagines she won't be too happy with going to his house, but he can't think of any better place to take her that won't get him skinned alive by Billy. That, and his momma knows how to deal with angry girls. She grew up in Susie's shadow. He turns the music down and gives Shelley a side glance. "Wanna tell me what happened back there?" He asks with a gentle tone.

"Nope," Shelley pops in anger.

"Are you going to call Billy?"

"So he can tell me to relax and take his momma's side again?" Her voice raises to a dangerous octave.

"Mmm, Or? He comes and makes it right." He tries to assure her.

"I'm not a home wrecker. He already chose his side."

"Yeah. He did. He chose you. Haven't you realized it yet? You could literally take a shuttle to the moon and that man would get in a rowboat row his way there."

"Just take me to the bus station, Tommy." She sniffles.

"You know, you'll break his heart if you run. Plus, where you gonna go?" Tommy's already connecting to Billy through the mind link. *"Hey man, you need to get to my house pronto."* Tommy exhales when he gets the affirmative back from Billy. He gives Shelley another side look. "Listen. I'm taking you to my parents' place. We'll get this sorted out. I don't know what's going on, but you owe it to Billy to at least talk to him before you run. If you talk to him and you don't like what he says, I'll take you to the bus station myself. Deal?" Tommy's being pretty honest with her, not wanting her to shut down. He and Billy talked about how she turns inward when people dismiss her.

"Fine. Whatever," Shelley mutters and looks out the window. Tommy will take whatever he can get.

******

David fishes out his phone as he sits in his office, calling his eldest son.

"Hey, dad," Matthias answers.

"Hey there, boy. I need to ask something of you that's... not easy." David rubs his hand over his face.

"Okay. What is it?" Matthias sounds worried.

"I need you to go out on the range. Find your mother and talk some sense into her. Remember how bad it was when you had your first son?" He sighs. "Shelley's taking it hard." He knows Susie will come back on her own, but it doesn't mean he won't worry about her. Not to mention, with the Appalachian Pack

Alpha stuff, it's not entirely safe for her out there. David wishes he could mind link with the patrols to have them keep an eye on her. It's the first time he regrets not being a wolf himself.

Matthias is quiet for a moment on the other end. "Dad, you know the solution was us moving away, right?"

"I know. Just... Please? We both know if we leave her out there. She is not going to come home for a week." David's sounds desperate.

"Is Shelley still there?" Matthias' question is simple, but David could hear the meaning behind it. He was asking if Susie physically hurt Shelley.

"Already called Tommy to take her away, and knowing that boy, the first thing he's going to do is call Billy." David grumbles. He hopes that Tommy just takes her to Billy. He can hear the irritation in his son.

"You sent her away?"

"No. I didn't send her away. She left. There's a difference." He snaps.

Matthias growls. David was right. This was not going to be easy. Matthias still hasn't forgiven his mother for causing that strife with him and his wife. "Fine. I'll do it. I'll let you know when I find her."

"Love you, boy. Tell her I'll have the good wine ready when she gets home."

His son grunts and hangs up.

CHAPTER THIRTY-FIVE
Do You Hear Me Now?

Billy had noticed Shelley has been unhappy since they settled in with Frances. Billy was sure going to see her parents would help with her tidal wave of emotions. For someone so tiny, she holds in a lot of emotions. The slightest thing brings her to tears. He hasn't seen her smile in several days. Then she started talking like a crazy person, afraid his mother was trying to take Frances away from her. He had tried to reassure her that pup raising is a communal task for the pack, and that his mother's behavior is normal. He forgot to mention this help was due to her being proud of her grandson. He thought it nice they get small breaks from the baby. He knew something wasn't right with Shelley, with the way she went quiet as he defended his mother. He doesn't think he has heard more than a few words from her the past few days.

"I don't know what to do," he grumbles to his partner on patrol.

He felt the sudden fear and an overwhelming sense of loneliness and grimaces. It's tearing him apart that he can feel all this from her and not do anything about it. When Tommy links him with the sense of urgency in his voice, he turns to his partner. "I need to go. I'm sorry. I'll send Tommy out."

"Bah... I got this. Go on. We won't tell Alpha," he smirks and winks. Billy laughs, then hot foots it to Tommy's house. It took him about an hour to get there. He enters his aunt's house as if he were approaching a crime scene. The pain he is feeling is dulled and when he sees Shelley asleep in the recliner, with Frances happily nestled against her, he starts to move forward to take the baby.

Out of nowhere, his aunt appears and has him by the ear. She drags him into the kitchen and forcefully plops him into the chair.

"Just what the hell are you and my sister doing to that poor girl?"

"Uh... what? We ain't doing anything to her," he grumbles in confusion.

"The hell you ain't. She is runnin', Billy. She has got a bag packed with her things, the baby's things, and she is holding about five grand," which tells Billy his aunt went through Shelley's things.

"What do you mean, she is running?"

"Why in the hell do you think she is at my house?" the woman crosses her arms and looks like a more feminine copy of his mother.

"Well, that's what I came here to find out."

"When Tommy brought her in. She was barely able to talk she was crying so hard. Something about judges and babies, and she'd just go find her sister. What's that shit about?"

"You got me. When I left this morning, she was feeding the baby like normal."

"Uh huh," his aunt crosses her arms and stares at him. "You listen here, pup. Your momma's been running roughshod over that girl. The whole pack's talking about how Susie's got a new baby and she is just lettin' that girl play at being momma to appease you."

"They're doing what?" His tone and expression darken.

"Oh yeah! Susie took him to the quilting circle. She took him to the pack meeting. She also took him out to lunch with her girlfriends. Shelley ain't been with her one bit. Don't you think it mighty weird that Alpha isn't takin' her grandson's momma anywhere with him? I bet she didn't even bother to ask if she could take him. That girl ain't said anything to you? Hard to believe, Billy." She frowns at her nephew. "Tommy said she said you took your momma's side. Told him to take her to the bus station. She wasn't even gonna say goodbye, Billy. You pickin' up what I'm puttin' down?"

Billy's shoulders sag. Why hadn't Shelley told him any of this? He wants to believe he would stop any wrong-doing against his mate. Billy thinks back over the past couple of weeks. His brow furrows. "She was halfcocked about Momma. Talking like she was trying to take the baby from her. But that won't ever happen. Momma knows that baby's mine and hers." He rubs his hand over his face and tries to link with his mother only to find the connection is blocked. He looks to the living room then and his frown deepens. "What do I do now?" He's afraid he is losing Shelley.

"You two need to talk. Not that pussy shit, either. You need to sit down and have it out until you work it out. Can you even imagine how lonely that girl is? She has got no friends here. No family other than you and that baby. And if I had to put my money where my mouth is, I bet that bitch sister of mine threatened to take the baby away when Shelley confronted her. Tommy wasn't sure, but it's your daddy that called him to come get her. Fuck, Billy. She is a baby herself. You gotta be the grown-up here. She needs *you* to help her do what's best for the both of you. If you don't get your head out of your ass, you're gonna lose her. She ain't like us, and if I know anything, she is not had any good role models either. She needs you to be on *her* side, even against your momma."

Billy makes a grunt of surprise. If his father was involved, it meant something happened between Susie and Shelley. He sighs and stands to go into the other room. Billy sits down on the couch, crosses his arms, and waits. He's not about to wake Shelley up when she is getting much needed rest, especially with Frances. By the little jagged hiccups in the baby's breathing, he can imagine the wailing that was happening prior to this nap. He's tempted to leave her here and go talk to his father before coming back, but he knows that at this moment he needs to be with Shelley. So he settles in, waiting. His aunt brings him a beer and hands him the television remote.

Two hours pass before Frances starts the fussy, hungry noises. Shelley stirs and sits up. Not even opening her eyes, she hikes her shirt up, pops the bra open, and shifts the baby around, gasping in pain when he clamps on. "Brute," she grumbles, but the relieved smile regarding him taking to her breast on the first try is on her sleepy face. She shifts to get comfortable, in spite of the tiny monster destroying her breasts. She hasn't noticed Billy there yet. It's then Billy gets a good look at Shelley. Her hair is pulled up in a ponytail, but it's wild and frayed looking, like she forgot she had it in said ponytail. Her eyes are puffy from crying and kissed with dark circles. She looks pale and tired, not her usual rosy sweet pink. Her eyes finally open and he sees the sad way her face turns down.

"Don't worry, Franky. I'll do the right thing," she whimpers at him. The way she brushes her fingers along him and admires him, Billy can tell she is trying to remember everything about him. The overwhelming sadness from her fills him again. "I just want a little more time with you."

Billy gets up off that couch then and scoops her, with the still feeding baby, into his massive arms, pulling them to his chest. Billy plops back down on the couch and holds them tight against him, not willing to let either of them go. Shelley stiffens in his arms at first. Her fear and anger ebbing the longer he holds her.

She squirms to get Frances in a good position again but doesn't fight to get out of Billy's lap. Silence fills the room, and all either of them hear is the steady suckling of the baby. When Frances is done she tilts him up, letting her shirt fall down to cover her breast and leans him against her shoulder, patting him. She has her head against Billy's chest, listening to his heartbeat.

"You gonna get in trouble for being here?"

"No. I'm with my mate, how can that be trouble?"

"What about patrol?" She is trying to avoid why he is here, or what she is planning on doing. Just the thought of her plan makes her squeeze Frances tighter.

"I got more important things than patrol at the moment." His arms don't loosen. Billy is trying to will her sadness away. Silence fills the room again and Shelley's emotions get the better of her. She cries. With his arms around her, she can feel his suffering as well. It's overwhelming and it leads her to turn her face into his chest, burying against him to hide the tears. He kisses her forehead and doesn't relax his hold on her. "Angel, talk to me." His voice is filled with frustration and desperation.

"Oh Billy. I ruined everything. I ruined your life. I ruined Faye's life. Frances hates me. He cries all the time when I hold him. Your momma keeps taking him and... and... now. Now she hates me and wants to go before a judge." She pulls Frances to her and cradles him as if someone might try to take him right then. "She is right. I'm just a dumb kid. And can't do anything right. I don't deserve such a perfect family. I... I... Was gonna give him back to you and go. I just... "

Billy's hand slides up and cradles the back of her neck. Then pets her back gently to soothe her. "You ain't going nowhere and neither is our baby."

CHAPTER THIRTY-SIX
The Prodigal Son

Matthias kissed his wife goodbye and took off. His mother could be anywhere. The fact he was having to do this at all infuriates him all the more. His mother isn't completely to blame. His father didn't understand how her hormones were in overdrive, especially around an infant. He would have thought after all this time with wolves, David would know better. He also wonders what is going on between them that his father would deny his mother another pup. But Matthias was not about to forgive his mother for trying to butt in on Billy and Shelley's baby. That poor girl couldn't even defend herself. All his mother was going to do was force Billy to fight her or abandon the pack.

Given the choice, Mathias would have left the pack and set out on his own. Early in his marriage, his mother had tried something similar with Bridget and his firstborn. He solved that problem by moving to his wife's pack. In the Appalachian Pack, the smaller packs aren't so separate they can't mingle. The hierarchy could get tricky, but he knew he couldn't just leave. His mother was tapped for the Appalachian Pack Alpha tourney. The founding Alpha had passed away, and the elders were flabbergasted that the rules for replacing an Alpha had not been modernized. To keep the peace, they are holding to the old ways, but limiting who can compete. When his mother told him she had been picked as one of the three, his plans shifted entirely to learning from her about being Alpha. Should she win, she would be the Alpha of the Appalachian Pack, essentially making her the leader over all packs from the Mississippi River to the East Coast in the United States. Should she lose, they will be in mourning for her death.

Either way, he was about to become Alpha of the Coeh pack.

He sighs and shifts down into his wolf form. Shaking out his fur, he tries to decide which way to go. Matthias looks like a massive black shadow with piercing blue eyes next to his SUV. He turns and takes off for his parents' house. Their kind can run at speeds as fast as any car on the interstate. He reaches the edge of their yard in no time. Silently, he sniffs around for the freshest impression of her scent. It takes several minutes, but then he's on her trail. It felt good to run like this. His mother was moving fast, he could tell by the broken foliage and the paw prints. She wasn't trying to hide. He thinks she is being terribly reckless. It's not out of the rules to kill a competitor before the arena fight. This spurs him on faster.

The hours pass and he is pretty sure he is well into Virginia at this point. Matthias slows a tad and sniffs for her scent. This causes him to veer west. He has every intention of giving her a run for her money as Alpha now. This is bullshit, running off into the night, and acting a fool. His rage is escalating.

It's well past midnight when he finds her. He stops dead, watching the clearing she is in. She had shifted back, and her pale skin in the moonlight made her look ethereal. She is on her knees, and her long, dark hair is draped over her shoulder, hiding her face from him. Her body is shuddering, and he lowers himself, resisting the urge to whine. Susie is distressed, more than he would expect for a spat between his parents. When she shifts her weight, he gets a good look at her face and sees she is crying.

His mother, crying.

His ears fold down in anxiety. He cannot recall the last time he ever saw his mother look so vulnerable. His rage begins to ebb with the sight of his mother. He had two choices. He could enter the clearing and talk with her or he could go back and talk with his father. His father would be the easier of the two.

"Matthias, it's not polite to lurk," she finally quips without looking at him. With a huff, he curls his lip, irritated that she knew he was there. He still doesn't know how she does it. "I'm your mother. I would know your scent anywhere." She is wiping her cheeks and starting to look for where he might actually be.

He gives her another snort as he eases into the clearing, still in wolf form. Slowly, he approaches Susie and lowers his head in deference to her.

"Oh, come on. I'm not Alpha here." She gently reaches up and runs her fingers through his fur. "I take it your father sent you?"

He sits on his hind legs and wags his tail but doesn't change just yet. At least in this form, he can hide his irritation and anger with her. For the moment, he feels like she could use a shoulder to cry on more than a lecture.

Susie raises a brow at him.

It's amazing to him how fast she hides her emotions behind the cocky Alpha. It makes him wonder just how much she hides from everyone all the time.

"I fucked up royally," she admits.

Matthias shifts then sits next to her. The memory of when he was thirteen, and she took him out to shift pops into his mind. He was over the moon at being a werewolf, then terribly shy at being naked when he shifted back. He isn't shy now. Susie had always been there for him and made sure he wanted for nothing. He remembers her standing between him and his father when he was little. This woman, who is beautiful, strong, and terribly pig headed, had always made sure her boys had the best and felt loved. He felt guilty about all the ways he planned to attack her on the run out here and rubbed his chin before he says anything. "Yeah, ya did. So what are you gonna do about it?" He gives her a side glance.

She growls, having expected him to coddle her. He wouldn't be her son if he did.

"You can growl all you want. But you're out of line, Momma, and you know it. She is a kid. One that's been abused. Everyone in her life who was supposed to protect and love her has hurt and abandoned her. And here you come, big bad Alpha, doing whatever you damn well please with her baby." Matthias gives her a pointed look.

Susie starts to protest and defend herself.

"Save it. I know how you think pack should work. You're wrong, Momma, and she ain't pack. Hell. The poor girl's probably suffering from postpartum. Have you even asked her how she is doing?" His piercing gaze levels with Susie's and she narrows her eyes at him. He looks so much like David when he's angry. She opens her mouth to speak again, then closes it.

Susie looks away from him and mutters, "No. I haven't. She is fine."

"She is not fine, and you know it. Or you wouldn't be out here being lectured by your son 'cause you ran out on your husband." He gives her a faint, tight-lipped smile. He swears this woman is so damn stubborn. "What's really going on?" He decides to get to the bottom of the matter. Just lecturing her and hugging it out doesn't work with Susie. He knows there is something else going on. She had talked with him extensively about Shelley. He had been tasked with finding out what happened that brought her to Susie's door, and what he found infuriated him. "You know she is not uncle Silus, right? That prick threw her out like trash, Momma. Her own damn mother hasn't come looking for her in how many months?" He has no idea that Billy took Shelley to see Paula and Silus. "Jasper and Faye are in Texas. You want me to put her on a bus to go live with them? How do you think that'll work out?"

"Fuck you, Matthias. Of course I know she is not Silus. What the fuck kind of monster do you think I am?"

"The kind that threatened to take away the only thing bringing happiness to that little girl." He doesn't back down. "Then had the gall to act so hurt by it, that your favorite son finds you crying in the middle of nowhere Virginia." He figures he might as well put the elephant in the clearing down.

Susie has been pushed to the limit. She is the fucking Alpha here. Not only is that little girl challenging her authority, but David's taking her side. Couple that with her son now calling her a monster and attacking her for having feelings. Without hesitation, she is shifting up into her werewolf form and lunging for him.

Matthias's eyes widen and he barely rolls out of her slash as he shifts into his werewolf.

Seconds later, the massive, nearly eight foot tall pitch black werewolf is snarling at the seven foot dark auburn colored werewolf. It is a clash of titans as they lunge at each other. Claws are swinging, teeth snapping. Susie throws him into the tree line, causing the trunks to crack and groan under his weight. He recovers quickly and throws her down on the ground hard enough to make a Susie-wolf sized dent in the soft dirt.

Around and around the two of them go until they are both standing in the clearing, panting at each other. Both are bloody and sweat covered. He doesn't shift down until she does. She is covered in bruises and scratches from his attacks, as is he.

"Feel better?" He breathes out. "It doesn't change that you are in the wrong, Momma. You need to make it right. Don't make Billy have to pick between you and his mate, like you did me." The resentment is heavy in his voice.

"David doesn't want me anymore," she finally blurts.

"What makes you say that, Momma?" He doesn't mock her or

dismiss her. If his mother says something like that, it's worth listening to.

"He doesn't want to have sex anymore. He's working all the time. He rutted with Carolyn the past two ruttings. And today... He," Susie frowns and clenches her jaw. "Not important. You're right. I need to make it right with Billy and Shelley. Then I need to focus on the Alpha fight." Susie walls herself up and doesn't thrust her personal problems on her son. It's not his problem to solve. It's killing Susie inside. If she wins the Alpha fight, she'll give David the option to stay here without her.

Matthias frowns at that response. His mother is shutting herself off from him after letting her feelings show for the briefest of moments. He believed his parents were madly in love, and happy. Seeing his mother's face makes him question that. She looked crushed for those few fleeting seconds. "You want me to run back with you?" He asks gently.

"Nah, baby. I'm sure your wife'll be happy to have you home. I'm just going to stay long enough to get my head on right, then head back."

CHAPTER THIRTY-SEVEN
The Key To A Good Marriage

By the time Susie is walking back onto her property line it's nearly five in the morning. She knows David will be asleep and doesn't want to face him. She is about ten feet from the tree line when she changes back into her human form to pull on the clothes she abandoned earlier.

"You and I need to talk," the deep voice of her Beta, Jacob, fills the air. While Matthias thinks he is an expert stalker, Jacob actually is. He had tracked Matthias as he took off after his mother and followed her home silently. Mostly to make sure nothing happened to her. He knows her son isn't the right person to talk to her. Whatever is going on with Susie, she needs to get her head on straight. "I don't know what the fuck is going on between you and David, but you need to fix it."

"I can't do this right now."

"The fuck you can't. You listen here, Susie. Your boys are in a tizzy. Tommy's bringing that girl to the house. And you're runnin' all over Hell's half acre. You're the God Damn Alpha."

Her eyes narrow and she squares up to put him in his place when he simply turns his head and submits.

"Don't get all riled up. I'm trying to help you, you pig-headed woman."

Her lip curls, but she relents.

"Now. Come on. Let's go talk." He motions and they walk down the path to the lake. A few minutes later they are sitting, looking out over the water. "Talk to me, Susie," he pleas. He had been honored when Susie tapped him to be her Beta. Jacob had always put money on it being the man that had been jockeying for her affection alongside the Baxter boys. He took it seriously and has always been there to keep her on the right path. Tonight is no different.

"I," she hesitates. For the first time in her and David's relationship, she is struggling to overcome that he is not a wolf. His philosophy has always been that he was born a human, he's dying a human. Susie found it was cute and adorable until fourteen years ago. He started using protection during the Rutting. They fought about it. Then neither took part in The Rutting, and it raised suspicion in the pack. Susie tried once, with another wolf. David's jealousy got the better of him. They were separated for a short while until her Beta went to David and beat some sense into him. Susie was too prideful to go to the man, but that had been years and years ago. Three years ago, she approached him again about having another pup, and he said no, without hesitation. Susie sighs. "I think David's done. Things ain't been right between us for a while. Tonight he turned his back on me and walked away."

"Damn, Susie," he frowns and puts an arm around her. Jacob doesn't believe for a second David would ever leave Susie. He can see it has Susie in a bad place, which concerns him. "You need to fix this shit with him. You go into that arena with your head all messed up, you're going to get killed."

"I know. I damn well know what's at stake. I'm not worried about that fight." She snarls at him. Her nerves are shot and temper short.

"You haven't even told him yet, have you?" Jacob grumbles.

"No. Between Shelley, the baby, and dealing with his fucking brother's bikers, I haven't had time to. He doesn't have time for me either."

Jacob knows better, and he nudges her. "Don't do that. He's your mate, Susie. He has a right to know. And you're being a damn coward about it."

She cuts him a side glance. "What the fuck is he going to do about it? Nothing. He's a fucking human. He can't do anything about it. Other than be pissed I agreed and have another reason to not want to be with me anymore." The next thing Susie knows, Jacob is throwing her in the lake. He shifted so fast she was in the air before she could respond. The yelp she lets out would be comical, other than her Beta just attacked her. Susie drops below the surface then comes back up furious.

Jacob is belly laughing on the shore. "You should see the look on your face. Oh God," he laughs harder. "Don't kill me," he holds his hands up. "You... deserved... it." He has tears in his eyes.

She is stalking toward him, dripping wet. The more he laughs the more she wants to murder him. She is pretty sure steam is coming from her ears. Her fists are clenched and she teeters between ignoring him by storming into the house and putting him back in his place.

He stands and wipes the tears from his eyes as he reduces his laughter to a chuckle. "Now you listen here, Susie. I love you to pieces. I'm giving you until five pm tomorrow to pack your shit. You and David are going to the boathouse. You ain't allowed back until your shit is right. He ain't treating you right, and you ain't treating him right. Fuck him, fight him, turn him. I don't care. But when I come to collect you for the tourney, you had better be prepared."

"You can't kick me out. It's my pack." Susie whines in surprise. The low growl she emits warning him that he has crossed a line.

"I can and will. When *you* made me Beta, *you* made it *my* job to protect *you* and *your* mate. That's what I'm doin'. You go to that house and get your answers. He'll either be with you, or he won't. And if he won't," he shrugs then, "Well, then you'll have closure and can move on." He's already moving away from Susie toward his house.

"Jacob!"

"Don't you Jacob me. Quit being such a pussy. You're the fucking Alpha, start acting like it." Jacob disappears into the tree line, leaving Susie by herself.

"Men," she snorts. She turns and makes her way into the house, stopping on the porch to strip down out of her wet clothes.

The house is quiet when she enters, other than the television running some terrible infomercial and David's light snoring in the recliner. Her eyes drift to the bottle of Jack Daniels well used on the table next to him. She continues down the hall and deposits the wet clothes in the washer before coming back. Scooping up the quilt that's piled on the couch, she opens it up. For a fleeting moment, she contemplates curling into his lap and pulling the blanket over the two of them. His cologne mixed with the whiskey sings to her, and in spite of her best efforts she is aroused. Susie wants him bad enough it hurts. His rejection to mating with her is eating her alive. It makes her clench her jaw and the bitter resentment fills her. She silently moves closer and gently drapes the quilt over him. Satisfied he is cared for, Susie turns on heel and leaves the room to go sleep in their bed.

David groans awake at about nine. The sun peeks through the window, burning against his cheek. He realizes he is covered up with the quilt. The television was on some morning news show and he ached from sleeping in the chair. His body is stiff and sore, not to mention his head reminds him he drained a fifth of whiskey. He can smell the bitter coffee wafting from the kitchen and staggers his way there. On the counter are two aspirin and a mug, waiting for him. He smiles. Only Susie would think to do that for him. God, he loves that woman, even if she makes it hard sometimes.

He pops the pills and pours himself a mug. His brow furrows as the house is rather quiet. It's downright peaceful without young Frances waking everyone up every few hours. He had to give that little girl props for being a good mother. Shelley goes to him every time he cries. He doesn't miss those days. It's too quiet as he makes his way into their bedroom, looking to see if Susie came back yet. He isn't expecting her. What he finds is Susie packing two large suitcases. A frown forms on his face as he watches her. Her brow has that cute crease she gets when angry and she looks like she hasn't slept a wink. Her hair is braided, and she is wearing fresh clothes. It's then he realizes she is putting his stuff into the suitcase.

"Mornin', beautiful," he rumbles in that sweet drawl of his.

"Mornin'," she murmurs before turning to go into their closet and retrieve more items. She returns with her stuff too, which only adds to his confusion.

"Need any help?"

"If you want to pack your bathroom stuff, that'd be great." He doesn't ask and turns to go into their master bathroom. Their travel bag sitting open with her things in it already. He grabs the anti-inflammatory the doc gave him for his shoulder, as well as making sure the pain patches are in the bag for when his back acts up. David checks to make sure he grabs all the normal items, brings the bag back, and sets it on the bed next to the suitcase. He knows better than to put it in the suitcase if she is not ready for it. He learned that lesson about thirty years ago.

David takes a seat on the bed, watching her.

Susie isn't meeting his gaze, and she is keeping herself focused on the task at hand.

He remains silent, enjoying the bitterness of the coffee as it helps to ebb the hangover brewing. David would rather leave her be until she is ready to confront him than force her and start a new fight. He can see his wife is anxious and still wound up from last night. He's not okay either.

She finishes putting their items in the suitcases and places the bathroom bag in one. With little effort, she zips them closed and sets them on the ground.

"Anything you need to do before we leave?"

"Nope. Where we headin'?" He stands then, taking one suitcase from her.

"Boat house. Jacob is kicking us out."

"And you let him?" His brow raises curiously.

"Well, he's not dead."

"Okay, well then I guess we're heading to the boathouse." He sets his half-drunk mug on the kitchen counter as they walk by. David fishes his phone out and texts his foreman that he's going to be out of town for a few days. The reply he gets tells him Billy already told him and said he was answering all questions until David got back. David cuts Susie a side glance, wondering what she is up to. He loads his suitcase in the back of the Suburban and takes hers from her to do the same. They're silent as they get into the Suburban. He doesn't ask anything further, as he starts up the truck and they roll out onto the highway.

CHAPTER THIRTY-EIGHT

It's My Baby Too

Billy and Shelley sit silently on the couch for hours before Billy's aunt finally came into the room to talk to them. "Miss Shelley, I'd be happy to watch your baby for you while you and Billy go sort this out." She doesn't move toward Frances, letting it be Shelley's decision what to do with the baby.

Shelley instinctively curls the baby closer to her at the mention of parting with him.

"I won't take him anywhere, and he'll be right how you left him with me. I thought it might be nice for you two to have some alone time tonight."

Billy frowns when Shelley doesn't respond at first. He is about to encourage her when she shifts and gets up.

His aunt gives a soft smile and takes the baby. "Now, you two get out of here for the night." She looks pointedly at Billy. "You best be on your best behavior, young man."

Billy stands and looks down at Shelley thinking she looks so beautiful in her disheveled state. He will never grow tired of looking at her.

Shelley catches a glimpse of herself when trying to wipe away old tears. Her cheeks flush pink and she hastily pulls her hair out of the loose ponytail to fix it. When she looks down at herself, she is in a pair of jeans, and her T-shirt has spit-up on it. Before Billy can do anything, she is yanking the T-shirt off and turning to rummage in her duffel bag. She retrieves a clean shirt and leaves the dirty one in the bag. Re-assembling her feeding bra, she pulls the shirt back on. Her cheeks are flaming red, and she is having trouble meeting his gaze.

His gaze is full of desire. His animal instincts are to mate with her again. Her very scent sends him into overdrive, and in her current state she smells doubly good. He pulls her into a kiss.

Shelley hesitates and shies at first. Her tender lips meeting his in confusion, and embarrassment.

"You are the most beautiful woman I have ever seen," he murmurs against her lips.

She was up on her toes and her eyes are closed from kissing him. The pink tint to her skin permanently in place with his affection.

"Where would you like to go?"

"Some place we can be alone," she finally responds. She eases back from him, he nods and the pair of them leave Tommy's house. Once outside, she stops, biting against her lip.

"What is it, Angel?" Billy looks down at her anxiously.

"It's just... I... Nevermind. It's dumb." She waves him off.

"No. Tell me," he insists.

"It's just... Well... I heard Tommy talking with his momma about how, running it off is probably the best thing for Momma Coeh to do. And... Well... I can't run like a wolf or anything. So... I thought... maybe you could... carry me. And we could... you know... go somewhere private, far away from everyone." She turns bright red at the request and Billy's expression is full of happiness and surprise.

He realizes she means to ride him while he runs. He could easily carry her, and he nods. "You'll have to hold on to my clothes. They don't shift with us." He strips down right there on the porch, which makes her cover her eyes and turn around.

A few seconds later she yelps in surprise when his cold nose touches her hand. She turns back around and scoops up his clothing he had folded.

His tail is wagging happily as he watches her. He lowers himself to let her mount onto him like a horse.

When he stands back up, she tucks his clothes under her T-shirt and leans down, lacing her fingers into his fur she nuzzles him. There is something insanely comforting in feeling his fur.

"Hold on," his voice fills in her mind and when he feels her squeeze against him he takes off at a dead run. He doesn't run anywhere near as fast as he can, but he is moving fast enough she has to cling to him and bury her face against him to keep from being whipped by the stray underbrush they are zipping through. She was surprised to hear his voice. David and Susie could communicate that way, but Shelley wasn't sure how to do it. She had so many questions about how they would be together. Shelley felt like she didn't deserve to have any happiness for ruining his life. Her eyes flutter closed, and she tries to push the thoughts from her mind to just enjoy this romp through the forest.

He runs fast and hard. She doesn't know how happy this time makes him. Her clinging to him and he just running free. Billy feared Shelley would reject his wolf's side when he discovered they are mates. Truthfully, he had no idea how to handle her. Her emotions are always extreme. He can't fathom how she functions with all that going on inside of her. He had tried to comfort her and show her he would be there for her, but that obviously wasn't right. He has been failing her in every sense of being her mate, in his opinion. Guilt washes over him and he finally slows. They had been running for an hour. He brings her to a small cabin. It was abandoned long ago in the national forest that butts up to the Coeh property. Billy spruced up the cabin for sleeping in when he goes running. He first came here as a teenager to get away from his brothers. Crouching down, he waits to move until she has her footing.

In his wolf form, he still stands just under Shelley in height. Their eyes meet for several moments before he nuzzles her. She fishes out his clothing and sets them on the ground for him. He motions with his head and she nods, moving toward the cabin. She glances back to see his bare bottom being covered by his jeans and underwear. Then he is to her and is guiding her into the cabin and leads her right to the couch. Billy rubs his hand over his face. He wasn't sure where to begin, or what to say to her. He is furious with his mother and wants to rip something to pieces. For all his pleasantness, Billy has a deep-seated rage that he keeps in check. It surfaced when that guy hit her at the bar, and again when he learned what Tommy had done to her. He promised himself that Shelley would never feel that rage turned on her. It breaks his heart that Shelley could be afraid of him.

"Billy, maybe your momma's right," she hiccups. "And I should let you and your family be happy..." Shelley trails off, not wanting to say the rest of her thought which is to mean they would be happy without her around.

Billy growls, then sighs as she curls up. "No. God damn it, Shelley, no. You're *my* mate. You were made for me! I was made for you! Meeting you was the best thing that has ever happened to me." He whines. Shelley gets the pouty frown that makes her absolutely adorable and he is getting distracted with wanting to kiss the pout away. "But this ain't gonna work if you and I can't talk to each other, baby girl. How am I supposed to fix it, if I don't know it's broken?" He is frustrated, and she furrows her brow at him.

"Don't you give me that, Billy Coeh," she huffs. He blinks and looks over to see her blazing angry look. "I did try to talk to you! I tried to tell you everything that was going on. And you know what you told me?" Her tone waivers as tears threaten her lashes again. "You told me to not be so paranoid. That your momma loves Frances and is just happy to have a baby in the house. You told me to just let her feed him in the middle of the night. You told me that your momma wasn't trying to take our baby from me. You took *her* side," she crosses her arms. To pour silver into the wound, "Now she wants to go before a judge to take him away."

"Well, that's complete and utter bullshit," Billy growls back. "Because any damn judge I can think of would leave that baby with his hard working papa. And his hard working papa ain't gonna be without his baby girl momma. So there! Let her take us before a judge. We'll win." He snorts.

"Oh. That so? She very much has no intention of takin' *you* before a judge. She wants me gone. So you can find a proper girl. You know... One that... your momma approves of." She huffs again.

"Damn it, girl! Your damn ovum... My damn seed... Meaning that it's *our* baby," his hands motioning between the two of them. "Therefore, you can't have the baby with a parent without the other parent. It just don't work." Billy's frustration is high, and he doesn't understand how his mother could think she is doing the right thing here.

"Single parents happen all the time, Billy! It's just here that people are weird about their families. Like all of you are one big family, just in different houses. It's creepy the way she thinks she has as much say as I do, when it comes to Franky. For whatever reason, all of you big, bad, scary werewolves," her hands flailing in the air for dramatic emphasis, "Just bow down to do whatever she wants. Making me have to be the bad guy who wants to know where the fuck *our* son is at all times."

Billy gives a heavy sigh. "Okay, I think we need to rewind and talk about what it is to be a werewolf, and what the pack is." He pauses to see if Shelley is willing to listen to what he has to say next.

CHAPTER THIRTY-NINE
Promises & Compromises

Shelley is prickly and raw from the day's events and doesn't want to hear a damn word anyone has to say. She realizes that Billy is trying to talk to her and work it out. She wants to just throw a tantrum and fling herself into the pity party of a pillow, but he is right, they are in this together. Even though she feels like she is on an island, alone, she nods for him to continue.

"Okay, where to begin? So, you know that feelin' you have when you look at Frances? That overwhelming need to protect, love, and adore?"

"I do,"

"The Alpha feels that for *every* member of the pack. You want to do what's best for everyone, even if what you think is best doesn't coincide with what the individual believes." He holds his hand up to prevent the angry reply he can see all over her face. "To allow an Alpha to do what is needed, in addition to the normal abilities a werewolf gets, an Alpha gains the ability to command other wolves. Momma can literally make us do what she wants us to do when she wants us to do it. Of course, there are drawbacks to her when she does it. But when she does use the command, it makes the person on the receiving end unable

227

to disobey. It's a form of mind control."

Shelley furrows her brow, thinking back to the arguments Momma Coeh and she have had. There was this awful sense of dread in the room, but Shelley didn't feel compelled to do what Susie was barking at her. "I think there's something wrong with me, then." She whispers. "She can't make me obey."

"That's probably because you're not a wolf, and not a member of the pack yet. The fact you felt the push is probably being mated to an Alpha. 'Cause regular humans? They'd just laugh in her face. It's crucial to have an Alpha for a pack. Without an Alpha, our kind turns rabid and become beastly, just like you see in the movies. She is more than in charge. She is the glue that holds us all together. She loves all of us with everything she has. Even you." He points at Shelley.

Shelley snorts in disbelief, but the way Billy looks, talking about his mother makes her jealous. She wishes her parents loved her like that. "I get all that. Still ain't right, Billy. I ain't ever gonna get better at bein' a momma if she won't let me be the momma. I need you to be there for me. I'm drownin'. I'm sad all the time. Frances hates me. I don't have any friends. Your Momma hates me too. I have to start school next week and I just know she is going to take Frances away from me." The words spilling out from Shelley sound fragile and scared.

Billy huffs in frustration and mutters. "She is not going to take Frances away. We are going to talk to Momma together and I will not fail you again. I promise." He pulls her into his lap, nuzzling her as she curls into him. "It's gonna be alright, Angel." His voice is low and gentle. Billy enjoys the silence that follows for several beats before he continues. "I want you to talk to the doc. What you're feelin' ain't right. Momma had plenty of babies after me and she never talked about feeling this way." He gently rubs her back. "We'll get through this Shelley... together."

Shelley relaxes and nods in response.

"Guess what?"

"What?"

He gets that easy going smile of his. "It's just the two of us here. No Alphas. No crying babies. And I got a nice warm fur coat for you to nestle into." Shelley's cheeks flush as she wasn't thinking about a fur coat when he mentioned them being alone. Then the surprised and mildly worried look on her face makes him laugh as he immediately knows where her mind went with the fur coat. "I'm talking about sleep," he laughs, and his cheeks turn bright red. "Shelley, as sexy as you are and as hard as it is to not just have my way with you, you're not old enough. What happened at The Rutting should have waited until you were."

Shelley frowns. "Are you seriously going to make me wait until my eighteenth birthday?"

"Well, technically, no. Not until we're mated properly." He looks sheepish. "That can't happen until you're eighteen and graduated from high school. Mates have to be considered adults in the pack. The rules were put there to keep hormonal teenage werewolves from doing really dangerous stuff."

Shelley huffs. "That's not fair. I'm adult enough." Petulance is laced in her reply. "Adult enough to have your baby."

"That right there is the *exact* reason that rule is in place." He chuckles and pulls her into a tender kiss. "Now, I say we get some much needed rest. How about you?"

"Fine," she mutters. The idea of uninterrupted sleep does sound amazing to her.

With her agreement, Billy scoops her up and carries her the few feet to the little rug in front of the fireplace. Then sets her down gently as he begins to strip.

Shelley gets this somewhat devious look on her face and waits for him to shift into wolf form before she strips as well. Not stopping at her T-shirt. Instead, stripping down until she is completely naked. The small whine from Billy lets her know that he definitely noticed. She curls into his massive form, getting comfortable on the floor and using him as a body pillows. It is not long before she is idly tugging on his ear in a petting motion as she drifts to sleep. He curls more, so he is around her, putting his muzzle on his tail, asleep soon after.

The next morning Billy wakes to find her sitting in his circle, gently petting him. He doesn't open his eyes, enjoying the feel of her hand running along him. He cannot help himself, and his tail wags at her touch, tickling her as it brushes along her. Her musical giggle fills the cabin and makes his heart swell.

With a devious a grin, she scratches the back of his ear harder.

He tries to resist. He tries so hard, but then he's leaning into her and his hind leg thumps rapidly against the floor.

This makes her laugh outright, then she does something he never expected her to do. She wrestles with him. She has him at a disadvantage and gets his belly exposed in no time, much to Billy's surprise. This cannot stand! He can't be defeated by belly scritches! He gives a playful growl and pins her.

The squeal she makes is hilarious. "Billy Coeh!" She teases. "Bad boy!" She then boops his nose like he's a pet.

He lets his tongue loll and licks her in retaliation.

She squeals and squirms again.

The pair of them are rolling around on the floor in a tangle of limbs and fur until he has her pinned again under his now human form. They are both breathless and flush, gazing at each other with him straddling her legs and holding her hands above her head, forcing her to arch up to him. The way her lips are parted, and how her chest rises and falls is making him hard. He wants her bad enough he can taste it.

The mood in the room shifts, and she gently frees her hands from his grasp. The sultry smile she gives him makes him raise a brow, now curious to what she is thinking. Then she wriggles under him. Confusion washes over him until her head disappears under his chest. He feels the shy lick of her tongue on the tip of his manhood. He pushes himself up, supporting himself by his hands as he looks down. His cock swells in response. He knows he should stop her. He starts to ease up further when she curls her fingers around the shaft, albeit awkward and a little tight for his liking. He stops retreating and twitches in her hand, instinctively pushing forward.

Billy is torn. He just told her they shouldn't be doing this, but damn her warm, wet mouth sweetly taking him further in is pushing any sane thought he might have had from his mind. His massive hand comes down and laces into her hair, tilting her head to the proper position. His grip firmly guides her in bobbing her head on his cock. At first, it is slow and gentle. He lets her get used to his size in her mouth.

"Breathe through your nose," he murmurs.

When she finally draws in the sharp gasp of breath and her mouth relaxes on him, he pumps more. His eyes close, and with the shift in her head he pushes further into her mouth, needing his cock sheathed in her sweet mouth. The soft whimpers from her, coupled with the suckling noises makes him harder still.

"Shelley," he moans.

Her delicate fingers trail down his shaft to tease the swaying sack below it as she allows him to move her head at the pace he wants. Her other hand grips onto his thigh to steady herself. She feels it then, the way his entire cock bounces in her mouth and throbs against the steady sucking. He is pushing more and more into her mouth, and she is starting to gag as he presses against the back of her throat. Billy's lost in the ecstasy of her sweet mouth on his cock and the sharp tingle as her fingers knead his balls. His hips are pumping steadily until he feels the surge of his orgasm. His grip tightens in her hair and he thrusts, pulling her head against him.

"Fuck," he moans when his cock pushes right into her throat and it milks him so tight. Her little fist is lightly hitting against his thigh as he holds her there, pulsing into her throat, forcing her to swallow him. He finally comes back to reality and eases back, bringing his head into her mouth. He feels guilty as she inhales sharply through her nose. The feeling of her mouth on his head makes him shiver. Everything is sensitive, and he eases back more, reluctantly drawing himself from her perfect mouth. He looks down at her, his gaze still full of lust.

If she keeps teasing him like this, he isn't going to make it to her eighteenth birthday.

CHAPTER FORTY

Making Waves

The car ride to the lake house was quiet. Only the sound of the radio fills the cabin of the truck. Neither David nor Susie felt the need to talk. When they pulled into the gravel driveway that winds its way to the lake, David glances at Susie. She hasn't looked at him once. He can see the way her face is drawn into a small frown and is pretty sure she hasn't been to sleep. She is out of the vehicle before he can kill the engine. There are still no words between them as they hoist the bags out of the back and stalk into the cabin.

This is going to be a rough couple of days.

David watches her move about the cabin. He helps her clean it up, unpack, and they check the kitchen to see it has already been stocked. This makes him realize someone has planned this for some time and he wonders how bad it must be for other pack members to intervene. He didn't think he and Susie were in such a bad place.

The rest of the day is pretty quiet. Susie handles pack business over the phone until he can hear her arguing with Jacob that results in her being hung up on. The last thing coming through the speaker was, "Get your shit straight. Then you can be Alpha."

It made David chuckle. What drew a frown from him is that the rest of the evening was pretty cold between them. It felt like they were two strangers trapped in this cabin together. He didn't want to be the first to back down. He knows he is right about Billy and Shelley. He could see the look on her face when she looked at him. She is good at hiding her emotions from everyone else, but not him. There is a hurt there he can't place.

The next morning David wakes to find himself alone in the bed. Coffee had been made, and she is outside, down by the lake. He frowns again. She didn't even kiss him good morning. He pours a mug of coffee and enjoys it before packing a cooler from the beer in the fridge, and stuff to make sandwiches later. It's after ten when he finally comes walking down the path. She hasn't moved from the spot she is sitting in. He doesn't say a word to her as he walks by. He pulls the tarp back on the pontoon boat, then checks everything over to make sure it's in working order. He secures the cooler, then he starts up the engine. Giving Susie a look, "You comin'?" his voice fills her mind.

She cracks an eye open and looks in his direction. With a nod, she pushes up onto her feet and joins him on the boat. A few minutes later they are out in the sunshine and chugging along at a good clip. His eyes keep drifting to her sitting on the bench seat. He hadn't realized she was wearing nothing more than a pair of shorts and a sports bra. She must have been training for that Alpha tourney in Tennessee. He was proud of her for being tapped for the position and hoped she gets it. Once he gets them secure out in the middle of the lake, he kills the engine and fishes out a couple of beers. He pops the caps and brings her one, then takes the seat across from her. He takes a long swig of his beer before he starts.

"You always knew I was an idiot. I think that's part of the reason you married me." He gives her a wry grin.

Susie was not expecting that, and she snorts her beer through her nose. "What?" coughing and laughing. She continues once under control, "What makes you say that? I always thought you played dumb."

"Oh, I have my moments of sheer brilliant stupidity," taking another long drag to collect his thoughts. "Take, for example, the moments that have led us here."

Susie's gaze darkens at his comment and he can see her body language. "Oh?" She carefully replies. She is trying to gauge where he is going with this.

Much to David's surprise, there is fear in her eyes, in spite of her calm demeanor.

"Mhm hmm," he then sighs. "Why does it feel like we can't talk anymore? We used to talk about everything. Now, it just feels like the boring daily shit is all that ever gets brought up. So here I am. Say what you're gonna say. I can take it."

Susie takes a long draw on her beer, thinking about his comments. Her gaze never leaves him as she assesses body language.

He can see the conflict between the woman and the Alpha going on without so much as a word. Until, "Just felt like there wasn't much else to say after the last time we talked about anything important. You were pretty clear on what you wanted. I didn't feel like pesterin' you over it."

"Nuh uh. Nope. You do not get to be vague about this one. It's just you and me out here, Susie. If you don't start, I will." His eyes narrow in challenge. That was completely the wrong way to say that cause she sits up, and he knows that posture. She is about to dig in.

"Go on then. Obviously, *you* got somethin' you want to say." He can see it again, that flash of fear in her eyes.

"That baby ain't yours," he looks at her pointedly.

To which she rolls her eyes and she nods. "I agree."

"Then why the fuck are you treating him like he's yours?"

"I'm treating *our* grandson like he is our grandson. I took him to fucking quilting and showed him off to the pack so she could sleep. Excuse me for being a proud fucking grandmother!"

"If you're so damn proud, then why'd you threaten to take her baby?" His words cut through her like a silver dagger and she turns to look out over the water.

"I was angry, and out of line," she mutters.

"What are you gonna do about making it right?" He presses.

Susie frowns then and looks at him without saying a word. Her expression grows cold and impassive as she walls up her emotions.

"Not sure yet. I'll take care of it before the tourney. Anything else?" Her voice is even and firm, but she is reeling on the inside.

"Oh yeah, there's more. I know you'll make it right for that girl. Now. What's got you twisted up like a pretzel on the inside? Your emotions are all over the place." He isn't going to let her weasel out of the rest of this conversation.

She sips her beer, ignoring him for the moment. She mulls over how to tell him the tourney is to the death. "Ain't nothin' you gotta worry about in a few weeks. Just stressed about the tourney. I'll be moving up to Virginia when I take over the Appalachian pack, you won't have to worry about me bein' damn emotional then." Her voice is soft and broken sounding.

"Susie Jeanette Coeh. You're a damn fool woman if you think I'm gonna buy that bullshit," he snarls.

She whips her head up at him using her full name and narrows her eyes. "What? You'll be able to retire in peace. 'Cause I'll either be Alpha or dead. Take your pick."

The spike of emotional turmoil that rockets between them nearly takes her breath away as David's expression changes entirely. She gives a bitter, small laugh.

"Oh, no. You don't get to be so damn concerned now. You walked away from me. You pulled away from me. You're the one that's been walkin' around like we're dead for the past four years. Leaving me to just focus on runnin' the pack and trying to figure out how to fucking rein in all the little bitches that want to fuck you. But, it's emotional Susie. It's way outta line Susie. It's fucking Susie who's stepping in that ring to fight for our packs and let you keep pretending you're older than you are. Heaven forbid, I get emotional thinking of what happens to everyone if I lose. Excuse me for wanting more kids and watching you reject me year after year like it's no big deal. You obviously have gotten what you wanted from this marriage. Time to hang up the hard hat, drink your beer, and just tell me to fuck off." Susie's voice is rising to that dangerous tone a woman takes when she is getting beyond reason.

"Nuh uh. NO! You don't get to throw that kid shit back at me. We talked about it. I gave you seven, strong, healthy pups. You're just pissy because I don't want to become a wolf and I'm getting old on you. I'm allowed to get old, damn it. It was damn hard raising those boys when little miss perfect Alpha was running around over Hell's half acre, reining in a bunch of mutts that weren't even her flesh and blood. I have worked thirty years of hard labor to provide a good life for us and to make our boys happy. To make you happy. So yeah, I have earned the damn right to get old. Yes, my back hurts. Yes, my joints hurt. I have earned the right to have pain. It's part of growing old. While I still have another fifteen to twenty years of work under my belt, or more, you aren't allowed to sit there and tell me to suck it up buttercup when you..." he gets silent. Tears well in his eyes, and "Damn it woman, I worry every day about what's going to happen to you when I die. All I want to do was enjoy our life with each other after the boys grew up and move out. I miss us. I mean, I want give you a good fifteen, twenty years before I became too decrepit to enjoy life with you. While you think I'm a young whippersnapper, I'm past the age of rearing young, bucking pups."

Susie says nothing at first. He cut her right to the core again. She couldn't even run away from him. It's the same conversation they had several years ago when she wanted another pup. He's breaking her heart as he rejects her wolf again. Her jaw clenches and she stiffens before she can get herself under control. Setting the beer aside she moves to her feet and begins to pace on the small boat.

"I'm sorry I'm not human," she whimpers out. Her cheeks flushing with shame. "I didn't realize I was torturing you so much." Her voice is so small as she shifts her weight again. "This was a mistake. I... I..." She turns to open the gate and to jump in the water to flee.

CHAPTER FORTY-ONE
Predator & Prey

David grabs her wrist and prevents her from running. His calloused hand grips hard enough it would hurt a more delicate woman. He knows she could easily tear herself free of him. "We're not finished with this conversation. I think it's one the two of us need to have."

"Ain't nothing left to say. You reject my kind and want to live your days happy. I'll oblige."

"What I'm trying to say is I love you, you stupid, beautiful, bull-headed, strong-willed, amazing woman. I love you. I love everything about you. The fact you are so strong. So amazing when it comes to corralling all the assholes in the pack. Handling and wrangling your children. You are perfect. To live my days happy, you have to be in them." He emphatically pleas. "Last I checked, you literally make the choice of being a wolf just that, a choice. While I love you, I prefer to stay human. It doesn't mean I don't like that our boys are wolves. It doesn't mean I don't like that you're a wolf. All it means is that I would prefer to not be one."

The overwhelming sadness that fills her is perplexing to him. He can feel her emotions full on, which is rare. Susie generally keeps herself walled away. The despair and pain at his words. A sense of profound loneliness. She knew this would be a problem when they fell in love all those years ago. Her father had tried to warn her. He even had tried to forbid her from being with David, or Silus. She had thought he would change his mind when he saw how the boys were as wolves, or that he would want to be with her longer.

"I love you," she breathes out in a whine.

She leaves the rest unsaid. She would not guilt him into becoming a wolf. It is his choice, and while it will destroy her, she will never make him stay with her.

"I'll be fine. It's just the tourney. It'll all be done in a few weeks and things will go back to normal. I promise. We'll be alright."

"No, we're not going to be alright," he says while still holding her wrist. "With talk like that. It means you've given up on me. I very much haven't given up on you. You say I'm the one that's pulled away, but here we are, you willing to throw away everything that we've built. Just because I'm not going to live as long as you. It'll hurt. I ain't denying that, but it's natural. Even if I was a wolf, nothing says I can't just randomly find myself dead. We lose pack members every once in a while."

He turns her to face him, "Susie, I am as much a part of your pack as any wolf out there. I will always support you in the end. Just because I may think you've overstepped yourself, because you decided you know what's best for everyone, doesn't mean I'm going to disrespect you in public. I'm allowed to disagree. It's a perk of being your mate. The other day, when I walked back into my office you were in no mood to listen to me, or to talk like an adult about what's going on between you and that girl. If this is truly about you wanting another damn pup, then just be the fucking Alpha and rut me. I seem to recall more than one evening where your back was turned to me in bed."

What could Susie do? David was supposed to love and cherish her. They were supposed to be together forever and as he turns her back to face him, he doesn't say the sweet nothings to make her feel that love. No. David accuses her of being a selfish bitch, and of throwing away their relationship. He's back to lecturing her about their fucking grandson. She stood there, held so close she couldn't think. His scent filling her and making her want him. He could take this big, bad Alpha and make her feel as small as a child. "Fuck you, David. Fuck you and your high horse. You don't know shit. You know that? You think you're being some altruistic bastard by staying human. That it's some God given right to feel pain, and to suffer. Do you even fucking realize what happens to the mate left behind in pairs like ours? No. I cannot fucking believe you right now. You stand there like you're the only one with feelings. With needs. What the fuck am I supposed to think? *You* said you didn't want anymore kids. I respected that. Then *you* REJECTED me again by telling me you didn't want to rut anymore. Then you're rutting with fucking Carolyn! *You* throw in my face all that running around and you being left with the boys. Well, fuck me. Maybe I should have just let those fucking rogues destroy everything *you* worked so hard for. Maybe I should just let the boys prey on humans and make 'em all wolves. I mean we're just a bunch of *mutts* who should be put down, right?"

Her temper is flaring and she cannot believe him right now.

"So you want, Alpha Susie? You want me to really treat you like the bitch you are? Fine." Her demeanor shifts than and she narrows her eyes. "Get naked," she growls at him, using the Alpha command. Letting him feel the full breath of what she can do to him and never has before.

His eyes narrow, and his lips crush against hers. The next thing she knows she is being shoved into the water. As she bobs under the surface, she rips off her shorts and comes back up in time to see him drop trou to jump in after her. She growls in irritation, especially when he smirks at her.

"Catch me if you can." He turns and starts swimming pretty

fast toward the dock in the distance.

Susie isn't amused, and David has pushed her to a point he may regret later. The inky blackness of her eyes suggests she is struggling to keep from shifting into her werewolf form. She watches him swim away and pushes off after him, swimming pretty damn fast. While he has that shit-eating grin, she looks murderous. She catches him about halfway there and snarls as she hooks her arm on him and starts dragging him back to the boat to do what she intended, which is to show him how and Alpha can be.

David's no wilting flower. He's in pretty top condition for a man his age and likes to make a big fuss of all his aches and pains. He is also an Alpha's mate. He wriggles free from her grasp in the water as she still hasn't shifted and takes off again.

His laughter making her blood boil. It's not long before she catches him again and tries to drag him off to where *she* wants to go. He will submit to her. He started this, he will damn well suffer its consequences.

He's wily and frees himself again, but heading towards the boat this time, still laughing at how mad she is.

She pursues slower this time, letting him go under the boat, trying to evade her. Smirking, climbs up onto the boat and quietly pads across, waiting for him to surface. Then she furrows her brow because she doesn't see him and it's been long enough he would not be breathing under water. Then she narrows her eyes and listens. She can hear him breathing under the boat. The longer he keeps this up, the higher her temper gets.

When he doesn't surface, he taunts her in a sing-song voice. "What? Big bad Alpha gonna let her prey get away?"

The growl he gets in response is anything but sexy. In fact, it's the menacing low growl she gets when dealing with asshole pack members. She jumps back in the water and the chase is on.

He sees her and turns to flee. He was just about to the shore when her hand wraps around his ankle and jerks him back. Try as he might, there is no getting free of her grip.

Her nails have extended to claws and are digging into his flesh as she tugs him back to the boat.

He struggles and fights properly. He's not a weak man.

When they are close enough to the boat, she jerks him forward and takes him by the throat. Her canines are extended, and she is in an in between state of human and werewolf.

He looks her dead in the eyes and says, "Kill me. Fuck me. Stop pussy footing around. Or do you like being my little bitch?" David is truly Silus's brother in knowing how to start shit.

She jerks her arm and throws him onto the boat like he's a doll.

He rolls with it, barely missing the table on the deck.

Before he can get his footing, she is on him, flipping him onto his back like a pancake on a griddle. Her fingers circle his throat and she pins him to the deck, leaning down and snarling against his tender flesh, threatening him with her canines. "Be a good boy and get hard for me," she growls. "And I might let you live."

He was already hard, but her threat definitely made him harder.

She leans up, using his neck to prop herself up as she thrusts her hips down on him. "Don't move," she orders him, using the Alpha voice again. She rolls her hips down to collide against him hard and fast. There is no love in this rutting. He wanted his Alpha bitch, he got her.

As he feels himself swell inside of her, he wants to put his hands on her waist, but the command holds him in place. He watches her riding him like a Valkyrie into battle. The way her lips part. How her breasts bounce with each buck of her hips on him. The way she looks primal and wild as she rides him. He can feel her emotions. Anger and hurt consume her. She stares him down as she offers no affection in riding him. Her breathing is erratic and quick. He can feel her tightening around his cock. He remains still underneath her, aching to thrust up into her and fill her until she screams his name.

"Cum, now," she issues the command, and his entire body tenses as he then gasps.

She didn't need to do it, he was almost there, but her eyes are blazing as she stares at him. She is the beast and the only thing he can do now is ride this out. He sees her teeth extend fully before she moved dangerously close to biting him. This is the cold stare of the Alpha staring down her pack member she is dominating. It's not Susie gazing at her husband when she gains control of herself enough to not force him into being a werewolf.

He erupts into her like a volcano and she rips herself off him. The Alpha command, used like that, takes its toll and she had held him under its spell for several minutes. She is shaking as she turns her back to him and tries to calm down. That's when David pounces and rolls her on her back.

"Now that you've gotten that out of your system," he smirks. "Let's do this right."

He goes to kiss her, and she turns her head.

David stops instantly and whispers, "Is that really what you want?" His voice is hitched and she can feel that overwhelming sense of rejection and hurt.

CHAPTER FORTY-TWO

Sun & Moon

"No," she confesses, looking back up at him. All of her fury punched out of her as if he had struck her.

His eyes are clouded with emotions as he gazes down at her.

She finally shifts back into human form and slams her lips into his. Needy and urgent is her kiss as she cries against him. "I want you, David. Forever. I need you. You're my moon and stars," she whimpers against him between kisses. "I can't do this without you."

He doesn't move, keeping her pinned underneath him. His heart both beats faster with joy at her words and breaks at how vulnerable she sounds. He doesn't dare ruin this moment or take away from her words as he gazes down at her.

She swallows hard. "It hurts that you don't want to stay with me," she whimpers. There is a reason the Alpha command isn't used very often. She is trembling underneath him and there is a lightness to her voice. She curls against him and he holds her, letting his weight cover her. "There is a very real chance I will lose the fight in Tennessee. The fight is to the death. In a few weeks, I'll either be Alpha of the Appalachian pack, or dead. After today, I realize how much you hate it all. It's too late to back out, and it's a chance to make a real difference in a lot of wolves' lives. I was convinced you were done with me, and it's been tearing me up. You've rutted with all these young pups, and I can feel you liked it, but when it was me talkin' about rutting, you were sore and tired. Now that girl. I've screwed it all up, and Billy's gonna run away like Matthias did. I just wanted to help her and show off how precious of a baby she made. Then... Then she doesn't respond to my command." She hiccups. "What kind of Alpha am I if I can't even make a human in my pack do what I say?"

David rolls onto his side then, pulling her into him. "You do have me," he murmurs against her. "I said 'til death do us part, and I meant it. With every fiber of my being." He kisses her. "While I may be your moon and stars, you are the wind on my cheeks and the sun in my sky. The idea of losing you is..." He stops, becoming verklempt. He has never, not once, in their thirty years of marriage thought he would ever face losing her. "I'm supposed to go first. It's the natural order of things."

He nuzzles her and she can feel the tears against his cheeks. "Don't you dare say you won't ever love again once I'm gone, Susie Coeh. You have too much damn life to live. I love you with all my heart and I will be here until the end." He reassures her. "And no, you haven't screwed up everything," He nips her shoulder. "All them kids ever wanted was a parent, or a grandparent. Someone to be proud of them. You gotta remember, with your kids, you gotta use kid gloves. They're fragile and easily broken."

Susie laughs then. "The irony of you throwing my own words back at me is not lost on me." She is referring to David's younger days when he was still trying to be like his father in raising his boys. "You remember when I told you those words? I had just gotten back from those attacks, and Matthias was being a normal four-year-old." She nestles to him, breathing easier with him holding her. "It wasn't pack members I was dealing with. We were so young when Daddy died and there ain't never been a female alpha, or an alpha that young. Hell, I'm still the youngest Alpha in recorded history." She adds. "I wasn't just out bossing people around, David. I was fighting, fighting for your life, our children's lives. And yes, for the pack. I killed more wolves than I ever care to remember to keep you all safe. There was a constant threat back then. They were following you to work. The kids to school. I couldn't let anything happen to you," she trails off.

"You never told me," he frowns. "I could've helped. Done something. Anything." He sounds disappointed that she didn't trust him to help her.

"David, you damn fool. You *did* help. You *do* help. You keep our family together. Without you, I would have had nothing to fight for and probably wouldn't be here now to fight with you. 'Sides. You're a human. I will never take you onto a battlefield with me."

"If Pop ever heard that I am hid behind your skirts, he'd tan both our hides and you know it." He laughs.

Susie laughs with him. "I didn't mean it like that. I meant, you would have been the target and I would have been forced to turn you, or suffer the loss of my soul mate." She holds her fingers up to silence him. "It's different for wolves, David. When you die, half of me is gone. It will take all of my strength to just will myself to live without you. It's the cruelest kind of joke that jealous bitch could play on us."

He studies her, their eyes mere inches apart. "What do you mean, gone?"

Susie bites against her lower lip, not wanting to fully explain it to him. He had made his choice and this would only guilt him into changing his mind. The intensity in his gaze, and the fear in his eyes causes her to relent. "Our souls are one, David. You are me, and I am you. It would be like trying to live in a house that a hurricane has ripped in half. There is no other that knows me as you do. Almost all wolves that lose their fated mate go feral or kill themselves."

"I... never knew." His voice is soft and solemn. "I never realized that would happen to you. For what it's worth, I truly am sorry you will have to suffer because of me. I know I could avoid all of that just by becoming a wolf. The boys love it. You love it." His voice is still soft. "Part of me always knew that you would outlive me, but I guess I never truly understood by how much or what it would cost you when I go."

"David. You will live another fifty years, easy. The only time I have seen a human mate die young, is when they're attacked. You aren't dying tomorrow, and I'm going to have to listen to you whine about your aching bones for years to come. That will be half of my life. I will live well into my hundreds provided I am not killed. The old leader of the Appalachian Pack was born before the Civil War. His mother is hundreds of years older than that and still Alpha of her pack." She kisses him softly and nuzzles him. "I love you, you stubborn asshole. I will never force you to stay with me. I want more pups, so I will never forget you. So I can look into their faces and see you smiling back at me when you are long gone."

He kisses her tenderly. "Since you are still such a young blushing bride, my love, I guess it is my honor to keep you barefoot and pregnant. After all, if you have a house full of pups, you'll be too busy keeping them in line to worry about me being gone." His kisses grow in passion and fervor.

"Mhmm," is his reply as Susie kisses him in return.

With an easy shift, he's nudging her legs apart with his knee and makes a graceful motion to cradle her to him as he brings his hardening shaft against her. They moan into each other as he eases his head in, feeling her already throbbing and wet. His strong hands glide down her back and cup around her ass as he rocks into her. He takes his time in filling her, only to retreat and listen to the little sighs escape her lips. His lips trail along her jaw and down her neck as he pumps into her. Her knees come up, allowing him better access. His eyes flutter closed as she peppers his jaw and neck with kisses.

He leans up when she arches underneath him and his hands follow the curve of her body around until he is cupping her full breasts. He gives her nipples a gentle tug to feel her tighten around his penetrating manhood. Her skin flushes pink, and he curls over her, pumping harder and faster. He suckles one of her nipples. He keeps his pace slow and steady until he feels her shudder on him, her orgasm washing over her in a tidal wave.

His smile is easy as he leans back up to watch her in the afterglow of her orgasm, knowing that his still throbbing cock inside of her only makes her more excited. God, did he love this woman. When he feels himself grow close to orgasm, his hands tighten on her hips and hold her still against him while he thrusts deep within. The little whimpers erupting from her only drives him closer. He pulls her against him as he buries himself hilt deep within her, moaning as his seed erupts inside her.

He collapses down and rolls onto his back, pulling her with him. David lies there looking up at the sunny sky as he trails small patterns along her back. "You know, darlin'," he muses. "That whole thing where you go all aggressive like? You should do it more often." He can't help but grin when she tenses on him and giggles.

"David Coeh, you're a pervert." She teases.

"And you like it," he wriggles his brow.

"I almost turned you earlier," she confesses.

"No, you didn't. I have absolute faith in you." He keeps trailing the patterns along her back.

"Hmm," she retorts. "Remind me of that when you're howlin' at the moon 'cause I lost control."

He chuckles, "Until then, I'll take my chances." It's then Susie's stomach growls like it's a wolf of its own. "Luckily for you, I brought lunch too."

"Uh huh," she chuckles easing up off of him. "You're such a

thoughtful kidnapper."

"Says the woman, who kidnapped me from our lovely home."

"Hey, don't blame me. Blame Jacob. He was going to kidnap us both if I hadn't done it. At least this way, we have clothes."

"Uh huh. Sure we do," he quips as he gives her an appraising once over. He pulls her into another heated kiss. "The food can wait," he smirks.

CHAPTER FORTY-THREE
Get Thee To A Nunnery

When Susie and David return from the boathouse, Susie seeks out Shelley. She treats her to a day of shopping for school supplies, along with Caleb.

"I'm bringing you along more often," Caleb teases Shelley. "She never lets us have half this stuff." He flashes Shelley a grin.

Shelley has reluctantly let Susie carry Frances around while she tries on clothes.

"No skirts," Susie chirps.

"What? Why not?" Shelley pouts. She had found a couple of really cute ones.

Caleb snickers and Susie cuts him a look. "'Cause of our beastly nature," he wriggles his brows at Shelley. "School implemented a no skirts policy to slow down eager... pups." He can't help but laugh. Caleb is a carbon copy of David, only broader in the shoulders. While he hasn't been very vocal about what's been going on in the house, he has silently been helping Shelley. His bedroom shares the bathroom with the nursery and in spite of her best efforts, there have been nights he can't sleep because of Frances. If his mother ever wanted to deter him from having pups, she succeeded by letting Shelley and Billy stay in the house with them. He had also been keenly aware of his parents fighting for some time now. Caleb is a people pleaser and wants happiness for both of them. He had tried to placate both Susie and David but had never been fully successful.

He could tell the difference immediately when his parents had returned from the lake house. It makes him breathe easier. He was going to talk to Billy about confronting their mother, when she and Shelley seemed to work it out on their own. Shelley agreed to let Susie have full access to Frances as she sees fit while Shelley is in school. She gave her ground rules about food, and his sleep schedule. She also forbade Susie from taking Frances up to her room at the house. Much to Caleb's surprise, his mother agreed. They spent the day shopping as a family. Both got new laptops, bags, clothes, and other various supplies. Frances came home with a new army of toys and clothes as well.

Billy's waiting when they get home. As the three of them slip out of the Suburban, Caleb unhooks the car seat and hands it to Shelley. He enjoys having a 'sister', so to speak, especially one that makes Billy get all worked up. He can see why Billy is so smitten with her. He hopes when he turns eighteen he'll find someone as sweet. His brows raise as Billy comes storming forward and begins his verbal onslaught to their mother. Susie and Billy stand pretty close to the same height and she crosses her arms, letting him rant and rave. Caleb's eyes dart to Shelley. She usually shrinks when people yell. Instead, he is surprised to see her trying to get Billy's attention to stop him. Caleb's eyes dart back to his mother, getting ready to guide Shelley into the house in case Susie puts Billy on his ass. What he didn't expect was the bemused look on her face.

"... And damn it, momma! He's our baby! You gotta ask permission to take him places. It ain't right how you been treatin' my Shelley." Billy finishes with a growl.

"Billy--," Shelley tries to interject again.

"No! I ain't gonna lose you cause she wants to get her damn

way. You're my mate and he's our son. And momma? Please..." the strength of his voice shifts to more of a whine, "Respect that." Billy looks imploringly at his mother.

Caleb holds his breath and eases closer to Shelley.

"Okay," says Susie in a calm manner.

"Okay then," Billy looks bewildered. That went way easier than he ever expected it to. He's not looking this gift wolf in the mouth. He smiles and takes Frances from Shelley.

Caleb sees Shelley roll her eyes and shake her head as she happily heads in with Billy. He then turns to the back of the Suburban to unload all the things they purchased.

******

Susie and David, along with several other pack members are heading to Kingsport, Tennessee. Susie had refused to let any of her sons attend. She wound up having to use her Alpha command to enforce them not attending.

Matthias and Samuel are furious with her, barking about how they could help protect her, and what if something goes wrong?

Brandon, who has been opposed to this fight altogether pretended to do as she asked with the plan on sneaking to the event until she used her command, forcing him to comply as well.

Billy is the only one she didn't need to use it on, as he understood her stance. She is protecting them. She may not have said it out loud, but he can read that she is afraid of the outcome of this fight. It had prompted him to give her some unlimited Frances time, much to Shelley's chagrin.

Jacob, agreeing with Matthias that Susie needs more than David as back-up, is en route with her, using his status as Beta to get his way. She finally relented after he explained his gut feelings about this event. This leaves the pack entirely in the care of the Coeh boys. Tommy assumes the responsibilities of his father as Beta, while Matthias assumes the duties of Alpha temporarily. This leaves Billy to manage Wolf Pack Construction, their father's business. Samuel and Brandon take over patrols and security. It is efficient and smooth, much to the pack's surprise.

Shelley has focused on school and Frances. She has little time to protest the situation as she had no idea what the event is Susie is going to. That and the private school differs vastly from her school in Savannah. She has been required to see the school counselor twice a week. They couch it as making sure she is adjusting to going to school with all werewolves, but it is also to address the other underlying issues.

Caleb has grown increasingly protective. He has been in two fights when young wolves get out of line with his sister-in-law-to-be. Shelley is a fascinating new toy to the other teens in the pack. Some of them have led highly sheltered lives away from humanity. Caleb, like the good little spy Billy recruited, reports about her progress and day in private. His irritation at what he thinks is flirting makes his older brother laugh. "She is allowed to talk to people, Caleb."

"It's not talking!"

"I trust her. She is allowed to 'not talk' to people too," he looks bemused.

"If she were my mate--," Caleb starts.

"She is not your mate, Caleb," The sharp warning in Billy's tone rings clear as a bell. "She is *my* mate, and she knows where the line is. She won't cross it. You just keep her safe."

Caleb chuffs at Billy and his cheeks turn red as he realizes he has crossed a line with his brother. "I don't like it. They think she likes them more than she does because she treats them like humans."

"Well, it's a good lesson for them pups to learn. They need to understand how to interact with humans. I've said it before and I'll say it again. That's one of the big failings of that school." Billy puts down the pen and closes his work binder to focus on his brother for a moment as he notices Caleb is still rather agitated. "What? You disagree?"

"No," he grumbles. "It's just... She is so... And they're..." He gets flustered.

Billy chuckles knowingly as he watches his brother suffer before him. "Boy, we need to find you a she-pup."

This promptly causes Caleb to blush and hurriedly leave with a bird flipped to his brother. He nearly knocks Shelley over when he barrels out of the office to run away.

"What's eating him?" Shelley asks.

Billy is still chuckling. "Nothin' a good ruttin' won't fix."

"What is it with you Coeh boys, and your fascination with rutting?" Shelley giggles.

Billy raises a brow, challenging her with a look. "You tellin' me you don't think about ruttin' as much as I do?"

The flush in Shelley's cheeks she tries to hide by turning to put Frances in the play pen gives him the answer. The scent of her arousal fills the room. Billy coughs lightly and shifts uncomfortably in his seat. If she were of age, they'd be fucking by now.

"When's your birthday again?" He rasps out.

"Hmm," is Shelley's reply as she gives him a coy smile. He can see what Caleb means. She doesn't realize just how alluring she is to wolves. That coy little smile she gives him suggests she knows exactly how she is tormenting him. "You have two hundred and twenty-nine days," she giggles. She gently trails her finger along his jaw when she comes close. "Unless you're up for feeding me," she winks.

Billy turns dark red at the memory of what she did in the cabin and immediately grows hard. He rubs his hand over his face, and in an overly dramatic voice, "Get thee away from me vile temptress!" He can't even finish the sentence without laughing as he pulls her into his lap and kisses her.

Shelley returns the kiss eagerly as she straddles his lap, "I believe this is what they call mixed signals."

"Woman, you keep this up, and you'll have two pups before you graduate." He grinds against her to let her feel just how aroused he is.

She then pats his cheek roughly and hops up with all haste. "I will get me to a nunnery, post haste," winking at him as she walks away.

Billy laughs, watching her leave before he tries to get back to work. "Note to self, don't mention another pup."

CHAPTER FORTY-FOUR
The Price Of Beer

The pecking order had been set. Matthias is acting Alpha. Tommy is acting Beta. Samuel and Brandon are sharing Gamma duties as heads of patrol, while Billy is filling in the Delta role. Beauregard is off at Savannah State University for his Freshman year of college, and Caleb is too young for any real pack work. Susie had only intended to take Jacob, her Beta, with her. But found the entirety of her pack leadership with her, leaving her boys to watch over home. Jacob and the others had made a compelling argument that David alone was not enough protection for her, unless David wanted to be turned. Exceptions had already been made for David's attendance at all, and the intelligence Susie received from Mehzebeen alerted her to the fact the Alpha known as The Beast had murdered the third competitor in this tourney already.

Shelley has noticed the entire shift in how the house operates. With all the brothers under one roof, Shelley hopes to God she doesn't have that many boys. There is so much testosterone it's distracting. Between random acts of prowess and the complete lack of privacy, she has half a mind to kick Tommy out of his house and trade with him until Susie and David come back.

Tommy's mom has been happily babysitting young Frances while Shelley is in school. Tommy has become her chauffeur as Billy is swamped between Wolf Pack Construction and Delta duties. With the best warriors in Tennessee, the Coeh brothers take patrolling more seriously. This would be an opportune moment for some of the wild wolves of the Americana Pack to try and stake claim on the Coehs' land.

Just when Billy thought things were going to settle down, Silus calls. He asks Billy if he would send Shelley down to the Six a few nights a week. Billy's knee-jerk reaction is to tell Silus to find someone else. He tells Silus it was up to Shelley.

"I'll see if we can arrange that, Daddy. I did make the cheerleading squad here, so I will have games, and only if I can find a sitter for Frances." She then hangs up. Her gaze falls upon Billy as she hands him his phone back. She hadn't given her parents her new cell phone number. While they had that one day, she was not fully sure she wanted them in Frances' life. The counselor at school has helped her to see how toxic that life was.

"He wants me to work at The Six on Fridays and Saturdays. What do you think?"

Billy's shoulders tighten and relax. He shifts uncomfortably. She can see he is conflicted. "I mean, if you think it's the best thing to do," he struggles to get the words out. It tells Shelley he wants to tell her no but is trying to treat her as an equal.

She furrows her brow and hesitates in response. "It would let me have time with my parents," she starts in hesitation. Billy's big on family ties. He knows how much she misses her family, Faye in particular.

"Well, I mean, yeah. But what about all those Angel assholes?" Billy grumbles as she opened the door for his side of the argument. All he can think about is the man that hit her, and how he would burn the place to the ground if she got hurt again.

Shelley raises a brow at him, crossing her arms. It's almost comical seeing him sitting on the couch, nearly as tall as she is standing. "Uh, huh? Those *assholes* have been there long before I met you, Billy Coeh." She doesn't deny that they're unsavory.

"And you still want to go back into that lion's den?" He raises a brow, trying to understand her logic.

"The way Daddy puts it, Mama's being run ragged because the girls he hired are too busy flirtin' with the Angels to get anything done. Faye and I had a pretty good routine when we worked there," she bites against her lip.

Billy sees that hopeful look on her face. She is trying to regain some sense of normalcy into her life. It reminds him that he, and his family, have very much kept her hidden away on pack land. "Fine," he throws his hands in the air. "But Tommy's gonna take you and stay the entire time."

Shelley narrows her eyes, "Just what do you plan to do on Friday and Saturday nights that you can't take me?" The little spark of possessiveness rises.

"Patrol," he grumbles. "With Momma and the others gone, we need strong fighters on patrol. 'Sides, Tommy owes us for getting us into this shit in the first place," he counters.

Shelley laughs at that. "When are you gonna forgive him?"

"In 217 days, when you're eighteen and I can fuck you like I'm supposed to," his gaze turns dark and heavy with desire as he catches her eyes. It makes her blush bright red. His hand rests on her waist and pulls her closer to him. The sparks between them are palpable. He leans up and offers a heated kiss to drive the point home, then sighs. "But we both know what Momma would do if we broke her rules."

The two of them linger in the embrace. She rests her forehead against his. Part of the tension between them is Billy trying to avoid being alone with Shelley. Just being in the same room with her makes him want to bend her over the nearest piece of furniture and have his way with her.

"I promise to not get in trouble," she chuckles. "And at the first sign of trouble, I'll go to Tommy."

"That's why he's there," Billy grins.

*****

Shelley is sitting in Tommy's pickup watching the tree line pass by as they head to The Triple Six. She had barely enough time after school to change, grab a bite to eat, and feed Frances. Grudgingly leaving him with Tommy's mother again. She was not about to leave her infant in a house full of rowdy alpha males. Even if Caleb offered to watch his nephew. She didn't want to saddle him with the responsibilities. He's a teen too and should be out having fun. As Tommy pulls his truck into the gravel parking lot, she looks hopeful. Maybe Faye has come back and their family will get back together, sort of.

"She ain't in there," Tommy mutters. "Last I heard from Jasper, they had just crossed the Guatemalan border. I'll tell him she needs to call you. Damn idiot probably didn't even think about it."

Shelley whips her head around to look at Tommy, and he puts his hands up defensively.

"I didn't know you didn't know, okay? If I did, I would have told them to tell you sooner."

"Hmph," she replies as she gets out of the truck.

Tommy just shakes his head and follows her. Once inside, he takes up residence in the corner booth. It gives him a view of the entire place and does not allow someone to sneak up on him. The young woman that approaches him is wearing a skirt far too short for her, and her make-up is on the heavy side.

"Why hello handsome, ain't seen you around before. You new?" She lingers with a tray of beers.

"Somethin' like that, darlin'" He watches as Shelley ducks into the back part of the bar, then quickly emerges without her jacket, an apron in place, and two trays of food.

"I mean, I would have noticed somethin' as smokin' hot as you being around," she coos.

It brings Tommy's gaze back to her with a curious look. "Darlin', just get me a beer. It's all I need right now." He winks and flashes that Coeh smile.

She pouts but then flops off to deliver the already ordered beers.

Thirty minutes later, Tommy can see that Shelley is really running the floor. She hasn't stopped moving once. She even delivered the beer he ordered from the other woman.

Two hours in, he sees the other girl come storming out of the kitchen and flop into the lap of a biker. "Well, at least I don't have to tip her now," he chuckles.

"Oh no, Tommy Coeh, you better damn well believe you're tippin' for that beer. Unless that's the only one you intend on gettin' tonight?" Shelley grins at him as she drops a second beer off.

"Yes, ma'am," he tips his beer at her.

The rest of the night is fairly uneventful. Tommy assists Shelley in busing tables after last call. He doesn't know what it is about mommas, but Momma Baxter walked over, shoved the bin in his hands and motioned. Next thing he knew, he was following behind Shelley as she filled the bin.

Shelley is chuckling at his perplexed expression. "It's paying for your beers," she giggles. "You help me, you get free beer, deal?"

"Deal." He grins in reply.

Once they are done, he waits for her at the entrance to the bar. While she told him he could wait in the truck, Billy had made it explicitly clear that he was to keep an eye on her, under penalty of death. Tommy guesses that there is something about Silus and Paula that Billy doesn't trust and being in the truck wouldn't let him protect her. The three of them are talking at the end of the bar, and he sees Silus pull Shelley into a tight hug, followed by Paula doing the same. Pure happiness is on Shelley's face as her parents embrace her. She settles up the tips and tab, then is happily coming to him. She offers him a small bundle of ones as he shakes his head, declining.

"C'mon. I tip my bus boys." She pouts at him.

"Nuh uh, missy. Yer mate'll skin me alive if I take any of that. I'm yer guard, not yer bus boy."

CHAPTER FORTY-FIVE
The Nine Lives of Jackson Pruitt

On Saturday, Tommy takes Shelley down to The Six early. They were having a live band tonight, and she wanted to get there to prep. He imagines it was more to spend time with her momma than prep. The two women have been hovering over Shelley's phone for the past hour, looking at photos of Frances. It makes him smile to see Shelley happy. The guilt of causing her so much heartache still weighs heavily on him. Soon enough the rumble of motorcycles fills his ears and Angels filter into the bar. They pay him no mind. Silus and a few of them are talking quietly on the other side of the room. They had no idea he could hear them plain as day, but that's alright. It'll give him more information to tell Billy.

In spite of Billy letting Shelley decide, he didn't trust Silus wouldn't hurt her again. Much to Tommy's surprise, Billy gave him permission to beat the shit out of Silus should he so much as bring a tear to Shelley's eye. Tommy thought he was being dramatic but would honor the request. What he did pick up from the men's conversation was that they are smuggling drugs and weapons up from South America, and that they figured someone named Pruitt was dead. The drugs had been lost in an accident and Silus was having to make amends with the Colombians. This drew a frown from Tommy. His gaze drifting back to Shelley at the bar. He knew once he told Billy that, he wouldn't let her work here anymore. But, that was a problem for tomorrow. Tonight, he is enjoying good beer, good music, and watching her pretty little ass shuffle about. One perk of being her shadow is getting to watch her without Billy murdering him.

As the patrons file in and take up their spots, he smiles at the cold beer set in front of him. Shelley passes quickly, not even stopping as she deposits the drink. Soon enough she is flitting around the room with drinks and food, like a nachos and beer fairy. It's an entirely different side of her that he doesn't see at the Coeh house. She is confident and sassy. Her sweet smile wins everyone over, along with her fast service. The men all seem to like her, and not a damn soul lays a hand on her. He can tell a few men want to. He imagines it is her father that makes them behave, but at least it makes his life easier. The band kicks up, and the little bar is loud and full of the steely blues music. He is starting to relax when he picks up the foul stench of a vampire.

He sets his beer down, and his gaze shifts to scanning the crowd. No one seems out of place until his eyes settle on hot little thing in a red jacket. Her pale skin and blue eyes settle on him. The two watch each other for a considerable amount of time before she winks at him and turns back to the drink she is not bothering to actually consume. Something niggles at the back of his mind, but he tries to let it go. Vampires could be in Savannah, so long as they followed the rules of The Accord. There is something about the red jacket that he knows he should know, but it eludes him at the moment. His gaze shifts from her back to Shelley. She had been swept into the arms of a drunk, wanting a dance. Her irritated chuckle made Tommy start to ease out of the booth to deal with the man, when his buddies pull him back into the seat and apologize to her. She laughs and hurries off to get back to work.

Tommy couldn't shake that horrible feeling building in his gut. It prompts him to stop drinking altogether and pay more attention to where Shelley is.

The band takes a twenty-minute break and the jukebox hadn't been fired up yet when the door to the front of the Six slams open. Strolling in like they own the place is a group of six men wearing Angel colors. The mini pack is led by a man about the same age as Billy. Tommy inhales, and the room is filled with the putrid scent of vampires. He cuts a look to the red jacket at the bar, then to the men. As casually as possible he stands and catches Shelley as she comes out the kitchen with a tray of food. He blocks her path, "Put the tray down. We're leaving through the kitchen," his voice is low and firm.

"What? No, Tommy. I got these three orders, and four more coming up. Not to mention the beers I need to get." She frowns up at him. He steps closer and gently takes the full tray from her, setting it on the bar.

"This is not up for debate, Shelley. It's not safe." Tommy glances over his shoulder to see if they have been noticed. His entire posture is massive near her, trying to shield her from sight entirely.

It's then, from the other side of the room, Silus's voice cuts over the crowd. "You part cat, Pruitt? You got a lot of balls showing up here." His growl lets Tommy know for sure there is about to be trouble.

"Jackson?" Shelley's voice squeaks, and Tommy narrows his eyes. Without another word, he is roughly shoving her toward the kitchen door. He knew the name Jackson. That dick had put his hands on Shelley and Billy is itching to give him a lesson in manners.

"Hey man, that prick Jackson's at the Six." Tommy links him as he continues moving Shelley through the kitchen in grim silence. His grip on her forearm is too tight for her to free herself.

"Tommy, stop! You're hurting me. What's going on?" Her

voice pleas with him as she stumbles along.

The two of them burst out of the back door and find themselves face to face with three more vampires.

"Fuck," Tommy growls, and shifts Shelley behind him, taking a more aggressive stance. "You boys don't start none, there won't be none," he warns. Their grins tell him it's going to be a long night, but he has to at least try to keep the peace. Momma Coeh drilled it into all the pack members.

"You go on back in Miss Shelley, Jackson's looking for you." One of them replies in a kind tone. Tommy's grip on her forearm tightens as he holds her in place. When their fangs come out, he doesn't hesitate. He shifts up into his werewolf and catches the jaw of the first one that attacks, ripping it apart until he's throwing the two pieces to the ground. The vampire's surprised look is forever etched on his face. Shelley screams and before the other two can act, he snatches her up like a thief in the night and takes off running.

"Vampires. At the Six. At least ten," his link this time went to anyone who would listen.

Billy, the moment Tommy said Jackson was at The Six, finished his patrol and was on his bike en route to the bar. He owed that boy an ass whooping. No one lays hands on his Shelley unanswered. It didn't matter that it happened almost nine months ago. Jackson'll be lucky that Billy isn't the killing sort. As he rides, the second message comes through and it's all he can do to keep from shifting right there on the bike. He speeds up, streaking through the night towards the Six.

"On our way. Get the Baxters out of there." Matthias' voice cuts over the link.

"No can do. Already gone. Parents still there. Chased by two. Headed to woods north of the bar." Tommy replies.

"Brandon and I are closest. We'll get the Baxters," Samuel chimes in. The two of them were already done with patrol and were coming to enjoy a few beers with Tommy.

Tommy focuses on running, pulling Shelley up from the pseudo football carry into a bridal style as he runs. He can feel her panic and fear. She trembles against him and has grown silent. He is sure it's because of seeing him rip that vampire's face in half. At least she is not putting up a fight with him. He knew vampires were fast as hell, and he's pushing himself to the limit running with her in his arms. He's thankful she is tiny and light. It's then one vampire collides with Tommy. He thrusts his arms forward, throwing Shelley away from them as the pair land on the ground.

"Run," He snarls at Shelley, forgetting that he can barely string words together in this form and it probably looks more like he's about to eat her.

Either way, it accomplishes what he wants, and she runs.

The vampire that collided with him is stunned and he turns as his buddy comes into the clearing, trying to chase after the prey that took off.

Tommy catches his ankle and throws him back against the tree behind him. He could take on these two, then go find Shelley. Her fear and prey pheromones are permeating the air, making it hard to concentrate. He rolls his shoulders and cracks his neck as he lets out a menacing roar at the two vampires. If they wanted to get Miss Shelley, they were going to go through him first.

Samuel and Brandon come barreling through the door at The Six. It's mass chaos. Dead on the floor is Silus Baxter. His throat torn from his body and his blank eyes staring into the ether. Scattered throughout the bar are Angels in various states of dying, or dead. There are people shrieking and running. Without hesitation, the two wolves shift to jump into the fray. They attack anything with fangs. Neither of them see Paula anywhere to speak of, but they had more pressing matters at the moment. A coven of vampires had preyed upon the Six, and it was their duty to put them in place.

"Silus is dead. Paula ain't here," Samuel links.

It's then Billy comes rolling up to the Six. His eyes are black with fury as he tries to contain his rage. He leaps from the bike, shifting into a copper streak as he catches faint hints of Shelley's scent.

CHAPTER FORTY-SIX
Alpha Games

Kingsport, Tennessee is not a large town. It's close to Johnson City and Bristol. It's a good place for the largest gathering of werewolves since the wars in Romania, as it is nestled in the Appalachian mountains. All the campsites and hotels are booked. The 'fair' is exclusive and kept well hidden from curious human eyes. In fact, the only humans allowed to enter the area are the mates of any wolves in attendance. This brings the total to five humans among a couple thousand wolves.

The exception had been made for Susie and David, as she was a competitor for Alpha, and the elders agreed that mates should not be separated. It would give the unmated competitor an advantage. The days leading up to the final battle were akin to the Highland Games. Wolves show their prowess in various feats of strength. It's mostly ways for Betas and Gammas to show off their packs. Jacob and Michael were no different. In fact, all the men in Susie's cadre were eager to show off just how much better Susie is as an Alpha.

Mehzebeen, along with all the other Tribunal members, are in attendance as well. Lucien Deveroux, the ruthless patriarch of the vampires in New Orleans. Patrick Howell, master of the vampire covens in New York, along with his teenage ward, Sabine. Last, but not least, Isaiah Belmont, a human and Hunter. All are in attendance as the Tribunal seat vacated by the deceased Appalachian Alpha will be given to the winner of this tournament.

The Tribunal is called so due to representing the three aspects of The Accord, humans, vampires, and werewolves. Some would argue that witches and fae are missing from this, but the leadership would not deny a representative so long as they agreed to The Accord. What is surprising to Mehzebeen was to see Una, the Alpha of the Britannia Pack. She is one of the most revered werewolves in existence. She is here to certify the results. It is her son who passed away, causing the tournament.

Mehzebeen, while knowing Lucien likes drama, was much relieved when they unanimously agreed to back Susie Coeh. The Beast would not hold to the bounds of The Accord and they would be forced to war with the werewolves. Everyone would suffer under his leadership. In spite of all her best efforts, she could not sway the elders of the Appalachian Pack to forgo the old ways and just appoint the next Alpha. It is the night before the big tournament, and they are sitting around makeshift tables at the "bar" created for the event. Near their group, a massive man, dressed like he walked out of a Davy Crockett show on Disney, is being boisterous and loud.

"She hasn't even shown her face yet. She is nothing more than a scared pup. I'll let her have her fun. Then I'll put her in place right there for all to see. I'd keep her as a pet if I didn't have to kill her after." The men chuckle and cheer, raising their glasses.

Susie raises a brow as she sees the grim expression on Jacob's face when he slams down his pint and gets up to stalk over to the blustering fur bag. She turns, easing up to intervene when Jacob gets into that Alpha's face, or tries to, as the man stands nearly seven feet tall in human form.

"She is twice the man you'll ever be and when she wipes the

floor with you, I will spit on your corpse." The room goes dead silent.

"Such big words, for such a tiny boy. Get out of my face, pup." He shoves Jacob. Susie eases forward more when Jacob stands his ground and growls menacingly at The Beast.

"That's enough, Jacob," Susie's calm voice holds a firmness that broaches no argument.

"Yes, little pup. Run back to your bitch's skirts." He gives a dismissive hand flick. "Your mate is awful pretty. Maybe she would like a real wolf." He gives Susie a grin and a wink.

Susie laughs then and Jacob's face is red with fury.

"Jacob, I said that was enough. Do not make me tell you again." Her hands are in her pockets with an all-around relaxed posture. Then her gaze flicks to The Beast. "You know, when I put you down tomorrow, I'm sure there's more than one pup who wants to spit on you." She flashes him a sweet smile. "There's still time for you to allow for modern rules, so you can tuck your tail and run back to your cave when I win."

The Beast's eyes narrow, and he looks her up and down. "So you are the beloved Susie Coeh." There is tension in the air as they stare at each other. He breaks first, "Good bartender! Drinks for everyone! Tonight, we celebrate! Tomorrow, we rip each other to pieces." With that, he hands the man a credit card and drinks are poured around.

Susie smiles at him but doesn't move until Jacob is back at his seat. She makes a point of showing The Beast she isn't intimidated by him. When she returns to her table, she shakes her head.

"You damn well know better," she points at Jacob. Then whirls on Michael, the Gamma. "And you're supposed to be watching him."

"Yeah. I watched him walk right over there. I had half a mind to join him. What he said ain't right, Susie."

"I don't give a fuck what he said. He's trying to get into your heads. Get you all riled up so you do something stupid," she growls, "making me have to deal with him before we're in the ring where there aren't any fuckin' rules. But, go ahead. Go provoke him again." She barks.

Jacob and Michael lower their gazes. "Sorry," they mutter.

David had thought the Coeh wolves were terrible about posturing. After seeing all these other wolves, they are downright tame. He has to admit the sheer size of The Beast is intimidating. Susie seems awfully calm about the whole ordeal. It makes him narrow his eyes at her. Usually, she is putting up a front and her emotions are all over her face, but all he reads right now is a serenity that makes him uneasy. Mehzebeen chuckles and shakes her head. She is projecting that she is human, as she learned a long time ago that werewolves are on edge with vampires around. Being as old as she is, she does not need to rile them up. It's then Susie and the other Coeh wolves stiffen.

Mehzebeen is standing as well.

"What is it?" David asks concerned.

"Vampires," Susie growls. "Something's happening at that fucking bar. We need to go." All the Coeh wolves start to get ready to leave.

"No. You need to stay," Mehzebeen looks at her pointedly. "If you walk away now, you will forfeit the fight, and he will be your Alpha. Can you live with the choices he'll make for you?" She looks right at David.

David hates when they do that. "I am right fucking here."

"Shush boy, the adults are talking," Mehzebeen flashes him a smile, showing him she is teasing him. "In all seriousness, he has made it clear he is impressed with you, Susie, and David is only a distraction to you in his eyes. You need to focus and win. I will go to Savannah and take care of whatever is happening at The Triple Six. You," she turns to the rest of them, "Are to make sure she is prepared for tomorrow. Including you, boy," she points again at David.

David gets a wolfish grin on his face, "Oh, don't you worry none. I know how to make sure she is properly rested for a fight." He eases up and comes to put an arm around Susie's waist. Even he is showing possessiveness regarding his mate. He knew how to fight dirty if it came to it. It's a secret Susie and he keep, the side-arm on him is loaded with silver bullets. Along with that, he has a stiletto switchblade made of silver as well. He and Susie had talked about it. He has always been a scrapper, having grown up in a biker gang and under an abusive father. Coupled with the fact he is mated to an alpha, he is stronger and faster that most humans.

Mehzebeen rolls her eyes, and when Susie relents, she vanishes into the night. Susie turns and sees The Beast staring at her. The jealous lust obvious on his face at seeing David touching her. He had not realized she was the Alpha he was going to fight. He has seen her around all week and had decided he was taking her home after he won. He felt the faint tugs of a mate bond between them and it is something he has never considered would happen to him. This complicated things, making him mildly sad with the fact that he would never get to experience that tight little girl.

Susie smirks and pulls David into a heated kiss, winning some whoops and hollers from the wolves nearby.

Soon, they were exiting the bar and heading back to their hotel. She felt guilty. David and she had been vastly improving since the boathouse and she hadn't told him yet that she is pregnant. David would try to stop her and stress them both out more if he found out about her being pregnant now. The weight of doing what's right for the pack over her personal life is heavy once again on her shoulders.

She spends the rest of the night making sure he doesn't worry about a damn thing other than making her howl.

CHAPTER FORTY-SEVEN
Cat & Mouse

Shelley runs for what feels like an eternity. Everything hurts. Her legs hurt, her chest hurts. Her cheeks are stained with tears, and she can't catch her breath. Her heart is racing fast enough she is sure she is going to have a heart attack. She can no longer hear the snarling sounds of Tommy and those other men. She doesn't dare look back as that's how people die in the horror movies. As she runs, she ticks through all the horror movies rules and panic fills her more, recalling she isn't a virgin anymore. Billy had told her if she ever wanted to lose a wolf to run into water. She has no idea where she is. It's dark and try as she might, she keeps stumbling and falling over the underbrush. She is scraped, dirty, covered in sweat, and everything in her body is telling her to move.

Jackson watches her silently. He had come upon Tommy fighting two of his Angels, and he left the other two that came with him to deal with the mutt. He could take care of Shelley on his own. Her fear is intoxicating and it makes wonders if he can keep her in this state of fear forever. Her heart is thundering in his ears. She was heading aimlessly, and the further she lost herself in the woods, the easier it would be for him to do whatever he wanted. He could tell she was getting tired. Sweet little prey like her always run themselves to exhaustion.

Adelaide had been right about savoring the hunt. As disappointed as his sire was that he still held a candle for this human girl, she catered to his wish to return here and collect what is his.

Silently he stalks forward, moving too fast for Shelley to see, or hear him. He brushes along her cheek before taking her by the chin and throwing her to the ground. She screams and rolls over to get onto her feet, not seeing anyone near her. He allows her to flee and watches as she scrambles away again. She is cut and scraped, so her blood is filling his senses along with her heartbeat. He can feel the hunger tugging at him. He allows her to run into the darkness, slowly pursuing her again. He lets her run for another ten minutes before he pounces her again, not letting her see what is tormenting her. This time he tears at her clothing as she tries to get away. He listens to her sweet screams and salivates at wanting to taste her.

By the time he catches her the third time she is limping and shivering. It's then he rushes into the clearing. "Shelley," his voice sounds panicked.

"J... J... Jackson?" She tries to stop from barreling into him but is slow and he's holding her. "W... What? How?"

He licks his lips looking down at her. Gently, he plucks the leaves from her hair and brushes her platinum blond curls from her face. "Shh... It'll be alright. I'm here now. You're safe." His voice is a purr and Shelley shivers in his grasp.

Shelley's not dumb. Not at all. If he had been looking for her, he would have been calling her name. She doesn't even know where she is, and he suddenly found her? She feebly pushes away from him. "Let go of me. How... How did you find me?" Her heart is still hammering, and she is positive at any second that Tommy is going to come snarling into the area and kill her. He looked so angry when he growled at her back there.

Jackson lets out a growl, and with a great deal of force he pulls her back to him, cupping her chin to force her to look at him. "Don't you fucking pull away from me. I gave up everything for you. You're mine. MINE!" he bellows. "All I ever wanted was you. You and me runnin' the Angels and ridin' free. But your fucking father," he snarls.

It's then that Shelley sees the fangs and her eyes widen in terror.

"Oh, yes, my little Angel. Yer lookin' at the new and improved Jackson. After I kill all those fuckin' Coeh mutts, you and I are gonna get real cozy." He forces her head to the side and brushes his nose against her neck, resisting the urge to bite her just yet. He settles for lapping his rough tongue along a small scrape on her shoulder, savoring the sweet taste of her blood. "You can be a good girl and come along. Or you can put up a fight. I'm sure your momma will understand why I had to take from her what you wouldn't give me." His voice is sultry and low, like it used to be when they were dating.

Shelley cries harder. "Jackson. Stop. Please. I... I... I have a son," she desperately cries. She doesn't know what else to say. All she can think about is that she was going to die and Frances would never know her. It is the wrong thing to say. Jackson's eyes turn a dark gold color and he snarls at her, jerking her to the ground.

"You fucking whore! While I was off doing your fucking father's bidding, what did you do? Fuck the whole gang? Who's the father? Who?" He jerks her underneath him. His fingers gripping onto her jaw so tight she is sure he will break her jaw. He bangs her head against the ground and she gasps, seeing stars.

"I'm sorry," she whimpers. "I... I... I'll be yours," she breathes out. "Just... Just don't hurt Momma or Frances. Please," she begs.

Jackson's temper is still running high. He would punish her for sleeping around on him. He would make her watch while he drains all life from Paula and whoever fucked her. She would learn who she belongs to and would be lucky if he lets her out of his bed from this point forward.

"Good girl," he coos. Then his entire demeanor changes as he is pinning her down. He looks purposely into her eyes, trying to bend her will to him. He watches as her eyes begin to gloss over, then flicker back to full recognition. His brow furrows, and he tries harder. She begins to comply and he sees the fog clear again. He would much rather she submit, as it will hurt her less. As she continues to resist his control, he grows frustrated and turns her chin up and away, forcing her neck to be exposed. He can hear her sniveling underneath him but has stopped struggling and is holding still.

He leans down, nuzzling her. "I'm going to enjoy this for the rest of eternity," he purrs against her earlobe. Then his fangs are exposed, and he lowers his mouth, inching closer to sinking into the sweet tender flesh of Shelley Baxter.

Adelaide had been watching Jackson hunt his Angel, as he called her. Her amusement at just how cruel he is being to her not contained. There is a tiny thrill that her chylde is as much a monster as she is. She is sure he will be a Red Jacket in no time, and with a pet to supply him with plenty of blood, he would thrive. His success pleases her beyond words. Quietly, she follows their cat-and-mouse game until he quits playing with his food. She would not intervene, as it's his game to have. Even if he kills the girl, it makes no difference to her. It would be one less tie to this fucking place. He could come to New Orleans and be a God among mortals. She listens as the girl pleads and begs with him, the surge of anger and jealousy from Jackson when the girl reveals she has a child is concerning. She is not taking a fucking baby back to New Orleans with them. They will have to locate the brat and end his existence. Or, if the father is human, just take Shelley and disappear, leaving the boy without her.

Jackson has come such a long way in a short time. There is a small amount of jealousy that his growth has been driven by the pretty girl he is now torturing. She turns to give him privacy and finds herself face to face with none other than Mehzebeen. Her eyes widen and she tries to make a sound to alert Jackson to the danger they are in, only to find she can do nothing. She just stares at the small woman in front of her. Mehzebeen's eyes are a vibrant gold color. Her skin shimmers the dark bronze of a goddess in the moonlight, and her lip is curled to reveal her fangs. Her posture and arrogant look reveals the air of royalty she possesses.

Lucien often warned and complained to Louise about how powerful Mehzebeen is. They had surmised she must be a second, or third, generation vampire from a Bride of Lucifer. Lucien is a fifth generation vampire from Bruji, the bride of his line. As she stands here, helpless as Mehzebeen looks at her, she realizes they are all wrong, she is much more powerful than that. She has not even said a word, and Adelaide can do nothing against her. With a sharp turn, Mehzebeen walks back to The Triple Six. Adelaide follows behind like a scolded child. Her body does not even jerk in resistance. She understands that Mehzebeen is controlling her, but her will is not being suppressed. How could she do this? "Who... who are you?" Adelaide stammers out.

Mehzebeen gets a small smile on her face as she continues walking. "You know my name, Red Jacket. Why are you attacking people in my city?" Mehzebeen never raises her voice and never threatens Adelaide as they continue strolling through the woods to return to the scene of the crime. She leaves Jackson and Shelley to their fates. She agreed to take care of the problem, not save everyone involved. Mehzebeen knew that Billy Coeh would not leave his mate to death. He will take care of the vampire in the clearing. If he cannot, she will deal with him after she cleans up the more pressing matter, the sudden influx of newly made vampires at The Triple Six.

CHAPTER FORTY-EIGHT

Here I Come To Save The Day

Billy picks up her scent in no time and is racing into the woods. It is a few short minutes later when he comes snarling into the clearing. Blood, sweat, fear, and Tommy fills his nostrils. Shelley's scent is faint. He looks around at the bodies and blood everywhere. Pressed against a tree, with his hand holding his abdomen is Tommy.

"I'm alright. She ran off that way. Just gonna take me a moment or two to heal. That damn vampire blood stings like a som'bitch."

Billy doesn't even bother to shift to human form or check on him further. Tommy wouldn't lie to him. He bolts in the direction he could still smell her. Her fear is pushing him faster and harder. The erratic running patterns and the fact she circled back on herself tells him she is being chased. The closer he gets the stronger her scent is. He can hear her before he sees her.

"I'll be yours. Just don't hurt Momma and Frances."

He sees red. Someone is coercing his mate by threatening her family. It doesn't matter that she hadn't say his name. He chose her and would protect her even with his life. As he reached the tiny clearing where he saw a figure over Shelley, holding her arched underneath him, he stopped thinking. He lept through the air and plowed right into Jackson, sending the both of them tumbling. He shifts mid-flight to his massive werewolf form. His claws and teeth slash and bite into Jackson with frantic fury.

Jackson is strong and brutal in return. His teeth snap at Billy and he throws him off.

The two of them collide into trees and each other as they battle for Shelley on the ground.

Billy is only vaguely aware Shelley isn't moving. That she is lying still where Jackson left her. Her hand twitches. If this cretin bit his mate, Billy would not only rip out his fangs, he would tear every piece of flesh from this vampire. Billy rips one of Jackson's arms off and tosses it aside as he lunges forward again, growling with all the ferocity of an Alpha wolf.

It wasn't a fair fight. Jackson tries to retreat then, seeing that Shelley has gotten herself mixed up with werewolves, and he will need to rethink his strategy. Billy isn't letting him go. He snatches him back and rips the other arm off. Billy looks like he is taking a toy and shredding all the fluff out of it the way his claws sunk in and tore out Jackson's flesh.

He then rips his head off and throws it away and impales Jackson's body on the nearest tree before turning to the center of the clearing. He is covered in blood and gore. His fur is matted with it. He seethes and clenches his fists, snorting steam into the night air. His eyes settle on Shelley, who is twitching more on the ground.

Panic fills him, thinking he was too late, and she was bitten. He stalks forward and her fear swells, and it stops him dead in his tracks. It crushes his soul that she is terrified of him. He roars and turns vent his frustration on the corpse impaled on the tree. Billy shreds and claws at the lifeless body until it turns to ash under his claws. He is panting and growling, with his back to her.

"Billy," her sweet voice finally pierces the fog of his rage. "Billy, look at me," she sounds firmer, but still scared. Slowly, the beast of a werewolf turns and looks down at his tiny mate. His piercing eyes looking all over her for any signs of being bitten. He sniffs the air and immediately is relieved that her sweet scent fills his nostrils. He stands frozen as she looks up at him, like she did the night of The Rutting. No matter how angry he gets, he would never hurt her. His ears fold down and he pants, as he fears she will reject him after seeing the monster he is.

"Oh Billy," she whimpers. She wraps her slender arms around his waist. He can feel her shivering and he scoops her up, wrapping her against his chest with his massive arms. It doesn't matter he was covered in blood and guts. She needs him to hold her, and while she is afraid of what has happened, he responded to her without violence. He holds her close enough she can't breathe. Then he turns, running with her, much like Tommy did from the bar. He leaves the clearing covered in blood and ash and makes a beeline for his aunt's home. They both need to know that Frances is alright.

Back at The Triple Six, Mehzebeen and Adelaide come walking up to the building. There is fighting going on around them as werewolf and vampire alike are unleashing unholy hell on each other. None seem to give either woman a passing thought.

Adelaide sees the vampires surrendering and walking into the bar, leaving the wolves standing there dumbfounded.

Matthias casts a single glance at Mehzebeen, bows his head in submission, and the fight is over.

Then Adelaide sees all the wolves quietly disappearing into the night, taking any vehicles and hints of their existence with them. She looks on worriedly and tries to stop following Mehzebeen. Only to pass through the doorway into the bar as if they were friends getting a drink. Inside, there are bodies everywhere. The scent of blood, booze, and fear fills every inch of this place and Mehzebeen keeps walking right by it all, into the back area of the building. She opens the door to an office and waits for

Adelaide to enter.

Paula sits on the couch with her hands in her lap, and head lowered. Mehzebeen takes her chin and lifts her face, inspecting her neck, then looking into her eyes. "Oh, you poor girl," she sounds morose as she looks at Paula. The vacant stare of the woman on the couch tells Adelaide that she is mentally gone. That Jackson had stripped her of her will and left her there. With a sad look, Mehzebeen gently guides Paula to sleep. "You won't feel any more pain," and leaves her on the couch. Mehzebeen turns and leaves the office.

Adelaide continues to follow obediently.

Adelaide is getting this nagging feeling that something terrible was about to happen here. Mehzebeen pauses and collects a few photos off the wall, making Adelaide hold them as they walk out of the bar again. Adelaide cannot understand why she would want the photos. Everyone who cared about them is dead.

"No, that Coeh boy saved his mate," she corrects Adelaide.

Adelaide's eyes widen in fear as she realizes Mehzebeen has been in her mind this entire time.

"You Cajun girls are always so slow," she sighs. "Now, for the fun part," Mehzebeen flashes a feral grin.

Adelaide swallows hard, in reflex, at the fear she feels standing next to this ancient being. She isn't a vampire, Adelaide is sure. For whatever reason, she portrays one.

"Oh, I assure you I am a vampire. Just not as young as any of you think. Now be a good girl while I do my work," Mehzebeen coos.

When Adelaide meets her gaze again, she can see the fire in her eyes. No longer just gold, but filled with a holy wrath of power that could only mean one thing, Mehzebeen is a Bride of Lucifer.

"Mhm, so you are slightly more intelligent than his regular jackets. I will tell you a secret, just between us girls, little Adelaide." With a flick of her hand The Triple Six erupts into an explosion, mushroom clouding up into the dark night sky. The entire building is engulfed in a searing, raging, inferno.

What few people that were actually turned by the vampires shriek in terror, along with the docile vampires that had surrendered. No matter how hard they try to get out of the building they find themselves held in place as the flames engulf them. Adelaide thought about the woman in the office. Her brow furrows as she had been led to believe Mehzebeen is a champion of humans.

"Oh, I am. But, your chylde removed any semblance of humanity from her. It would have been crueler to allow her to continue her existence." There is a pain of regret on Mehzebeen's face momentarily, but it is soon replaced with indifference.

"I believe I was letting you in on a secret," she smiles at Adelaide then and turns to walk back towards the woods. Adelaide is confused by this action. Why would she take her away just to bring her back. Mehzebeen sighs, takes hold of Adelaide and in a blink they are back to the clearing where Jackson and Shelley had been. Adelaide is crushed, seeing the pile of ash and traces of blood everywhere. Mehzebeen walks into the clearing and has Adelaide sit on the very spot Shelley had been pinned down at.

"Stay," Mehzebeen boops her nose.

"You are correct. I am a Bride. You and your little boy violated the rules of *my* Accord. There is no forgiveness for your crime. Now, give me those photos and your jacket." She takes the photos from Adelaide and waits for the jacket. Once in possession of both, she disappears, leaving Adelaide in the clearing.

Try as she might, Adelaide cannot move. Fear wells inside of her as the dark night sky gives way to gray hints of dawn. Bloody tears stain her cheeks as the grays give way to the pink horizon. She had not seen the sun in nearly two hundred years.

"I forgot how beautiful sunrises were," she murmurs as she turns to ash.

CHAPTER FORTY-NINE
Underworld Sovereigns

Mehzebeen appears just outside of the hotel where the Tribunal is staying. Her posture is confident and relaxed. The problem in Savannah was no more troubling than irritating children rebelling. With a thought, she summons the other Tribunal members to the sitting area in the lobby. Isaiah is the first to arrive. He looks as though he had been asleep. Howell, without his ward, is next. Lucien is the final to arrive. When they are all settled, she throws the red leather jacket at Lucien.

"You would do well to remember that Savannah is my city, and those thugs you call Red Jackets are not welcome if they cannot behave."

Lucien raises a brow and disdainfully sets the jacket aside. "They are my Louisette's friends," he looks bemused. "Should one act out of line, I would hope you deal with them swiftly."

"It is not out of my purview to deal with the one in charge of the city from which they spawned. Without our support, you would be handling the Americana Pack on your own, or have you forgotten that? I believe Marie Laveau was quite clear about how you were to run *her* city." Mehzebeen's eyes are burning bright.

Isaiah Belmont watches the woman who is their leader. He had hoped to spend some time with her at this event, but it seems a leader's work is never done. When his father passed, she quit coming around altogether. They had been close when he was younger, and now she keeps an aloof distance with him. He has learned she does not act without reason. She has proved to be fair in how she handles anything that belongs to the Supernatural world. He can tell she is furious, and the hint of smoke that clings to her makes him worried for what has taken place.

"Did you not think I would find her? Or that I would not demand repercussions for the insult? Their Alpha is here, fighting for her life, and you send your peasants to attack her family!"

Isaiah gives Howell a frowning look, and both men shift as Lucien moves to stand and face Mehzebeen.

The tall and slender vampire narrows his eyes down at the petite woman. He wants to attack her and put her in her place for insulting him in such a manner. He knew that Adelaide had no intention of breaking rules in Savannah. That boy she turned must have led her down the foul path that was her demise. He looks Mehzebeen over and bares his fangs.

Howell stiffens, as does Isaiah.

Mehzebeen cants her head at Lucien and a feral grin forms on her lips.

Without a word, Lucien immediately drops to his knees and bares his neck to her.

The look of utter shock on his face would make Isaiah laugh if he didn't realize what is happening. His father, Josiah, had always warned that Mehzebeen is not what she appears, and to lose her confidence is a dangerous thing.

Howell raises his hand to stay Isaiah but he does not remove his eyes from the pair.

"H... How dare you do this?" Lucien croaks. His entire body is being held in the submissive position to her. Try as he might, he cannot even summon the shadows to attack her. For the first time in hundreds of years, he feels fear.

"As I said," she coos to him. "You would do well to remember who needs who here. I choose not to rule you with an iron fist. Push me, Lucien, and you will learn how insignificant you are."

She releases him.

"Savannah is *my* city. Until your kind can learn to restrain themselves, they are not welcome within its limits." She leaves the three men to deal with her ultimatum and finds herself standing next to the matronly figure known as Una in the elevator.

"It never ceases to amaze me the lengths you will go to regain what you lost in Egypt," Una's graveled voice fills the elevator.

Mehzebeen cuts the elder woman the dirtiest of looks, which wins her a peal of laughter from Una.

"Oh, sweet child, I have no desire to out you. I think what you are doing here in the States is admiral," her crisp British accent cuts across the tiny box they are trapped in. "I am merely making conversation, young Pharaoh. If they knew who you were, they would not be so cavalier in trifling with you. Why do you keep it secret?"

"Why do you keep your lake hidden away, old one?" Mehzebeen gives her a faint smile.

Una responds with more laughter. "I knew this trip would be worth it." She wipes the tears from laughing away. The elevator chimes and the doors swoosh open. Una steps out of the box, without looking back, leaving Mehzebeen to ride on to her floor. She had business with the two Alphas that will be fighting.

Una knocks firmly at the door to the Beast.

He pulls open the door and narrows his eyes down at her. "What do you want," he leans in the door frame, watching the older woman.

"Seeing as we may work together soon, I wanted to get to

know the man who will assume my son's pack."

He furrows his brow, and steps back, motioning for her to enter the room.

Una smiles and takes in the earthy scents of the Beast. His father and mother had been murdered at a young age by hunters, and he has been ruling his pack since then. He lives in the New England area, which afforded him less human interaction than most, and his pack is known for being quite feral. Even his clothes are more of a natural ilk. She sits on the edge of his bed and watches him in silence. The longer the silence lingers, the more agitated he gets. Una does not react to his frustrated growl. He is a pup in her eyes. She could see the merits of his way of life. Humans are weak and inferior. Vampires are a blight on all that existed. They are a creation born of the betrayal of Lucifer to Lilith. Wolves were born of a need in the world.

Constantine Trudeau held to the old ways. Wolves are out of sight and out of mind guardians against all else that goes bump in the night. His ruthlessness and brutality won him his nickname, but he loves his people fiercely. He would be the iron fist that would stamp out the rebelliousness of the Americana Pack and swallow the Northwest Pack. What concerned her was his boasting about the other Alpha pup in this fight. Why must the fate of the world always rest upon the shoulders of pups barely off their mother's teats? The way he talks concerns her that he will give up the old ways and murder Susie's mate. Una will not stand for that.

Mates are sacred.

They are the gift Lilith promised Una for her to forsake her life in Avalon and enter the realm of man.

"What do you want, old woman?" He growls at her again. "Speak your mind or get the fuck out."

"Manners, young pup. I am a guest and you should remember how to treat me," her sharp look turns to the mini-bar in the room. She is rather surprised when he blushes and frowns.

He stalks to the bar, pours a couple of drinks from the mini-bottles, and brings one back to her. His muscles tense as she watches him.

She can tell he is nervous about the fight. This eases her mind. If he was not nervous, she would think him too confident. She accepts the drink and sips it without speaking still.

He sits down like a sulking child with his drink.

"Much better. Now, to begin. Tell me young Constantine, do you have a mate?" His eyes dart to her and he furrows his brow.

"Listen, Alpha Una. You're lovely and all, but I have more important things to deal with than rutting." He takes a firm swig of his drink.

Una laughs, "Oh pup, you could not handle me in a rutting. Stick to your pretty little pups. I am asking because of your rather forward claim on Alpha Susie."

She listens as he informs her it is just boasting and that the only way he would lay claim to her is if her mate were gone. For all his bravado, it eases her mind to hear him value the relationship. She finishes her drink and leaves shortly after the conversation, giving his shoulder an encouraging pat. She then makes her way down the hall to Susie and David's room and gives a firm knock.

David answers the door. "I swear to God, Jacob, you're worse than a damn toddler with all your--" He stops mid-sentence and looks the older woman up and down.

Una raises a brow with a tight grin on her face.

"Mr. Coeh," she greets him formally.

"Uh, Susie, it's for you." David retreats into the room, and Susie comes around the corner in a bathrobe. She and David had been trying to fornicate, only Jacob felt like they needed a play-by-play update on Savannah and had interrupted them at least three times now.

"Alpha Una," Susie smiles. "Come in. Would you care for

something to drink? Pay him no mind. He's just frustrated with our Beta." Susie gives David a patient look.

"Thank you, I won't take up too much of your time. Yes, tea, please." Una comes in and takes up residence at the edge of the bed, as she had done with The Beast. She watches Susie brew her that God awful cheap tea in the little coffee pot in the room, but at least she offered without being reminded.

Susie then settles down in the chair. David kisses her on the temple and murmurs something about texting him when they're done. He leaves the room and Susie can hear him pound on Jacob's door down the hall. She chuckles and shakes her head.

Una watches the exchange and, to look at Susie, you wouldn't guess she is an Alpha. Her calm demeanor and the way she interacts with David makes her question how things are done in Savannah.

"As you know, the winner of tomorrow will be one of the few leaders of a major regional pack, and we will likely work together. I wanted to come and learn about how you intend to run the Appalachian Pack, and deal with the other American packs," Una says as she ships her tea.

Susie is a baby compared to the other Alphas at this level. Most don't come into being an Alpha until they reach about a hundred years old. A wolf's longevity depends on many factors, but to have Susie, who is not even fifty years old, considered for the head of a large pack is perplexing. Susie is a capable warrior. Her instincts are brutal and fierce. Her rise to her current position has been meteoric. Una regards her with an ambivalent gaze. Much to Una's surprise, Susie lets her sit in silence.

She picks up a small stack of papers to look through while she thinks about how to respond to Una. After a considerable pause. "I plan to run them how I do my current pack. Along with the help of the other Alphas. As for the Americana and Northwest. Well. The US is a pretty big place. I think it would be unwise to combine them all under one umbrella. So long as they aren't hurtin' no one, I don't really give a shit what they do."

Una raises a brow. She does not agree with the sentiment, but can see Susie's point of view on the matter. She shifts gears, "Tomorrow will be brutal. I am surprised you have not asked for a delay because of your condition." Una's smile turns into a smirk.

Susie looks up from her paperwork then and gives Una a faint smile. "Alpha Una, I am well aware of the level of battle I will face tomorrow. I will do what needs to be done. But, no offense, my *condition* ain't none of yer damn business."

CHAPTER FIFTY
My Pack My Rules

Susie wakes just before dawn. The light snore of David beside her tells her she didn't rouse him. She rolls over to face him and nestles close. His hand instinctively goes to her waist and pulls her against him before it grows heavy on her hip again. She traces her fingers along his cheek. Her eyes follow her finger trail, memorizing every tiny little nuance of his face. How lines have formed at the corners of his eyes. How his dark hair is just starting to salt at the temples. It gives him the look of a sly old fox. Her fingers trail further down. They walk the map of the chest and torso she knows all too well. He has a terrible scar across his chest where Silus and he had gotten into a horrible bike accident as kids. Jacob had been right to send them to the boathouse. It dissolved the wall they had built between themselves. Their discussion about this fight had ended with him supporting her, and telling her he loved her.

As she watches him sleep now, she prays to the Moon Goddess for the strength to win this fight. With a small nuzzle against his jaw, she gets him to roll onto his back, and she follows him. Susie straddles his legs where she feels him spring to life. His eyes haven't opened, but she knows he is awake. With a gentle shift of her hips, she is drawing him into a tender kiss before lowering herself onto his manhood.

His hands caress up her thighs and grip her hips as she leans up. He opens his eyes slowly to look up to his dark auburn-haired goddess. The way her body rolls on top of him is the most beautiful thing he has ever seen. He dares to slide his calloused hand up her soft skin, and fondle her breasts. Their love making is sweet and tender. Sadness fills him to think this might be the last time he gets to be with his wife. He gives his head a light shake to push those thoughts from his mind and focuses on her. The intensity of their lovemaking increases as he begins to thrust up to meet her hips as she crashes down on him. He reaches up and pulls her down roughly, smashing his lips into hers as he rolls her over. He guides her knee up with his other hand as he pumps down into her harder. The memory of the first time he had her fills his mind. She acted confident and cocky until he actually got her undressed. She had lied to Silus and him about her experience. Much to David's delight she wasn't experienced at all that night. His gaze holds her and they don't say a single word, not until he feels her shuddering underneath him, his own orgasm soon following.

"I love you, Susie Jeanette Coeh," he murmurs against her lips.

"I love you, David William Baxter," her reply is breathless against his skin.

They showered together, ate breakfast with the other Coeh Pack members, and the entire morning held a somber tone. Not much merriment and cheer came from their table as they all worried for their Alpha. The Beast isn't anywhere to be found this morning. It's quiet in the gathering room. All their lives were going to change in a few short hours. Susie gives David one last kiss goodbye and parts from him, entering the fighters' tents.

Jacob clamps a hand down on David's shoulder as they watch Susie walk away. "She'll win. It'll be alright," Jacob is assuring himself as much as he is David. "She has to. I don't want to be fucking Alpha."

David cuts Jacob a look, "You're right. She has to win. I'd hate to be fucking the Alpha," He gives him a wry grin and bumps him on the shoulder.

"Hey! I'd be gentle... at first," Jacob laughs. The other men following along are mortified at this conversation.

Michael pipes in, "Does that mean your wife's fair game if you become Alpha?" He sounds far too hopeful.

"I'm not beyond killing you for even thinking about her like that." Jacob dead pans as they take their seats.

The coliseum style ring is a cleared field with bleachers circling around. Susie had stripped out of her clothes and sits with her legs crossed in the tent. Her eyes are closed as she severs the link between her people and her. She doesn't want the distraction, or for him to feel her fear. She can hear the roars of the people outside the tent. There are hecklers there rousing the crowds. They are rattling through all the deeds of each Alpha. She has to admit that for all his faults, Constantine is a strong Alpha. She doesn't believe in the same way of doing things he does, but that doesn't make him wrong. She quietly sits and listens to the crowd.

When Alpha Constantine takes the battlefield, his pack is on their feet, growling and stomping for him.

She is getting swept into the momentum and stands. Dropping the little robe they offered her for modesty, she steps through the tent flaps. The sun is peeking over the tree line and it forces her to blink a few times as she moves to the center of the ring where the naked beast of a man stands with his arms crossed. The surprised murmur that falls over the crowd at her naked body makes David laugh.

That's his girl alright.

The terms and rules are read aloud. Each Alpha takes the blood oath to uphold a fair fight, and they turn to face each other. The bell chimes and both shift.

The Beast towers in at eight foot four inches, his shoulders easily three men side by side. His fur is a mismatch of browns and golds with a white belly. His massive hands swipe at Susie's head. He roars at her, trying to assert dominance with his howl.

Susie is just over seven feet in height and her shoulders are as broad as a man's. Her arms are long and slender and her fur is a dark auburn color. Where The Beast has brute strength, she has speed and agility. He lets out a violent roar and in the stands several wolves begin to submit. Susie feels it in her bones, his attempt to dominate her. It wasn't the first time a wolf tried to use their command on her in battle. She roars right back at him, sending the onlookers into confusion about which Alpha to submit to.

Constantine is thrilled she doesn't submit. He would have been disappointed.

Then she leaps on him and he tumbles with her, only she doesn't roll away from him. Instead, her knees lock onto him and she swipes at him with fast and furious strikes. The attack isn't enough to do lethal damage, but it's enough to draw blood. Lots of little tiny scratches pepper his arms and chest, stinging like deep paper cuts. His body steams in the brisk morning air as it kicks into overdrive to heal him. He finally gets a firm hold on her and throws her off of him. The second her foot touches the ground she is rolling as he is leaping at her. She balls up, protecting her stomach, and grunts as his knee slams into her forearms, bouncing her away from him.

Jacob frowns in the stands. His eyes narrow as he cuts David a quick look. He and Michael are sitting on either side of him in case this goes south. Susie took a defensive pose there. He has never seen her fight like that. She is usually balls to the wall, leaving herself completely open when she attacks. His gaze darkens as he looks back to the fight. There is only one reason she would defend instead of attack, and this was one hell of a time for that to happen.

Maybe he should not have banished them to the boathouse.

Constantine's fist connects with Susie's jaw, and it sends her sprawling. Blood fills her mouth, and she spits, growling at him. Their arousal is clear and makes those closest to them uncomfortable.

Then they are colliding and she bites his ear, hard, jerking him to the ground.

He rolls with it, letting out a yelp as he tries not to lose his ear. He lands a blow to her ribcage and Jacob tenses oddly. It draws David's attention to him.

"You alright, man?" David's voice is grim and low. He hadn't seen Susie fight before, not in anything serious, anyway. It's violent, and primal. No room for the tender woman he knows to exist. It's giving him a raging hard on.

"Fine," Jacob snaps, which only tells David he is not fine.

It's then Constantine who has the upper hand. He has Susie on her knees and he laces his fingers into her hair with every intention of snapping her neck.

Only, before he can get a full hold, she sinks her claws right into his balls, looking up at him.

The moment of mutually assured destruction brings the fight to a sudden standstill, every man in the stadium collectively holding their breath in anticipation. Sure, he could kill her, but she would take something extremely valuable with her.

They circle each other as they leap apart. It's then Susie shifts down into her wolf form.

This confuses Constantine, who is still in werewolf form. He watches her prowl around him in the circle. She is the most beautiful thing he has ever laid eyes on, and jealousy wells in him that she belongs to another. She takes advantage of the distraction to leap at him, a streak of dark fur. They are a hurricane of fur and teeth.

Constantine, struggling to keep her jaws from his throat and not lose his footing sends them crashing to the ground and Susie relentlessly pursues him. Her assault gives him no room to think or react.

He's bigger and slower in spite of his power. He finally bear hugs her and tries to squeeze her to death as he thrusts his weight on top of her, but he left himself open.

With a loud grunt, his back thuds against the ground and her teeth are in his neck. He squeezed tighter, trying to break her back, but only felt her mouth clamp tighter on his throat. Her growl is dark and menacing, warning him to submit.

The audience goes deadly quiet.

Another growl and light shake from her tells him she could easily tear his throat out if he tried to pry her off, or didn't submit.

He could not believe it. He lost to this woman. His body relaxes, and the stunned look on his face tells her he is submitting. She gives another growl, and a shake. His arms lax from around her and he's breathing hard. He shifts down into human form and looks up at the piercing gaze of Susie as a wolf. What he sees is her begging him to submit and not make her kill him. This makes him chuckle.

"I am not afraid to die," he rasps.

A small whine emits from her, but she does not murder him. Instead, she relaxes her bite and she nips his ear, taking a small chunk of it from him.

Susie shifts back into her human form and stands. "Submit. I am your Alpha," her voice booms over the crowd.

Jacob and David look at each other. Jacob lowers his gaze and turns his head in submission to Susie. David looks from him to the others and while he is not affected by this Alpha Command, he does submit out of respect, not wanting to cause a political shit-storm for Susie. Slowly but surely each wolf in the arena, except Una, lowers their head in submission. Even Constantine, who is at her feet, exposes his neck to her. She is bloody and bruised, flush from the exertion and excitement. Her eyes positively wild with the power surging through her.

"Respect the old ways," Una snarls at Susie with irritation. "It is not legitimate without his death. His blood seals your bond."

"No. It does not." Susie snarls back at her. "This is my pack. I will not needlessly kill a good man for power. My bond is sealed with their submission." Her hand motions. "The old ways are just that. Old. They have no place in this pack. If you cannot respect our ways, you are free to return to Britannia's territory with no ill will between us."

Una's eyes widen at Susie's defiance. She watches Constantine, who is healing under Susie.

Susie then turns to offer a hand down to him. "Do not feel shame, Constantine. You fought admirably. If you will accept it, you will be my Beta. I will take care to respect your way of life as much as my own."

Jealousy clouds Jacob's face. He thought if she won, he would be her Beta still.

Una, as the arbitrator of the power transition, gets a small smile on her face. As she suspected, Susie is a brilliant politician. To be Alpha does not always mean being the strongest. It means being the best leader for those under you. It makes her proud that Susie sees the value in life and will respect that over power. She is about to commend her for making such a wise decision when Constantine's voice cuts through the air.

"I accept, Alpha Susie. It is a great honor to help you guide our people." His deep baritone rings with sincerity. He leans in close and murmurs against her ear, "I owe you my life. I will never forget that, Susie Coeh. Thank you."

The area erupts into cheers. Una narrows her eyes at Susie, and the younger Alpha meets her gaze. The smirk on Susie's face tells Una that Susie had no intention of killing Constantine, ever. There is a nod between the two women, and Una leaves quietly. She had no desire to remain and celebrate with these American pups.

Constantine follows Susie's gaze. "That'll be fun to deal with." He misreads the silent interaction between the two women.

"Eh, she is a cantankerous old cunt. She was testin' us. I ain't worried 'bout her." Susie shrugs and it causes Constantine to erupt into full on belly laughter.

Susie feels hands on her shoulders, turning her. She started to bring up her clawed hand when she sees David standing there, beaming from ear to ear. She grabs the front of his shirt and pulls him into a rough and needy kiss.

"Now that you got that out of your system. Let's get some clothes on you," He smirks and tries to lead Susie to her tent.

Isaiah Belmont is the Tribunal representative that actually attended the fight, along with young Sabine Howell. The three vampires were forced to remain at the hotel due the fight being held during the day. He cuts into the celebration to congratulate Susie on her victory, informing her there would be a Tribunal meeting after sun-down to accept her officially into The Accord.

Constantine gives a snort at this, but keeps his mouth closed with the look Susie gives him.

Isaiah doesn't hide his excitement that it is Susie and not Constantine as the werewolf representative.

Sabine turns her gaze up at Constantine. "At least now we don't have to worry about putting you down." That makes Isaiah's eyebrows raise, and forces Susie to step between the young girl and Constantine. From behind Susie, Sabine lifts her chin defiantly. "What? You had no intention of joining The Accord, and we would have been forced to eradicate the wolves to keep the peace. Much like they did in Russia, centuries ago."

Susie inhales sharply and keeps her eyes on Constantine. He can feel her rage at Sabine's comments as well.

"You cannot hurt her. Go run it off." Her voice holds authority, but she doesn't use the command on him.

It makes Constantine look at her oddly. He has no issue with using his Alpha command to make wolves do as he wishes.

"I'm not you. Now run it off before I have to whoop your ass again." Susie flashes a grin.

He snorts and turns to walk away.

"He wouldn't have done anything," Sabine taunts and Susie turns around to face her, stepping into Sabine's bubble.

Isaiah stiffens, and he watches anxiously as the naked and bloody Susie reaches up to take Sabine by her chin.

She leans in close, her eyes dominating the younger woman's gaze. "Little girl, your arrogance is gonna get you killed one day. You'd be smart to not provoke a werewolf by callin' us mutts." She watches and waits for Sabine to realize she is without her vampire for protection.

Sabine turns her gaze in Susie's hand to Isaiah to help her, only to find he is standing there with a cocked eyebrow and bemused look. He has no intention of intervening, as he knows Susie won't hurt the girl in earnest. While she may be rough and tumble at the moment, she was not going to risk everything by abusing Howell's pet.

Susie gives a tight smile, then shoves Sabine roughly. "Insult my kind again, and we're gonna take it up with Patrick about what I get to do to you. I promise, ain't either of you gonna like it."

Isaiah exhales and helps Sabine up, before heading back toward the hotel, his hand never leaving her elbow.

David interjects then and takes Susie up over his shoulder to stalk back to the tent she came out of. The wolves around them growl and start to move forward to protect their new Alpha. David flips them the bird as he walks by.

Susie laughs and squirms, causing them to just watch in fascination. "Brute," she chortles.

Her wolves whistle and cheer David on. The flaps to the tent close and Jacob takes up guard duty. Nobody is getting by him while they celebrate.

* * *

Billy lies still, watching the sleeping forms of his mate and child. He is worried about Shelley. She hasn't said more than a few words since he found her last night. They showered when they arrived and he didn't protest one bit as the three of them curled into a bed together. The baby is sleeping soundly between the two of them. Billy, more than once, felt her jerk and whimper in her sleep. He is furious again for what Jackson has done to her. He did find comfort in the fact she had not been bitten. All her physical wounds were superficial and from her fleeing. He comforts her in her sleep, and murmurs soothing words until she settles again. She is clinging to Frances for dear life. They both had fussed over him after the shower, afraid that he was threatened. Guilt fills Billy at knowing that her life would be completely different if they hadn't rutted. He couldn't let her leave even if he wanted to. He is positive, without her, he would just die. As much as he wants to respect her being a human, he can feel the pull to turn her and give her the strength of a werewolf.

Tommy clears his throat in the doorway causing Billy to shift his glance to it.

Billy kisses Shelley on the forehead, then eases out of the bed to go talk with Tommy. He gives Tommy a once over, checking his wounds. While Tommy has cleaned up, Billy can tell he is pretty injured.

"Do you need anything?"

"Nah, man. I'm good, but we need to talk about Shelley," he frowns. "You need to get that thought right outta your head about turning her."

Billy raises a brow. "It has always been her choice to make, Tommy."

"Uh, huh. I see how you keep lookin' at her. Like she is a damn porcelain doll. Billy, that girl took a full on Ruttin' with you. Then spit out the watermelon of a son you gave her. 'Sides, you'll regret it. Part of you likes her as human." Tommy crosses his arms and takes the firm stance of a Beta.

"Anyway, it's not even up for discussion for another two hundred and fourteen days. At which point, whoever's Alpha will offer that to her. Regardless, it won't be my choice." Billy grumbles.

"Jasper didn't give a fuck about Alpha with Faye," Tommy lets slip.

"That's between the two of them. Plus, he set out on his own. He ain't rogue, but he's makin' his own pack with his own damn rules." Billy gives Tommy a pointed look.

"I know. You need to knock some sense in that asshole. Tell him to have his woman call her sister." Tommy mutters.

"What the hell do you mean she ain't callin' her sister?" That explained a lot. He had just assumed Faye was talking to her.

"And Shelley was fuckin' pissed when I told her Faye was alright." Tommy confesses.

Billy's eyes glaze as he roars into Jasper's head. *"Damn it, Jasper!"*

"Uh... A little busy, Billy. Can we talk later?" Jasper's voice is distracted, like he is fighting.

"No, you fuckin' prick. Tell your damn woman to call her sister!" Billy growls through their link.

"Yeah. Sure. Talk later," Jasper cuts the connection. Billy shakes his head.

"That damn fool is probably in a bar fight right now. No more talk of turnin' her. She is got enough to deal with. You understand me?" Billy points at Tommy.

"Yes, sir," he smiles. "Oh, and Matthias said you two can't leave property for a while. If you see any kind of press sniffin' around, tell 'em to get lost, and that it is private property."

"What are you talkin' about, press sniffing 'round?" Billy's eyebrow raises.

"You haven't seen it?" Tommy's face lights up like a kid on Christmas morning. "Oh, man, have you gotta see this."

He and Billy head into the living room where Tommy turns on the television. All over the local news are tales of a freak gas explosion at The Triple Six which killed upwards of twenty people.

CHAPTER FIFTY-ONE
The Aftermath

November 25, 2004

Susie is trying to escape from the sterile office that is her new work home. The Appalachian Pack was traditional in keeping the Alpha home and Pack house together. She hates that shit. No one in the pack needs to see her personal business. This will be changed when she moves here. Across from her is Constantine who looks sharp as hell in a suit. It's distracting. Constantine growls, "Tell me again, why am I in charge of The Rutting? Aren't you Alpha?" He flashes her a grin.

"You shut yer yap! It's called delegating." Susie grumbles.

"Won't it look bad, you missing the first Rutting of your reign, *Alpha*?" His voice is laced with humor. He enjoys riling her up.

"I'm gonna put you through that wall," she motions flippantly towards a wall. "I'm still Alpha of the Coeh pack, and they're whippin' themselves into a frenzy 'bout who the hell is going to replace me. Shit, even my granddaddy is talkin' about being Alpha. Damn fool ain't got any teeth and can't see past his nose, but he sure as shit wants to run the pack," she throws her hands up in frustration. Constantine laughs at the image of an old, gummy wolf trying to rule over the pups.

"Just tell them who is going to be the next Alpha. It's your choice." He's still laughing.

There is a knock on the door and David pops his head in. "Woman, I told you ten minutes ago we needed to go. If we don't leave now, we ain't gettin' dinner. And I am *not* puttin' up with your grumpy ass if you don't get to eat. Whatever the hell you two need to settle, settle it."

Constantine's brows raise and he narrows his eyes at David. He is quite surprised Susie allows him to talk to her like that. Even if he is her mate, he is not a wolf. In Constantine's eyes, that makes the man a lesser being.

"You stop rushin' me. I'm makin' sure Constantine has everything he needs to take care o' The Rutting. Unless you want to stay and we rut here." She had a sneaking suspicion Constantine wanted just that, as David had already made it clear he wasn't taking part this year unless it was with her. Especially in a strange pack where they didn't know who has dipped what into whom.

The two men lock eyes and Susie finds herself mildly aroused at the idea of them fighting over her.

"Susie Coeh, I'm gonna whoop your ass. You ain't avoidin' tellin' your family what's going on. You know damn well they're expecting us. Now get your shit and get your ass in the truck." David sasses her. "And you," pointing to Constantine. "If she don't get her ass out of this office in the next ten minutes. You have my permission to whoop it." He flashes Susie a devilish grin.

Constantine shifts uncomfortably, and a hint of a blush falls on his cheeks. Clearing his throat. "Yes, Luna," he smirks as he teases the other man.

David storms out after that, heading to the truck.

Susie and Constantine look at each other. He can see the look on Susie's face as she contemplates testing David's threat. Her eyes have an odd gleam in them as she looks at Constantine. He clears his throat and looks away first.

"I should get going," she chuckles. "You'll be fine. Find a nice young girl and show her what you're made of, champ," Susie pats Constantine on the shoulder.

"I did," he mutters to an empty office after the door closes behind her.

Back in Savannah, the entire Coeh pack has turned up for Thanksgiving weekend. The first full moon after Halloween fell just perfect for them to enjoy two holidays in one. With Susie as the new Alpha of the Appalachian Pack, the Coeh Pack has been in a tizzy about who will be the next Alpha. Most assume it will be Matthias, while others believe it will be Jacob. The tenuous balance that Susie held as their leader is crumbling. Old feuds and slights are starting to rear their ugly heads, causing strife throughout the pack.

Billy and Shelley have since moved back into the main house, and Billy is worried about her. She isn't engaging with him and the others. She focuses solely on Frances and school. When they try to broach the topic with her, she shuts down entirely and begins to shake. Billy can feel her pain and fear, and it's killing him. He holds her tight at night to keep the shaking and nightmares away. He and Matthias stand in the doorway and watch her in the kitchen with Bridget. Billy has a small frown on his face.

"I don't know what to do. I'm afraid she is never going to recover," he voices to Matthias through their mind link.

"She will. She is strong, Billy. It takes time. She was attacked and lost both her parents at the same time. The girl has fucking PTSD. She is going to be scarred the rest of her life. I still can't believe she resisted his control. Billy, humans can't resist vampires like that." Matthias looks at him pointedly.

"Maybe humans can't, but mates can. You've heard the stories." Billy looks back at Matthias. Humans who mate with a werewolf are gifted several boons. Good health, longevity, stronger will,

and better reflexes are the ones at the top of the list. The stronger the bond to their mate, the more powerful their gifts. Billy feels the thrumming connection between them. All the mess after their first rutting didn't make one difference.

"Just keep taking care of her. She'll come around," Matthias assures him. Then he pushes off the wall to head outside and settle whatever the latest fight has been started.

All the Coeh boys are being run ragged with putting out all the little fires. Working together, the eight men have been playing referee, placater, and sympathizer based on the situation. Billy sighs and follows him out to knock a few heads together.

Billy is about to approach two young pups brawling over who will get to sit next to Alpha when Hank, non-ranking wolf, crosses his path. Hank is a deputy in the Savannah police department. "We need to talk, Billy," he starts.

"You and everybody else," he straightens up and looks at Hank. "What's up?"

"That social worker ain't going away. She is called my office three times this week lookin' for Shelley. Almost have half a mind to invite her to Thanksgiving with how tenacious she is." He flashes a grin.

Billy grumbles and rolls his eyes. "She ain't ready yet, Hank. She may never be."

"Did you take her to the damn counselor like I told you to?"

"She sees the damn counselor twice a week, asshole."

"I ain't talkin' about Agatha at the school. I'm talking about a real head shrinker. Somebody with one o' them fancy degrees hanging on a wall."

Billy snorts. "It's on the to-do list. There's a lot of shit going on," as he motions to the two pups now rolling around on the ground snarling at each other.

Shelley comes walking out with two dishes in hand to set on the table. Her eyes narrow at the two pups on the ground as she sets the dishes down. "You get your asses up and act right. This ain't some inbred hoe down. You're about to sit down with family and give thanks, and this is how you act?!" Her voice hits a hysterical note as it hitches and tears cling to her lashes. The whole area goes quiet. All of them are well aware of who Shelley is, and what has happened to her.

"No! Bad!" She baps both of them on the nose with her dish towel. "Now you go sit at those trees until you can act right. Ain't no one sittin' at my table actin' a fool."

Hank and Billy share a look, but not a word is said between them.

Shelley crosses her arms as the two pups tuck tail and run for the tree she pointed to. As they are running, they are muttering at each other about whose fault it is they are now banished. Shelley whirls and looks at the rest of the group. "And don't you think I'm not above making the rest of your asses act right. This is Thanksgiving. Not the WWE. I don't give two shits who you think should be in charge. I'm in charge of this meal, and I'll be damned if it's getting ruined by some dick swinging contest. Is that understood?!" She shrieks it across the yard.

"Yes ma'am," Susie's voice cuts in behind her.

Shelley stills and she goes wide-eyed as she becomes cherry red. She turns to see the rather tight smile of Susie, who is angry with her pack and not Shelley.

David then chimes in, "Don't beat yourself up, darlin'. Someone's gotta wrangle these pups, and let me tell you, it is a full-time job." His smile is gentle as he tries to lighten the mood.

Shelley frowns, then runs into the house. The rest of the wolves settle down and start to take their seats without any more fuss.

Susie comes alongside Billy and rests a hand on his shoulder. "Go on in and make sure she is alright. I'll take care of these assholes." She gives his shoulder a gentle squeeze.

Billy finds Shelley in the nursery where she is sitting in the rocking chair. Frances lies sleeping in his crib next to her. Her face is drawn into a small frown as she looks out the window, watching his family carry on. Billy is at a loss of what to actually say to her. He knows she is not alright, but he has to break the silence and it's the only thing he can think of. "Everything alright, Angel?" His voice gentle and tentative.

This only draws her sweet face more into a frown. But she turns to look at him and sees the worry on his face. He has looked like that from the moment he rescued her. She sighs. "No, it isn't, Billy." She stands then and comes to him. Her tiny frame nestles right up to him and she buries her face against his chest.

His massive arms come around her and hold her tight. He can feel the tension ebbing from her as she stays against him, her emotions leveling out. "You wanna talk about it?" He kisses her temple.

"No," she mutters in a petulant tone.

"Let me rephrase that. Talk to me about it." He chuckles against her.

She hmphs at him, but nods. "Not in here. It'll wake Frances." Both of them agree that waking the tiny terror is not a preferred plan.

With an easy turn, he motions her out and they walk across the hall to their bedroom. He is much surprised when she curls right into his lap as he sits down. He had expected her to sit next to him. He doesn't fight it as he is elated she wants to be near him. Instead, he lets his hand wander in aimless circles along her back.

"I just wanted it to be perfect. No fighting. No one yelling. To see what a normal family looks like," she whimpers.

It breaks his heart to hear her, but he forces himself to focus on her. Then he chuckles. "That family out there does love each other. Don't you, ever for a second, think they don't. It's because they love each other so much they argue and bicker and carry on like three-year-olds," he confesses to her.

She groans, "That just means I was a total jerk then," she whines.

"Nope," he grins. "Means you're one of us. And you ain't weaselin' out of it. Trust me, if they didn't respect and love you, they wouldn't have agreed to your demands." He gives her a light squeeze. "And Angel, you're allowed to be emotional. You can be as emotional as you want. We're still gonna love you. You don't have to hide, Shelley. Ain't no one here gonna hurt you, I promise. I'll always protect you," he murmurs against her. Guilt wells in him that she was even put in that situation. "Plus, them two pups knew better." He can feel her relax.

"I don't know, Billy. One minute there's nothing. No feeling, no sadness, no happiness. Just nothing. The next, I want to scream and rage at everything." Her voice is quiet, causing even him to strain to hear her as she confesses her fears to him.

"Well..." he starts awkwardly, "Not to appear the overly insensitive asshole boy, but," he hesitates, knowing what he is about to say might get him slapped. "You women do have patterns where your hormones get cranked to eleven. Could it be something like that?" He exhales when he feels her shoulders shaking from laughter against him.

"Oh Billy Coeh," she sighs into him. "No. This is different. That," she chuckles again, "Is when the entire world is against me and nothing you say is right, and I feel ugly. Totally different."

"Okay," he nods, not fully understanding how she can spectrum such a thing, but he's going with it. "Just throwin' out ideas."

"I thought it was because of Momma and Daddy. But truth is, I'm relieved about them." She whispers it and he wouldn't have heard it had he not been a wolf. He pulls her tighter, understanding her emotions regarding her parents. "This nothing feeling is different, Billy. It's *nothing*," she emphasizes the word as if she could explain it through her tone.

"There is one option," he starts. "And you ain't gonna like it."

"I'm not turnin' into a werewolf, Billy. You think PMS is bad now," she chuckles.

"No, what I was going to suggest will be worse than that," he then gently eases her back to look at her. "I was going to suggest you talk to Momma."

Shelley's eyes widen and there is a mix of fear, irritation, and curiosity in her gaze. "Someone killed her parents too?"

"No, not that I'm aware of. Momma has dealt with a lot of shit and knows a lot of shit. She always has good advice when we need it. I figured the same might be true for you." He looks on hopefully. Billy has always revered his mother. His father is a good man too, but his mother is amazing in his eyes.

Shelley simply nods in agreement, not giving him any flack about it.

The pair linger on his bed for a few more minutes before his mother links him, *You two better not be doing anything. Get your ass down here, I'm hungry.*

Billy chuckles, "Not to make you feel worse about yourself, but everybody's waitin' on you 'fore they get to eat. I mean, If you really wanna show 'em whose boss, we could find something to do up here." He wriggles his brows at her. Shelley's cheeks flush bright red as she takes his offer to the dirtiest place he meant.

"Billy Coeh, you're incorrigible." She eases up off his lap, but then kisses him fiercely. "And I love you," she murmurs.

"Yes ma'am, I am. And I love you," as he follows her from the room.

She pauses in the nursery and scoops up the sleeping baby. Then the pair head down to the meal.

"Nice of ya to join us, Miss Baxter," Susie teases. She pats the empty seats next to her that the two pups had been fighting over. "Now that everyone's with us, enjoy!" The entire group of them dig in. There are at least a hundred people spread across the several tables strung together. There is enough food for at least twice that. Soon the table erupts into the bustling noise of people gossiping, eating, and kids playing and laughing.

Shelley happily holds the sleeping Frances in one hand while she eats with the other.

Susie is watching the Coeh Pack enjoy Thanksgiving. Matthias has done a wonderful job preparing for this and The Rutting. She is so proud of him. She had been mulling over what to do about Alpha for the Coeh pack the entire way home. Jacob doesn't want it. Matthias doesn't appear to want it, but fell into the role dutifully. She can't just pick another son, as it would cause an uproar throughout the pack. Especially if she picked one of the turned boys. In spite of the pack being welcoming to all wolves and humans, there is a big difference between a natural born Alpha and a turned one.

Any of her sons would make an amazing Alpha. She then looks at David, who is now holding Frances. The tough man cooing down at the child brings a smile to her lips as she rests her hand on her stomach.

Shelley takes this chance to devour her food.

Susie hopes it is a girl. She doubts it. She is eight for eight on boys, after all.

After about an hour, the meal comes to a close and they are sitting around, talking. "Alright, you mongrels," she chuckles. "We got some pack business ta deal with, and I'm not gonna spend all Ruttin' dealin' with your asses. So here's what's gonna happen. Matthias, Billy, and Caleb are gonna go through a proper Alpha challenge. Anyone else that thinks they can take on one o' them is welcome to join the challenge. Ain't no killin', and all pack laws apply. The winner is your new Alpha. That understood?"

There is a hushed murmur down the table and Shelley frowns. "What's a proper Alpha Challenge?"

Susie can see the worried look on the girl's face. "It's just a free-for-all boxin' match. Strongest survives. Seein' as I can feel about eight of 'em who want to play, it'll be kind o' like the Sweet Sixteen in basketball with the final two dukin' it out to be Alpha."

"Oh," she bites against her lip.

"Don't worry none. Billy's a pretty damn good fighter, even if he doesn't like to show it." She winks at Billy.

Matthias and his wife exchange a look. The silent conversation tells Susie all she wants to know about his thoughts on being Alpha. She purposely didn't say you couldn't just submit. Her boys are smart and will work it out.

Caleb chimes in. "I'm out! Good luck! I'm not even out of high school yet, and our pack already had one Freak Alpha," he grins at his mother. "It don't need no second one." The group erupts into laughter. It shows a great deal of wisdom to not just battle for the power of Alpha. Susie smiles, knowing Caleb will be a great man someday.

"Any other damn fool things we need to talk about?" Susie cuts across the laughter. When no one else brings up anything, she nods. "Then, as of tomorrow, I'm no longer your Alpha. I am the Alpha of the Appalachian Pack. The Elders will handle the Alpha Challenge. Tonight, we celebrate!"

CHAPTER FIFTY-TWO
Circle Of Life

December 2004

When Hank got blown off by Billy, he turns to David and Susie. He explains the situation, and how the social worker has been breathing down his neck to find Shelley.

David tells the man he will take care of it. He waltzed into that social worker's office, sat down, and explained just how Shelley came to be in his and Susie's care. He took the time to explain the abuse his brother had given both girls, and how he didn't discover it until it was too late. He provides verification that he is her uncle. He signed all the paperwork to foster her until she turned eighteen.

Faye and Jasper arrive on the fifteenth, almost a year to the day Shelley found out she was pregnant. They flew in from somewhere in South America.

Shelley, carrying Frances in a carrier, teeters anxiously to see her sister. Billy had taken the day off of work to take Shelley to the airport. He has been overly attentive to her since her confession at Thanksgiving. Shelley had talked with his mother, but Susie didn't have an answer. She offered encouragement and promised her that they would dig deeper if she wasn't feeling right after a few months. He has noticed little moments where Shelley seems to just stop functioning and stands stock still. The only sign she is present is her hand will twitch. It hasn't seemed to affect her day-to-day life, so he hasn't pressed the matter, but it worries him.

Billy grins and takes the carrier from Shelley, allowing her to pace and fidget properly. Billy sees them first, Jasper's broad shoulders and piercing gaze. He stands a head-and-shoulder over the general crowd. Jasper looks every bit like David, with lighter hair. Then his gaze takes in Faye. She looks lean and fit next to his brother. Both are sun-kissed, and she is holding his hand as they come strolling down the concourse. Billy can sense the change in Jasper, and is happy he found a pack where he feels like he belongs. The squeal of delight from the two women makes Billy and Jasper wince, then chuckle.

Faye and Shelley hug each other tight enough to make them gasp when they part. Each look the other over to make sure they're alright. Faye's tall and athletic build is only accented more by being a wolf now. It makes Shelley look even more dainty and feminine. Both girls tear up and hug each other again. There aren't words to say between each of them, but the men can feel it, the swell of relief from both of them.

Jasper and Billy give each other a tight hug.

Then Faye spots Frances. She scoops him right out of his carrier. She cradles him to her and coos down at the child.

Billy smirks and Jasper grimaces. The way she is holding the baby as they are walking, and doesn't even cast a glance upward, tells him he's in trouble.

"Oh, he's perfect, Bratnik. Look he even has your nose. And he smells so good."

"So when are you gonna get one o' yer own?" Billy teases Jasper.

"Fuck you," Jasper retorts with a grin. "She don't want one either."

"Uh, huh. 'Cause that looks like a woman who wants nothing to do with a baby," he teases as he watches Faye cradle the baby tighter.

"You both know I can hear you, right?" Faye coos in a baby soft voice, not even bothering to look at the men.

"Sure do," Billy gives a shit-eating grin. "So when you gonna have one?"

Faye snorts. "Yer daddy's an asshole," she coos to Frances who erupts into shrieking giggles.

It makes Shelley stop dead. That's the first time she is seen him act like that with anyone other than Billy.

Billy has a soft smile of a proud papa, as his son happily laces his fingers right into Faye's hair and pulls.

Jasper groans as he can smell the change in Faye. "I hate you," he eyes Billy.

"Don't blame me, man. This is Tommy's fault." Billy laughs and claps a hand on his brother's shoulder. "I'm surprised you don't have one already. You two have been hot and heavy since we met and I am sure you rutted like a good wolf. Means he's definitely on the way."

Jasper cuts him a dirty look. They have rutted, and Jasper realizes now they didn't use any protection. The way his momma talks, there isn't anything other than the mushrooms for protection in a rutting. "So, Ruttin' in South America... Them Brazilian girls do weird shit?"

Faye snorts.

Shelley blinks and turns bright red at Billy's crassness.

Jasper busts out laughing. "Nah, man. I wouldn't know. I was busy with my All-American girl. But the whole party leadin' up to it... Hot damn, it's crazy."

The four of them banter as they pile into the suburban and Billy drives them back to the Coeh house.

Shelley and Faye talk non-stop the entire way home. Billy enjoys watching her animatedly talk to her sister in the rear-view mirror.

The Coeh house is bustling with preparation for the funeral. While Silus was a bastard, he was David's brother, and the girls' father.

Faye hasn't mentioned her parents once, and Shelley isn't inclined to bring it up either.

Billy is much relieved that Shelley seems to have perked up with her sister's presence. He almost selfishly wants to ask Faye and Jasper to stay longer, but he knows the answer to that already. They are only here for Shelley. Jasper made it clear he was done with the Coeh pack last year when he left with Faye.

He laughs when he sees what used to be his room, decorated in cute baby animals and bright colors for Frances. He rubs his neck and smirks at Faye. "Wanna go sleep by the lake?"

"I'm in," she grins.

"Alpha," his mother's firm voice fills the hall behind him and Jasper stiffens.

Faye gives him a soft look, trying to encourage him to bury the hatchet with his mother.

With a sigh, he turns and looks at Susie, stuffing his hands in his pockets. There is silence between them as Jasper and she lock gazes. Jasper feels Faye's hand on the small of his back and he squares his shoulders, "Alpha," he responds quietly.

Susie wouldn't admit it out loud, but she is damn proud of Jasper. For all of his hot-headed and reckless actions, he has grown into his own. Her new position afforded her better knowledge on his whereabouts and actions.

Faye holds her breath as Susie steps forward. She exhales when Jasper is pulled into a tight hug by his mother.

He sniffs. "Fuck, not you too?" he whines like she has betrayed him.

Susie laughs and eases back. "Me too what?" She gives him an incredulous look.

"Nothing," he snorts, and turns his gaze to Faye.

Billy calls from in the nursery, "Faye's got the fever and Jasper's scared shitless. Don't you worry none, Momma. He rutted like a good boy."

Susie gets a knowing look on her face as she looks between Jasper and Faye, not saying a word.

"For fuck's sake," Jasper groans. "It doesn't happen *every* time you rut. We got shit to do. Ain't no time for a baby." He grumbles, but then bites his lip as Faye's shoulders droop.

Susie boxes his ears hard, which makes him growl and whine. "Ow. Shit! Momma!"

"You're still a damn fool, Jasper. Now get your ass downstairs and help your brothers with the hors d'ouerves." She barks like she is still in charge here.

Jasper looks between his mother and his mate.

Faye shoves by him without a word, angry and hurt.

Jasper locks eyes with Billy, who has come to the door.

"You should go after her and apologize," Billy offers softly. "She may not be talkin' about it, but her emotions are high today. As they should be." He reminds Jasper that they are at her parents' funeral.

"Think I could borrow him for a minute," Jasper gives a sheepish grin.

Billy smirks. "Nope. Get your own."

Jasper throws his hands in the air, exasperated. "The more things change, the more they stay the same. Fuck both of you, assholes." He turns and trots after where Faye disappeared.

The rumble of motorcycles can be heard as the remaining Angels come to pay their respects. The sea of Angels colors brings tears to Faye's and Shelley's eyes. When Faye turns, Shelley's wearing Paula's jacket. It had been at the house when her parents were killed. The Wolf Pack bikers show up in full force as well. Several other colors are seen and Shelley had never realized just how many people her parents had touched.

The two girls are standing numbly when David comes up

behind Faye, draping his old Angels jacket on her shoulders. "I know they ain't yer daddy's colors. They were *his* father's, and he'd want you to fly them proud," David's voice is gentle as he kisses her temple, then joins Susie with the rest of the guests.

Faye's jaw clenches and she slips her arms into the jacket without hesitation. She turns to give her sister a tight hug before they follow the procession down to the lake.

David steps up in front of the crowd, "Silus was a hell of a brother. Best wing man a man could ever ask for. Hell or high water he had your back. Until you crossed him. Or at least he thought you crossed him," the crowd chuckles in agreement. "When our momma, Francis, died, it created a rift between us. And while we had tried to patch it up here or there, that son of a bitch could always hold a grudge." More laughter from the crowd. "And somehow, by the grace of God another Frances came into our lives," then David tears up, "and with the shit he put his little girl through... Somehow, some way, her love for her Papa healed what twenty years of bad blood had severed." He looks at the jar in his hands and his breath grows ragged as he continues. "Silus, you truly were the best damn brother a man could ask for. Kick all their asses in Hell for me." With a tight nod, he hands Silus' ashes to Shelley as Faye takes Paula's ashes and the two girls spread them over the lake.

An hour later, people are meandering back up to the house for the wake. The crowd is gone, leaving Shelley and Faye standing there with Billy and Jasper. Shelley has fallen quiet, her hands at her side as she stares out over the lake.

"He is dead. Stop waiting for him like he commanded," she thinks to herself, trying to will her body to move and can't. Her hand twitches. To the other three she looks passive and quiet. Her cheeks are red and puffy from crying throughout the day. She is only staring blankly out over the water. Billy is filling Jasper and Faye in on what really happened and Faye frowns, looking at her sister.

"No wonder she is catatonic. Fuck. Did he bite her?" Her tone is pinched as she comes closer to her sister. "Earth to Bratnik!" She takes a deep inhale of her sister. She doesn't care how weird it looks. "Nope, no vampire."

"I'm right here, being a good girl. No! I don't want to be a good girl," Shelley's thoughts spiral as her hand twitches again. She struggles to shake off the lethargic desire to wait obediently for Jackson. She has not said a single word out loud. In spite of him being dead, and knowing that he was left as a pile of ash in the woods, there is something in her mind trying to consume her and make her surrender to his commands.

"Billy, has this happened a lot?" Faye frowns at Shelley and waves her hand in front of Shelley's face.

"Shelley," his voice calls to her in a low and anxious manner, and he places a hand on her shoulder. It jolts her body into responding and she blinks, looking between them. The fog lifts and she is confused for a moment by their worried expressions. She looks from Faye, to Jasper, to Billy.

"What?" Her mind locks away what she just went through. All that is left is a blank spot where the last several minutes should have been.

CHAPTER FIFTY-THREE
A Penny For Your Thoughts

March 2005

Shelley's eyes fly open. It's quiet. She looks up at the ceiling and furrows her brow. Above her is the far too familiar popcorn ceiling of her old bedroom. She sits up suddenly and looks around. Confusion and fear wash over her. She is in the twin bed that's shoved against the window wall. Faye's bed is neatly made, and the room is dimly lit. The only light is from the little unicorn night light plugged in at the foot of her bed. Shelley looks down at herself and she is in a T-shirt, one too big for her, and as her bare feet touch the old carpet she curls her toes. She eases up off the bed and gingerly walks out of the room.

From downstairs she can hear some sort of sports game on the television. It's surreal to her. The house looks exactly how she remembers it the night her father threw her out. She feels tired and drained, like she isn't getting enough sleep. The nagging feeling that something isn't right fills her. She distinctly remembers her father saying he had better not see her again, and the fear that he'll be downstairs and catch her floods through her. She looks down at her hand and on her finger is a ring, sparkling and bright, with sweet little sapphires laced in diamonds. This only draws more confusion from her as a dull ache forms in her temples. She shakes her head to clear the cobwebs and cautiously continues down the stairs.

When she reaches the bottom of the stairs, she stands stock still. In her father's big recliner chair is the perfect specimen of raw male, his blondish brown hair cropped, and his wind kissed skin tanned from days spent under the sun on his bike. When he turns his gaze to look at Shelley, his eyes pierce right into her. His stormy blues meet her pale blue ones. His smile is gentle, and he eases up off the chair. "Angel," he rumbles low and gentle. "Have a good nap?"

As Shelley struggles to process what is happening, Jackson's arms are sliding around her and he is kissing against her temple. He is warm and safe, like he was before that horrible night in Hilton Head where he abandoned her. "Y... You're..." her words slip away as she struggles to remember the thought that just slipped her mind.

"Shh, Angel, it's alright. You're safe. He can't hurt you anymore." Jackson's voice is tender and loving. His strong hands rub her back gently. Shelley begins to shake more. Her hands push against his chest and she looks up at Jackson's face. His grip tightens on her, like he's afraid of losing her.

"W... Who can't hurt me?" She frowns, perplexed on who he is referring to. His cologne fills her senses and reminds her of how much she missed clinging to him on the back of his bike.

"Your daddy. I took care o' that bastard and you're safe now. Here with me." Jackson's entire demeanor is off. He has never been so tender with her. He has always been possessive and controlling. The way he nuzzles her and holds her close leaves her feeling serene.

Her eyes are then drawn onto the simple white gold band on his ring finger. She frowns, struggling to remember anything about their wedding.

"Now, go on, Angel." She is drawn back to his gaze, the

wedding band dissipating like smoke in her memory. "You need to get dressed before you cook us dinner. Unless, you're trying to rile me up while cookin' in nothing but my T-shirt." He flashes Shelley a wicked grin.

It gives Shelley the impression he might thoroughly like that option, which causes Shelley to blush fiercely and tug the hem of the shirt down.

He gives a soft chuckle, pinching her butt as he sends her back upstairs.

Slowly, she makes her way back up the stairs and heads into her room. She finds it odd that if they're married, then why is she sleeping in her bed? She opens the closet, and it's empty. This makes her furrow her brow and look around. The entire room looks empty and abandoned in the dim light from the unicorn on the wall. She quietly returns to the hall and turns to go into the master bedroom. It's vastly different from what she remembers. The large bed with dark sheets and a quilt under the window looks far too plush to have been her parents' bed. Her jewelry boxes are open on the dresser on the far wall. She opens the closet to find a mix of her and Jackson's clothing. She steps into the closet and brushes her fingers over the clothing. A sharp pain stabs in her temple and she rubs her fingers over it. She chalks it up to a storm front moving in and her sinuses are acting up as a small peal of thunder ripples over the house.

"You alright, up there?" He calls from downstairs. "I'm starvin' down here. You wanna hurry it up?" His tone sounded more normal, with a hint of menace if she didn't comply.

She hurriedly pulls the dress she was fingering off the hanger and slips it on. As she leaves the bedroom, she catches a glimpse of herself in the full-length mirror and realizes she put on one of her momma's dresses. "Why do I have momma's dresses?" Shelley lingers, looking at herself in the mirror. She is having a hard time focusing on her face.

"Shelley," Jackson's voice growls up, breaking her glance from the mirror.

"I'm coming," she calls hurriedly, not wanting him to get angry. Fear washes over her at the thought of making him angry.

As she comes back down the stairs, he smiles at her and watches her head into the kitchen.

Everything was the way she had left it. The dishes in the sink had the remains of Christmas dinner. It makes her shake her head and frown as Christmas was several months ago.

Then he's pressing against her back and kissing against her neck, tilting her head enough to make her entire body go rigid. Something was terribly wrong here. Jackson kept touching her and when he does, her mind gets all muddled. What are they doing in the kitchen again?

"Everything alright, Angel? Make me some o' that stuffin' stuff you like. I'm famished." He purrs against her neck then leaves her alone.

Shelley is standing there, looking at the kitchen and breathing harder. She looks down at her hand again. The ring glimmers shiny and bright in the dim kitchen, almost like it's out of place on her finger. The entire room feels queer as vertigo causes her to swoon. With a small shake of her head, the room snaps into focus and she obediently begins cooking the dinner he requested.

Not long after she starts to cook, the wind picks up and howls around the house. The entire house shakes like an earthquake and she is terrified. Then Jackson's there again, wrapping his arm around her waist as she cooks. "It's just a storm, Angel. Don't worry your pretty little head about it." He kisses her temple softly. Shelley nestles into the warm comfort of his arms. She feels the tension ebb from her body and the pounding in her head subsides.

Dinner is quiet between them, but the howling of the wind is picking up and the rain machine gunned against the house. It is like the storm was trying to jar her into paying attention.

"Enough. It was wonderful, Angel." Jackson grips her hand tightly as he pulls her into the living room with him. The two of them settle down on the couch to watch television as he keeps her close. His arm is around her, and occasionally he leans over and kisses her temple. A roaring thunderclap shakes the house again and Shelley hops up before Jackson can keep her in place to go to the window.

"Angel, it's just a thunderstorm," Jackson's voice sounds like it is far away to her as she pulls the curtain back. Outside the window is the most violent and terrifying sight she has ever seen. The rain is bright and coppery, like little comets of fire showering down through the jet black sky, and a hurricane of copper fire lit by thrashing white claws of lightning was spinning right for the house.

"Jackson! Jackson! There's a hurricane coming." She turns to run with him to the basement of the house, only she is alone. She is standing in the living room, but there is no Jackson. Jimmy Kimmel drones on in the background from the television, the audience laughing loud at some crass joke.

"Jackson!" She shrieks in fear. The house shakes violently again. She covers her ears and drops to her knees, sobbing. Shelley squeezes her eyes shut as the house explodes around her, leaving her in total darkness.

"Shelley!" Billy's voice is full of urgency as he shakes her gently. "Shelley, look at me," he begs her. She is standing in front of Frances' crib, unmoving. Her expression as she looks down at the screaming infant is blank and passive, like she isn't even there. The only sign she is still conscious is her hand occasionally twitching. Frances is howling at the neglect of being left in his crib well past his feeding time. Billy places both hands on her shoulders, turning her to face him. "Shelley, wake up," he growls in anguish.

"Billy? What? Who? Oh, Frances," she frowns and tries to free herself of Billy's grasp to pick up the screaming infant as if she hadn't just been standing there catatonic.

Billy watches her in silence as she soothes their son. He realizes that there is something not right about this entire situation. This isn't PTSD or postpartum. These episodes are getting worse, and more frequent since her parents' funeral a few months ago. As they approach Spring Break for Shelley, Billy is beginning to question not forcing her to see a therapist. He has never seen her let Frances fuss for more than a few seconds, and by the time he came into the room, their son had been screaming for a good five minutes.

Once she gets Frances soothed, he pipes up. "You sure everything's alright, Angel?"

Shelley furrows her brow as she looks at Billy, getting another weird sense of déjà vu. Her head begins to throb, and she gets the horrible feeling she is forgetting something important. "Of course. Everything's alright, Billy," her tone is soft as she kisses against Frances.

Billy's expression draws more into a frown. "If you say so. You know you can talk to me, darlin'. I'm here for you."

Shelley gives him a soft smile that melts his heart and closes the space between them with a few steps. She leans up to kiss him softly. "I know, now go on back to bed. I got him."

CHAPTER FIFTY-FOUR
Brotherly Love

Saturdays are Billy's favorite days. No work, no chores, no pack business. Matthias and he had planned this fishing trip since the Alpha challenge was announced. Both men have been making their way through the bracket created by the elders and there are four wolves left. Billy and Matthias are due to fight each other next weekend. Matthias and his wife have talked it over at great length. He has been offered the Beta position of his wife's pack. He didn't have the heart to just bail on his family's pack. Finding his wife pregnant again and with the new offer from her pack, he had already decided to either become Alpha and pick one of his brothers, or hope that one of his brothers wins the challenge.

The two men load up the supplies and are out the door while it was still dark out. They drive to the boathouse and load up the pontoon boat. The sun shines brightly in the eastern sky as the two men are sitting on the front of the boat, their feet in the water. They don't have to fill the air with noise and chatter. They are fussing with their fishing lines and baiting the hooks to avoid talking. The incident with Shelley and Frances weighs heavily on Billy's mind. Shelley is furious with him and has moved into a guest room.

It hurt like hell when she accused him of treating her like a pet. That when she didn't do what he wanted, he forced her to get all sorts of medical attention. That it had to be something wrong with her. It just wasn't like her and it gnawed at him. Through the bond, he can feel she is afraid and angry all at once. He didn't leave her any room to argue. He forced her to go to therapy. He also forced her to get a real check-up, with the pack doctor. The loneliness of Shelley not being in his bed has made sleeping even more difficult. He knows there's something wrong with her. People don't just stop moving like that. She doesn't know this, but she is no longer left alone with Frances. He hired a nanny to care for Frances under the guise of helping her with her final month of her junior year of high school. She had relented only when she realized she was in danger of failing a class.

"We're pregnant again," Matthias cuts the silence.

"Congratulations," Billy smiles. The worried look on Matthias' face makes him chuckle. "What's this? Four? Five?"

"Six and seven. It's twins. She is over the moon," Matthias rolls his eyes at Billy. "I've been offered the Beta position in her pack. Her father's health is ailing, and he is stepping down."

This raises Billy's brows, and he gets a perplexed look on his face. "How is that going to work when you become Alpha of our pack?"

Matthias chuckles and shakes his head. "I already told the Elders I wasn't fighting you. That I forfeit, and you're moving into the finals."

"You did what!?" Billy chokes on a mix of shock and anger. He had mildly been looking forward to fighting his brother. "You can't quit. You're supposed to be Alpha." Billy frowns at his brother and is suddenly feeling the pressure that he must win the final fight to honor their mother's legacy.

"Billy, I never wanted to be Alpha of the Coeh pack. I left to get away from these assholes. Our kids have grown up in Bridget's pack. It's peaceful, and none of the bullshit like here. I already accepted the Beta position. I only stayed in the fight to make sure one of us was in the final round. If any of the other brothers had made it this far, I would have done the same for them." After getting it out, Matthias noticeably relaxes.

Billy had a million protests and is more irritated with his older brother now, but the look on Matthias' face silences him. For all his ire, Billy understands, and he nods. They fall into an amiable silence again. The fish aren't biting. They can sense the nearness of the two predators and won't get anywhere near their bait. Billy stares at the water again and finally sighs. "Shelley is getting worse," he starts. "There is something going on in that pretty little head of hers."

"She has been through a lot, Billy," Matthias offers gently. "I mean, it's not even been a full year since her parents were killed and she nearly died."

Billy rubs his face in frustration. "God damn it, Matthias. Don't you think I know that? Fuck. It's not that. I can feel there's something wrong. We've seen what traumatized humans look like, and this ain't that. She just checks out. Like a damn vampire's kiss has her enthralled, but she ain't been bitten. She is coming up aces on all the tests Doc gives her. But it's happening more and more. Harriet tells me she'll see her just standing there, staring at Frances with this look on her face like she hates him. She does it at school too. Caleb says she'll just stand there, staring blankly at him, then doesn't even act like she has done it. She is moved out of our room and doesn't want me to get anywhere near her."

The hurt and fear in Billy's voice makes Matthias take pause. He reels in his line, sets the pole aside, and turns to face his brother.

"Billy, do you feel your bond getting weaker when this happens?"

"No. That's the damn weird part about it. I thought that, too," he gives his brother a look. "Like maybe she was losing interest and had found someone else. But when I feel her, it's as strong as ever. Maybe more so. When she blanks out," he frowns at the water. "It feels like the bond is the only way I get her back out of the spell. These last few weeks I've had to shake her to get her attention. Every time, it's like she is afraid of something, but then suddenly right as rain."

"Hmm," Matthias nods in response. "And you said she is physically alright? It's just these random episodes of nothing?"

Billy nods in response. "It's all I can do to concentrate when fighting. It's driving me so crazy. I just want her to be happy, and to give her the world, but it feels like all I do is mess up her life."

"Billy," Matthias sounds irritated, "that girl loves the shit out of you. Do you know she asked me to take back the rules Momma put in place about her bein' able to rut with you?" He gives him a smirk. "She gave a very compelling argument about the fact that if she weren't with a bunch of stuffy werewolves she would be old enough to give consent in the eyes of the State of Georgia. It took all my strength to not laugh her out of my office. She has been telling Bridget all about how you and Frances act when you are together. She even confided in her that she hopes you still want her when she graduates."

Billy blushes and grins. "She was counting the days down until her eighteenth birthday, the first of May. I didn't have the heart to tell her that Momma threatened to castrate me if I touched her before she graduated high school."

"She is aware. She asked me to reverse that too. Said it's not fair and she should get to decide what she does with her mate. She *actually* used the mate card." Both men laugh at the idea of Shelley throwing that fit to Matthias.

"What did you tell her?" Billy raises a brow, trying to keep the hopeful look out of his eyes.

Matthias snorts and rolls his eyes. "I told her that if I changed the rules, Momma would have my balls too, and I just couldn't bring myself to sacrifice them on her behalf. Then I suggested she find creative alternatives to scratch that itch." Matthias laughs when Billy punches him hard in the jaw. Both brothers are smiling then. "Listen, Billy. I think you need to prioritize. I'm not saying to forget about Shelley's issue. I'm just saying you need to focus on becoming Alpha. Once you're Alpha, deal with her situation. You'll have more power, and your bond will be stronger. You'll be able to help her better if your attention isn't divided."

Billy nods, but the idea of putting pack over his mate makes him sick to his stomach. He grimaces and turns to face the water again.

CHAPTER FIFTY-FIVE

Preparations

June 2005

Shelley is in a full on panic. She is keenly aware that she is not alone in her body. Three days ago she fought against the numbing sensation. She was sitting with other women of the pack, and realized she was fading out. She had focused on what the women were saying and doing, trying to engage with them. It was then it happened. He laughed and mocked her as he took control of her body. Shelley felt her very being shoved to the back of her mind, like she was being locked in an invisible cage.

"You will always be mine," Jackson's voice purrs in her head. *"Now be a good girl and play along."* She had tried to go to Billy. No matter how hard she tried, her body avoided him. Surely he would notice she is acting strange?

Caleb has noticed and growls at her every time she gets anywhere near him. Her body doesn't react right. She doesn't cry in spite of the silent plea in her mind to help her.

"Don't worry, Angel. You'll be happy soon enough. We just have to wait for the right moment. Then you'll be mine." Jackson coos in Shelley's mind.

"Please, Jackson, don't do this. Please. I love Billy. We're mates. Please." Shelley begs of him constantly.

The only response she gets from him is anger and jealousy. She is shoved further into the back of her own mind. He is allowing her to see what he is doing, which terrifies Shelley. She can feel every sensation, hear every word, but it is like she is watching television and she can't change the channel.

Billy has been avoiding her. She can feel his loneliness and frustration. The amount of hurt coming from him makes her heart break. Their bond is deepening, and she knows that he is struggling when it comes to her. Try as she might to use that bond, she is thwarted. In horror, she feels Jackson responding to his wants. He manipulates her emotions to send him reassuring vibes while allowing her love for him to blossom to the surface, appeasing the beast.

The way he handily plays as Shelley makes her lose all hope of Billy ever coming to her rescue. Was he planning to possess her forever and just never let Billy have her again?

"Oh no, Angel. I fully plan to be your mate forever. Don't worry that pretty little head of yours. You'll have your mate. He'll just be... improved."

Billy had tried to take Matthias's advice and focus on the Alpha challenge, but he feels her inner turmoil. Panic and fear mix with emotions he can't readily process, like anger and jealousy. Billy has done nothing to provoke her ire. Try as he might to focus on the challenge, his mind wanders back to Shelley.

Caleb has cut himself off from her. He told Billy that wasn't Shelley. That it looked like her, smelled like her, but there was something wrong about her.

The fight this evening is going to be bloody and violent. His cousin Darryl came from his eldest uncle and had Alpha genes in him as well. Not to mention, the man is a few years older than him. He had wanted to spend the morning with Shelley, snuggling and cooing at Frances. Instead, he found Shelley was not in her room. Her panic and fear thrum in his chest, making him want to go hunt her down and hold her close. He checks the nursery and sees Frances is still sleeping. He steps in and scoops up his son. The baby looks tiny as he cradles him to his massive chest. It makes Billy smile as he nuzzles the boy's tiny head. The imagery is completely reversed when Shelley is holding her massive child. "Where's your momma, buddy?"

Billy wanders the rest of the house, casually looking for Shelley and frowns when he cannot find her anywhere. *"Tommy, you got eyes on Shelley?"* Billy tries to sound casual over the mind link.

"Nah, man. I'm at the arena, getting things ready here. Pop, you got her?" Tommy loops in Jacob.

"Haven't seen Shelley since school ended a few weeks ago." Jacob's calm voice comes over the link, but in person he is getting his stuff together to find Shelley.

Billy's fight is in a couple of hours, and this is the last thing he needs.

"Maybe she just went shoppin'? Or she is out for a walk?" Billy offers hopefully, but dread fills him. He closes his eyes and he tries to feel her through their link and is met by a crashing wave of fear and panic. Something has happened. Then it's gone, and she is sending him encouraging vibes. The love she feels for him hits him like a Mack truck. His brow furrows deeper, and he rubs his hand along Frances's back. "Buddy, we're gonna help your momma. Just one more day. Then I'm gonna fix it. Ain't never gonna let her suffer again. I promise." Billy possessively keeps Frances with him until it is time to get ready for the fight.

Shelley still hasn't come home. Jacob gives him progress updates every thirty minutes, but trying to locate her is proving daunting. He tracked down that she had been at the arena near sun up then wandered off in the woods.

"Find her. I need to focus on the fight. If someone has hurt her..." Billy's voice fills not only Jacob's ears, but the Delta and Gamma as well.

The men agree. They leave Billy to his brothers and the pack begins to search for their potential future Luna.

"We'll find her. I've already got her scent." Jacob calls to them as he stalks along a faint scent trail he picked up. It's tracking deep into the woods, and it's concerning to him that she would wander this far without someone to help her.

"Miss Shelley?" Jacob's voice is soft as he comes into view of her. She is standing stock still. Her hand is twitching and when he comes around to look her in the eyes, they are out of focus, like she is staring at something far out of his sight. He reaches up and takes her chin, turning her head this way and that. "Shelley," his voice is firmer now. He sniffs, but he does not sense anything else around her. There is still no response. *"I found her. She is safe."* He quickly calls off the search, and hopefully sends Billy the ease of mind he needs to focus.

When Shelley doesn't respond, he simply picks her up over his shoulder. She weighs nothing to him and he starts back to the arena. Doc would be there and could check her out. She is limp in his arms. Jacob is grimacing as he walks. He can hear her heartbeat, and there is otherwise nothing wrong with her. It's the damnedest thing. *"Doc, be ready. I need you to look at Shelley."*

"Bring her to the medical tent."

Ten minutes later, he is gently putting the catatonic girl on the make-shift medical table. "How long has she been like this?"

"Not sure, at least thirty minutes. That's the way I found her." Shelley's hand twitches and both men watch. The doctor checks her vitals, flashes a light in her eyes, and frowns.

"Everything looks normal. If I didn't see it, I would say she is faking it. But *that*," he motions to her hand, "is not something people fake."

"Do you want me to get Billy?" Jacob frowns and rubs his cheek as he looks down at Shelley.

"No. He is already amped up because of her. This will just add to his stress. Unless, you're *trying* to make him lose?" the doctor's grin broadens as he looks at Jacob.

"Fine. Keep her here?" Jacob grumbles as he leaves the tent. The crowd begins to gather. The battle for Alpha has drawn people from all over the pack territory. Billy and Darryl would both be good choices as Alpha. Darryl Coeh leans more to the wolf-friendly policies, while Billy takes after his mother. As they get closer to sundown Mehzebeen and Isaiah roll up in her car. Billy's head is killing him. The wild roller coaster of emotions from Shelley is causing him to struggle. Frances is with Harriet, and he hasn't seen Shelley all day. Jacob said she was alright, but Billy doesn't believe that horse shit for one second.

"Look at me," Matthias's firm tone pulls Billy's gaze to him. "Clear your fucking mind right now. There is nothing you can do for her if you don't keep yourself in check and win." He rests his hands on his brother's shoulders.

"Darryl likes to pin his opponent and use his weight to keep them down. As long as you keep him moving, you have the advantage. He's slow and favors his right side." Samuel and Brandon are offering their input on Darryl's fighting abilities. "Hands down you are the more rounded fighter, and stronger if you can get him off his game."

"Gentlemen," the elder wolf pops her head into the tent. "It's time."

CHAPTER FIFTY-SIX
The Cat Came Back

Billy and Darryl emerge from their tents and their families take their places in the stands under the pale moonlight. Billy frowns when he doesn't see Shelley anywhere. Both men are naked and showing off their prowess. Billy looks wild with his hair tousled from running his fingers through it relentlessly. Darryl's longer hair is neatly pulled back. Both men are in prime physical condition for young Alphas. It is difficult to tell who is being cheered on as the roar of the crowd engulfs the area.

Shelley's eyes open in the medical tent, and she is alone. Doc has gone to the arena to be ready should the boys carry the fight too far.

"Just gotta look pretty, Angel." Jackson's voice fills her mind and tears begin to stream down her cheeks.

She sits up and places her feet on the ground. She purposely doesn't think about her plan, and she walks. She had every intention to turn and run into the forest, far away from Billy so Jackson can't hurt him.

"Oh, Angel, so heroic," he coos in her mind, *"but there is nothing you can hide from me now. Don't worry, it'll soon be over."* Her body jerks as she tries to resist, and she turns to approach

the arena. She finds herself in the entrance Billy had just emerged from, holding still in the center.

Mehzebeen and Isaiah are sitting on a raised platform as guests of honor for the fight. With Suzy still off doing Alpha work, it fell upon them as Tribunal members to oversee this fight. Mehzebeen furrows her brow. "Vampire," she murmurs, and her eyes flicker from the gold color to the fiery blazes of Hell.

Isaiah shifts uncomfortably and looks around with her, trying to pinpoint the source. While he could not smell them, like Mehzebeen can, he usually can pick them out of the crowd. Both of them were on edge. The threat is proving elusive, making them even more wary and distracting them from the fight about to begin.

The elders of the pack set the two boys loose on each other and it's terrifying to watch. They both morph into their werewolf forms without hesitation. Claws tear and teeth rend as howls and snarls fill the air. Isaiah had never watched such a thing before the Appalachian Pack's challenge. While he knew this one was not to the death, the very nature of their fight looks like they will tear each other into pieces.

Darryl immediately has the advantage. His size is massive next to Billy, which is an impressive feat considering the mountain of a man he is fighting. Darryl lands hit after hit and it draws gasps and cries of joy from the crowd.

Billy staggers back from the onslaught and brings his clawed hand to his head. It feels like someone is taking a silver axe to it. Another heavy blow comes crashing from above, and he tries to roll it off his shoulders, but cannot deflect the blow. Darryl's slashing and rending force him to the arena's edge. The voices of his brothers roar into his head, telling him to move his ass. Billy's vision is blurry and off. The sharp stabbing pain will not leave him.

Shelley's shrieking in the distance. He can hear her, but it's like she is far away.

Darryl lands another left hook, and it sends Billy staggering until he's on his knees.

Ten feet from him is Shelley, stock still and watching with bland indifference. He can see the tears streaming down her cheeks and her entire body trembles.

"MOVE!" The cacophony of voices in his head solidify as all his brothers agree what to say, and Billy rolls just in time to miss the pinning blow from Darryl.

The sudden lurch from Billy leaves Daryl off balance and he careens towards Shelley.

She stares at the hulking beast crashing towards her, unflinching and unblinking.

Billy catches the other man before he can hurt her and throws him off in the other direction. Darryl grunts as he rolls along the ground, slowly getting to his feet. That's when Billy smells it. His eyes widen and a vicious snarl rips from his throat. It is the same scent he smelled that night he found her in the forest, being pinned down by that vampire. He looks around, wildly, and can't see him anywhere. The scent intensifies, then loud and taunting laughter fills Billy's head.

"Oh, hot damn, you're a strong beast," the bastard's voice hisses in Billy's ears. *"I'm gonna love fuckin' Shelley like this,"* he purrs.

Billy is sent sprawling as Darryl's fist connects with him again.

"Oh, I bet that hurt, Billy boy. Just relax, so I can take full control, I'll let you still watch when I have her. I've been itching to feel my Angel for at least two years, so it'll feel all the better knowing my first time is your last."

Darryl lands another blow as Billy feels the crushing heaviness from Jackson's attempt to take control of his body. It's all falling into place. The way Shelley would stop moving. How she feared nothing at all. How she looked like a shell of a person. She had been battling Jackson all alone, and it crushes Billy that he didn't do something sooner.

"Awe, don't beat yourself up Billy boy. She didn't figure it out until I let her. She is such a sweet little ride, and I spent all these months getting to know you well enough she won't know the difference." Jackson tries to assert dominance again as Darryl lands a blow to Billy's gut that sends Billy to his knees.

He could feel himself losing on both fronts. The voices of his kin are silent to him, as he struggles to keep his defenses up. His eyes move to Shelley. She has dropped to her knees as well. He's being shut into a cage in his own mind. Another blow lands from Darryl and Billy is on all fours. The massive werewolf is bleeding, broken, and slowly losing all control of his own body.

"Goddess, please," Billy pleads, his eyes on the moon above them. "I can't fail her again."

The wind howls around the arena, and Darryl is barreling forward to attack again.

"She deserves to know love." Billy lets out a mournful howl as the heavy blow flies towards him.

"Help me, I beg of you." Shelley is his mate. He will not let some punk vampire come between him and her. His jaws open wide as he arches towards the heavy silver moon in the sky, and his howl transforms into a deafening roar. Power rages through him as he stands, his coppery fur flaring to life in the silver light. Around the arena, silence falls across the spectators as everyone submits. Their heads are turning down and their necks expose. Even Isaiah and Mehzebeen feel the compulsion. Darryl stops in his tracks and blinks as he drops to his knees and submits.

Dark madness grips Billy's mind as Jackson thrashes against him. His howl peters out, and Matthias answers him. Soon the entire arena echoes with the packs' call. An ear-splitting screech of a howl rips from his throat, shattering the grip of the vampire as his eyes flash silver in the moonlight. Billy stands tall in the clearing, shimmering in the moonlight as he pants from the exertion. His eyes burn with white fire instead of inky blackness. The rest of the pack members are kneeling in submission and their calls to the moon settle into an eerie silence as they watch him.

"Get the fuck out of my mate," he demands of the shadow that had tried to claim his mind. He's not sure how he did it, but power floods through his bond and Shelley wrenches over, her porcelain skin shining in the moonlight. A black, vile tar flows from her mouth as she retches onto the ground. The crowd watches in silent fascination as the emulsion slowly grows in mass, the small woman retching and convulsing as the foul substance pushes its way out of her tiny mouth.

It grows and twists, finally manifesting into the man known as Jackson Pruitt. Like a streak of lightning, Billy puts himself between Shelley and Jackson. Matthias, Samuel, and Brandon move to join him, protecting Shelley.

Billy doesn't spare a thought and strikes for the creature that had wounded his Angel. His claws swipe through the oily mist as Jackson literally dissolves before him into a dark cloud.

"See ya 'round, Billy boy. Better take care of my Angel."

Billy snarls at the fading laughter of Jackson. Then the man is gone: no scent, no trail, nothing. The only thing Billy can hear is the roaring cheers of the crowd mixed with the heart wrenching sobs of his mate. He turns to see Darryl on one knee before him accepting his loss. The power coursing through Billy is overwhelming. He can hear all of them and feel all of them. He feels like he could lift an entire house. He turns to Shelley. His brothers step aside as he scoops her up into his arms.

"Oh Billy! I'm sorry! I was trapped. I couldn't stop him. Please, please don't hate me. Billy, please," she pleads to the werewolf holding her against his chest. The soft whine from him as he cradles and nuzzles her makes her calm down. She wraps her arms around his neck and he pulls her closer. A few quick looks around and he starts to turn to flee.

Mehzebeen and Isaiah, along with the elders are blocking his path.

"Alpha Billy, we need you to put your mate down and shift back." Mehzebeen's voice is loud and demanding The power coursing through Billy is terrifying. She is quite certain that he just manifested a vampire back from the dead out of his mate. Concern fills her that she didn't pick up on the vampire in the girl sooner. Why hadn't they trusted her and told her there was a problem?

Isaiah steps up next to Mehzebeen and holds his hands up. "C'mon big fella. We don't want to hurt anyone. We just want to finish the formalities and hunt down the vampire that was hurting your girl."

Thirty miles away, Jackson manifests, looking back to the arena. This is not how he expected tonight to be. Yet, he couldn't be happier to have his body back again, or at least most of it. Tendrils of mist curl oddly from him if he doesn't hold concentration. He was completely confident that Shelley was only a human, and didn't think werewolves had that kind of oomph.

"That's because you're young," Lucien's irritated voice fills the clearing. "The fact you survived means you have potential. Now let's see if you are smarter than your sire at playing with wolves." Lucien clamps his hand down on Jackson and drags him through the shadows with him back to New Orleans.

CHAPTER FIFTY-SEVEN
Put Your Alpha Pants On

Billy's nostrils flare. All he can smell is Shelley. The sweet scent of lilies and watermelon drown any thoughts other than he wants his mate. His muzzle nestles into her neck, and his claws are tearing at the cute little sun dress she is sporting. It doesn't matter that they are standing in the arena with his brothers all around him, a vampire in front of him, and a hunter beside her. His erection grows and the entire crowd averts their gazes, but not wanting him to go further.

"Whoa! Hey! Put that thing away! Momma's gonna kick yer ass," Matthias is grinning and shielding his eyes as he tries to get Shelley from Billy's grasp.

Billy snarls at his brother for coming anywhere near his mate. Shelley is giggling as he's tickling her with his nose, but then gasps as his claws desperately pull along her back, shredding the dress.

"Billy James Coeh!" Shelley laughs and squirms, which is only inviting him to mount her more. It's then she feels him press against her thigh and her eyes widen.

"Oh, no, you don't, Mister!" She baps him on the snout.

Billy's experience at being bopped like a disobedient dog is very little and causes him to blink in disbelief at his mate. He gives her a loud chuff in frustration and shifts her more. It looks like he is going to take her, regardless of her opinion.

Shelley slaps him then. "I said no." She is no longer giggling at him and her tone is very serious. "Look what you did to my dress. You should be ashamed of yourself."

Billy shifts back to human, not letting her go. A serious pout graces his face as he submits to his mate's wants. "But I'm Alpha now, and get to make the rules." He sulks more.

Shelley rewards him with a sweet kiss before she squirms to stand in front of him, allowing him a modicum of decency.

"Yes, you do. And if your rules involve taking your mate when she says no, we're gonna have another Alpha battle and we'll see who wins," she brandishes her finger up at him. It's comical to see that tiny girl make the massive man behave. Mehzebeen laughs and cuts Isaiah a look to make sure he's not about to shoot Billy Coeh.

Matthias hands his brother a pair of shorts. "At least pretend like you're some kind of civilized wolf." The grin on his brother's face says he is teasing.

Billy returns to ignoring the rest of them after shimmying into the shorts. He pulls Shelley closer to him again. "I love you, Angel." He kisses her tenderly. "No one will ever hurt you again."

"I love you too," she coos up to him and wraps her arms around his neck as they kiss. The wind picks up around the pair of them and it feels like a gentle embrace. He knows it's the Goddess showing her approval.

Their loving moment disappears when Caleb invades the small group. "His scent's gone. There was another vampire. Old as fuck. It's about thirty miles from here, but their scents are just... gone."

Billy turns to Mehzebeen. "Want to explain to me what the fuck just happened?" His arms cross and his posture falls right into the Alpha role.

Shelley is standing beside him, but her hand is rubbing his back. It's making it hard for him to remain angry. With a brief glance, he realizes Shelley does not know Mehzebeen is a vampire. He sniffs the air and both his brows raise at the vampire having a human scent.

Mehzebeen's tone was serene and nonchalant. "Do you wish to tell me how you fucking manifested a vampire back from the dead?"

Billy snorts and replies, "Would if I could. Tell me why there was a vampire in my mate's head."

Mehzebeen draws a sharp breath. It's showing her irritation, as she does not need to breathe at all. She looks at Isaiah, who asks her the same question with his gaze. This is a new trick for vampires. She looks like she doesn't have an answer, and it bothers him more than almost having a front seat to werewolf porn. Mehzebeen shrugs and turns back to Billy and Shelley. "I need to enter her mind."

Billy's eyes narrow. He mulls it over for a few moments. "I think we need to take this conversation into private. Away from prying ears."

"My limousine should suffice," Mehzebeen offers before they have to negotiate allowing her across a threshold.

Mehzebeen's limousine is quite luxurious, but Billy ends up looking like they stuffed him in a sardine can. It causes Shelley to giggle as she squeezes in next to him. "What do you mean by enter her mind?" Billy doesn't beat around the bush. "My momma may trust you, but this is my mate." His teeth bare and Shelley gives him a light nudge.

"Be nice."

"This *is* me being nice, Angel." He looks down at Shelley and offers a gentle smile.

"I mean, I need to look through her memories of that night. I do not know any vampires with the ability to possess a human physically." Mehzebeen's voice is full of irritation and worry. It's making Isaiah even more anxious. This is a tiny space to have an Alpha and vampire fight.

Billy snorts. He doesn't like this one bit. He shifts and pulls Shelley into his lap to hold her closer while also freeing him to splay out across the seat. "Not to frighten either of you, but we should focus on the fact someone helped him leave without a trace, and that he is very much back amongst us. What I do won't hurt, Miss Baxter. It will give us insight into his abilities. And," she pauses for emphasis, "allow us to prevent him from doing it to you again." She looks back to Billy, "Unless your intention is to keep her locked in a windowless dungeon for the rest of her life?"

Billy frowns. He could decide for Shelley. It's his right as Alpha and as her mate. Billy respects Shelley too much to do that to her. This had to be her choice.

"I can't breathe," she squeaks up to him and he relaxes, muttering an apology in her ear. "If it will help, I'm willing to do it. Are you a witch? Do I have to drink a potion? Or something?"

"Something like that, my dear," Mehzebeen reacts with a rueful grin. "No potions. I just need you to face me and relax."

Shelley complies and squirms in Billy's lap to face Mehzebeen.

Billy can feel his shorts tighten as his body reacts to his mate's contact. He rests his hands on his knees and behaves himself. Mehzebeen leans forward and brushes her fingers along Shelley's temples. Her eyes light up with a vibrant gold color as she stares deep into the girl's eyes. Shelley's pretty blue eyes glass over and her breathing evens out, like she is sleeping.

The entire affair takes about thirty minutes, and Mehzebeen has to recollect herself to get her fangs to retract before Shelley comes out of her daze. Leaning back, she looks between Isaiah and Billy.

"The night he sought to claim her, and you intervened," she motions to Billy. "He was struggling to dominate her mind. He had dominated her mother's mind, but Shelley was resisting him. I believe that's because of your bond. He was in her mind when you attacked him. As best I can tell, a piece of his soul manifested in her mind, allowing him to torment her through visions until you ripped him from her body today. We watched the fight, Billy. What did you do to rip him out of her?"

"I don't know. One minute I'm getting pummeled by Darryl, then I felt him in my head. Jackson was trying to take control. It felt like a dead weight on my whole body. My link was severed and Darryl wasn't lettin' up. So I howled to the moon." He says that like it is perfectly ordinary and explains everything. "By the grace of the Goddess, she gave me the power to kick him out of my head. Then I felt how he slithered back into Shelley and I wasn't lettin' that fucker have her. So I did what came naturally and booted him out."

"You just booted him out?" Mehzebeen's voice is deadpan as she raises a brow at Billy.

Shelley, who has been rather quiet, has a pensive look. "I felt you in my head," she responds to Billy. "You demanded I get rid of him. Your voice was weird and I could only obey you."

Isaiah pipes up, "That, darlin', was the werewolf Alpha command. It has quite a kick to it. It's rare for it to work on a human, but we do know it works on mates." He pats Shelley's knee. "Now, Mehzebeen and I have some research to do regarding our undeceased deceased friend."

"You'll keep me in the know," Billy's request is more of a demand, and Isaiah nods. "I will. Come by my office in Savannah in three days and we'll chat." Isaiah gives him a tight smile.

Billy and Shelley shuffle out of the car. His grip tightens around Shelley as the elders bombarded Billy with the details for transitioning to Alpha. Darryl retracts his claim to Alpha and hugs his cousin. Shelley uses the chance of being free of Billy's embrace to slink from the pack members and find her son. He is sleeping in the nursery and she scoops him right up and squeezes him to her, waking the boy and letting her tears fall as she thought she would never see him again.

CHAPTER FIFTY-EIGHT
Pomp & Circumstance

After much discussion and discoveries with Lucien and Jackson, Billy reluctantly talks Shelley into spending the rest of the Summer in South America with Jasper and Faye.

Shelley and Frances left a week after Billy became Alpha.

It makes for a rather moody Billy. Billy's first act as Alpha is to make Caleb pack his shit and head to their mother's house in Virginia. Caleb, despite his treatment of Shelley, had grown too attached to her. Billy wasn't about to get into a fight with his kid brother over his mate. He had to chuckle at his mother's bitching about how Caleb fluctuates between sulking and taunting Constantine. This leaves Billy and Tommy to work out official duties between the two of them, and Beauregard falls nicely into the Gamma role even while still in school. Making amends with Darryl, Billy makes him the Delta.

Billy takes this time to travel the entire Coeh pack territory. The four men introduce themselves and deal with business in each area as needed. It wasn't until Pensacola that they had trouble. Trouble being a tall beach bunny named Claudine that Beauregard fell for harder than a ton of bricks. Billy and the others had to laugh at how lovesick Beauregard became. When she agreed to come back to South Carolina, Beauregard was over the moon.

Tommy keeps humming the hook to "Another One Bites The Dust" every time Beau is around.

Darryl then opens his mouth and spouted off about never wanting a mate. Not as much trouble as women are. Billy and Tommy grin at each other. Darryl just triggered the jealous bitch hiding in the moon. She never lets a challenge go unanswered.

Sure enough, Jacksonville happens.

They spend a few days dealing with pack business, and once finished, Darryl disappears with a few good old boys. Two days later, he comes back nervous as hell, and eager to get home.

******

A firecracker red-head comes rolling up on her Harley to Billy's work site. She raises holy hell about how her mate's a no-good deadbeat, and how much of a deadbeat the Alpha was that condones it. Billy is thankful that all of Wolf Pack Construction are pack members. He stands with his arms crossed, listening to her rant and rave in a mix of Spanish and English. She carries on about how the man was such a worthless bootlicker. How he promised her the moon and told her he loved her. How he ran off in the night like a coward. How he abandoned her, and she was not raising his pup alone. The longer she paces and rants, the more bemused Billy becomes.

"Mind tellin' me his name, darlin'?" His voice rumbles and is low, but the sense of authority is present.

She turns and narrows her eyes at him. "Darryl Coeh!" Her voice echoes across the work site and silence fills the air. Billy's eyes take on a mischievous twinkle at that.

"C'mon. Let's go to the house and sort this out"

Two hours later, Darryl comes rushing into Billy's home. "What's the emergency? Who's hurt? Who do I need to kill?"

He looks frantic as he steps into the living room. Billy had just linked him that there was a situation he needed him there for immediately. Darryl freezes and sniffs the air. He would know that scent anywhere. "Fuck," is the only word he gets out when she comes leaping at him like she is going to murder him.

As the pair of them tumble out the front door, Tommy's pulling his truck up and Billy's following them outside. Poor Darryl is trying not to hurt the little firecracker as she lands blow after blow on him. Her rants and growls in Spanish are making Billy chuckle.

"You think we should save him?" Tommy's chuckling as he comes to stand next to Billy.

"Nah. He brought this shit on himself. Plus, we should be sellin' tickets." Billy steps forward then, wrapping one massive arm around her waist and hoisting her up so Darryl can get up. No matter how hard she tries, she can't get out of Billy's grasp. "Honey, you're just gonna hurt the pup."

"Pup?" Darryl looks pissed. "I ain't no damn pup! Hell, I'm older than you, *Alpha*." Billy just smirks at Darryl, letting the man dig his own grave. His grip on the squirming firecracker is firm and unrelenting. It takes a second for Darryl's light bulb to come on. His eyes flit between Billy and his mate. "Who the fuck did you sleep with?" He snarls at the woman.

Billy's eyes narrow at his cousin. "That boy's a damn fool. I think you *should* whoop his ass," he suggests as he releases her.

"What?" Darryl's eyes widen as the woman turns into a blond she-devil of a wolf.

Billy steps back next to Tommy to watch.

"Did he just call his mate a whore?" Tommy sounds stunned.

"Pertinear just about," Billy drawls in response.

The fight lasts several minutes until Darryl gets the upper hand and pins her by biting the back of her neck and forcing her to the ground. His large tawny colored wolf blanketing over the blond one. Both are panting and tired, bleeding from their efforts.

"Are you done being a damn fool?" Billy's voice cuts across the yard. "Darryl Coeh, you're gonna do right by that girl." His voice is full of anger at this point. He waits for the two of them to shift back into their human forms, and Billy pulls his shirt off to offer it to the girl for modesty. "You," he points at her, "Are going to calm down and use your words to talk to him." He then points at Darryl, "You are going to sit there and listen to your mate. If you call her a whore again in my presence, you won't like it. Now both of you get inside to talk like grown-ups."

******

Pack life returned to normal once Darryl and Cody got resolved. Shelley returned a week before school started. The entire pack fell into a peaceful rhythm. Billy had to deal with all the responsibilities of running the pack, along with his newfound position as manager of the construction company. Shelley threw herself into her schoolwork. Shelley and Billy didn't take part in The Rutting that year. The pack understood, as she has not finished school yet. All of Susie and David's worries about not mating were unfounded. Shelley's first act as Luna was to transform the pre-Rutting ceremony by creating a mass public wedding ceremony for anyone who wished to take part. The pack took to her like ducks to water.

The lack of information regarding Jackson Pruitt gave Billy a reason to be paranoid. This meant that either Tommy, Beau, or Darryl guarded Shelley, even while she was in school. Darryl loathed what he called "teen duty". Beau and Tommy found it amusing, but neither man was interested in any of the advances of Shelley's school mates. Graduation day finally rolls around. Shelley had long since moved back into Billy's room.

It is hell to not mount her every night, but he survives. Billy gazes up at his Angel, and smiles. Feeling the warm wetness of her engulfing him. It's as divine as the rutting. It's making him throb as he grapples her thighs to hold her close. Her soft moans only egged him on further. His hips buck up into her and his eyes roll back. Only, it felt odd. Like she had fur. His senses come to and he realizes he is holding onto someone's head. His eyes snap open and the dream of him fucking his mate gives way to the sight of his hands cupping her head as he thrusts into the back of her throat. Hastily, he pulls back, and she inhales sharply through her nose.

The light chuckle that erupts from her drives him crazy and, without warning, he leans up, keeping her head on him. He grabs her ankle and spins her like a top around until she is laying on his stomach. "You think that's funny, do you?" He purrs at her as she yelps on him. With his one hand, he laces his fingers into her hair and bobs her head on his throbbing cock. He then curls up, forcing his face between her legs and buries his tongue deep into her folds. He bounces her between burying his cock in her throat and burying his tongue deep inside her.

She moans, and he feels her body jerk with the onslaught of her orgasm. He licks faster and pumps harder into her mouth. Soon following with an eruption that has him gripping onto her tight as his cock pulses in her sweet mouth. She gets even as her thighs clench hard around his ears, drawing his tongue deeper into her as she shivers against him.

When he finally relaxes back on the bed, he is content and allows her to wriggle off of him so she can properly snuggle against him.

"Two can play that game," he chortles.

"Mhm hmm," she hums in a dreamy, euphoric state. He turns his head, and it's only about six in the morning. They had three hours before they had to be up for graduation.

He felt her relax against him and he chuckled softly.

"Oh, no you don't," he rumbles as he kisses her temple.

He rolls on top of her and easily parts her legs. His rough and calloused fingers probe and tease her already sensitive skin. She arches and sprawls open for him and he pauses in his teasing to admire her. She truly looks like an angel before him. His manhood is already rising to attention for a second time. He has waited two long years to feel this taste of heaven again. He wasn't waiting a moment longer.

CHAPTER FIFTY-NINE
Worth The Wait

Shelley's hips roll up to meet his fingers and she gives a coy smile. "Billy Coeh, you ain't breakin' yer momma's rules, are you? I ain't graduated yet."

Billy raises a brow and presses his finger deeper inside her. "Is that so, Miss Shelley? My momma ain't Alpha anymore, now is she?"

"Mhm, you're right. She is Queen of the Alphas. Still the boss of you," she moans as he keeps teasing her.

He chuckles at her sass, "Well, then I guess I get a few more hours of shuteye," he stops touching her and rolls over to face away from her on the bed. His raging hard-on painfully reminding him how much he wants her.

"Awe, don't be like that, sugah," she coos against his back, rubbing herself against him. "I'm sure we could find some way to ease your need," her delicate fingers trailing down his hip.

"No ma'am. That boat has already sailed. And you're the one who put it to sea, remember?" He is grinning. She bites him hard.

"Suit yourself. I'll just get--" but she never finishes as Frances cries. With a small frustrated sigh, she rolls out of bed and pulls on one of Billy's T-shirts. Once she is gone, Billy rolls onto his back and closes his eyes. One hand behind his head and the other reaching down to finish what she started.

"Yer daddy is naughty," he hears her coo on the baby monitor. "He better not be in there doin' bad things without me, or he'll get a spankin'."

Then he hears Frances' perfect little laugh.

"Now, you go back to sleep. It's too early for this," she sets him in the crib and he fusses again.

"Frances David, that's enough," her voice takes a tone Billy hasn't heard before. "You don't have to sleep, but you have to lie there."

He hears the petulant huff of his son in reply.

When Shelley comes back in the room, he is already satisfied and laying on his side to face her. Patting the bed, "Ready to get a little more sleep?"

She giggles and crawls into the bed with him. She snuggles right up to him and bites his chest again. "You finished without me," she pouts.

"You can't prove anything. You'll never know if I did or not." He purrs to her.

The rest of the day went well. Susie and David came in for Shelley's graduation and quality Frances time. The graduation party was in full swing by two in the afternoon. Pack members flit back and forth between all the kids who are graduating, since it is one big party for all of them.

Shelley's positively glowing throughout the day. She laughs and smiles with her friends.

Billy keeps getting pulled into pack business and finally growls at them that today wasn't for business, it's for family. Not even that allowed the pair to be together. They lock eyes across the yard and give sheepish grins at each other throughout the day.

There is live music, grills burning all day long, and Frances has spent all day with Nana. It was his first word and happened early at the party. Susie was sure he called her a banana, but when he made grabby hands at her and said Nana again, it was all she wrote. Susie Coeh is now Nana.

"If I find out which one o' you taught him that..." she brandishes a finger as she is holding her grandson, leaving the threat empty.

David laughs, "C'mon Nana, let's get you two some food." A shit-eating grin is plastered all over his face.

Billy can't take it anymore. Her sweet scent is tempting him, even from afar. He stalks toward the gaggle of girls she has spent the afternoon with. Without saying a word, he unceremoniously scoops her up and tosses her over his shoulder like a sack of potatoes. His large arm clamps over her legs to hold her in place as he heads to the path that leads to their cabin.

"Billy!" She squeals at him without trying to free herself.

"Hush Angel, you've been tauntin' me all damn day. You're gonna get yours." He pats her butt with his other hand.

"Think we should stop 'em?" Caleb asks the gathered family members.

David smirks and shakes his head no. "Hell no. He's Alpha. He can do whatever he damn well pleases. You gonna stop him?" He eyes his youngest son.

"Just kind of rude, that he took her away like that," Caleb mutters as he tries not to stare at Shelley.

"Boy, there's a whole gaggle of girls just waitin' for you to notice 'em. Get yer eyes off yer brother's girl 'fore I do it for you." David's expression turns serious as he stares at Caleb.

Caleb's cheeks burn red, but he obliges his father by going to talk with the other girls. Soon enough he's grinning and flirting just like a Coeh, but his eyes wander back to the trailhead every once in a while.

Billy doesn't shift, but he hurries through the woods, taking them to the cabin. All he can think about is the image of her sweet mouth wrapped around him the first time they came here.

He had put some time into sprucing up the place even further than before, it cozier and warmer for her. As they come to the front door, he sets her to her feet.

She is blushing and giggling as he pulls her into a kiss. Her lips are soft and sweet against his.

He presses her to the door, caging her with his body as he drinks from her intoxicating kisses. Only pausing for air, he eases the door open and walks her in.

Shelley is drunk off the bliss of kissing Billy. His scent is strong and fills her with every breath. His lips taste of beer and remind her of the night they met. She doesn't say one word as he closes the door behind her. Instead, she turns her back to him and starts to peel out of her clothes. They had both been anticipating this moment for two long years. First her sandals, then her jacket hit the floor. Her cute little sun dress follows and lands on the back of the couch. Leaving the white lace bra and panties the only clothing she is wearing. She pauses and purposely bends over to slide down the panties, giving him a show. Her skin flushes pink at the soft growl she hears from him. She leans back up to move around the couch. Her hands reach behind her and unclasp the bra, leaving it tossed aside as she moves to the fluffy fake fur on the floor.

Billy's eyes are wide with lust as he watches her strip tease. His heart hammers in his chest and his cock gets harder with each piece of clothing that comes off. He unbuttons his dress shirt slow and steady as he moves forward. He steps out of his shoes and lets his shirt hang loose as he removes his socks. Soon his shirt and undershirt get draped on the couch with her dress. His hands deftly unfasten his belt and pants, letting them hit the floor as he steps out of them. Billy's boxers are the last to hit the floor as he pauses behind her. His breath catches as she has positioned herself in offering to him, coyly looking over her shoulder to watch his reaction. She is the sexiest thing he has ever met. He positions himself behind her as he drops to his knees. His knee brushes hers to spread her legs wider. His cock twitches in anticipation as it brushes against her wetness.

Before she can say a word, he thrusts in deep. His hands taking hold of her hips in eager roughness. His moan fills the room, and he nearly loses himself in her tight and wanting depths. He lets her get used to him, hearing her whimpering below him. She isn't pulling away.

Shelley pushes back against him, begging for him to go deeper. When he doesn't move, she whines and rocks her hips back against him, trying to encourage him to thrust again.

"That's right, Angel, take it all." His voice is husky with desire. "Show me how much you want me." Billy leans over Shelley more, pumping into her nice and slow. He was drawing this out for as long as he can. He closes his eyes, panting and resisting the urge to shift into his werewolf form. Memories of their Rutting flashing before his eyes.

Shelley's soft mewl and squirming body are driving Billy deeper into euphoric bliss. He growls in response and his grip tightens on her ass, squeezing as he thrusts deep again.

"Billy. Oh God, Billy," her voice is breathless under him. "Don't stop, please," she begs.

She tenses on him, and he feels her jerk as her orgasm washes over her, causing her throbbing and milking him as he continues to pump into her. With a howl of a moan, he buries himself as deep as possible and bursts inside of her. They are both covered in sweat and breathing hard. His muscular hands are petting along her as he then folds her to spin her on him without pulling out of her.

With her back on the rug, he resumes pumping into her. Her fluffy blond curls partially hide her face. Her skin glistens pink in the dim light. He leans over her, his mouth eagerly seeks her nipple, drawing it into his mouth as he squeezes and pinches the other. It rewards him with the precious yelp he wanted and makes him grin as she tightens around him.

"Mhmm, so tender," he purrs against her. He turns his head to repeat the suckling of her other breast.

Shelley's fingers lace into his hair, and her back arches under him.

"Angel," he breathes against her skin.

"Take me, Billy," she moans. "How you want to." She rolls her hips to meet his. His heart races at the way she begs him. "I need you, Billy," she moans again.

Who was he to deny her? Her sweet whines called to his inner wolf. Shelley's eyes flutter open as she feels him swell inside of her, and she sees the copper fur sprouting from Billy's tanned skin. His thrusts grow harder and wilder, making her cry out. He nuzzles and licks against her skin as he claims her, being careful to not bite her in this form.

Lost in ecstasy, Shelley gives herself over to her beast.

All she will ever need is him.

There was no fear this time. No hesitation to let him near her. The copper werewolf leaned up and pumped hard and fast into her until she felt him shudder, then howl proper above her.

He collapses on top of her, not shifting back. He leaves himself buried deep inside of her as he pulls her close.

"Mine," she murmurs against him.

"Mine," he growls in response, the word harsh but loving from him in his werewolf form.

CHAPTER SIXTY

Welcome To The Triple Six

Halloween 2006

"Mommy!" Frances' little voice wails up at Jasper. His face is red with crying and he is throwing an absolute wall-eyed fit. He has not seen his mommy all day.

Jasper looks down at the pup and is chuckling. He squats down to get eye level with him as Billy's still in the shower. "Hey little guy, it'll be alright. You'll see mommy soon."

"NOW!" he shrieks at Jasper.

Jasper inhales to not murder his nephew.

Caleb and Beau are laughing from the couch, where they are playing video games in their tuxes.

"You assholes know how to deal with this?" Jasper growls at his brothers.

"Nope!" they reply in unison. "We don't have pups."

"Tranquilizers maybe?" from Beau.

"Duct tape?" from Caleb.

"Shelley uses candy." Billy's voice filters out from the bathroom. "But you give him candy before the ceremony and I'm lettin' his momma whoop you. If he gets that tux sticky, she'll have my balls." All the men in the room chuckle.

"MOMMY!" young Frances shrieks and stomps his foot in demand.

"Come here, buddy." David swoops in to save his sons.

"NO UP! MOMMY!" He growls up at him and runs.

"Yes, up!" David, with lightning reflexes, catches the toddler, and in one swift motion, scoops him up. "It's Pops, Grandpa, Pop-Pop. Really, anything but Up, buddy."

"Up," he whines as he curls into grandpa.

"Don't tell yer mamma," David's voice pitches conspiratorially low as he pulls out a sucker.

"Up!!" The tantrum vaporizes instantly as the boy reaches for the sucker.

Billy laughs and shakes his head as his father takes his son out of the room.

Jasper exhales.

"Thought you'd be used to it by now. Seein' as you have a short person too." Billy grins.

"Listen man, my little princess ain't nothing like that ball o' crazy." Jasper counters.

"Just you wait," Billy grins. "I give her six months. That's when your second one's due, right?" Billy smirks, knowing that Jasper and Faye are in for it if he has another girl.

"Look who's talkin'. I've heard shotgun wedding more than once today," Jasper jabs.

"Low blow," from the guys on the couch. All of them erupt into laughter.

Tommy enters the room. He is ready for the ceremony. He looks handsome and proud. His goofy grin hasn't left his face all morning, "Been on reconnaissance. Y'all need to up your game. They have food."

"Well, yeah. Two pregnant women in a room alone? They probably would have murdered somebody if there wasn't food, seein' as they've been gettin' ready since before dawn. You should have gotten up to eat breakfast with us." Billy chuckles as he is pulling his tux on. He glances at his watch and verifies they still had plenty of time. "How are the girls?"

"Right as rain. Faye's complainin' about Jasper makin' her fat."

"Uh, huh? She is the cute pregnant type according to my mate." Billy counters.

The men chuckle again, and Tommy continues. "They were cryin' and laughin' when I left. Shelley told me to remind you that if your son soils his tux, you don't get no more pups."

Billy laughs and motions to the door. "Then you should rescue him from Up."

Tommy shakes his head and heads out the door. A few minutes later, you can hear Frances shrieking. The sound is fading as Tommy takes Frances to see his mother, leaving the sucker behind.

"MOMMY!" Frances shrieks at Shelley, who is in a robe still. Her hair is up in rollers. Her stockings are on, but she is not in her gown yet.

"Frances!" Shelley lights up. "Thank uncle Tommy," she coos.

"Tanks Tata," his cute little voice chirps.

"I swear to God, that kid gets cuter every time I see him," Tommy chortles as he leaves the room.

Faye's shy little girl comes up to Frances while sucking on her thumb. Her cute, chubby little hand that isn't in her mouth clamps onto his hand as she teeters. She is still new to walking. Frances looks between his mother and this thing attached to him.

"Go on," Shelley encourages.

"NO!" Frances barks up at his mother.

"Frances David," her tone changes instantly to mom voice.

"Hmph," Frances let the little girl hang on him, but it looked like it was killing him. Soon enough, they are playing on the floor with her toys.

The next few hours are a whirlwind for Shelley. Faye helped her into her dress. Both women are round-belly pregnant. Faye is due in a few weeks. Shelley in a few months. They filled the little park they chose with flowers and people.

David is beaming from ear to ear as he gets to walk Shelley down the aisle. Billy is a bundle of nerves until he sees her coming to him. She is the most beautiful thing he has ever seen. His megawatt smile threatens to never fall off his face again.

Susie officiates their ceremony, and it's full of family and friends. Frances is adorable as he holds up the rings for his mommy and daddy. It is hilarious when he tries to keep his daddy's ring for himself.

"NO! Me!" He makes a kissy face at his mother.

After cajoling and laughing, Shelley finally gets Billy's ring. Her secret weapon to get him to relent was the promise of ice cream afterwards. Pictures take forever as the guests are ushered to the reception.

Billy has kept the reception location a secret from Shelley. The banquet hall she chose had to cancel suddenly, so far as she knew. Billy took over reception hall duty to keep Shelley from breaking down. It was all going according to his plan. Billy just grins and he places a white scarf around her eyes, blindfolding her as they make their way to the destination.

She waits with a smile on her lips. Her hand in Billy's the entire ride. When they pull into the parking lot, she cants her head, hearing gravel crunch under the tires. Billy eases her out of the car and leads her forward a few steps. She can hear the murmurs and voices of people around them. Billy moves behind her and undoes the blindfold. She blinks under the bright sunlight, then gasps. Shelley takes in the new building. Billy and David had recreated The Triple Six, right down to the three neon sixes above the door. "Oh, Billy!" she turns and throws herself into his arms, kissing him as tears cling to her lashes.

"Don't thank me, thank Pop. It's his gift to you," Billy

murmurs in her ear.

David and Susie, along with Frances, come walking up.

"Yeah. Insurance finally came through. Found out the bar was still in my old man's name. So it went to me. Now, it's yours, darlin'. Paperwork's already taken care of. Just waitin' for you to sign it." David's smile matches Billy's.

Billy and Shelley move to the entrance of the bar. The couple is giddy and beaming in front of the crowd.

"Thank you y'all for sharin' this day with us! Hope you enjoy the food," Billy's voice carries over the crowd. He then looks down at Shelley, who cannot contain her excitement.

"And welcome to The Triple Six!" Shelley squeaks out as Billy sweeps her into a bridal carry over the threshold of the bar.

CHAPTER SIXTY-ONE
Epilogue

August 2005 - New Orleans

Jack Talbett stands at the corner of a building in downtown New Orleans, thankful that his heavy body armor blocks the driving rain. "Everybody in position?" he comms the team.

"Yeah, if by position you mean having a fucking hurricane shoved up my ass," Buck growls in his comm.

"Awe, we both know you like shit up your ass," Tabatha chimes in.

"We've been over this. The hurricane gives us enough cover to strike and washes away the evidence we were ever here. Everyone, quit fuckin' around and time to get your game face on." Jack barks.

Trevor sits at his perch. The rain is blowing sideways as the storm rages into the city. Their intel suggested the vampire's lair was near the water's edge.

This four-man team of Night Rangers are the best of the best. The Night Rangers is the US Military's secret organization of hunters,. Their uniforms are black tactical armor and they have full clearance to do what is needed to protect humanity, even within the borders of the States. Tonight, they are here to deal with an abomination that has been terrorizing the wolves in Savannah. A vampire that can turn itself into mist and possess people. "Overwatch is green," Trevor gives the all clear.

The three shadows move with an eerie precision. Jack pulls them into position, water streaking across his visor as he pulls a UV grenade from his vest. Popping the door open, he chucks it in and pulls the door closed to shield them from the light. The blast is like lightning in the room, and when it subsides, the soldiers filter into the room. Bullets whiz in the air. The wind howls more. The three soldiers move without hesitation. They fire without remorse. The four vampires had been sitting around a card table.

One had been instantly ashed by the grenade.

Another tried to spring into action only have a heavy stake slammed into its chest by Jack.

The third is ripped to shreds by the rifle fire.

The fourth, wearing a red jacket, snarls at Jack, but then levels his gaze on Tabatha. She sings to him. His eyes lock with hers and she freezes. She is the closest to the door.

"Shit. Tabby!" Jack shouts in the comm to pull her out of her daze.

She had been through the holy water treatment once already and it still eats at Jack that he let her get bit.

Jackson takes the opportunity and bolts for the door, his mist pooling around the woman to take her with him.

Trevor is watching. He doesn't wait. He fires a UV grenade at the entrance, then another and another. The wind catches them as they flare to life and create a purple vortex of sunlight in the otherwise black sky.

Jack and Buck come to the door. They witness the most gruesome sight they have seen to date. The flashes and swirling purples of the UV light have tiny bubbles of blood exploding into the air and spraying the entire area in gore.

Jackson Pruitt had just spent his last life in New Orleans.

Jack turns to Tabatha and injects her with tranquilizer. He hoists her over his shoulder as she passes out. He wasn't risking anything with her. The doc at the bunker could sort her out.

The three men, with Tabatha in tow, book it to the safe house. They intend to ride out the storm. Buck doesn't let Trevor show him up on this mission. Jack just shakes his head at the somewhat unhinged joy from the other man as his present causes the building to implode, just one more building lost to the storm raging around them.

Biography

J. R. Froemling was born in Indiana, the second eldest of three. She met her first husband in an online writing community. She met her second husband at a board game convention in 2015. She has a Bachelor's of Science in Information Technology from Western Governors University of Indiana. She got her start in an online writing community for Star Wars fan fiction. Over the past twenty years she has transformed that love of fan fiction into works of her own.

Want to find out more about J. R. Froemling and how to keep up to date with her?

https://jrfwriting.com

Other Books By J. R. Froemling

The Wolfe Legacy

Mistress Giselle - Book One of Hope-Marie

The Naughty List - Book One of Elijah Joseph

Chronicles of Nodd

Fall of Avalon - Verse One

Immortal Love Saga

My Viking Alpha